W9-BLD-762

EVERYONE LOVES *BELOVED*

Also by Antoinette Stockenberg

EMILY'S GHOST

ANTOINETTE STOCKENBERG

Beloved

A DELL BOOK

Published by
Dell Publishing
a division of
Bantam Doubleday Dell Publishing Group, Inc.
1540 Broadway
New York, New York 10036

ISBN: 0-440-21330-4

Printed in the United States of America

Published simultaneously in Canada

October 1993

10 9 8 7 6 5 4 3 2 1

RAD

For Dad

AUTHOR'S NOTE

I'd like to thank Miss Barbara Andrews, now-retired librarian of the Nantucket Atheneum, for her kindness (and for the Fig Newtons); Glen Austin of the Antique Rose Emporium for taking the time to walk me through the process of budding a rose; Rebecca Lohmann, currently Nantucket's town clerk, for her patience and courtesy during several long phone calls; and Frank Crandall of Wood River Evergreens, who knows everything about hollies. Thanks to Blue Balliett, whose charming books of Nantucket ghosts got me in the mood. And I'd like to thank John for his inspired contribution to this novel; who knows better how to smell the roses?

The reader might be interested to know that the incident behind my Legend of the Cursed Rose—the removal of a rose planted to make a grave—is true.

CHAPTER 1

"**D**o you think she's really dead?"

"Man, we don't even know if she's *in* there." The boy reached out a grimy hand and laid it gingerly on the closed lid of the gleaming casket.

His pal—younger, cleaner, better behaved—sucked in his breath. "You're not supposed to touch it!"

"What's she gonna do? Open it and come after us?" The older boy's voice was defiant; but he glanced around furtively, then rubbed away his smudge marks with the sleeve of his jacket. "Come on, let's go. It looks like we have to take their word for it."

Watching the two from her seat in the front row of folding chairs, Jane Drew tried not to smile. *You never should've kept their baseballs, Aunt Sylvia. Fifty years from now they'll still be saying you were a witch.*

The kids made a run for the door around a plain-dressed woman, who promptly collared the younger one.

"Walk. This is a place of respect."

The boy squirmed out of her grip, then walked briskly the rest of the way out. The woman, sixty and bulky, shifted her handbag from her right forearm to her left and glanced tentatively around the room, taking in the closed coffin, Jane, and the two visitors chatting quietly in the back.

Jane went up to the new arrival. "I'm Jane Drew, Sylvia Merchant's great-niece," she said with a smile.

The visitor stuck out a well-worn hand. "How do you do. I'm Mrs. Adamont. Adele Adamont. I work at the A&P where Mrs. Merchant shopped," she explained. "I wanted to pay my respects because, well . . ." She nodded to the empty chairs. "You see for yourself. When a widow has nobody, this is how it ends up."

Surprised by the islander's bluntness, Jane said something dutiful about her great-aunt having outlived most of her friends.

"Oh, no; she never had none, not that I recall," Mrs. Adamont said evenly. "Everyone on Nantucket knew that. They say her husband died in the First World War; I suppose she never got over it. She was always one to say good morning, but never one to stop and pass the time of day. She was funny that way. How old was she?" the woman added.

"My aunt had just turned ninety-four. The last two years were hard for her," Jane volunteered. "She didn't like living in a nursing home, away from Nantucket."

"I did wonder why she decided to go into a home off-island. Was she all right—you know—up there?"

"Sharp as a tack," Jane said, taken aback again.

Leave it to an islander to think anyone living on the mainland must be insane. Jane racked her memory, trying to remember whether her aunt had ever mentioned a Mrs. Adamont. But the visitor was right; Sylvia Merchant had had little interest in other people. In the nursing home she'd reminisced about her house, and her garden, and the two cats who'd shared it with her. Books were important to her. So were movies: she'd had a VCR in her room, and her own copy of *Casablanca.* But as for friends and neighbors . . .

"She did give me zucchini from her garden once," Mrs. Adamont said, as if that were reason enough to pay her last respects. "So then, you're all there is for family?"

"Almost," Jane answered, drawing herself up to her full five-feet-seven, trying to make up for lost relatives. "There's an elderly cousin no longer able to travel. I have a sister living on the West Coast, and of course my parents;

but unfortunately they're in Europe right now." Not that they'd come in any event, Jane knew. Other than an occasional exchange of Christmas cards, there'd been no contact between her parents and Sylvia Merchant for decades.

Mrs. Adamont looked Jane up and looked Jane down and Jane's first thought was that the pale gray suit she was wearing just wasn't funereal enough.

"I see. You're the one who'll be getting the house, then."

Jane blinked. She was thirty-three; a career woman (even if an unemployed one); and reasonably sophisticated. Hosting a wake shouldn't have been a daunting social challenge—but this portly, plain-spoken visitor wasn't making it easy.

"As a matter of fact . . ."

As a matter of fact the cottage *was* Jane's now. She'd found that out just two hours earlier from her aunt's attorney when he picked her up at the ferry.

"Oh, you don't have to say if you don't want to, dear," Adele Adamont said, seeing that Jane was reluctant to talk about it. "Everyone will know soon enough. You're not *staying* at Lilac Cottage, are you? The place does need work. Well, never mind. All in good time. Let me just say my good-byes to poor Sylvia. She had a long life, and—despite all the silly gossip—who's to say it wasn't a good one?"

Mrs. Adamont wrapped her coat around herself a little more snugly and approached the coffin. She bowed her gray head and murmured a short prayer, ending it with the sign of the cross, a kind smile for Jane, and a purposeful exit. She had done her duty to the deceased.

The two women visitors in the back—elderly sisters who had no idea who Sylvia Merchant was but who never missed a wake in town—left shortly afterward. For the next hour and a half Jane sat alone in the second row, her heart steadily filling up with sorrow, unwilling or unable to believe that no one else would be coming.

Finally, ten minutes before the end of the wake, someone did show.

He was a few years older than Jane and had the look of
a man who's had to juggle his schedule ruthlessly to find
the time to break away. He nodded to Jane and walked
directly up to the casket, where he stood for a moment of
quiet reflection.

As for Jane, she could hardly keep from staring. He was
almost the first person under sixty that she'd seen all day,
tall and good-looking and handsomely dressed, with an air
of quiet confidence. He was, she knew at once, a man of
some success.

He turned to Jane again, his face sympathetic. It was a
handsome face, chiseled to near-perfection and framed by
dark hair.

"I'm sorry to barge in so late," he said.

Jane had become so used to the thick sound of silence
that she jumped a little. "Not at all; I'm glad you've come,"
she said, as if his showing up made a quorum. "I'm Jane
Drew."

"Sylvia's great-niece. Of course. I'm glad to meet you at
last. Phillip Harrow," he said, taking her hand in his. "I'm
sorry about your great-aunt, Miss Drew," he said softly.
"Ninety-four is a wonderful old age, but a hundred and
ninety-four would have been better still."

Somehow Jane didn't want to argue with him, didn't
want to admit that just a month earlier her aunt had
slammed her tiny fist on the bedstand and shouted, "I'm
ready to go, goddammit!" So Jane nodded and said simply,
"Yes." She added, "How did you know my aunt?"

"She was a neighbor. She—"

Just then the funeral director, his lips pursed in sympathy, appeared in the entryway; it was time to close up shop.
Phillip Harrow acknowledged him with a somber "Evening, Fred," and turned back to Jane. "I'm leaving the

island tonight. I'm sorry—I won't be attending the funeral," he said, his voice low with regret.

Jane was sorry, too, though for a split second she wasn't quite sure why. *Because I want* someone *else to be there,* she decided as she shook Phillip Harrow's hand good-bye. *I want* someone *else to care.*

Harrow began walking out, then stopped suddenly and turned. "Will you be staying on Nantucket past tomorrow?"

Jane smiled and lifted her shoulders. "I don't know . . . maybe a day or two. . . ."

His blue eyes—piercingly, hauntingly blue—settled on her for a long, long moment. And then he, too, smiled and shrugged. "Well, good-bye, then."

There were seven people huddling under seven umbrellas at the funeral. Jane knew only one of them: her mother. Gwendolyn Drew had flown from London to Boston, caught an air shuttle, and much to Jane's astonishment, arrived at Prospect Hill Cemetery right in the nick of time.

"I had to come back to the States early and it wasn't that out of the way," her mother whispered over the eulogy. "And after all," she added with a sigh, "Sylvia *was* family."

The morning was wet and cold; Jane felt pierced through to her bones. But her mother faced down the weather with a kind of noble indifference, as if she were waiting in her BMW at a red light in her beloved San Francisco.

How does she do it? Jane wondered, not for the first time. Her mother couldn't possibly have got more than a couple of hours' sleep, even in first-class. And yet here she was, fresh and poised and uncomplaining. Every highlighted hair was in place; the belt of her trench coat was tied exactly so. The makeup she wore was perfectly applied and unstained by tears.

Jane's eyes, on the other hand, were puffy from weeping,

her nose bright pink from blowing. She'd forgotten to open her umbrella at one point, and now her long auburn hair was plastered to her face in dark wet ringlets. Yesterday it hadn't sunk in, but sometime during the night she realized it: Aunt Sylvia—funny, eccentric, shrewd Aunt Sylvia—was gone.

The minister finished with a short prayer and offered his condolences. The service was over; the small gathering began breaking up. Gwendolyn Drew took her daughter aside with a look of loving horror.

"Darling, you look positively awful," she said, peeling a wet strand of hair from Jane's forehead. "Would you rather skip lunch and go to bed, and I'll be on my way?"

"No," Jane said quickly. She flapped open her big wet hanky and blew one more time. "I'll be all right. I don't know what's come over me . . . I knew Aunt Sylvia was ready to . . . but I never knew she cared enough about me. . . . Oh, mother . . . *she left* me *Lilac Cottage.*"

Gwendolyn's eyes opened wide. "She *did*? That *is* a surprise. I assumed the house would go to an animal shelter or some such. Well!" she said, lowering her voice in deference to the one other mourner who remained. "That really is a surprise."

The mourner, whose back was to them both, was a solidly built man with shaggy hair. In one hand he held a big black umbrella; the other was jammed into the pocket of his canvas jacket. As they watched, he took something from his pocket and tossed it into the open, still-empty grave. His profile was grim as he turned and left without acknowledging them.

There was a finality in the man's gesture that made Jane say, "I guess we should go."

She touched her fingers to her lips and blew a kiss gently in the direction of her aunt, then fell in alongside her mother. But at the grave's opening she stopped, attracted by a small red spot of color in the dirt at the bottom. It was a rose, tiny and exquisite and impossibly out of place in February, in a grave.

The two women moved on.

They had lunch in town at the Crowninshield Saloon, a casual bar and restaurant with a scrubbed wood floor that was popular with the locals and one of the few that remained open all year long. At her mother's insistence that she eat something, Jane forced down a bowl of hot kale soup, a Portuguese speciality that took away some of the chill that had plagued her since the night before.

Her mother had a chicken salad and a glass of Perrier. Her mother *always* had a chicken salad and a glass of Perrier whenever she was in what she called "a place like this."

"Nantucket. What a desolate place to live," Gwendolyn said, staring out at the rain pounding the bare windows. "Fog . . . rain . . . penetrating cold. . . ."

"Mother, you live in San Francisco," Jane said, recovering her sense of irony. "*You* have fog and rain and penetrating cold."

Gwendolyn Drew gave her daughter a good-natured grimace. "Yes, but we're open all year. We also have compensations: opera and ballet, museums and theaters, not to mention charity balls for all of them. But here! What does one do on this . . . this rock?"

"One sits by the fire, just as we're doing now, and warms one's buns."

"One gets rock fever."

"*I* wouldn't."

"Jane. If you're thinking what I think you're thinking— don't. You couldn't possibly afford to keep Lilac Cottage as a weekend retreat. You have no job. The property taxes alone—"

"I didn't say I was keeping it," Jane answered defensively. She hated when her mother acted like her father.

"I should hope not. This inheritance is an absolute god-send. You've been living on your savings for six months now; how long could you have gone on? The mortgage on your condo alone . . . and what about your father?" she said suddenly. "When he learns about the inheritance, of *course* he'll want you to sell." She brightened. "You can go back to school and retrain; law school maybe—"

"Mother, I'm not going to become a lawyer just because Dad's one. And I *like* being a graphic designer. This down-turn can't last forever. I'll get another job. Eventually." She spread a hard pat of butter so viciously onto her slice of bread that it fell apart in her hand.

Her mother circled her daughter's wrist and said sooth-ingly, "Don't blame me, darling. Blame the economy. Blame the advertising sector. Or better yet—blame your father," she said with a smile. "He's not here; he'll never know."

"Oh no, Mother, I blame *you*," Jane said, only half kid-ding. "You stopped having kids one boy short. Think how much easier my life would be if Dad didn't look to me to carry on his tradition of workaholism. If you'd had a Neal Drew, Jr., *he* could've been the lawyer."

Her mother shrugged and said, "Well, it's too late now. Anyway, we've been all through this. If you don't want to be pressured by your father, you should find yourself a nice rich man and settle down with a family. Like your sister."

"Those are my choices? Law school or marriage? This is practically medieval," Jane said, throwing her hands up and rolling her eyes. It was an overly dramatic gesture, she knew; but she wanted to irritate her mother, and being melodramatic in a public place was a quick and easy way to do it.

Her mother gave her a sit-up-properly-and-eat-your-food look. Jane went back to her Earl Grey tea.

"I feel really guilty about the house. What will Lisa

say?" Jane murmured, wrapping her hands around the tea mug to warm them.

"Your sister is married and financially secure. She won't begrudge you your cottage. Besides, *she* didn't spend a summer with Sylvia."

"I only spent a month."

"And *she* didn't visit her in the nursing home for the last two years."

"It wasn't that often," Jane said sadly. "Not often enough. I wish I'd known before then that Aunt Sylvia was willing to see me."

"Well, what do you want to do? Give it back?" her mother said, exasperated.

"I'm beginning to think so!" It seemed an incredible act of betrayal, having to sell the cottage her aunt had loved so dearly.

"Sweetheart." Her mother's smile was meltingly tender, the kind of smile a mother has for a daughter who's tried to tie her shoelaces for the first time. "Before this windfall there was no way you would have survived without your father's help, sooner or later. We know what a fiercely proud brat you are; wouldn't you rather have the help from Aunt Sylvia than from your stubborn, domineering father? Who, incidentally, loves you more than life itself?"

"Well. Once you put it that way . . ." Jane made a little sound of frustration and gazed out the window, chewing on the inside of her lip.

"It's stopped raining," her mother said, glancing at her watch. "I just have time to make a quick run out with you to see the place—"

"Look!" Jane cried, pointing out the window. "There's the guy who threw the flower in the grave!"

He was sitting in the driver's seat of a rusty, dark green Ford pickup with J & J LANDSCAPING AND NURSERY painted on the door panel. His expression was as grim as ever, which cast a malevolent shadow over the craggy, weathered features of his fortyish face. He looked like a man capable of anything.

"It's hard to imagine him carrying a tiny rose in his pocket," Jane murmured, frowning. She was absolutely put off by the man.

"No mystery about that; Aunt Sylvia must have been a client," her mother said as she dropped her Visa card on top of the tab. "She had to have needed help keeping up the property at the end."

She signaled for a waiter to square up the bill. "Rain or not, I'm looking forward to seeing your Lilac Cottage. As I recall from an old photo, it's an adorable place with lots of shrubs and flowers. We'll have to be very clever marketing it, especially in this economy. . . ."

"Hmmm." But Jane wasn't listening. Her attention was fixed squarely on the driver of the pickup, who'd rolled down his window and was yelling across to someone she couldn't see.

"I want the burner, you moron!" he shouted. *"Bring it over!"* He threw the truck into gear and tore off down South Water Street.

"Charming," Jane's mother remarked, slipping her credit card into her wallet.

"People never shout in San Francisco?" Jane asked dryly.

"Not where we live," her mother said without a trace of irony. "That's the trouble with an island: There's nowhere to run, nowhere to hide, from these types."

Gwendolyn Drew was of the Miss Manners School of Snobbery. As far as she was concerned, you could be rich, or you could be poor. You could be educated, or you could be not. But you had better *behave,* or you were nothing at all. Jane smiled to herself, shook her head, and slipped on her coat. "Ready, Mother?"

CHAPTER 2

Lilac Cottage was a shambles. Jane had tried to prepare herself for the inevitable wear and tear that two years without an occupant can mean to a house. But she hadn't taken into account the savagery of Nantucket's storms, or the corrosiveness of its year-round fog. And she hadn't taken into account her aunt's reluctance to spend any of her savings on the property.

She turned off the key to her rental car and sat, stunned, staring at the tiny two-story Gothic cottage, whose front door was nearly hidden by two massive holly trees flanking either side. Peeling paint, sagging gutters, missing roof shingles, rotted steps . . .

"This isn't the place," Jane said flatly. "I remember a long flagstone path that wandered through a high pergola covered with purple clematis, and there were green shutters all around, and a potter's shed off on the right, and . . . and it was all much *bigger*."

Her mother was more philosophical. "That was a quarter-century ago, darling. You were little. Things looked big. Still, I must admit it's been far more neglected than I thought. This will be a hard sell." A thought seemed to occur to her for the first time. "Poor Sylvia," she said softly, her hand resting on the door handle. "She must've had to watch every cent."

They got out of the car and began picking their way through the front lawn, which had the look of a mowed-down hayfield. Jane moved some of the dead grass aside.

"See? Flagstone. I was right. And this," she said, pausing

before a six-foot post leaning over what used to be the front path, "this must have been part of the pergola." She tried to push the post upright; it made a dull snapping sound at the base and fell to the ground.

"Rotten," her mother said, stepping over it. "Do you have the key?"

But Jane was still riveted to the spot, staring at the post as if it were a soldier felled in some hopeless battle against time. *"I climbed up this pergola,"* she said in an awestruck voice. "I picked a bunch of clematis from the top and wove them into a purple crown for Aunt Sylvia . . . and she let me unpin her hair and brush it out . . . and I put the crown on her head."

She looked around, dreamily, and said, "She sat on a wooden chair right there, next to the house, and the sun picked out the red that was left in her hair . . . and she told me that hers was once the same color as mine. . . ."

"Jane?"

"I can't believe it's all gone," Jane said, still in a faraway voice.

"The key?"

Jane stared at her mother. "To what?"

"Your *future*, ninny!" Jane's mother pointed a manicured finger at the front door. "Open it, dreamer," she commanded, laughing. "Before I grow as old as that post."

Jane searched through the ring for a likely match to the old lock in the door and came up with it on the first try. She turned the tarnished brass knob and, after putting her shoulder to the heavy, sticking door, managed to swing it open. The two women stepped inside to a world of mildew and cobwebs.

Gwendolyn Drew made a face. "God, it smells awful," she said, flipping a switch. When nothing happened, she went up to one of the low windows and flung open its moldy drapes. Weak, gray light spilled into what must have been a front parlor, revealing a boarded-up fireplace and a dreary collection of budget furniture standing on a carpet remnant of some indeterminate color.

"Is there a Goodwill dropoff on the island?" was all Gwendolyn could think to say.

"I don't know. This isn't at all what I remember," Jane said, walking around the room, disappointed that nothing in it reminded her of her aunt. "What happened to Aunt Sylvia's old stuff? She had such nice things."

"Probably she sold them," her mother remarked, looking at the peeling ceiling with dismay. "What kind of nice things?"

"Nothing fancy, but just, you know, nice. There was a slant-top desk I used to sit at to write you and Dad that summer . . . it had pigeonholes and a secret compartment. . . ."

Jane thought of the desk and sighed. "Well, this is too bad." Somewhere in the middle of the night she'd comforted herself with the thought that she'd haul that desk back to Connecticut and somehow reconnect with Aunt Sylvia.

She followed her mother into the kitchen, which had little to recommend it: doorless cupboards, worn-out linoleum, a freestanding porcelain sink. In a little pantry adjacent, an ancient Frigidaire and a three-burner stove were crammed side by side under a high, tiny window. It was all as inefficient as could be.

The two women crossed the hall and peeked into the bathroom.

"Not as bad as the kitchen," Jane's mother decided. "Black and white deco tiles are a good, classic treatment. And clawfoot tubs are still in."

Upstairs there were two small bedrooms which had casement windows and a cozy, steep-eaved charm. At the end of the hall was an even smaller room filled with boxes, some broken chairs, and the head and footboards of a small spindle bed.

"I like the view," Jane said, looking over the top of a huge bare lilac just outside the window. "This would make a nice little office."

"I think, more of a nursery."

Jane closed her eyes and began counting to ten. "Mother—don't start."

"Start what?" Gwendolyn asked blandly. "I wasn't talking about you."

"Of course you were."

They began to retrace their steps downstairs. "Well, can you blame me?" her mother asked in a plaintive voice. "Jane, you're thirty-three years old, and I don't see *any*one *any*where on the horizon. Your sister—who, I might add, is five years younger than you are—has found herself a nice hard-working doctor and is soon to give birth to her second child."

"Whereas I am—"

"Not even dating, are you?"

"Not in the way *you* mean."

They stopped in the middle of the dingy kitchen, and as her mother exhorted her for the umpteenth time to shape up her life, Jane found herself scanning the open cupboards for some bit of crockery, a teapot, anything, to remind her of the summer she'd spent here when she was eight. She wanted so desperately to hold on to the memory of her aunt.

"Darling, I'm only going on about this because I love you very much, and I don't want . . ." Her mother sighed, took her by her shoulders, and said, "It's true, what they say: Youth really is wasted on the young. Jane—don't you see? Falling in love takes time. Building a family takes time. You act as if time is some endless resource you have."

"I haven't met the right man, Mother," Jane said absently. "I'm not going to force a relationship where one doesn't want to grow."

Gwendolyn Drew sighed again, heavily, and Jane noticed almost for the first time the lines that ran from her finely shaped nose to the corners of her usually animated mouth. And her gray hair, so much more than before. Her mother was no longer young . . . fifty-nine? Was it possible?

Her mother seemed to be reading her mind. "All right, I admit it: Yours isn't the only biological clock I'm worried about. Your father and I are getting on; *this* is our time for grandchildren. You know how much we adore little Jonathan."

Grateful at least for her mother's candor, Jane smiled and shook her head. "I need more reason than—"

"Of course I know that. You can't rush these things; haven't I just said as much? But in the meantime, shouldn't you be doing something more with your life? Being a graphic designer was very nice, but the advertising industry isn't going to bounce back for a long, long time. Aren't you just, well, treading water?"

She seemed to be choosing her words with infinite care. "I suppose what I'm saying is, it's *fine* if you take a career track. It's *fine* if you take the mommy track. Our great fear is that you're not taking *either* track."

It began to dawn on Jane why her mother had really detoured to Nantucket: it was to jump-start her daughter's flagging ambition. "Well!" Jane said with a false, bright cheerfulness. "It beats having a heart attack trying to do both tracks at once."

But her mother was right, and Jane knew it. She'd become so discouraged by the job market in the last few months that she'd stopped looking. If that free-lance assignment hadn't fallen into her lap . . . She gave her mother a tremulous smile and put out her arms and hugged her.

"Anyway, here we are, trying to figure out how to sell this house. Am I on the right track now?"

Gwendolyn Drew kissed her daughter on the cheek, wrapped her arm around her waist, and whispered in her ear, "I'd rather have the grandchild."

"You're hopeless!" Jane said, swatting her mother's shoulder.

"True," her mother admitted with a sigh. "But . . . lately I've been wondering more and more: do you want children, or don't you?"

"How can I know, if there's no one in my life to have children *with*?" Jane wailed.

Her mother gave her a quick, sympathetic squeeze. Having declared a truce, the two of them went arm in arm into the last of the rooms together; and in the last of those rooms, Jane found what she was looking for.

It was large, bare-windowed, and even on a wet day like this one, filled with light. A cherry-manteled fireplace dominated one wall. The windows opened to a view of gently rolling terrain, dotted with bayberry bushes and low evergreens. Outside, a soft gray fog suffused everything, fuzzing the edges, intensifying the greens. Jane suddenly remembered that a tiny old burying ground nicked one corner of the property.

The room itself was attractively furnished: a Persian rug, an Empire bed covered in kilims, an old brass table lamp. The whimsical iron plant stand was still there, and the old rocking chair—Jane remembered it well, having spent afternoons petting the cats in it—and best of all, the slant-top oak desk, tucked quietly in the corner. Bookcases on each side of the fireplace were still half-filled with books, as if Sylvia Merchant had been fully planning to come home on sunny weekends.

"I *remember* this room," Jane cried. "I remember the fireplace. It was August, and we couldn't have a fire, and I prayed for just one night of frost. . . ."

"Look at this—some sort of old portable kerosene

heater. I wonder if the furnace even works," Gwendolyn mused. "Oh dear; that'll cost you."

The old and faded wallpaper was exquisite, a restrained floral of ivory, rose, and green. Jane remembered tracing the tendrils of ivy with her mind's eye as she sat at the desk and struggled to write clever notes to her mother and father. It all came rushing back, her connection with the place.

"It's obvious that Sylvia retreated with her favorite things to one-room living," Jane's mother said thoughtfully, stroking a soapstone figurine of a cat that sat on a side table. "I've seen it happen before," she added. She wandered over to a small inlaid table that stood next to the Empire bed. "It's an economizing gesture . . . a last, desperate attempt to parcel one's resources. . . ."

Suddenly she stiffened. Her voice coiled tightly around a gasp. "*Tarot* cards. So she *was* some kind of witch!"

"Witch? What witch?" Jane walked up to the gaming table and stared at the pack of symbol-filled cards arranged across the tabletop. "Do witches use tarot cards?" she asked, amused by her mother's overwrought reaction. "I thought only psychics did."

"Well, who*ever*," Gwendolyn said testily. "It just shows that your father and I did the right thing, keeping you away from her."

The bemused look faded from Jane's face. "What do you mean—keeping me away?"

Her mother made an impatient sound. "What do you think I mean? When you got back from your summer on Nantucket, your head was filled with paranormal gibberish. All you could talk about was ghosts and goblins. It frightened your father and me half to death. We decided to . . . well, discourage . . . any further association between Sylvia and you."

She picked up a card with distaste and tossed it back on the table. "And I can see now, we did the right thing."

Missing pieces to one of the puzzles of Jane's life suddenly fell into place. Her parents' insistence that she begin attending summer camp; her letters to her aunt that went unanswered; her mother's vague explanations for her aunt's aloofness—suddenly it all made sense.

"You kept me away from Aunt Sylvia because she told me ghost stories? But I don't even remember them!"

"Of course not; we stopped things in time."

"You can't be serious! I don't believe it—Aunt Sylvia would have said something when I began visiting her in the nursing home."

"We had asked her not to."

Yes. It all made sense.

"This is—how *could* you?" Jane said in a shaking voice.

Her mother shrugged unhappily. "We did what we thought was best for you at the time, Jane. Maybe we were right, and maybe we were wrong. But you were such an impressionable little girl. Anyway, how could we know that Sylvia was going to leave you her house?"

Exasperated, Jane threw up her hands and let them fall with a flop at her sides. *"That's not the point!* Aunt Sylvia was left *alone* all those years—"

"I know, I know," her mother said, wincing. "But what's done is done. It's always easy to—for goodness' sake! There's the fellow in the pickup, driving right through your yard!" She nodded out the window at the dark-green truck marked J & J LANDSCAPING AND NURSERY that was speeding past the side of the house.

It was a transparent ploy, but the distraction worked. "That's not my—Aunt Sylvia's—land. It's the neighbor's land," Jane said, feeling angry and contrary.

"Oh, yes; I see that now. It's a nice property. The house has been done over beautifully. Who lives there?"

"Apparently some New Yorker who uses it on weekends," Jane said stiffly. "He has a sister living there at the moment."

"And meanwhile, Mr. Oak Tree has disappeared," Gwendolyn said, peering through one side of the window. "Do you suppose there's a shortcut across the property next door? That could be very annoying—at least, until Mr. Oak Tree gets his muffler fixed."

"Mother, will you stop obsessing on real estate and just—"

"Just what? Apologize?" Gwendolyn Drew shook her head sadly and fixed a sad, pale blue gaze on her daughter. "Wait until *you* have an eight-year-old, darling. If she came back from someone's house with stories of hauntings—if she woke up soaking wet from nightmares she was too frightened to recall—what would *you* do?"

Jane compressed her lips and lifted her chin up. The truth was, she didn't have a clue. She'd never had an eight-year-old.

"I just wish I'd known," was all she could think to say.

Jane drove her mother to the airport in moody silence. Her mother, who did not believe in coaxing people out of moods of any kind, sat amiably beside her, ready to chat if the need arose. But the day had been an overwhelming one for Jane. With a melancholy hug she put her mother aboard the commuter back to Boston.

After that Jane returned directly to the Jared Coffin House where she was staying, and borrowed a copy of the Yellow Pages. By six o'clock she'd been able to cajole a plumber, an electrician, and even a roofer into meeting with her the following day, Friday. Things were going well; her spirits began to lift.

Jane slept better that night, and by the time the sun finally poked its nose over the horizon, she was putting away a big breakfast at the inn. Her first stop was at the hardware store, where she bought a couple of smoke alarms. Her next stop was at the A&P, tucked hard by the harbor, where she picked up cleaning supplies, food, can-

dles, and an Igloo cooler. After that she bought a pair of
overalls and a workshirt, and after *that*, a bottle of Bermuda rum. She was ready to take on Lilac Cottage.

By all rights Jane should have been depressed when she
saw the cottage in bright morning sun: there seemed to be
less paint and more weeds than she remembered from the
day before. But even in its state of forlorn shabbiness, the
cottage beckoned to her. Maybe it was the fond memory of
her summer there, or maybe it was her natural desire to
put things right; whatever the reason, Jane found herself
standing in the middle of the mowed-down lawn, hugging
herself with anticipation.

*It has so much charm, so much potential. It may not be the
biggest cottage, but it's in a wonderful location. And it's so
sweet. You can tell it wants to be friends. You can just tell.*

She swung around, searching for the ocean that she
knew was out there not far from where she stood. But the
house was on low land; there was no water view. It didn't
matter. She inhaled a lungful of cold salt air, her chest
expanding from the effort. *Now* this *is living,* she thought,
grateful simply to *be* alive.

It was at that exact, precise moment of gratitude that
Jane found herself slammed violently in the back, so hard
that she went sprawling on the soggy grass in front of her.
Shocked and winded, she rolled over on her elbows and
found herself staring at the massive head of a dog—or
some cross between a dog and a mastodon—that was hovering over her. Drooling.

"Buster! Dammit, Buster! Come back here!" It was a
woman's voice, high and musical and totally without au-
thority.

Jane didn't dare take her eyes off the panting beast, who
seemed to be regarding her as he would a smallish par-
tridge. It was only after the woman—pretty, twenty, and
dressed in jeans and a bomber's jacket—grabbed the dog's
collar with both hands, that Jane allowed herself to sit up.

The collar, which looked pretty much like a large man's belt, seemed sturdy enough, but Jane wasn't so sure about the woman. She looked as fragile as stemware.

"He's just a puppy; he won't hurt you," the girl said with an apologetic grin.

"That's what they all say," Jane said with a shaky laugh, wiping the drooly sleeve of her jacket on the grass. She stood up.

"I'm Cissy Hanlin, by the way," the pretty blonde said, not daring to let go of Buster's collar. "I live next door."

Jane introduced herself, and Cissy explained that she'd always wanted a dog but her husband didn't like animals but now they were separated and so the first thing she did was get a dog, a big dog, because she felt safer being so all alone and it was *so* lucky that she discovered Buster, who was a cross—could Jane tell?—between a black Lab and a Saint Bernard or at least that's what the waitresses who brought him to the shelter before they left the island after summer was over said.

She paused, at last, for breath.

Jane said, "Yep. He looks like a black Saint Bernard."

At this point Buster's tail was wagging furiously, landing with quick hard thumps on the back of Jane's thighs. It did not seem possible that an act of friendliness could inflict so much pain. The interlude ended abruptly when a squirrel —dumber or braver than most—scampered across the lawn not far from them. Buster took off in loping pursuit, his tongue lolling out the side of his mouth, his paws ripping out consecutive mounds of earth.

He crashed through a rhododendron, breaking off several branches, and plowed over an azalea before fetching up at the trunk of one of the huge hollies that blocked Jane's front door. His bark, like the Hound of the Baskervilles', came straight from hell. From somewhere high, high in the holly tree, the squirrel twitted him.

"*Silly* puppy," Cissy cried. She turned to Jane with a helpless shrug. "I can't seem to get him to *stay.*"

And I can't seem to get you to go, Jane thought, surveying the damage. She smiled weakly, her thoughts turning to stockade fences, and said, "Maybe it's just a phase."

Cissy rolled her eyes and said, "I *wish.* Well, it's nice that you're going to be around for a little while; I get so bored by myself. If you need help with anything, just shout," she added, and began whistling her dog away from the tree.

Eventually Buster came and dragged Cissy off, and Jane was able to unload the car. Her plan was to spend the next week cleaning, seeing to critical repairs, and talking to realtors (once she'd deodorized the place a bit) about listing the house in spring.

But first things first, she thought, taking down a jelly jar glass, which she wiped clean with her shirt. She took the rum and the glass into the fireplace room and poured a tot for herself.

Then she lifted the glass to the fireplace, the focal point of the room, and said, "Aunt Sylvia—thank you. I don't deserve this, but I thank you. I'll make this place pretty, and someone with children will live here and love it, and you and I will somehow share in their joy."

She tossed off the glass, and the odd-tasting rum shot through her winter-chilled body like a ball of flame. Her aunt had visited Bermuda once, and brought back the rum, and that's the only kind she drank for the rest of her life. (Jane used to smuggle a flask into the nursing home, and the two would sneak a tiny ceremonial drink together before she left for the night.)

The thought that there would be no more smuggling hit Jane hard; she poured another ounce, this time for her aunt, and sipped it as she wandered around the room, pausing to stroke a worn chair cover, taking a moment to scan the titles of the books on their shelves. How sad, she thought, that there were no framed photographs of loved ones anywhere in the room, not even of Sylvia's cats. All Jane saw was a charcoal sketch of a young woman in a plain gown, with a coal-skuttle bonnet lying on the floor beside her. A nineteenth-century Quaker, Jane decided, and an unhappy one at that.

She walked up to the framed sketch, which was hanging in a quiet corner of the room. All in all, it wasn't badly done. Perhaps it was her aunt's work. Sylvia Merchant had enjoyed dabbling with charcoal and pastels, although her subjects had generally come from the garden. Jane looked more closely and saw that she was right: In the corner of the drawing were the initials *SM*.

Jane took the frame from the wall and walked over to a window with it. There was evidence of erasure, as if her aunt had struggled to capture an exact degree of unhappiness in the young woman's face. And what unhappiness! Her brows were tilted upward and toward one another; tears rolled down her face. Her full mouth was partly opened, as if she were imploring someone, while her hands were curled tightly around one another in obvious distress. As for her long dark gown, it hung a little too closely to her body to be historically correct. Like the curls that ringed her brow, the clinging garment gave the woman a voluptuous air that was at odds with the modest intents of Quaker fashion.

Jane shivered, deeply moved by the subject's distress. The drawing had the immediacy and power of a photograph. *Well done, Aunt Sylvia,* she thought, hanging the sketch back up on its hook. *You should have done figures more often.* She wondered who'd posed for her aunt. An island girl? Or had Sylvia merely copied someone else's work? But no; the sketch had too much emotion in it. Jane looked around the room, half expecting to find a companion sketch, this one of the brute who was causing the Quaker woman such pain. But there was nothing else.

She finished her rum and put the bottle away. There was

work to be done—and in the next several hours she found out just how much, when the contractors dropped by one by one with their estimates.

The roofer looked things over, frowned, and said, "Five thousand dollars."

The electrician looked things over, laughed, and said, "Five thousand dollars."

The plumber shook his head and said, "Torch it."

By the end of the day Jane was bloodied but unbowed. *Okay, so the house isn't perfect,* she admitted as she boiled some tea water in a pot that looked as if it had a questionable past. But at least now she had heat—in most of the rooms, anyway; and water—even though it was flowing through lead pipes; and as for the roof, well, it wasn't supposed to rain for a day or two.

But now it was one in the morning; it was time to drag herself back to the Jared Coffin House. She sipped her Earl Grey tea tiredly, eyeing the Empire sofa in the room. Tomorrow she would definitely sleep here. She simply couldn't afford not to. She went around turning off the lights, aware that she hadn't even allowed herself the diversion of going through the boxes and closets. Today it was all Lysol and Tilex; maybe tomorrow she could relax and poke around a bit.

And tomorrow she would pick up a book on interpreting tarot cards before she packed away the deliberate arrangement that had been left sitting on the game table. *That,* she was determined to do.

She was just switching off the red ginger-jar lamp in the fireplace room when she heard the unmuffled roar of the dark green pickup turn in from the road again and race past her house. Buster, next door, heard it too and began woofing maniacally. The pickup had passed in and out at least half a dozen times in the course of the day, setting off the beast each time, and now it was one in the morning and they were both still hard at it.

What's going on? she wondered, disturbed by the implications. *Short hops, in and out. . . .* The only other time she'd noticed a travel pattern like that was when she was in college: The guy in the house across the street used to zip in and out all day and night, and eventually he was arrested for dealing drugs.

Terrific. She was beginning to think just like her mother. Surely there must be some everyday explanation. The man was probably . . . probably . . .

But she couldn't come up with an everyday explanation.

CHAPTER 3

Saturday morning dawned sunny and dry. After checking out of the Jared Coffin House, Jane bought the cheapest sheets she could find, a book on the tarot, and half a dozen gallons of white paint. Her plan was to paint the interior entirely white, which would end up looking clean and offending no one.

She bought coffee and a sticky bun and headed for Lilac Cottage, mentally revising her calendar as she drove. One week for the cleanup would not be enough, but two might do it if she worked like a fiend. After all, she did have the time. If only she had the money. At the moment it was a toss-up between trying—ha!—to get an equity loan or spending the last of her rainy-day fund.

She shook off the sobering thought. The morning was too wonderful, all bright and mild and unlike March. Even Lilac Cottage seemed to have thrown off its winter chill. With all the shades pulled up and the drapes pulled back, the tattered house looked as relaxed as an old, sun-warmed cat.

Jane opened her car door and had one foot on the ground when she heard the by now familiar *woofwoofwoof* of Big Buster, hell-bent for her car. She yanked her leg back and slammed the door just in time: Buster's muddy paws landed on the car's window, not on the front of her jacket. She cracked the window open and was trying unsuccessfully to shoo him away when a shrill whistle pierced the air. It came from a man walking in the road. Buster took off for him like a bat out of hell and Jane thought, *Does the dog have any speed besides* full *speed?*

The man, tall and blond and about her age, and with a good-natured smile very much like Cissy's, threw a stick the size of a railroad tie in the opposite direction from Jane. Buster bounded after the stick, scooped it up in his massive jaws, and kept right on going. Jane got out of the car. The man walked up to her, smiling ruefully and shaking his head.

"He doesn't have the concept of 'fetch' down yet—praise the lord. He'll turn around eventually. By then you should be safely inside."

Feeling cowardly, Jane felt forced to explain. "As it happens, this is my last clean jacket."

He nodded. "Say no more. My cleaning bill's quadrupled since my sister adopted that mutt. I'm Bing Andrews, by the way. Cissy told me about you. Jane Drew, isn't it?"

They shook hands and Bing said, "I was sorry to hear about Sylvia Merchant. I didn't know her personally—I bought my place just after she left the island—but I've heard that she was . . . a very interesting woman."

"You mean you heard she was a witch." The words blurted out before Jane could think to stop them.

There was the smallest of pauses. Then Bing burst into a laugh and said, "That's exactly what I heard!"

By rights Jane should have been offended. But Bing's laugh was so infectious, so good-humored, that she found herself laughing with him. Maybe it was the warm sun, bouncing off his blond hair; or maybe it was the way he cringed and crossed his forearms when he saw Buster loping back toward them—whatever it was, she liked his style. And besides, *she* was the one who'd brought up the subject of witches.

"My aunt told me the kids around here really believed it," Jane explained. "When you're an old woman without children or friends—and you refuse, for example, to give back a baseball that's gone whizzing through your living room window—the witch thing becomes inevitable."

Bing was watching her with a lively, appreciative look on his face. "Ah, but *I* heard—this talk doesn't bother you?"

"Not at all. What did you hear?" Jane asked, curious.

"I heard that she used to walk around talking to some-one—"

"To herself. Old people do that. Heck, *I* do that."

"*—who talked back,*" he said, finishing his thought. "In another voice. A man's voice."

There was an openness in his look that kept the chill out of what he was saying. He spoke completely without malice, and that made it impossible to get angry with him. "Who told you this?" she asked, wondering.

"The people who sold me my house. Actually, it came from the wife, who was a bit of a crone herself."

"Well there you *are!*" Jane said, relieved. "It's one old woman's word against another's."

Bing grinned, and she caught her breath. He was almost *too* handsome, in a Robert Redford, boyish kind of way.

"She seemed sharp as a tack to me," he was saying. "But then, so does your Aunt Sylvia. Since they've both passed on, I guess we'll never know." He loomed over her, tall and friendly and completely at ease.

Jane was remembering that he was a bachelor. She folded her arms across her chest. *Oh yes. Definitely a heart-breaker,* she decided. She found herself nodding with herself in agreement.

"Will we?" he asked, misinterpreting her response.

"Uhh-h . . . well . . . who knows?" she said vacantly. She had dropped the thread of their conversation, and now she cast her eyes downward, looking for it. Instead she found Buster, sniffing interestedly at her ankles. She jumped away.

Bing grabbed Buster's collar and said, "Don't even think about it, pal."

Jane was deciding whether or not to run for it when a dark burgundy Mercedes slowed to a halt in front of Bing and her. The driver was Phillip Harrow, casually but still beautifully dressed, in turtleneck and designer jacket.

"Hey, you two," he said, rolling down his window. "How about dinner at my place next Saturday? It'll be a chance for you to meet your neighbors, Jane."

Bing waited for Jane to answer. Caught off guard, she stammered an affirmative. Bing said to Phillip Harrow, "What time?"

"Say seven thirty. Strictly casual." Harrow put the Mercedes in gear and drove off.

Bing began hauling the dog toward his house. "Let me give you a tip," he said to Jane. "Phillip's idea of casual is a doublet and waistcoat."

"Dear me," she answered with an ironic flip of her wrist. "I shall have to wear tea-length, I suppose."

Hell and damnation, she thought, going into the cottage. *I don't have time to socialize. I just want to fix up the house, sell it, and get on with my life.*

Her mother was right: She couldn't afford to keep the place, so what was the point of getting to know the neighbors? Besides, now she'd have to go back home for dressy clothes.

"Ah, well," she said, sighing for the benefit of no one in particular. "If I go home, I can get my own car and turn in the rental."

Jane worked diligently through the morning on the Lysol/Tilex detail, and when she couldn't stand it anymore, she went for a walk in fresh air. She had no clear remembrance of just how much land went with Lilac Cottage, and it seemed like a good time to find out.

There was hardly any. Lilac Cottage was shoehorned in between Bing's more generously sited house to the east, and a really grand parcel called Edgehill, bounding hers to the north and the west, which belonged to Phillip Harrow. Somewhere in the northeast corner lay the tiny old graveyard, and beyond that she saw a row of arborvitae that blocked off the view. That was where the green pickup truck kept heading in and out.

There was also a wet gully, from a spring perhaps, with a tiny and quite charming old footbridge over it, on Phillip Harrow's land behind Lilac Cottage. As Jane drew near, some furry thing scampered out of the gully and waddled away.

Jane Drew was a city girl and proud of it; she knew the New York subway system like the back of her hand. But she was taking to this rural side of Nantucket like—*like that furry thing to water,* she thought, smiling to herself as she picked her way through crunchy-cold brush toward the northeast end. Her breath came fast and frosty as she tramped on at a bracing pace. And yet, here it was, March, the worst month of the year—Hate Month, the islanders called it. What would a good month—a June, or a September, say—be like on Nantucket?

Oh no you don't, girl. You are going to sell the house and use the money to start a new career. Boutique, yogurt bar, graduate school. Whatever. Fortunes are built in times like these. She could hear her father saying it. And he was absolutely right.

She almost missed the little graveyard that was snuggled between the adjacent properties; grasses and bushes obscured most of the dozen or so historic, crooked gravestones that stood like drunken sentries over their forgotten captives. It saddened her; somehow the neglect was less tolerable here than on her aunt's property. She wondered who 'ad the responsibility to maintain the burying ground —surely, the town of Nantucket? Her recollection of the place was that it had been neat and well kept.

A wistful thought came to her. *Too bad Aunt Sylvia couldn't have been buried here, almost in her own garden.*

She wandered from gravestone to gravestone, wondering when the most recent burial was. But among the Obadiahs and Elizabeths, the Mitchells and the Whitsons, there was no end date later than 1854. Her aunt had died a century and a half too late.

One of the gravestones was half missing; but it, too, must have dated to the period. JUDITH, it read, and 1802. But the last name was broken off, and the end date. Jane wondered about vandals; but the damage seemed to have been the work of a thorny, robust shrub rose that was growing atop the grave.

The roots have gone under the gravestone and broken it in two, she decided. Part of the broken stone lay under the thorny canes. Jane reached in gingerly to turn it over. It was blank. Disappointed, she began to stand up, but she was careless: she suffered a sharp, long scratch through the sleeve of her sweatshirt. With a yelp of pain she fell back to her knees and carefully disengaged herself from the thorny cane.

Serves you right, stupid. You're supposed to be cleaning house. She took it as a sign that there was no place in her life just now for idle curiosity. So she returned to the cottage, took up her Tilex, and attacked yet another colony of mildew. By evening her hands looked like prunes and her lungs felt scalded; but the house was beginning to look and smell undeniably clean.

When the knock came at the door, her first instinct was not to answer. She was a mess, and she had no wish for distractions. But the drapes were still open, and it was obvious she was at home.

It was Cissy. "Have you seen my dog?" she asked with a hopeful smile. "He's run away again."

"I heard him bark not so long ago. The last time that green pickup drove past."

"Oh, yeah; Buster really gets into it when he goes

through. So you can hear Buster barking?" she asked naively.

"*Seattle* can hear him," Jane couldn't help saying. When Cissy looked crestfallen she added, "But it's not a problem. Really."

"Oh, good. After a while you hardly notice." She peeked around Jane at the horribly furnished parlor beyond. "I've never seen this place before," she said, pretty much inviting herself in.

With a silent sigh Jane stepped aside for her to come in. "It's not much to look at right now."

"My God; I *guess,*" Cissy agreed, looking around her. "Who would've thought a place like this could be located right next to my brother's?"

"Gee. Go figure," said Jane laconically.

"I didn't mean that the way it sounded," Cissy said quickly. "It's just that I've heard such *weird* stories about this place and the lady—your great-aunt, I guess she was— who lived here. Like how one of her cats only had three legs because she needed the fourth one for a spell. Whereas my brother is just so, you know, *normal.* Like *you,*" she added brightly. "You're normal."

Jane laughed out loud. Cissy seemed so young. She made Jane feel so old. "I'm sure you mean that in the very best way, Cissy; but it's late and I have an awful lot of work to do."

"Oh, okay," she answered, taking no offense. "I'll just take a quick peek around and go. I really should find Buster before he ends up at the shelter; he's been there twice this month already."

She went through the rooms with Jane in quick succession, finishing up in the fireplace room, which in the soft glow of lamplight looked warm and cozy. Almost immediately Cissy spied the tarot cards spread out on the inlaid table.

"Tarot! Cool!" She ran over to the table and said with

real enthusiasm, "This is a beautiful deck; I've never seen one this old before. Will you give me a reading sometime?"

"I wouldn't know how," Jane said simply. "Those cards were there, arranged just like that, when I arrived."

"Really! So you don't know what the question was that was put to them." Cissy lifted a card from the center one on which it lay. "Hmmm . . . the significator card is the Lovers . . . I wonder if your aunt was doing a reading for someone."

"You understand the cards?" Jane asked, surprised.

"Well, no; but one of my sorority sisters used to do readings for us."

Cissy pored over the layout of cards attentively, sweeping her blond hair away from her face, drawing her brows together in concentration. Finally she shook her pretty head. "Nope. Without knowing what's called the 'situation,' I couldn't tell you."

She looked up; the expression in her blue eyes was uncharacteristically serious. "But I can tell you one thing. If this was a random spread, it's a very powerful one."

She motioned Jane to the inlaid table and said, "Out of seventy-eight tarot cards, only twenty-two are what're called the Greater Arcana—somewhere I heard that that works out to two out of seven. But look at the ten cards dealt here: *Seven* are from the Greater Arcana. That's really rare. Here's the High Priestess, here's the Moon . . . Temperance . . . Judgment . . . the Charioteer . . . and—anyone would recognize this one—Death."

Jane studied the beautifully illustrated antique cards at length. Their rich colors and intricate designs seemed to blend perfectly with the worn Persian rug in the room. Part of her wanted to believe that the cards were nothing more than her aunt's decorative arrangement of *objets d'art*.

The other part of her wanted to know how long her aunt had been a witch.

Cissy left and Jane, suddenly unable to keep her eyes open, decided to wash up and call it a day. She was changing in front of the old, beveled mirror that hung in a simple frame in the bathroom when she saw the scratch she'd got on her left shoulder from the rosebush. All day long she'd been bothered by a stinging, burning sensation. Now she knew why: the scratch had gone deep, drawing blood. The blood had smeared across a broad section of her shoulder and breast, making the wound look much worse than it was. Jane had no antiseptic, of course; so she cleaned the scratch with soap and water, slipped into a warm flannel nightgown, and went to bed.

As she dropped off into a troubled sleep, the last image to flit through her mind was of richly designed tarot cards smeared with blood.

It was pitch black out, wild and wet and frightening. She was hovering over a precipice, inches away from a drop that she knew fell thirty feet. She didn't care. She had been there many times before, straining to see into the blackness, over the precipice, into the distance beyond. It was impossible, of course. She knew that. She always went there when the weather was foul, but when the weather was foul, she could not see. It was an infuriating, agonizing conundrum.

Her hands gripped the rough and weathered wood railing as she leaned into the fury of the wind, squinting into nothingness. Tomorrow morning her hands would once again be filled with splinters. She knew that, too, but it made no difference. Nothing could change her behavior, because her actions were driven by fear—fear that this time, he would not come back. How could he possibly come back? She brought both hands up against her mouth, warding off a vomit of terror. He *would* come back; he'd done it before. He knew she couldn't live without him. He *must* come back.

The rain drove sideways into her face, soaking her gown, blowing her bonnet from her head. Held in place by the ties under her chin, the bonnet flopped madly back and forth across her shoulders like a kite on a short tether. She didn't care. Her mind was racing ahead, through a life lived without him. But it raced through blackness, like a meteor through space, because without him there was nothing.

She clung there, wet and wild with fear, waiting. But she waited in blackness.

When Jane woke up, she was drenched in sweat. At first she thought she was soaked from the rain; and then she remembered the dream. The strange and terrifying dream; it came back to her in bits and pieces as she staggered out of bed and into her morning routine. She remembered the terror of it with an intensity that even now made her shiver. And yet she knew in her soul that the terror had had nothing to do with the high and windswept place where she dreamed she'd stood, watching and waiting. No, the terror had come from the thought that she'd never again see this . . . this *someone* she loved so immeasurably.

Who?

She wasn't in love with anyone, had never *been* in love with anyone, not to that degree. Why would she dream that she was? Or maybe she hadn't been dreaming of herself. Maybe it was one of those dreams where you were in the character and yet somehow out of the character, watching from the front row. She had a vivid image of that bonnet, flapping back and forth across someone's shoulders.

Whose?

The dream bothered her more than she wanted to admit; it was just so . . . *intense.* And yet, as all dreams do, this one faded, and by the time the coffee was brewed, Jane was convinced that it was the result of late-night snacking and an overactive imagination.

She'd been tired the night before, that's all, and she'd let Cissy spook her. New house, long hours, no phone, no TV —that kind of isolation was bound to make a person think funny. But now it was a bright new day, and Cissy was coming over to help paint, and she was even bringing along a radio.

"Tomorrow's Sunday and I have nothing to do," she'd insisted to Jane the night before. "Please let me paint. Please please please."

So Jane had let herself be talked into accepting Cissy's help later, and now she was lingering over her Cheerios and reading the preface to her book on the tarot. She was glad to read that tarot had nothing to do with either witchcraft or fortune-telling—meaning she and her mother were *both* wrong—and that it was to be regarded, instead, as a body of wisdom.

That made sense. Aunt Sylvia had been nothing if not a seeker of wisdom. She'd read Scripture, she'd read Shakespeare, she'd read the Koran. She'd read anything she could get her hands on. Naturally she would've read the tarot.

Jane put the book aside, then sipped the last of her coffee while she studied the kitchen with an eye to improving it. In a way, it would be nice to leave it just the way it was, right down to the collection of old spoons that hung in a little wood rack next to the door. But the layout was hopelessly inefficient; it would surely kill a sale. The pantry would have to go and new cabinets be installed.

She heard a sound, turned, and saw Cissy's nose pressed up against the window in the back door; the girl waved energetically and let herself in. "Where do we start?" she asked, hiking up a pair of oversized painter's pants and

adjusting the red kerchief on her head. She looked charming but inept—kind of like a Barbie doll with a paint
bucket.

Jane poured her a cup of coffee and said, "So where did
you end up finding Buster last night?"

"I didn't, exactly," Cissy said with a guilty smile. She
scooped two teaspoons of sugar into the mug. "But don't
worry; I promised I'd help you paint, and that's what I'm
going to do."

"Cissy! What about Buster? I thought—"

A heavy rap at the kitchen door sent Jane jumping.
Through its window she saw the man from J & J Nursery,
with what could only be called an evil look on his face.
When she opened the door, it became clear why: He was
holding a rope attached to Cissy's dog. There he was, big,
dumb Buster, panting expectantly, all set for the next adventure.

The dog saw his mistress and tried to make a dash for
her, but his holder said *"Stay"* in a voice that suggested
there were few other options.

"Sorry to bother you," he said to Jane—although it
looked like he didn't care one way or the other—"but I
was on my way over to return the dog to Mrs. Hanlin,
when I saw her come in here."

"Oh *thank* you," Cissy cried, rushing up to them.
"Where was he?"

"In our barn. Nose to nose with a racoon. I considered
bringing him over after I split up the pair, but I didn't think
you'd like being rousted from bed at three A.M."

"God, no. Good thinking," Cissy answered, completely
missing the irony in his voice. Without any apology she
took the rope from him, wrapped it twice around her fist,
and said gaily. "Be back in a sec."

That left Jane trying once again to make eye contact
with the square-jawed and evasive stranger. He had known

her aunt; she wanted to know how well. Was that asking so much?

He was already turning to leave, so she said quickly, "You're from J & J Nursery. I've seen your truck."

His smile was thin and ironic. "You mean you've heard it."

"That too," she admitted with the exact same smile. Hoping to get some clue who he was, she asked, "What does J & J stand for?"

"Jim and John. Is it important?" he asked, cocking his head just enough to show insolence.

His uppityness seemed uncalled for, so she dug her heels in, ignoring it. "I see," she said with deliberate brightness. "So are you Jim, or are you John?"

"I'm Mac."

"Ah. Neither." *A hired hand, then, with a chip on his shoulder.* "I'm Jane," she said, matching his tone exactly. "Pleased to meet you." With that, she let him go.

He went—but not before tugging at the brim of his cap in a yes-massah way that left her embarrassed and indignant.

Really! she thought, closing the door after him. *What did I do? Try to start an innocent conversation?* She slammed her cup on the porcelain drainboard of the sink. Her mother's first impression of the man had been right: it was obvious that he lacked any manners at all. She folded her arms across her sweatshirt and glared at the kitchen floor.

But after a moment her anger relented. *After all,* I'm *the one who didn't bother at first to introduce myself.* She'd treated him like some hired hand before she'd known he *was* a hired hand. And she shouldn't have done it even then. *What a rotten start,* she thought, dispirited. *I'll never get him to open up about Aunt Sylvia.*

Why *did he throw that flower in her grave?*

CHAPTER 4

Cissy showed back up, this time with the radio, and after that, Jane was too immersed in giving painting lessons to worry about Mac and his flower. It turned out that Cissy was hopeless—hopeless!—as a painter's assistant. She dripped, she slopped, she couldn't cut in a straight edge to save her life. Jane, who could paint and wallpaper with one arm tied behind her back, was spending half her time cleaning up after the girl.

Still, it was almost touching to watch Cissy dip the brush into the paint, take aim, and swing it like a bat at the wall, all the time happily chatting nonstop about the men in her life, good and bad.

"I can't believe that with a role model as perfect as my brother, I went and married a stinker like Dave. I was too young—nineteen is way too young—but how could I not see that Dave only cared about football, beer, and D-cups, in that order? I mean, unless there was a game on TV, I couldn't ever count on his being at home—no, wait, I'm a liar; once he cheated on me during a *Superbowl*—and after a while that gets really tired, y'know?"

She frowned and took aim at the wall again. "So I left him. It wasn't easy, but Bing has been *so* supportive. He's basically raised me since our parents died. I came to Nantucket because Bing said it would be a good place to sort myself out."

She noticed a huge paint blob on the floor, lifted her shoe, checked the sole, wiped it with a rag, and kept on painting, kept on talking. "Well, I'm sorted out now. I want

to go back to New York, but Bing says Dave will make
trouble for me if I do. Dave's not taking the divorce so
well. So I'm supposed to stay here until it's final. But, like,
there's *no*body here in wintertime, only old people. Well,
your age."

She stepped back in the blob and then wandered over to
tune the radio, leaving little white pawprints on the only
section of floor that Jane hadn't covered. Her knack for
mess was almost uncanny. Resigned, Jane had already decided to have the floor sanded and varnished later on. It
was in poor condition anyway, and anything was easier
than trying to clean up after Cissy.

"Your brother does sound too good to be true," Jane
said thoughtfully. She remembered his chivalric attempt to
lure Buster away from her car and smiled to herself. "I
always wanted a brother," she added. "It would've taken
some of the pressure off me from my dad."

"Oh, you mean your dad wanted you to play basketball
with him and stuff like that?"

"Yeah—stuff like that," Jane said, cutting in her brush-
stroke with an expert hand.

"Have you ever been married?" Cissy asked absently.

"Nope."

"How come?"

In new company, as at family weddings, the question was
inevitable. Still, it didn't get any easier to answer with practice. "I dunno," Jane said vaguely. "Haven't found anyone,
I guess. Besides, haven't you seen the infamous Harvard
study on single women my age? Our chances are better of
getting killed by a terrorist."

"That's crazy. Look at you: tall, auburn hair, good voice,
green eyes. You could have about anyone." Paint was ooz-
ing from the brush down Cissy's forearm; she tried rubbing
her arm on her pants and became more thoroughly covered with paint than the wall she was working on.

"Have you ever been involved, at least?" Cissy persisted.

Jane was glad not to have to disappoint her. "Yes," she said, "I *was* involved once—when I was at Rhode Island School of Design. But he got a job in Chicago, and I chose not to follow him out there."

"Why not? Didn't you get along?"

"Sure we did." Maybe too well; he bored her.

"Too bad, then," Cissy answered promptly. "That was your mistake. What would you do if Phillip Harrow asked you out?" she suddenly asked.

"He'd better not; I don't have a thing to wear," Jane quipped. After a moment she added, "Phillip's not married?"

"He was, to a wealthy woman. But his wife died five or six years ago. They were out sailing and got caught in a squall. He almost drowned trying to save her. They were only married a year, I think. Everyone said he just about died over it. It's only recently that he's started seeing women again."

Jane poured some paint into her roller pan. "You seem to know an awful lot about his love life," she teased.

Cissy's cheeks took on a pretty shade of pink. "Well, I was kind of interested for a while. But he's too old—forty."

"Oh, yeah," Jane agreed. "One foot in the grave."

By the time Phillip Harrow's dinner party rolled around, Jane had gone back to her condo in Connecticut for her car, her clothes, and her own linens. The week had flown by. She'd spent one day sorting and piling up furniture for a dump run. Another day, talking to every house painter on the island. Another, collecting estimates for knocking out a new kitchen. Before she knew it, the week was over and she wasn't any further along on the white-paint front.

Which was just as well. Because the more she studied the room she and Cissy had painted, the more boring it looked. The house deserved better. It had lots of charm

and character and old-fashioned detail. She began to think
about wallpaper instead.

After all, the town was full of inspiration: the beautifully
papered rooms in the shingled and clapboarded houses
that stood cheek by jowl on every street and lane. Some of
them were stately homes built by whaling captains, and
some were simple lean-tos built by ordinary folk. Some had
elegance, some had charm, some had both. Most had wallpaper.

At first it was the wallpaper that drew Jane out for a
quick walk through town every evening. Most of the houses
were closed down for the winter, of course; but she did her
best to peek into the ones that weren't. She'd drag her
steps to get a better look into the open-shuttered parlors,
or suddenly decide to retie her shoe in front of some door
with sidelights. Through the glass she'd see wonderful pat-
terns and colors: florals and bamboos, stripes and Orien-
tals; rich reds, deep greens, subtle off-shades of every color
in between.

Before long she was hooked on the houses themselves.
She became quite shameless, hopping up and down the
brick sidewalks when the windows were too high to see
into, pausing on every incline to see what she could see.
From the pediments outside to the curved staircases inside,
she couldn't get enough of the antique homes. By rights
she should have been arrested for peeping. But she convinced herself that the owners understood that the historic
treasures they lived in belonged, in some small way, to
every American.

The more she prowled, the more Jane saw that somehow
Nantucket Town had been spared the ravages of modern-
ization. There were no ugly apartment boxes; no factories;
no malls; no office blocks. The town was wonderfully con-
sistent, with its lane after lane of eighteenth and early
nineteenth century houses. The saltboxes, Federals, Greek
Revivals—even the whimsical Queen Annes, with their tur-

rets and towers and verandas—she loved every house without reservation.

And she loved the ghosts that went with them. In every foggy, lamplit lane she could see them: well-dressed ships' captains arm in arm with their wives; ordinary seamen, relishing their time ashore before shipping out for another two- or three-year voyage; young Quaker girls in their coal skuttle bonnets, chattering and giggling on their way home from Monthly Meeting. They were there, the ghosts were, because there were no apartment buildings or office centers or mini-malls to block Jane's view of them. It was that simple.

"Well? What do you think of our Little Grey Lady?"

The question was put to Jane by Mrs. Whitney Crate, a sharp old woman who lived down the road, and she was apparently referring to Nantucket, not herself. Mrs. Crate had been the first to arrive at Phillip's dinner party and would no doubt be the first to leave: probably at nine-thirty, whether her husband was done with his coffee or not.

Jane tugged the black sheath she wore over her knees a little more primly and smiled. "I haven't seen much of the island, only Nantucket town," she said. "But the town itself seems nearly perfect."

Mrs. Crate smiled importantly and said, "*We* like it."

Mrs. Crate had a forty-something daughter who lived with her. Like her mother, Dorothy Crate was smug and slow to warm up. She was sitting next to her mother, sipping sherry and sizing up the new neighbor.

"Has Phillip told you? I dabble in local history," Dorothy said to Jane with a fluttery wave of her hand. "I'd always meant to get an oral history from your . . . aunt, but somehow things never worked out. Mrs. Merchant wasn't the most . . . approachable woman, you understand. One never knew what, exactly, to expect. She was *quite* the character around here. A very . . . *mysterious* woman. Yes . . . hmmm . . . mysterious."

Jane murmured something noncommittal in response and wandered over to the sideboard to accept a sherry from Bing, who was pouring for their host.

"Oral historian, my eye," Bing whispered to her as he handed her a glass. "She is *such* a fraud."

Jane caught her breath, afraid that Bing might have been overheard. But no; Cissy had taken Jane's seat and was filling in mother and daughter on the progress at Lilac Cottage.

"There's just nothing Jane can't do," Cissy was saying in an awestruck voice. "This morning I dropped in and there she was with a sledgehammer, knocking out the rath and plaster—"

"*Lath* and plaster, you noodle," said Bing. His voice was warm and amused and his gaze equally so, as it passed from his sister to Jane and lingered there. "Is this true, Jane? Are you superwoman?"

Jane flushed and said, "Anybody can tear down a wall. The question is, who'll put it back together for me? I haven't found a contractor yet."

"You might want to call the guys who did my place," said Bing. "Remind me to give you their card before I go back to New York Monday. Phillip put me on to them. Where *is* our host, anyway?"

Their host was in the kitchen, consulting with the cook. When he came out, he rubbed his hands together and said, "All here except for . . . hmm, McKenzie. Bing? Any sign of him?"

"Haven't seen him all day."

A shadow passed over Phillip's face, like a hawk's over a pond. Then it was gone, and Jane was left with only a vague sense of unease, nothing more.

Phillip's smile was urbane. "We won't be able to wait

dinner, I'm afraid, or it'll be *my* head that ends up on the platter." He glanced in the direction of the entry hall.

On cue, the doorbell chimed. In half a dozen strides Phillip was in the hall. Jane heard a low exchange of voices, and then Phillip ushered in his truant guest: Mr. McKenzie. Mac, that is, McKenzie.

At first Jane thought that he was merely there on some errand, because somehow he didn't quite fit in with the rest of the company. He was dressed acceptably enough—a tweed jacket over a dark plaid shirt and wool slacks—but it was a far cry from Phillip's Ralph Lauren look and Bing's loose, New Yorky elegance. His shaggy hair was neatly combed, but certainly not styled; Jane was willing to bet it had never, ever, been touched by mousse. He towered over the others, but that wasn't it, either. He looked out of place most of all because of his hands: big, powerful, un-manicured.

He's country, Jane decided. *And not just fashionably so.* Mac McKenzie was the real thing—for better or worse.

He greeted the women with a stiff smile and shook hands with Bing and poor Mr. Crate, who'd finally come out of hiding from the corner bookcase where he'd spent the past half hour browsing.

Phillip filled in the last of the evening's introductions. "Jane Drew, I'd like you to meet John McKenzie."

"We're already on a first-name basis," McKenzie said dryly.

"I'm just not sure which one," Jane replied with her mother's smile. So he *was* one of the owners, then. "Is it John, or is it Mac?"

"Mac, to those who know me."

"Well, John, then I guess 'Mac' will have to wait." *God. What is it with this guy? Just getting his name squared away is going to take a U.N. effort.*

A look of sympathy for Jane flashed over Phillip's face, as if he understood her sense of frustration with the man.

"Shall we go in?" he suggested to the company.

The group fell into the kind of disjointed chitchat that usually accompanies a move from one room to another. Cissy was demanding to know how McKenzie had got Buster to "stay," and Mr. Crate was asking Phillip about a first edition of *Great Expectations* that he'd been thumbing through. Bing was chatting amiably in Jane's ear about contractors.

And from behind her Jane heard, or thought she heard, Mrs. Crate murmur to her daughter, "What's that felon doing here?" But she couldn't be sure. Maybe Mrs. Crate had said, "What's that fellow doing here?" Felon or fellow, she didn't seem to want McKenzie included in the company.

The table setting was quietly spectacular, thoroughly in keeping with the rest of the furnishings: antique Meissen and Waterford on satiny damask, and heavy silver candlesticks surrounding a floral arrangement of breathtaking loveliness.

"I have always loved this room, Phillip," Dorothy gushed. "What a shame it's dark out; your view of the ocean is so much better than ours."

"I keep forgetting there's an ocean *out* there," Cissy said, craning her neck. "All *we* see are bushes—look! You can see the lights of a big ship!"

"That's not a ship, Ciss; it's a fishing trawler," said Bing.

"Don't be silly; nobody would fish in March," Cissy retorted.

"Ah, sweet Cissy," said Phillip, slipping his napkin from its silver ring. "Where do you suppose the 'fresh fish' we buy locally comes from?"

"Well, I suppose I thought—from warmer water. You shouldn't make fun of me, Phillip," she added with dignity. Her cheeks were deeply flushed.

She does *have a thing for him,* Jane decided. It was really very sweet. Of course, Cissy was too hopelessly naive for a man like Phillip; his type would have to be able to recognize Meissen at a glance and understand the dollar value of a water view. Someone like Dorothy Crate, for instance. Jane was sitting diagonally across from her and had the chance to study her. Dorothy was attractive, carefully preserved—despite her lightly grayed hair—and well spoken. Her manners were impeccable, even if she *was* a bit of a fraud.

The first course was brought out by a jacketed butler: a bisque of lobster. *All that's missing is the string quartet,* Jane thought, impressed.

Dorothy Crate batted her eyes at Phillip. "I understand congratulations are in order, Phillip; you've sold the property in Bourne! How wonderful for you! Who bought it?"

A look of bland reserve settled on Phillip's handsome brow. Clearly he preferred not to discuss his business dealings at his own dinner party. But he answered easily, "A designer outlet. They'll do well. It's a good location."

End of story. Dorothy swung her gaze carefully over the top of Mac McKenzie's head and focused on Bing Andrews instead.

"And how goes the Melowe Museum, Bing?" she asked. "Are the funds still flowing? It can't be easy being the Director of Development nowadays when so many others are chasing the same few dollars."

"I do my best to outrun them," Bing acknowledged, smiling.

"My brother knows *every*body worth knowing," Cissy added. "You should see his Rolodex. Just last week he managed to shake down someone for a thirty-thousand-dollar contribution to the museum. It's true what they say about him: When Bing Andrews walks into a room, hold on to your wallet," she said cheerfully.

"It's for a noble cause," Bing said, laughing; but he was obviously embarrassed by his sister's effusiveness.

Jane gave Bing a sideways look. Yes, she could see it: He

was clearly the type who could charm a possum out of a tree. If he were less well born, he might have been selling time-shares, or conning little old ladies into buying triple-paned windows they didn't need. But he was as rich as he was engaging, and so he spent his time extracting money and art out of acquaintances who had too much of both. It was a perfect fit.

The conversation turned to the halting state of the economy, although it seemed pretty obvious to Jane that most of the guests had nothing to fear from it. No one asked her what she did for a living, which spared her from having to admit she'd lost her job. The presumption seemed to be that she was a millionaire.

"Will you be living in Lilac Cottage year-round, Miss Drew, or just the summers?" It was Mrs. Crate, and she was giving Jane precisely two choices.

Before Jane had a chance to speak, Cissy answered for her. "Neither! She's dumping it!"

Instantly Jane felt the temperature drop ten degrees. Several of the party had lived on the island all their lives; naturally they would resent a money-grubbing carpetbagger. "Well, I wouldn't say *dumping* it, exactly. I . . . I plan to make every effort to properly restore the cottage."

"No kidding?" said Cissy. "You said you wanted to slap a coat of paint on it and sell it. But a *restoration*—you'll be here for a year. Cool!"

The girl was infuriating. Jane glanced around the table, wondering why on earth she'd blurted out a commitment she had no intention of fulfilling. Phillip, on her left, was giving her a look so penetrating that she wilted under it. McKenzie was sipping his soup, oblivious to her embarrassment. Bing's smile was, as always, sympathetic. As for Mrs. Crate and her daughter, they were wearing carbon copies of the same expression: suspicion.

Damn it! she thought. *This is what comes from getting to know your neighbors personally. You begin not wanting to disappoint them.*

"Excuse me," poor Mr. Crate mumbled into the painful silence. "Would you please pass the salt?"

Thankful for the diversion, Jane lifted the shaker nearest her, even though there was another at Mr. Crate's elbow, and handed it to him. The simple act of lifting made her wince in pain; her shoulder had been aching for a week now.

"What's wrong?" Cissy demanded to know. "You made a face."

Jane tried to make light of it. "I got a deep scratch from a rosebush in the graveyard behind the house the other day, and I think it's got worse. I suppose my urban immune system hasn't adjusted to country living."

"For goodness' sake," said Mrs. Crate. "I've been a gardener all my life. Nothing's ever happened to me."

Bing also was puzzled. "Are you sure the infection is from the rosebush, and not from some rusty nail around the house?"

"Did you put Bactine on it?" asked Cissy, pushing away the bisque as a child would her spinach.

"Do you know," mused Dorothy, "this reminds me of an old Nantucket legend. I'm not quite positive about the details, but there's a story of a grieving mother who planted a rose on the grave of her convict son. She couldn't afford a stone, you see. The rose is supposed to have been cursed ever since."

"You're quite right, dear," said Dorothy's mother. "I remember it now. Except that it was the convict's *wife,* not his mother, who planted the rose. Or—was it a father and not a son who was buried? I can't recall."

Mr. Crate took off his wire-rimmed glasses and began polishing a lens with his handkerchief. He cleared his throat. "I believe the legend is that it was a murderer who planted the rose on his victim's grave, out of remorse."

"Nonsense!" snapped Mrs. Crate. "I never heard that. It was a wife and her husband. Absolutely."

"Really," said Jane, fascinated by all the versions. "Do you remember where this cursed rose is supposed to be growing?"

"In the North Burying Ground, wasn't it, dear?"

"No, Mother. I think, the South."

"North, South, whatever. Surely the important part of the legend is that later someone scratched herself on a thorn and her *hand fell off—*"

"Mother, I do hate to argue but I think the victim actually got brain fever and died."

Bing was sitting opposite Jane; she felt him give her a gentle kick in the shin. She looked at him and ventured a tiny smile. He was right; these people were a piece of work.

Jane wondered what Phillip Harrow thought of the whimsical, if not downright absurd, argument the Crate family was having over the Legend of the Cursed Rose. Presumably he'd had higher hopes for the level of dinner conversation.

"What do *you* think, Phillip?" Cissy asked, voicing Jane's thoughts. "Who's right?"

Phillip shook his head diplomatically. "We have three different opinions: from an amateur historian, a retired scholar, and a woman of immense experience. I couldn't begin," he said dryly, "to choose among them."

"Get it looked at by a doctor."

All eyes turned to McKenzie. It was the first thing he'd said since they sat down at the table.

He was looking directly at Jane. His hazel eyes were intensely expressive.

"Excuse me?" she said, puzzled.

"You should get the scratch looked at by a doctor," he repeated. And then, as if that expanded version of his remark had exhausted him, he stayed silent throughout the entire next course.

The conversation during the fish course drifted amiably around the problems and pleasures of living on an island thirty miles from the mainland. All the while Jane was wondering why Phillip had invited McKenzie. His interest in being there seemed to range from zip to nil.

After a while, Phillip tried to draw out McKenzie. "Mac, how's Jeremy? Your boy must be, what—seven, eight years old now?"

"He's ten. And he's fine."

"And Celeste?"

"She's well."

So. He was married. Or divorced. Divorced.

"Good. Is she still with Rooney, Smith and Amel?"

McKenzie nodded, and that was that. Really, he was practically rude. If he hated being there that much, why come at all? Shyness was one thing; but *this*. . . .

Jane decided, almost from a sense of perverseness, to make him talk. "I was wondering, John, how your property runs. You must have a long, narrow strip of land between Bing's house and mine?"

McKenzie looked up from his cranberry-stuffed bass, warned her away from the topic with a level look, and returned to his food. "Nope. I don't."

Bing laughed rather self-consciously and explained. "Mac's property is what realtors call 'landlocked'; it doesn't front on the road. He drives over my land—which used to be owned by relations of his—to get to his own. It's not all that unusual with these old plats. Have you traipsed over to his place yet, by the way? Wonderful property. Great views, good acreage—and you can't have a quieter neighbor than one with a tree farm."

"Oh, I see," Jane said, thwarted in her effort to make McKenzie talk. "What you mean is Mr. McKenzie has an easement over your property."

Phillip interrupted. "No, Mac has something better: Bing's word as a gentleman," he said blandly.

Mr. Crate chimed in with a gracious, "Hear, hear."

Bing colored and changed the subject, leaving at least one puzzle solved. *McKenzie is here because he has to be,* Jane realized. *He has to stay on friendly terms with his neighbors.* Judging from the black look on his face, that took an effort.

Cissy had been uncharacteristically quiet for the last little while. Now, like a child too long ignored, she became restless. "What I want to know," she said in a fretful voice, "is who actually carries out the curse when a rose is cursed? Is it some kind of ghost? A ghost in the garden?"

"Cissy, really," her brother said. "It's not as though we can look it up."

"Is it the ghost of the one in the grave?" she persisted, ignoring her brother's halfhearted attempt to shut her up. "Or is it God? Or the devil? Or even Nature, some kind of vindictive Nature?"

She was deadly earnest, and Jane found that endearing. "Yes, and what *about* that curse of the Mummy's Tomb, now that we're at it?" she threw in impishly. "Who's responsible for that one?"

"You laugh, Jane," said Mrs. Crate. "But some say Nantucket has more ghosts per square mile than anywhere else in America. There are whole books written on the subject."

"You're not serious," Jane said, grinning. But she was scanning people's faces, aware that everyone at the table—except Cissy, of course—seemed to know something that she did not. It was hard to pin down: a veiled look of reserve; a sense that some subjects were better left alone.

"Perhaps it's because we have so many old houses," Dorothy volunteered nervously. "So many people have passed through them over the centuries."

"I suppose that's true," Jane answered, changing her tone. "You do get a sense of it when you walk around. Almost since the day I got here I've felt . . . I don't know, a sense of *déjà vu* . . . almost as if long ago someone had once . . ."

She looked around, embarrassed. She had become the absolute focal point of the table; everyone was watching her intently. Her mind flashed back to a moment a couple of hours ago, when she was slipping on a pair of plain gold earrings. Her plan had been to get in and out of the evening without anyone taking much notice of her.

Her plan had failed.

CHAPTER 5

"**Y**ou can't walk home."

"You'll freeze to death."

"We'll drive you."

The combined forces of Mrs. Crate and her daughter Dorothy were too much for Jane. Despite the fact that she'd enjoyed the walk over and was looking forward to a brisk return walk to clear her head after the dinner party, she agreed to let them drop her at her door. Phillip began sorting out guests and coats and scarves in his elegantly paneled entry hall. In the inevitable crush of people, Jane found herself tucked between Bing and McKenzie.

"Damn," murmured Bing, holding open her coat for her. "The Crates have no right to take you home. Look," he said in a low voice. "Will you be home tomorrow afternoon?"

Jane laughed and said, "Where else?" Then she saw that his blue eyes were dancing with interest. Or maybe it was just the wine. She couldn't tell; she was feeling a little pleasure-hazed herself. "Tomorrow, then," she murmured, smiling.

"Tomorrow's going to be foul. Plan on snow."

She'd been so intent about Bing that she'd forgotten about McKenzie, who was standing behind them.

"Oh?" Jane said. She was still annoyed with him for snubbing everyone all evening long.

McKenzie flipped up the collar of his heavy jacket and pulled down a floppy tweed hat over his brow; he had the look of a man battening down the hatches. "That's a nor'easter brewing out there," he said, as if it were *her* fault.

"Is that something I should care about?" Jane asked coolly.

McKenzie shrugged. "Only if you'll need to get your car out of your driveway."

"Mac's right!" Bing said. "Have you made arrangements to have your driveway plowed when it snows?"

"Well, no," Jane confessed. "I'm from condo country. What do I know about snow plows?"

"I'll take care of it," Bing reassured her. "And think about getting a phone, would you?" he added in a plaintive voice. "How the heck do I reach you from New York? Smoke signals?"

Wine or not, Bing seemed to be coming on strong. Wine or not, she seemed to be liking it. Everyone said good-bye to everyone else, except that Bing took her hand and held it longer than anyone else, and then they were out in the cold, being swept along to their cars by a raw, scudding wind. She was surprised to see McKenzie set off on foot.

"Mac! Want a lift?" Bing cried out.

McKenzie waved him away with a "Thanks, I'll pass," and was quickly swallowed up by darkness.

No one lived all that far from anyone else, but in March, on a dark road, the distances were just enough to be awkward. Jane was glad she'd accepted a lift from the Crates after all. The thought of ending up walking alongside a ditch with McKenzie was strangely unnerving.

As for Mr. Crate, he drove the way he spoke and the way he ate: slowly. While they sat waiting for the car to warm up, Mrs. Crate said to her husband, as if Jane were not present, "Why does Phillip persist in treating that man as if they were equals? They're nothing of the sort. Phillip's an Andover man. I'm not sure Mac even has a diploma, for God's sake. After all, he spent his high school years in reform school."

"He stole a car, dear, that's all," said her husband mildly.

"He stole a *Porsche,* is what he stole. And sank it!"

"Some boys are wilder than others, especially when they're stuck on an island while their friends go off, as Phillip did, to grander things."

"And what about that other time, when he was called in for questioning?"

"Nothing ever came of it."

"What Celeste saw in him, I will never know. That tells you something about summer romances. She was absolutely right to accept that position in Boston three years ago. Look at her now—a shoe-in for partner in a prestigious law firm. Where would she be if she'd stayed behind to water his trees for him? Penniless! That's where. Mac McKenzie hasn't got two nickels to rub together. There's no money in nurseries. He should've sold that land years ago, at peak. He could be a wealthy man now."

"There *is* the problem with access, dear," Mr. Crate said, throwing the car into reverse and backing ever, ever so cautiously out of Phillip's driveway.

"Don't be silly. Watch that tree. Do you think Bing wouldn't be willing to sell him the rights to a permanent easement across his land? That's what covenants are for. Or Sylvia Merchant's property; he could drive over *that,* if he had to."

"But as you say yourself, Mac has no money to buy the right—"

"He would if he were *selling* the land; it's all in the timing—oh, never mind. I just don't like it when he shows up at these things. Nothing will ever change that."

Her voice became low and anxious. "You've seen him with that ax. It looks natural on him. I'm afraid of him. And Phillip knows that. Stay in your lane."

She's as much as calling him an ax murderer, Jane thought, amazed at the tenor of the conversation. She swung her head, looking back along the road. If they'd driven past McKenzie, she'd missed it. The thought that he'd be passing her house quietly on foot sent the hair on the back of her neck rising.

In a moment they were at her door. Mr. Crate slowed his Lincoln to a gradual stop—actually, Jane could have stepped out any time along the way and not even twisted an ankle—and she got out of the car. Dorothy, who'd been sitting next to her in silence, suddenly stuck her head out the window and said ominously, "Single women take *nothing* for granted."

They left Jane, mouth agape, standing there with her keys and thinking, *What a timid little family they are.* It was catching; she was regretting not having turned on the porch light. The problem was with the two huge hollies that flanked the door: fifteen feet high, they blocked light from the inside, as well as any view of the outside.

Jane let herself in and instantly she felt the cold: the furnace must have blown another fuse. *Damn.* The electrician had warned her that the burner was old and inefficient and the sixty-amp service not up to the task. She'd laid in a supply of fuses, but an expensive upgrade looked inevitable. *Damn.*

She rummaged through a kitchen drawer for a flashlight and, since some of the inside stairs to the basement were missing, went back outside in the whistling wind to enter through the heavy cellar bulkhead doors. The dirt-floor basement was less than six feet high and filled with moldering lumber and rusted, broken-down machinery. The basement light was on the same fuse as the furnace, so when the furnace went out, the basement went black. After the electrician explained all this the first time, Jane had hoped never to return. Fat chance.

She groped toward the fusebox, arcing the flashlight back and forth through the debris. She swung the beam where she thought the box should be and it lit, instead, on two bulging yellow eyes placed squarely over the most vicious fangs she'd ever seen. Jane screamed. It screamed. She dropped her flashlight and felt something scurry past her legs. She jumped back, instantly wrapping herself in a cobweb of repulsive size. The sense that spiders and dead flies were all over her hair was overwhelming. She cried out in revulsion and fled, slamming into hard metal and scraping her shin on the way out.

She ran straight into the bathroom, tore off her clothes, and jumped into the shower. There was, of course, no hot water. It hardly mattered. She shampooed, and scrubbed, and shampooed again. Clean and frozen, she checked out the damage to her shin, amazed at the depth of the gouge and the size of the goose egg on it. There wasn't a doubt in her mind that the plow, or whatever it was she ran into, was rusty. *Oh, fine. Tetanus, too.*

Clearly I'm not yet ready for prime-time country, she thought wryly. *What was the worst it could have been—a weasel? A possum?* As for the spider web—*I go running off hysterically like Little Miss Muffet, and now I'll probably die of blood poisoning.*

She put on a pair of heavy Levi's and an old jacket and tried changing the fuse one more time, with a better flashlight. All went well and ten minutes later Jane was upstairs in bed, listening to the wind sending the door of the potting shed thwacking back and forth on its hinges. Jane counted the thwacks, like sheep, and in five minutes she was sound asleep without a thought in the world for weasels or ax murderers.

And yet somewhere in her subconscious she was dreaming about the storm that raged at the island so alone and exposed, thirty miles from its motherland. She was dreaming of Nantucket's children, huddled under warm blankets, and its wild creatures, sheltered in its nooks and crannies. She was dreaming of its women—fewer than in years gone by—who tossed in their beds as they waited for their men to come home from the sea. And she was dreaming of its fishermen, not daring to return through the island's infamous shoals, holding their vessels into the wind and praying for the storm to be over, while they no doubt swore never again to go to sea.

When the explosive, sickening crash came, Jane was ripped from the deepest of sleeps and sent careening from her bed. She charged for the door only half-conscious, and then stopped herself. Her heart was pounding, her senses alert; her breathing was fast and shallow. Her body was ready to do battle.

But against what? And *with* what? Jane had come to sleepy, deserted little Nantucket expecting to be completely safe. She had no gun, no Mace, no phone, and—after dinner with the Crates—no confidence.

Calm down, she told herself. *Think about what you're doing.* Tiptoeing back to a lamp, she turned it on, then took up a crowbar she'd left propped in a corner of the bedroom.

Will I use this if I have to? she wondered, gripping the cold metal bar as she moved from one room to the next, switching on lights. *Crash it through someone's skull? Could I do that?* It was a horrible thought, a sickening thought. The answer to it was no. She laid the crowbar quietly on the floor of the hall. Why hadn't she just gone with the hair spray? At least there was an outside chance she'd have the guts to spray it in someone's eyes.

She felt sickeningly vulnerable. What did *she* know about Nantucket? Nothing. Obviously the island had its share of burglars and maniacs. Obviously. She tried very hard not to recall anything Mrs. Crate and her daughter had said. But she remembered every blessed word.

She made her way through the upstairs floor, room by room, then crept down the steps. There was no one in the parlor . . . no one in the kitchen . . . no one in the bathroom. There was only one room left. By now the house was lit up like a Christmas tree. Jane peeked into the fireplace room, the last room, and was shocked to see that a huge oak bookcase had been hurled flat on the floor, and all its books scattered like November leaves on a lawn.

Still, it was obvious that there was no one in the room; Jane even made the effort to look up the chimney. The doors were still locked, the windows closed. *This is bizarre,* she thought, walking around the fallen bookcase.

She leaned against the sill of the nearest window, trying to figure it out. The wind was forcing itself through the cracks in the window frame, cutting through her with its cold. It was howling in earnest now; through her nightgown she could feel the house shake.

That's it! she thought, jumping up. She flattened her hands against the wall where the bookcase had stood: it was vibrating perceptibly. And the pine floor underneath it was uneven and buckled, the way wide-board floors can be. The *house* had knocked down the bookcase.

Relieved, Jane stepped over the mess—it would just have to wait until morning—and retraced her steps, turning off each of the lights behind her. She thought about her mother, living in California. Gwendolyn Drew had been visiting a friend in Santa Cruz during the '89 earthquake; the house had slid off its foundation and the two women had gone sliding with it. When it was over, Jane's mother had poured both of them double scotches and managed to joke about it. Jane was in awe of that in her mother—that tough-minded fearlessness.

I just hope I inherited my fair share of it, she thought wearily, switching off the bedside light.

The next sound she heard was that of heavy metal scraping asphalt. It was new, loud, and unexpected; she threw on her red chamois robe and made her way groggily to one of the front windows. It was gray out, barely dawn, she guessed. And it was snowing; there must have been half a foot on the ground already, with more coming down in heavy, wet flakes. The snow didn't surprise her, but the sight of Mac McKenzie sitting on a John Deere tractor fitted out with a plow and clearing her driveway—that surprised her.

Splaat! A fat snowball hit the window in front of her face and slid down the pane. It was Cissy, dressed in jeans and a parka with a fur-rimmed hood, jumping up and down and waving.

"Get dressed! Get dressed and come on out!"

Jane slid the window up and said, "Are you nuts? It must be six in the morning!"

"No, it's not—it's nine o'clock!"

Splaat! Another snowball, this time from the side—and this time, right through the open window and down the middle of her nightgown. Jane cried out from the cold shock of it and turned to see Bing with a wickedly boyish grin on his face. "You heard my kid sister! Come on out— or are you too chicken?"

"Chicken! We'll see who's chicken, you . . . you cluck!" Jane yelled. She slammed the window down and marched back to the bedroom with a determined glint in her eye. She dressed quickly for battle in heavy pants, a turtleneck, a tasseled cap, and a down jacket. Then she slipped into the backyard, packed a dozen snowballs into a galvanized bucket, and sneaked back around to the front.

Bing was throwing a fluorescent pink Frisbee across the snow for Buster to fetch and had his back to Jane; he never knew what hit him. *Bam! Bam! Bam!* Three in a row, all in the back. Her shoulder hurt like crazy from the effort, but it was worth it: the last one knocked the ski cap he wore right off his head. Bing swung around, laughing and stunned by her ferocity.

"Hey! Where'd you learn to shoot like that, pardner?"

Jane gave him an arrogant look, then blew smoke from

the barrel of an imaginary six-shooter. "Don't start nothin'
you don't mean to finish, pal," she said, feeling like a flirt.

Cissy was getting the bottom of a snowman going.
Buster, wanting desperately to be a part of things, came up
and put his huge paws on the rolling ball, just as his mistress was doing. Cissy laughed and stood up and tried to
push him away. The dog stood up on his hind legs and
pushed her back—such fun!—and Cissy fell on her behind
in the snow.

It *was* fun, the way fooling around in fresh and falling
snow is always fun. But it was impossible, at least for Jane,
to ignore the fact that their fellow dinner guest was twenty
feet away, working hard at plowing her driveway clear. She
sidled up discreetly to Bing and said, "Why is he doing
that? Just being neighborly?"

"Hell, no; I'm paying him," Bing answered cheerfully as
he shaped a snowball in his gloved hands. "The regular
service wouldn't be around to your place for hours."

Shocked, Jane said, "You're *paying*—"

"Don't think twice about it, fair one," he said gallantly.
"It's no different than picking up the cab fare into Manhattan on a dinner date."

"But we're not *on* a dinner date—"

"Which is why I was coming over. Will you have dinner
with me tonight?" he asked. His eyes were sparkling with
interest, and this time there was no wine to blame.

"Tonight?"

The revving of a tractor engine behind them sent Jane
jumping: McKenzie seemed to want to plow the exact spot
they were standing on. He was wearing a duckbilled plaid
hat with fold-down flaps, but even that wasn't enough to
prevent him from having to squint in the driving snow. He
looked fiercer than ever. His lips, normally set in a firm
line, shaped themselves silently around one word: *move*.

He was being deliberately annoying; surely there were
other parts to plow. *That damn chip on his shoulder,* she

thought. She'd been wrong about him being a hired hand at the nursery, but she hadn't been wrong about the chip. Anyway, right now he *was* a hired hand. And in this case, she didn't like it. It offended her that he'd accepted money for plowing her drive. If their positions were reversed, *she* would've done it for nothing, just to be neighborly.

"I would *love* to go to dinner tonight, Bing," she said, stepping nimbly aside just as the plow was about to take out an ankle. "What time?"

They made arrangements and then Bing took the huge snowball he'd been shaping and, grinning, calmly dumped it on her head. "Now we're even."

Jane was still sputtering from it when she felt an avalanche of snow being plowed into the back of her legs, filling her boots. She whipped around, furious. McKenzie shrugged and said "Sorry," and backed the tractor away for another pass.

Bing, laughing, swatted as much of the snow off Jane as he could, then said, "You look like a Quaker Oats commercial. C'mon, let's go in and I'll make us breakfast."

Jane agreed, mostly to prove that she wasn't a bad sport. She waited as Bing helped Cissy roll the bottom of her snowman into a monstrous ball, and then they all headed for Bing's house. McKenzie was just finishing plowing her drive. Bing paused alongside his tractor.

"Thanks again, Mac," he said, slapping the side of the tractor as if it were a farm horse. "And hey—how about some bacon and eggs?"

The snow had dribbled into Jane's socks by now. If there was one thing she hated, it was snow in her socks.

McKenzie gave her a cool, infuriating look and said, "Breakfast sounds good."

Jane's instinct was to turn on her heel and leave, but again: she wouldn't give anyone the satisfaction. So they all piled into Bing's enormous designer kitchen, which came straight out of *House and Garden,* and stripped off their snowy jackets and hats. Bing hauled out a carton of eggs and a slab of bacon and got to work, while McKenzie went to the fireplace at the far end of the room and coaxed the dying embers into a comfortably roaring flame.

Cissy brought out dry socks for Jane, so she peeled off her wet ones and draped them over the big brass screen that protected a handsome hand-knotted rug from the crackling fire. The women dragged a couple of chairs, overstuffed in creamy tweed, closer to the fire and put their feet up on a shared hassock between them. Buster lay down alongside them, his big tail thumping contentedly on the wide slate hearth. Jane offered once or twice to help with breakfast, but Bing wouldn't have it.

"How's your shoulder, by the way?" he asked suddenly.

"No better, I'm afraid. Must be old age," Jane said, rubbing the spot. "I doubt that I could lift that cast iron pan right now."

"Bing's got even bigger pans than that," Cissy piped in, slipping off her sheepskin slippers and curling her toes in front of the flames. "He's a way better cook than I am. But then, he's had sixteen years longer to learn."

"It's the *practice* that makes perfect, Ciss," Bing said in gentle reproach.

It was obvious that Cissy thought that cooking skills, like crow's feet, came automatically with age. Jane shared a sympathetic smile with Bing and turned her attention to the rugged, taciturn man on her left.

McKenzie was sitting in a chrome-and-leather director's chair, his elbows resting on his thighs as he stared at the leaping, crackling flames. His ruddy skin had kept its high color from the outdoor work; his hair, damp from the snow, looked darker now, almost black. Unlike the others, he seemed oblivious to the cold, oblivious to the wet. He seemed, in fact, oblivious to their presence.

Fine. Why the heck did he join us, then? Just to throw a

pall on the merriment? In the meantime, she wasn't even sure the man could form two sentences in a row.

"Isn't a fire a wonderful thing?" she asked him, trying to force him into speech. "I suppose our fascination with it goes back to Prometheus," she added, sure he couldn't have a clue who Prometheus was.

McKenzie turned to her with a look of pure irony. "Actually, I was thinking that Bing has been burning too much pine."

"How did you know I burn pine?" Bing asked.

"I smell it when I drive by."

"What's wrong with pine?" Jane wanted to know.

"Creosote. It builds up in the chimney. You're asking for a chimney fire, Bing."

"No problem," Bing said cheerfully. "I'll get something else. Is oak okay?"

"Sure," McKenzie said. "And have a chimney sweep look at it before too long." He fell back into moody contemplation of the fire.

He looked so deeply philosophical; it was disappointing to know that he was analyzing the ash content of the logs. Jane tried again.

"I can't get over how deserted the island is in March. When I was here last it was in August, at the height of the season."

She said it in a general way and was surprised when McKenzie turned to her and said dryly, "I know. We met."

In an equally dry tone she said, "I doubt it. I was eight."

"And I was fifteen. Your aunt used to hire me now and again to mow her lawn. I remember having to mow around you; you wouldn't budge." He snorted, a barely audible sound. "Nothing much has changed."

"You're in for it now, girl," Bing interjected. "These islanders have long memories. Come 'n' get it, people."

"I don't remember that," Jane said, wondering. "I don't remember *you*."

"No. I don't expect you would." McKenzie stood up at the same time she did. She was close enough to see a dark, angry flush intensify the ruddiness in his wind-whipped cheeks. It occurred to her that she would not want, ever, to anger this man.

They took their seats around a scrubbed pine table and were treated to a simple but wonderfully filling breakfast of thick Canadian bacon, scrambled eggs, and fresh-baked sourdough bread that Bing had brought with him from New York. Warmed outside and inside by the fire and fresh coffee, Jane felt more relaxed and at home than she'd been in months.

They talked about anything and everything, from the great October nor'easter of 1991, the worst storm to hit the island in a hundred years (even McKenzie admitted it was a big one), to local efforts to relocate the historic Sankaty Lighthouse before it tumbled over the bluffs into the sea. They talked about the fire that burned down Downy Flake Restaurant (before Jane's time) and the great home-team advantage the high school football team enjoyed (think how tired the mainlanders got just getting to the field).

They talked about a lot of things, and when there was a lull, easy and relaxed, Jane sighed and said, "This is really nice."

"It is, isn't it," Bing said, getting up for more coffee and to stir the fire. "So why do you want to sell?"

It caught Jane by surprise. Still, it was a simple question, and it deserved a simple answer.

"I need the money," she said.

"For what?" he asked casually. Presumably he was expecting her to say, "For a Ferrari."

But she said, "To eat. To pay the mortgage. To buy gas. To start up a new career. I don't have a job," she finally confessed. Somehow, suddenly, she needed to admit it.

"But I thought you were a graphic designer," Cissy interjected.

"I am. An unemployed one. I did have some free-lance work, but that finished up the day before my aunt died. Needless to say, there's nothing else at the moment."

She was very aware that McKenzie was following the conversation. She could tell by a kind of stillness in him; he reminded her of a cat, ready to pounce. "What exactly is a graphic designer?" he asked, looking over the rim of his coffee cup into indeterminate space.

He seemed not to want to ask her the question directly, so Jane addressed her answer to Buster, who was stretched out at her feet, snoozing. "I did the layouts for an ad agency in Connecticut. I worked mostly on two or three accounts—perfume, lipstick, vodka, mineral water, that kind of thing."

McKenzie put down his cup and leaned back in his bleached-oak chair, balancing it against the wall. "I see," he said with a dry and appraising look at her. "All the essentials of life."

"Well, no," she admitted, flustered. "Obviously not. That's why they have to advertise: to create the need."

He frowned. Naturally. She could see the disapproval in his eyes. Impulsively she added, "I wish I could tell you I was working on something monumental when they let me go, Mr. McKenzie—"

"For Pete's sake, call him Mac," Bing chimed in, watching the two of them nervously.

"I wish I could say I was creating a new vaccine, or a cure for cancer. But I wasn't. I remember very well what I was doing when I got my pink slip: sketching a chair for an ad for an interior design firm. That's all. A chair. I'm sorry I'm not Mother Teresa, Mr.—Mac—Kenzie," she said, stumbling once more over his blasted name.

There was a surprised little silence, and then McKenzie surprised them even more by standing up and drawling, "I suppose there are more useless things. You could've been a goddamned lawyer."

He unhooked his jacket from the back of his chair and slapped Bing on the back. "Thanks for the chow, man," he said, and he left.

"Geez," said Cissy. "What's with *him*?"

Bing blew out a stream of air through puffed-up cheeks. "Well, let's think about it. The guy's wife has left the island and taken his kid. He's probably up to his neck in debt and banks aren't lending. And late winter isn't exactly a boom season for nurseries, here or anywhere else."

"Oh. So the problem wasn't really the chair?"

"Not the chair, Ciss," Bing said, with a soft laugh.

Things got a little quiet after that. Jane insisted on cleaning up the dishes, and Cissy played old-sock with Buster while Bing went out for more wood. It was all very relaxed, almost domestic, and Jane managed to salvage some of the mellowness she'd been feeling.

They're really very nice, she thought. *Cissy's a ditz, but she's a sweet ditz.* And as for Bing, he was about as different from McKenzie as a man could be: loose, easy, friendly, generous, kind. . . . It beat uptight, tense, aloof, stingy, and mean any old day.

Jane left Bing and his sister a little while later and waded through the blinding, drifting snow back to her cottage. She stood on the little hooked rug inside the back door, shaking the snow from her clothes and stomping her boots free of it. When she pulled her boots off, she had to steady herself against the door jamb.

That's when she noticed that one of the antique spoons was missing from the wood rack that hung on the wall beside the door.

CHAPTER 6

Who would want a spoon?

That was the first question that popped into her head, and it stayed there as she searched under the table, alongside the stove, and in the silverware drawer. It had been there yesterday morning; that, she knew. She remembered staring at the dozen different spoons in their rack as she ate her toast, and wondering about their value. She remembered that she'd decided it was mostly sentimental.

So who would steal a spoon?

The one that was missing was nothing special; it was pewter, as she recalled, with a sort of cut-work handle.

Kids? Anything, she supposed, was possible; she'd left the door unlocked, after all. A sinking thought hit her. *Did it just happen?* She ran to her purse, which she liked to leave on top of an antique pot cupboard in a corner of the kitchen, and checked its contents. Nothing was missing. So it wasn't a break-in; just . . . a prank?

But who? She swung open the back door and stuck her head out into the slanting, stinging snow, hoping to catch sight of footprints. But her own deep prints had almost drifted over; the nor'easter had destroyed any evidence.

If there was *any evidence.* It was eerie, it was creepy, and she didn't like it at all, the thought that someone had come and gone through her kitchen. For the first time since she'd arrived, she decided to lock the door even though it was daytime. She slipped the button down on the lock, then headed for her bedroom to change into workclothes. On the way there, she tripped over the scattered books.

Nuts. This was a distraction she didn't need. She tried to lift the heavy wood bookcase from off the floor. It didn't budge. She stood up, arching her strained back, and her glance fell on the sketch of the bonneted woman that hung on the wall opposite.

The bonnet. Of course! It was the Quaker woman in the sketch who'd been the star of Jane's dream. She should've known the bonnet, the dark coal-scuttle bonnet. Ugly and defeminizing, it was nothing more than a constraint designed to keep its wearer from flirting or taking an unseemly interest in her neighbor's business.

Like blinders on a horse, Jane thought, feeling a surge of sympathy for the unhappy subject of her aunt's sketch. *What a miserable thing to be forced to wear.*

She backtracked to the kitchen, intending to shanghai Bing into helping her lift the bookcase, and found him on the other side of her door, dressed for travel and gripping an attaché case. He looked distracted.

"What's wrong?" she asked.

"Nothing much," he said, stepping inside. "Just a routine crisis at the museum."

"You mean someone wants to donate the painting but keep the frame—that sort of thing?"

"I *wish,*" Bing said with a wry look. "No; someone wants to donate the Homer but keep the Hopper. We want the Homer *and* the Hopper."

"Aren't you being selfish?" she said lightly.

"He promised."

"I can see why the Melowe Museum has such a rounded collection."

"We've scheduled an exhibition of Depression Era art. We *need* the Hopper."

His eyes burned with a pure blue flame, the fire of a man with a mission. If he had the painting, the exhibition would be complete. Anything else was less than perfect, and that was unacceptable.

"I've got to go back to New York," he said with grim determination. "No chance of taking a plane in this snow; I'm making a run for the noon ferry. So much for my Monday holiday. Can we reschedule dinner for another time?"

"Oh, sure," she said with a polite smile.

"I feel like a rat, finking out on our first date."

"No, really, don't think about it," she said with a nagging sense of *déjà vu*. "If I had a nickel for every time my dad stood me up on business, I could start my own foundation."

She listened to the self-pity in her voice and groaned. "Will you listen to me? I'm laying on guilt with a trowel," she admitted. "I'll tell you what—help me lift a bookcase and we'll call it even."

"Your wish, m'lady, is my command." Bing set his attaché on the kitchen floor and followed Jane out to the fireplace room. "Good lord, Jane," he said, surveying the mess, "you must've had some pretty heavy reading on those shelves."

"Very funny, smart aleck," she said, thinking uneasily of the book on the tarot that she'd put on an upper shelf. "The darn thing just . . . fell over, in the middle of the night."

"Really. C'mon; take that end. Ready?" They wrestled the bookcase back in place.

"There's a reason it fell over, of course," she said, pointing out the buckled floor. She hesitated, then added, "But I'm not so sure about the spoon."

"A spoon fell over in the middle of the night?"

"A spoon is missing from my aunt's display rack." She added dryly, "Maybe it ran away with the dish."

Bing's eyes were dancing with amusement. "Hey, diddle diddle. So what're you thinking? Ghosts?"

She'd been leaving *that* thought unformed, at least until he said it. "Please forget I mentioned it," she said, coloring.

Bing put his arm around her and walked with her from the room. "I guarantee you're as safe as gold bullion here. I'll see you next weekend."

He brushed her lips with his own and released her. "And see about getting a phone. *Not* because I fear for your life," he added. "But because it would be nice to hear your voice before Friday."

"Maybe I will."

He took up his attaché case and swung open the kitchen door with great drama. "I'm off! For the sake of art!" The wind ripped through Jane as she watched him charge through the snow, turn and wave madly, and then disappear. She came back in, touching her fingers to her lips, thinking of the kiss. His breath was very nice, warm and intimate and . . . very nice.

Gawd. Here she was, going on about a man's breath. It was pathetic. How long had it *been* since she was with someone? She remembered, then blushed, remembering. The guy had worked with her at the ad agency. They'd dated for weeks and weeks, and he'd begun to press. She liked him, and she'd been without someone for what seemed like forever, and so she went to bed with him. Once.

It was a disaster. They were as different as could be. He'd kept a television on his dresser turned on to the Financial News Network the whole time. As a courtesy, he'd kept the sound off. When they were done, he'd turned that on, too. Jane remembered Cissy's complaint about her football-crazed husband and smiled grimly. Football came to an end, eventually. But *money*—money was always in season.

For the next week Jane kept her nose pretty much to the grindstone. On Tuesday she had a message relayed to her through Cissy that Bing was not going to be coming to the island for the weekend. Phillip seemed to have disappeared, and Mac as well. Jane began to understand Cissy's lament that on Nantucket "the dead of winter" was not just an idle expression. The only breaks in the sounds of Jane's silence were in Cissy's visits and in the tour Jane gave to Mrs. Crate and Dorothy when they stopped by.

She spent the week stripping old, painted-over wallpaper, which was dull and slow but oddly pleasant work; it left her mind free to daydream about life, and where she was going, and why. She'd begun, lately, to think about opening her own ad agency with the proceeds from the sale of Lilac Cottage.

Why not? Sooner or later every bad economy turns around, and when it did, she'd be positioned to turn around with it. She was experienced in logo design, brochure and catalog layouts, magazine ads. Heck, she could write commercial jingles if she was forced to. The important thing, the critical thing, was to be her own boss. Never again did she want to be confronted with a pink slip. Never again would she trust a company that promised her the moon and then pulled the rug out from under her as she reached for it.

My own boss. The words lingered sweetly on her lips as she scored and soaked the painted wallpaper, then peeled it away in long, ragged strips.

By Friday, Jane's shoulder ached so much she wasn't able to continue, so she dropped in at the emergency room of Cottage Hospital. A physician looked at the rosebush scratch, which was healing very slowly, and ordered a blood analysis; but he seemed as puzzled as Jane was about the cause of her pain. He put her on antibiotics and sent her packing.

On her way back to Lilac Cottage, Jane detoured for groceries into the A&P, where she ran into Adele Adamont working behind the checkout counter. Mrs. Adamont was the type never to forget a face; she recognized Jane instantly from her visit to the funeral home.

She took Jane's bag of A&P coffee and dumped it into the hopper for grinding. "I understand you're living in your Lilac Cottage while you fix it up for sale. And have you decided definitely to redo the kitchen?"

This is a small community, Jane thought, surprised by the woman's up-to-the-minute analysis of her life. "If I do, it will be a very limited redo," she said over the whirr of the coffee grinder. "I've knocked out a wall, and I'll be having cabinets and new linoleum put in. That's about it." *And unless I get my hands on some cash, the cabinets are going to be made of papier-mâché.*

"Yes, I expect you're feeling the pinch like the rest of us," said Mrs. Adamont. It wasn't a probing remark—simply one of her statements of fact.

Sighing, Jane nodded and opened her wallet. It had not escaped her attention that food cost more on an island than on the mainland. She wondered how ordinary Nantucket folk managed. Maybe the checkout clerks got discounts on the merchandise.

Mrs. Adamont plucked out the Sarah Lee coffee cake from Jane's groceries and said, "Don't buy this. We have a bake sale going on at St. Michael's bazaar tonight. It's a good cause—for abused children on the island—and *my* coffee ring is ten times better than store-bought."

She laid the Sarah Lee aside, just like that, and rang up the rest of Jane's purchases, giving her directions to St. Michael's Day Care. "You make sure you come, now. Seven o'clock. There'll be games of chance."

Jane walked out clutching her paper bags, briefly tempted to drive to the other, newer supermarket for the darn Sarah Lee. But that would mean going right back where she'd come from; and besides, after shopping at the A&P for the past couple of weeks she felt a surprisingly strong loyalty to the old store.

Good lord, she thought as she eased her car out of the pretty, cobblestoned lot. *I'm bonding.* In her whole life she'd never felt loyalty to a supermarket, probably because she'd moved so many times: Providence, Boston, New York, New Haven. Wherever the meat was cheapest, that was good enough for her.

So many moves, so many jobs, and where had it got her? Clinging to a career ladder with broken rungs and living in a condo that she couldn't sell if she wrapped a big red ribbon around it and threw in her Volvo. No wonder she liked Nantucket so much: it was someplace to run, someplace to hide.

After she got home, Jane decided against doing any heavy work and contented herself with sorting through some of the boxes in the room that her aunt had used for storage. They were filled with the usual leftovers of a long life lived without heirs: clothes too good to toss, too tight to wear; appliances that stayed broken because there was no husband to fix them, no money to pay someone else; pots that were too big to cook with for one; and photos and prints with broken frames or no frames at all.

One box, and one box alone, interested Jane. It wasn't very big, just big enough to hold a harmonica, a slender bundle of airmail letters bound in a faded blue ribbon, and a group photo of a dozen or so World War I soldiers. There was an empty bottle of Paris perfume, very old, called *Dangereuse*. A newspaper clipping, and that was all.

It was obvious that the items were all related and had had some significance for Aunt Sylvia. But in that case, why hadn't she taken the box with her to the nursing home? Jane untied the brittle ribbon from the letter packet and lifted the top one from the rest. It was addressed in a different hand from the others—French, judging from the stylized numeral "one" and the slashed "seven" in the address. Jane unfolded the single sheet of onionskin. It was dated December 3, 1918, from the French town of Sedan.

Dearest Sylvie,

This is the hardest thing I ever had to write. I won't be coming back. I've thought about it until my head hurts, but I can't leave Sedan. Everything I want is here. I've fallen in love, Syl. With a Frenchwoman. She's married too. I didn't mean to and neither did she. But when the armistice was signed three weeks ago, we both knew I couldn't go back to the States.

You can have the house, Syl. It's the least I can do and I know you're fond of it. I didn't mean to hurt you, honest. If you want a divorce, that's all right too, but I don't know if they'll let you divorce a fellow you can't find. I'm sending along the harmonica your dad gave me. I never learned to play it and I know he had it all his life. I don't know what else to say.

Your dearest husband,
Sam

Shocked, Jane sat there for a stretch of time, then automatically slipped the letter into its envelope and put it back, as if she'd stumbled into an extremely intimate scene between a man and a woman. This was a secret her aunt had very nearly carried with her to the grave: of a husband who had betrayed her in the worst possible way.

It explained so many things. Was it any wonder that Sylvia spent the rest of her life withdrawn from the Nantucket community? What would her choices be whenever the subject of her husband came up? To lie, or to humiliate herself. *Dear, poor Aunt Sylvia.* No wonder they thought she was a witch.

It explained something else as well: her aunt's vague story that she had had her husband's remains cremated and scattered at sea. The real reason there was no grave was because Sam had never come back.

Jane couldn't imagine what it must have been like to open the envelope addressed in someone else's hand; to read the crushing message within; to fold the letter up and put it away; and—eventually—to make supper, or do the laundry, or a little Christmas shopping. In short, to go on living, in the house Sam was letting her keep as a consolation prize.

In the house that Sylvia had bequeathed to Jane.

Good God, she realized suddenly. *The house may not even be mine to have.* What if Sam was still alive, or had remarried—*did* Aunt Sylvia ever divorce him? Or what if he had children in France? And how had Sylvia Merchant managed to convince her attorney that she was a widow? Overwhelmed by the possibilities, Jane went back to the cardboard box, looking for an answer.

She found it almost at once, in a brittle newspaper clipping dated a month after Sam's letter to his wife. It was an obituary, cut out of the *Inquirer.* Sam Merchant had died on December 11, 1918, exactly one month after the armistice was signed at Compiègne, when the transport vehicle he was riding in overturned.

So the Army had never found out, and neither did Nantucket, that Sam had made other plans for himself. Which had come first to Sylvia Merchant, Jane wondered—the news from the Army, or the news from her husband? The postmark on Sam's letter was illegible, and Jane couldn't find any death notice from the Army. Either way, it was a sickening one-two punch.

And who had posted Sam's last letter? The handwriting on the envelope was French, undeniably. His mistress? Could any woman be that cruel? Or was she just doing the rational thing, the French thing, and tying up loose ends?

A kind of morbid, fatalistic curiosity overtook Jane, and she began reading Sam's letters—there were a dozen or so —from the earliest to his last. They were short, sweet, and simple, spanning about six months. There was the initial excitement of landing in a foreign country; predictable raves when he passed through Paris; some gossip about the men in his unit; expressions of hope that the Germans would soon be defeated.

Sam also wrote of the French people, whom he found aloof and indifferent—that is, until he met a soldier who was a fisherman by trade, with a boat on the Meuse. After all, Sam was a fisherman, too, with a boat on Nantucket; they spoke a common language.

After that, Sam became more enthusiastic about the French. By the time the Germans abandoned Sedan, and the U.S. military respectfully encouraged the French to re-enter their town first, Sam was a staunch ally. That was the day before the armistice was signed. Three weeks later, he didn't want to come home.

What had happened? Was it really love at first sight, or was it the war? How could he be so sure it was love?

Jane stood up and wandered over to the window, the one that opened onto the huge lilac bush, and stared out at the bleak late-winter landscape beyond. For thirty-three years Jane had been waiting to fall in love at first sight. How hard could it be? All her friends apparently had done it. She'd heard all about the symptoms: pounding heart, stumbling speech, sweaty hands. But the only time she'd experienced *those* symptoms was when she had to make a presentation at the office.

Jane picked up the photograph of the Army unit again. She had no idea which of the soldiers was Sam Merchant. They all looked alike: young and naive, and new to the game. How could any one of them have made a decision to go AWOL in a foreign country and leave behind a wife and a home—and a boat? It seemed such a monumental, passionate thing to do. She felt a sudden stab of jealousy for someone so thoroughly ravaged by love.

She laid the curled photograph face down on the letters and tied them up with the ribbon. *Never mind,* she told herself. *You have a list of the symptoms. When it happens, it'll be obvious.*

She thought about it and smiled. *Just like the flu.*

That evening Jane decided, after all, to go to St. Michael's bazaar; with any luck she'd find out something more from Mrs. Adamont about her aunt. She put on a black wool skirt and a bulky teal sweater, and black leather boots which weren't very waterproof, and headed off for the day care center.

St. Michael's Day Care was a small gray-shingled house standing alongside a small turreted church of the same name, near the Nantucket Airport. The area was one of the less fashionable in Nantucket, probably because it was too far inland for the pied-à-terre set. The parking lot was reasonably full. Jane followed the signs and ended up in the church's basement, a wide-open, well-lighted room filled with tables and tables of . . . stuff. She had no idea what to expect—she'd never actually been to a church bazaar—but this one looked like fun.

There were raffle tables, a take-a-chance display, a handmade crafts and linens table, a book sale, and a white elephant section. There was even a concession table serving up pizza and Coke. A long table set up at the far end held a mouth-watering assortment of baked goods, including three still-warm coffee cakes Mrs. Adamont had just put out.

"Isn't that nice, you've come," she said to Jane when she saw her. She leaned over and whispered, "Buy this one; it has extra apricots."

Jane bought it. And two slices of baklava. And two cupcakes with sprinkles. And a Napoleon. She and Mrs. Adamont were arranging the haul in a brown paper bag when the churchwoman spied someone behind Jane. "Hey! Mac! Come over here!"

Jane whipped around in time to see Mac McKenzie

laughing with a couple of men behind the pizza table. It was like being splashed with cold water. McKenzie—laughing! McKenzie—at ease with other human beings! So he *wasn't* a misanthrope. And he didn't look anything *like* an ax murderer. He glanced over with a wave of acknowledgment and sauntered toward them, hands in the pockets of his corduroy slacks. If he was surprised by Jane's presence, he didn't show it.

"Mac, you never endorsed that third-party check over to St. Michael's," Mrs. Adamont said, rummaging through her handbag for it.

She found the check and laid it on the table, then dove back into her purse for a pen. Jane, normally the soul of discretion, read the front of it. It was from Bing Andrews to Mac McKenzie for thirty dollars. On the memo line, Bing had written "plow J.D. drive."

"There's a pen here somewhere," said Mrs. Adamont. "I'll find it." She plunged into her purse with both hands, like a clamdigger with a bull rake at low tide. "I'll find it."

McKenzie turned his back to the bake table and murmured pleasantly to Jane, "Slumming?"

It was uncalled for. Almost everything he'd ever said to her was uncalled for. "Not until now," she said, just as pleasantly.

Mrs. Adamont brandished a pen in triumph. "I found it! Sign it over, Mac. Before you change your mind!"

McKenzie bent over the table to endorse the check and Jane found herself assessing the broad expanse of his back. She averted her eyes, she wasn't sure why. She studied his signature instead: strong, quick, illegible. His personality exactly.

"Thank you, Mr. McKenzie, sir," Mrs. Adamont said cheerfully, snatching up the check. "This is a lovely donation. But take something with you, at least. For dessert."

McKenzie grinned and said, "Okay. If I can't have you, Adele, then I'll take one of those Napoleons I saw earlier."

Mrs. Adamont looked crestfallen. "I sold the last one to this young lady."

Instantly Jane said, "You're welcome to it, I have more than enough of everything—"

"That'd be my guess, too," he said dryly.

"Lighten up, McKenzie," she said through a clenched smile. She opened the top of her brown A&P bag and said, "Help yourself. It's right on top."

He bent over to see at the same time that she bent over to check, and they knocked heads. Jane let out a little cry of pain and annoyance. McKenzie said, "We seem to do a lot of this, don't we?"

"Yes! No. Here you are," she said, reaching in the bag and pulling out the pastry. "Take it."

It wasn't exactly a peace offering, not in any real sense of the phrase. But Jane wanted to be on the granting end, not the receiving one, with this man. It was important to her. She wondered why. Maybe she knew, instinctively, that he'd resent it. The way he must've resented Bing's check.

She watched him take the sweet, and for a second she thought he was going to donate it back to Mrs. Adamont. But instead he smiled and bit down on it with strong, white teeth, savoring it, and that made her instantly want the Napoleon more than anything else in her bag.

This is absurd, she thought, compressing her lips. *This guy drives me nuts. He does it on purpose.*

She passed her grocery bag over the table to Mrs. Adamont. "Can I leave this with you until I've looked at some of the other tables?"

"Sure you can. Mac, you take this girl around and show her the bazaar. She was very nice, giving you her Napoleon." She dismissed them like two preschoolers and turned her attention to the next customer.

As they walked away, Jane said quickly, "I'm sure you have other things to do."

McKenzie polished off the last of the cream-filled puff

paste and reached into his pocket for a handkerchief. "If I get a better offer," he said, wiping his hands clean, "I'll let you know."

"Please do," Jane said coolly, and stopped, ignoring him, to peruse the white elephant table. It held the usual array of castoffs: awful bowls and orange vases, odd glasses and gold-trimmed pitchers, and linen calendar towels, never used, from years gone by. There was also a wooden crate filled with old and broken tools.

McKenzie beat her to it. She watched out of the corner of her eye as he poked around in desultory fashion through the collection of screwdrivers, coping saws, planes, and chisels. One of the things he laid aside in the process of sorting through them was an old-fashioned rotary hand drill.

"A hand drill!" Jane said, delighted. "I've been looking for one."

McKenzie looked almost embarrassed. "I'm, uh, sorry . . . I took it out to buy."

"Oh. Well, naturally, since you saw it first . . . Ah, the handle's missing," she added quickly. "I wouldn't have wanted it anyway." She picked up the next thing she saw, a Phillips screwdriver for fifty cents, and paid the man in a Bruins cap who was standing guard.

Incredible. Twice in five minutes they'd gone after the same thing. Men and women *never* wanted the same thing. That was one of nature's laws. What would they be fighting over next, she wondered. A shower curtain?

The next table was overflowing with crafts and linens. McKenzie ambled past the crocheted doilies and corn husk dolls with hardly a glance, but Jane stopped and sniffed each of the potpourris, grateful for the chance to regroup. What was it about him? Every moment they'd ever spent together had been awkward. And she was just as much to blame as he was. She'd never met anyone who'd got so much on her nerves. Oil and water, that's what they were.

And it was also true—she was ashamed to admit it—that she still didn't trust him. Some people were open books; Bing, for example. But others . . . well, she was beginning to understand the expression "Still waters run deep." Oh, she'd known quiet men before. But they were merely dull, sometimes transparently so. They were not men she'd call *deep*.

She'd been staring for a small eternity at what looked like a pink-and-purple crocheted top hat, without having a clue what it was. When the sweet old lady behind the table said, "I made it myself," Jane had no choice but to buy it. She handed over two dollars and fifty cents.

"You might not be able to fit it over the fluffier kinds," the elderly volunteer advised. "I use Scott brand."

Baffled still, Jane turned and walked virtually into Mc-Kenzie's arms.

"A screwdriver and a toilet paper cover," he said with an absolutely impenetrable expression. "You're really making out tonight."

"A *what*? Oh, you mean the . . . yes, the toilet paper cover. Well," she said, tossing off a shrug, "that's what tag sales are like. Something for everyone."

He smiled—in a way it was an attractive smile, even if it was a snotty one—and said, "We'll see if it ever ends up on your bathroom shelf."

"I doubt very much that you'll ever get the chance to know," she retorted, and then she turned her attention to the next table.

It was the take-a-chance table, with a big fishbowl filled with little folded slips. The prizes were mostly stuffed animals; but there were three grand prizes of a blender, a coffeemaker, and a toaster oven, to lure the high rollers. Jane plunked down five dollars, assuming she'd get five chances, and was astonished when the vendor said, "Twenty chances, young lady. See what you can do."

She plunged into the bowl and pulled out her first slip of

paper. *Sorry,* it said in a neatly written hand. She pulled out another. *Sorry.* And another: *sorry.*

McKenzie was still standing there, enjoying her rotten luck, she supposed. "You know, Mr. McKenzie," she said, still simmering over the toilet-paper-cover crack, "I'm pretty tired of you treating me like some snob."

She pulled out two slips at once by mistake. *Sorry. Sorry.* "Apparently you have some problem with people who inherit real estate"—*sorry*—"although I can't imagine why, since you own an old family business yourself." *Sorry.* "But I'm a little tired of your attitude." She opened three more slips while she waited for him to respond: *sorry, sorry,* and a *sorry.*

"My attitude," he said at last, "is to live and let live."

Sorry. "You know that's not true," she insisted. "You know you resent me living in that house. You know you resent me getting ready to sell it. There's no way you *won't* resent me. You're determined, because I'm an off-islander." *Sorry! Again?* "Well, there's nothing I can do about that." *Sorry.* "Maybe my aunt should've left *you* the house, but she didn't. I'm *sorry.*"

She opened the next slip: *You win a stuffed toy.*

"Hey! I won!" she cried. "I won I won I won!" she repeated in a laughing babble. "This is incredible! I won!"

She waved the paper at the vendor in high spirits, then turned around in time to see McKenzie staring at her with a look of . . . she didn't know what. She'd never seen a look like that on a man's face before. Good, bad, up down —she had no idea. "Well, I did," she repeated, altogether confused.

The vendor said, "Pick any toy you want, miss, any at all."

Jane studied her choices. She passed right over the teddy bears, the poodles, the fuzzy red lobsters. "The little whale. I want the whale." The vendor handed it over just as three men and an attractive woman dressed in a skin-tight mini-skirt came up to McKenzie and her.

"Mac!" one of the men said, slapping him on the back. "We're goin' for a beer. Wanna come?"

The woman looked deliberately from McKenzie to Jane and back to McKenzie again, but nobody was introducing anyone.

Mac said, "Sure. I'll come." He turned to Jane and gave her a brief, ironic smile. *You know that better offer I mentioned?* it said. *Here she is.*

He walked out with them.

Jane blinked, then bit her lip and turned to go. She'd never won anything before, but she'd never been cut like that before, either. *Oh, well. It's a wash,* she thought sadly, clutching her little gray whale and turning to go.

"Miss—you still have three more chances," the vendor said to her.

"Oh. Do I? I wasn't counting." She reached in and pulled out three more slips, then opened them all in a row.

Sorry. Sorry. Sorry.

7

Jane hadn't seen Phillip Harrow since his dinner party, and when he stopped in she was surprised; she'd assumed he was off the island.

"I was, last week," he admitted. "But I spend most of my time on the island—more than Bing, although far less than Mac. And of course, all of us are home less than the Crates, who prefer to live as if they're under house arrest. Some islanders are like that."

Jane laughed and offered him coffee and a tour. Phillip declined the coffee, but politely agreed to let her show him the house.

She took him first to the fireplace room. He had good things to say about it—everyone did. He ignored the tarot cards that were still laid out, just as Jane had found them, on the little inlaid table.

"I assume by now all the neighbors have trekked on through," he guessed aloud. "With your aunt having been a recluse, everyone's worked up a fierce curiosity about the house," he said as she led him through the rest of the place.

"It's true. Dorothy Crate and her mother have already been by, and Cissy and Bing, of course. I get the impression that people on Nantucket know every one of the older houses, that they regard them kind of like community elders. A total stranger knocked on my door yesterday and asked to see the place."

"And Mac McKenzie?"

"He's been here," she said briefly. *As far as the back door. Any farther will be over my dead body.*

They were in the kitchen now, with its knocked-down wall and exposed timbers. Jane explained her plans, and Phillip nodded without commenting.

They retraced their steps to the front room. In the empty parlor Phillip saw a stack of wallpaper books piled in the middle of the floor and said, "You won't think I'm out of line if I give you a tip, I hope. But my business *is* real estate, after all."

He ambled up to the opened page of the top book and said, "You don't want to spend too much time and money papering walls with, say, this floral chintz, because the buyer may own Arts and Crafts Movement pieces and prefer a minimal look.

"In general, you'll want to avoid putting the stamp of your personality on a property you mean to sell—no matter how charming a personality that happens to be," he said, smiling. "Let's face it: the renovate-and-flip age is over," he added. "You should be watching every penny you put into this project."

Grateful for the advice, Jane said, "I'm glad to hear you say that. After talking to the Crates I felt an obligation to restore Lilac Cottage to museum condition. To be honest, I just don't have the money," she said, closing the wallpaper book with a slap. "I'm looking for a job right now, and I have a condo in Connecticut to pay for.

"I wish I could keep this, I really do," she added with a sigh, watching the lively play of sunlight through the diamond-paned windows. "There's just something endearing about this place, even in March."

"That's a good sign, Jane. If you like it, someone else will, too," he said reassuringly.

Phillip had his hand on the front doorknob. Suddenly he turned to ask Jane if she'd decided on a realtor yet, and whether she had a ballpark figure in mind. Jane hadn't talked to any realtors, but she had a price in mind and said so.

"Too high, I think," he said thoughtfully. "For these times, anyway. But I'll tell you what: before you sign a listing agreement, let me ask around. I may be able to find you a buyer and save you the commission."

"*Would* you? Oh, that would be fabulous," Jane said, her hopes beginning to soar. Phillip was just what she'd been missing—a disinterested, impartial advisor. She herself knew nothing about real estate. How else had she managed to buy a condo at peak, in a development that remained half-empty to this day?

"No promises, now," he warned, taking out a pair of elegantly thin calfskin gloves from the pocket of his top-coat. "But I'll make a few calls. In the meantime, don't go boxing yourself in by signing a contract with somebody."

Delighted, Jane walked with him to the door and waved him a friendly good-bye as he slid behind the wheel of his burgundy Mercedes.

Jane's giddy optimism lasted all of thirteen minutes, which was when she picked up the wallpaper razor and lifted it to the next wall due to be stripped. The searing pain in her shoulder returned, and she was plunged into instant depression.

The antibiotics had done nothing. The wound was healing, but the pain itself was worse than ever. And yet she'd been told that her blood test results were within normal range. *What is going* on? she wondered, becoming frightened. Some form of premature arthritis? Lyme disease? *What?*

Feeling frustrated and defeated, she threw on a jacket and a woolen cap and went out for a walk. It was cold; her breath came out in smoky billows. Inevitably, inexorably, her steps took her to the little burying ground behind the house and the rose that was growing on Judith's grave.

Jane paused, her mittened hands jammed in the pockets

of her jacket, and studied the thorny shrub. It was very old, that was obvious. The shrub wasn't tall, perhaps four feet, but it was dangerously thorny and sprawled all over the grave.

Was this rose the cause?

She circled the grave slowly, staring at the shrub. How could she have become infected by it? Just suppose that's really what had happened—never mind that her doctor had laughed at her theory. Then where did the poison, or the fungus or the virus or whatever it was, come from?

The roots are growing on a grave.

That thought had first formed at Phillip's dinner party, when the different versions of the Legend of the Cursed Rose got passed around. Jane had pushed it to the back of her mind, and there it had germinated, probably in the dreams which seemed to trouble her almost nightly. Now it was emerging, fully formed, a frightening, demonic thing: *The roots are growing on a grave. Over it, through it, part of it.*

"Oh, God," she whispered, crouching down for a closer look. How deep did the roots of roses go? She was no gardener. How deep were bodies buried? She was no gravedigger. Was Judith buried in a coffin? Had the coffin rotted away? And Judith? How connected, in nature's grand recycling scheme, *were* Judith and the rose?

She pushed herself away from her crouching stance and jumped to her feet, shaking violently. *This is dumb, this is stupid. You're letting yourself fall under the spell of this . . . this* other *side of Nantucket. Just because a little bookcase goes bump in the night, you're ready to call in an exorcist.*

She wasn't forgetting, either, what her mother had told her on the day of her aunt's funeral: that when Jane was eight years old, Sylvia Merchant had spent the summer filling her head with "paranormal gibberish." *Gibberish. Yes. You are predisposed to gibberish.*

And yet . . .

She circled the grave again. Was it her imagination, or was the dull, ever-present pain in her shoulder easing? Or was it just the anesthetizing effect of the cold? She circled the grave once, twice more, trying to determine if the relief was measurable. When she looked up, it was to see Mc-Kenzie's dark green truck stopped in the lane nearby.

Unfortunately, McKenzie was in it. He was sitting in the driver's seat, watching her. The sun was slanting off the window, so she couldn't see the expression on his face. Amusement, contempt, menace, bafflement, all four—anything was possible.

Oh, fine. Here I am, behaving like a puppy at a fire hydrant. What must the man think of me? She decided to preempt the obvious guess—that she was insane—by confronting him. She walked boldly up to the car. He rolled down his window.

"Hi, Mac, I see you've got your muffler fixed. How've you been?" she said in her breeziest way. "I haven't seen you since . . . since . . ." *Since you walked out with a gorgeous woman hanging on your arm, you jerk.*

"Since you got lucky," he said with that ironic smile of his.

"Funny; I would've said that described *you* to a T."

He thought about it a second. "You must mean Miriam," he drawled. "Miriam's one of my cousins. I would've introduced you, but I didn't want to seem impertinent."

"Oh, for—! Why do—?" She looked down at her shoes, suppressing a snort, wondering whether there was any way they could have a simple conversation without exploding into class warfare.

In the meantime it occurred to her that he could've done *some*thing on his own to level up the playing field. *Some*thing to put them on terms of friendly equals. He could've said, "That's a pretty jacket you've got on." Or, "You look nice in blue." But no. He just sat behind the wheel of his pickup, watching and waiting. What was he waiting for, a work order? Why did he make her feel like an overseer on a cotton plantation?

"Well," he said at last, rolling up his window.

"Before you go!" she said quickly. "I wonder if . . . if you could give me some advice. About the two hollies on either side of my front door. They're way overgrown; I can't walk up the steps without getting tangled up in them. Something has to be done."

"All right," he said with a look almost of concern. "An hour from now okay?"

"I'll be there."

"By the way . . ." He reached for something on his front seat and passed it through the open window to her: it was the rotary hand drill, with a brand-new wood handle varnished to a brilliant finish.

"I once saw a woman break another woman's finger at a flea market over a shoe rack," he said. "I guess we stopped just shy of that last week. I've got other hand drills," he added, rolling up the window.

Before she could respond, he was bumping down the lane toward his place and Jane was left standing in one of the sandy ruts, with the drill in one mittened hand, thinking, *Damn. He did that on purpose. To have the upper hand. Well! We'll see who's more gracious than who.*

For the next hour Jane worked diligently on the wall of the parlor, ignoring the pain in her shoulder. By the time she heard the loud thunk of the old brass door knocker, she was more than happy to stop what she was doing and answer it. She'd made a pot of extrastrong coffee and defrosted the second half of Mrs. Adamont's apricot coffee cake, just to show how gracious she could be.

But when Jane opened the door, she saw at once that McKenzie was on his way to a boat. Dressed in a heavy navy blue sweater and yellow oilskins over olive green rubber boots, he looked like the picture on a box of Gorton's Fish Sticks.

"Come in while I put on a jacket," she said, oddly disappointed that this was just a pit stop for him.

As he stepped into the parlor, he pulled off his watch cap; she was struck anew by the almost boyish wildness of his thick, curled hair. A lot of men his age had begun to cling for dear life to what hair they had left on their heads. Jane felt sure McKenzie had never given it a thought.

Stuffing the cap into his pocket, he looked around the room. "It's too bad she closed in the fireplace on this side," he remarked as Jane slid her sore shoulder carefully into the sleeve of her jacket. "This was always a good room for a fire."

"You've been here before?"

"Once or twice," he said noncommittally. He was rocking back and forth on the heels of his boots, obviously in a hurry.

With someone as tight-lipped as Mac McKenzie, "once or twice" could mean once or twice a day, or once or twice in his life. She knew from Bing that McKenzie's people had been farming the land behind her for two hundred years. In the forty years he'd lived there, McKenzie must've learned *some* damn thing about Sylvia Merchant.

"When was the last time you were here?" she asked him.

"The day before your aunt closed down the house. When she gave me her cat."

"She gave *you* her cat? I didn't know that! Where is it now?"

He shrugged. "Mousing, probably. You must have seen him around. Big, gray, yellow eyes. Kinda wild."

She remembered the creature in her basement. "Does he have a face like a Gremlin, from the movie? I was attacked by something gray downstairs a couple of weeks ago."

"Could be Wicky. As I recall, he liked to squeeze through a missing piece of granite in the foundation and sleep on the furnace. Look, I don't mean to press, but the tide is falling and I mean to do some clamming."

"Sorry," she said quickly. "Let's go outside and have a look, shall we?"

They stepped out onto the sagging front porch together. The overhanging hollies, like dancing teachers nudging their students to waltz, forced them uncomfortably close to each other.

"See?" Jane said in an edgy voice. "There isn't room for both of us on the porch." *There isn't room for both of us on the* planet, she thought, catching her breath at the nearness of him. What was it about him? He emanated a kind of strength that she found almost threatening. "They're just too big."

McKenzie stepped down two steps and looked up at the majestic hollies. "Someone probably dug up a couple of wild seedlings and just stuck 'em in the ground on a whim, never considering their ultimate size.

"I grew up with this pair," he added with obvious affection. "When I was a kid the first thing I learned to watch for were the boy holly, and the girl holly with the bright red berries; they marked the turn home."

"Yes, but now they're too big for the site they were planted on," she repeated, feeling like the other side of a custody battle. They were her trees, after all, to do with as she wished. "I wanted to get a quote from you for cutting them down."

His look turned instantly dark. "Are you *kidding*?"

"Or," she added quickly, "cutting them way back. You could kind of take out a semicircle from the inside half of each one. On each side of the porch. Do you know what I mean? Kind of like . . . *this*," she said, gesturing with her arm in a wide semicircle.

But her shoulder wasn't up to the task. "*Ayyii*," she said, gasping from the pain.

He gave her a sideways look, as if she'd dribbled tea down her chin. "Did you ever get that scratch looked at?"

"Yes, yes, yes," she said, wincing and rubbing her shoulder through her jacket. "The blood tests, whatever they were, all showed normal. *I* think it might be Lyme disease."

"They would have tested for that."

"Okay, then it's the curse of the Cursed Rose," she snapped.

"If you're talking about the rose I saw you moping over a little while ago, I guess you've got the wrong rose. That's a rugosa rose on Judith Brightman's grave. God only knows how long they've been around—England had them two hundred years ago from Asia. People make tea and jellies from their hips, which are full of vitamin C. It's not a real dangerous rose," he said in his deadpan way.

She made a face. "All I know is that I was fine before I scratched myself on its thorn, and now I'm not. In any case, it's *my* problem, isn't it?" she added sweetly. "And so: Will you cut the hollies down, or will you prune them?"

"Neither."

Neither. Of course.

"Do you run a landscaping service, or not?"

He sighed and said, "Let's try this another way. A holly grows very slowly. These hollies are irreplaceable. They're also a valuable asset to your property, whether you realize it or not. Last but not least, that pair has overseen a fair amount of Nantucket history. I know that doesn't mean much to you nomadic types. But around here it counts for a lot."

"They're not appropriate for their location," she said, digging her heels in.

"Appropriate, my *ass!*" he said, his patience exploding. "I'm sick of the word 'appropriate'! That's all we ever hear: It's not *appropriate*. A tree farm's not *appropriate*. The noise from a chipper-shredder's not *appropriate*. The tractor's too noisy, the rooster crows too loud for a . . . a *residential neighborhood,*" he said, spitting the last two words out with contempt. "Well, I've got news for you and yours, lady. The farm was here before half these houses, and those holly trees were here before *you.* And if you don't *like* it—"

He brought himself to a screeching halt and stared at her with an absolutely furious expression on his face, as if she'd been some jaywalker who ambled onto the highway as he was rolling through in his Mack truck. Then, just as suddenly, he shifted down to a lower gear and continued quietly on his way.

"Look . . . Miss Drew . . . I was way out of line, there," he said, taking a deep breath. "Obviously there's a solution to this problem."

"I should think so," she said, wide-eyed and breathless, stunned by his vehemence.

"Just move the front door."

"What?"

"Sure. The porch is rotten anyway. Have your contractor move the doorframe to the east and rebuild the porch there; it's not that big a deal." McKenzie's face took on a relaxed, almost joyful repose; he'd solved the problem, at least to his satisfaction.

*"Mis*ter McKenzie. In the first place, I haven't found a contractor I can afford yet. And in the second place . . . in the second place, *I want the hollies out.*"

McKenzie pulled out a small, battered notebook from inside his shirt pocket. "Here's someone you can afford," he said, ignoring her demand. "His name is Billy Butkowski—Billy B., everyone calls him," he said as he scribbled the name and phone number. "His wife just had their second kid; he's hungry for all the work he can get."

He tore off the sheet and handed it to her with a neutral look.

Obviously they were at an impasse. Jane stared at the slip of paper through glazed eyes. Then a thought occurred to her. She said, "What if we dig them up and move them? Could that be done?"

"With enough time and money, anything can be done," McKenzie said. He stepped down and around the trees, gauging the distance between the roots and the house. "It's iffy. I don't know that I can get a tree spade in there."

"So how much would it cost for me to have them dug up and planted nearer the road?" she asked, pleased that the damn issue of his heritage, or whatever it was, could be resolved without bloodshed.

"It's early in the season . . . they're still dormant . . . if you do it now, before the spring rush—say, five hundred dollars a tree."

"*Five . . . ?* Oh, I can't afford that. Really." Her tone was calm, dignified, and final.

He seemed, at last, to understand. "All right," he said after a pause. "Then what about this: I'll remove one of them, for nothing, and keep it to plant on my own property."

"Done," she said at once, relieved to be finished with the subject. They shook hands on it—she was surprised by the calluses on his palm, and the way his hand engulfed her own—and he left after setting a tentative date to begin removal of the tree.

"He's exhausting," Jane said after he was gone. She sat back on the sheet-covered Empire sofa with her eyes closed and her feet up on a milk crate, recovering from this latest military skirmish. She wondered whether McKenzie had been like that with his wife. Of course he had.

We're all the enemy to him—every one of us who's had the misfortune to go to college or, God forbid, had parents who did.

And yet, to see his hostility as town versus gown seemed oversimplified. Jane began to think it was subtler than that. Mac McKenzie wanted things kept just the way they happened to be when his mother gave birth to him: women in the kitchen, men in the field. He felt threatened by progress of any kind, whether it was the cutting down of trees, or a wife with a law degree.

Granted, Jane didn't know him very well—he was the kind of man who would let only one or two people in his life do that—but if she had to guess, she'd say he put everyone he met in one of two camps: those who were out to preserve the world, and those who were out to rearrange it. Maybe that explained his obvious contempt for Phillip. He wouldn't think much of a developer.

She tried to put McKenzie—and the headache he'd given her—behind her as she dragged herself back to work. Maybe she'd been going at the house too hard: twelve-hour days, almost three weeks without a break. She needed a night off, a little fun and laughter. She needed Bing.

So after she couldn't push herself any longer, Jane wandered over to his house, at the risk of being mauled by Buster, to borrow some coffee from Cissy and to find out when her brother was due back on Nantucket.

"Tomorrow," Cissy told her. "He called a couple of hours ago, hoping you'd be here. But I told him you never break away for anything but food and drink. And," she said, holding up a can of Folger's, "I was right."

"Well, considering how hard I'm supposed to be working, the house doesn't seem to be getting anywhere," Jane said, discouraged.

Buster came over with a sad-eyed, sympathetic look and laid his massive black head in her lap. She rubbed his floppy ears and sighed. "I think if someone walked in off the street right now and made an offer, any offer, on Lilac Cottage, I'd jump at it. Every time someone gives me an estimate for something, I go into shock," she said, thinking of McKenzie's tree-moving quote. "Condo dwellers are used to fixed-price living."

Cissy snapped a Tupperware lid on a container she'd filled with ground coffee for Jane. "You're just tired, that's all. But the days are getting longer, and the coldest weather's over, and things will get better, you'll see."

Jane remembered that McKenzie had given her the name of a contractor. "Can I use your phone while I'm here? Mine won't be installed until next week."

Cissy said to go ahead, and Jane made a call to a pleasant and eager-sounding young man who said he'd be by the next day to look at the job.

It was a quick call, but Cissy seemed to spend it staring at the big quartz clock that hung impressively on the opposite wall. Aware that the girl was carefully made up and dressed a little provocatively in tights, a short skirt, and a plunging Lycra top, Jane said, "Am I keeping you from something?" *Lunch at the Espresso with her pals,* was Jane's offhand thought.

"Yes, you are!" Cissy blurted. "I'm in love!"

CHAPTER 8

"In love? Really?"

"Yes!" Cissy said, hugging herself with quick little rocks of joy. "I can't tell you who it's with, he's forbidden me to say—he's a really private person—but he's just so *wonderful* and a fantastic lover and I never *dreamed* this could happen. You know how unhappy I was about being here all alone on the island and yet here he was, under my nose! I think I've been confused—emotionally—and he just seems to understand all of that so well! He's so deep. He takes everything so seriously. I think that's why before he met me he was so miserable. Oh, Jane, I'm *so* happy."

"I can tell," said Jane, laughing at her sheer ebullience.

Cissy looked truly radiant. She was young and hadn't yet learned how to dress with any sophistication, but it didn't matter at all. With her glowing cheeks and her hands dancing expressively and her voice ringing with happiness, she was the prettiest thing on the island and, very possibly, earth. *It's true what they say,* Jane decided. *Everyone loves a lover.*

"You're not going to tell me who it is?" she asked, fishing shamelessly.

Cissy shook her head resolutely.

"He's not *married,* is he?"

"Not anymore."

"Ah, but what if Phillip finds out?" Jane teased, remembering Cissy's recent crush. "Won't he be jealous?"

"Ooohh-h," said Cissy with a distressed look; apparently she'd forgotten all about Phillip.

"I was kidding. Don't worry about Phillip," Jane said softly. "Just follow your heart. Anything that makes you look this good can't be all bad."

So much for my flu-symptom theory, Jane realized. Love at first sight looked pretty good. Dammit.

"You haven't known him very long, I take it," Jane added, almost wistfully.

Cissy whispered, "It seems like all my life." The words fluttered through the air like a butterfly in a garden, and Jane was left with a sense of awe and of great, great deprivation.

That night Jane dreamed not of thorns and blood, but that she was eight years old again, on a sweet, warm summer's day on Nantucket. In the dream she was weaving a coronet out of daisies and purple clematis, but behind her she was hearing a sound, monotonous and droning. It was very bothersome; she couldn't concentrate on her task, although it seemed critical that she finish it. She tried and tried, but the relentless noise was making it impossible.

Jane woke up. The relentless sound was of Buster, barking. Over and over again, the same pattern repeated itself: three woofs and a growl, three woofs and a growl. Bizarrely, it sounded like it was coming from deep in the house, in her basement. Jane lay there for a half-conscious moment, and when it didn't stop she dragged herself out of bed and put on her heavy chamois robe and camp shoes and staggered downstairs into the kitchen. She flipped on the basement light switch at the top of the missing stairs, then forced herself out into the night air, which was surprisingly mild, and around to the outside bulkhead doors.

The doors were wide open.

The doors had very definitely *not* been open that afternoon. She'd made a point of closing them, because the forecast had been for rain. The ground was wet but the clouds were parting; the rain had come and gone. Jane crouched low and peeked down through the open inner door into the dimly lit basement. It was Buster, all right, on the loose again. When he heard his name, he stopped barking immediately, lowered his head, and came shuffling meekly toward her, his big tail wagging apologetically.

"C'mere, boy," she said, reassuring him with some pats on his rump. "Whatsamatter? Racoons again? Is *that* who opened the doors? Yeah . . . people say they're clever with their hands." She paused to consider what she was saying, and to whom she was saying it.

Yikes. This place is getting to you, Jane Drew.

She circled the basement warily, keeping alert for just about anything—racoon, Wicky, snakes, owls, lions, tigers. . . . Nothing would surprise her. The basement was small; the search did not take long. Jane found nothing, which somehow bothered her more than Wicky or snakes would have. She began to second-guess whether she'd left the bulkhead doors open, after all.

She led Buster out of the basement, holding on to his collar so that he wouldn't run away—although for one evil second, she toyed with the idea of letting him loose to wake up McKenzie again. Obviously she couldn't take Buster over to Cissy in the middle of the night—Cissy might not even be home—so she brought the dog into the house and waited a moment to see if he'd settle down. He did, quite contentedly, in front of the fireplace.

"How dumb can you get, dog? There's no fire. There's not even any wood." She laughed softly and turned to go and Buster, realizing his *faux pas,* got up and followed her sheepishly into her bedroom.

He stretched out on the floor beside her bed, which was fine with Jane. So far she'd been trying hard to be blasé about the goings-on around Lilac Cottage; no doubt they were pranks by local kids. She even thought she knew who the ringleaders were: surely the two she'd seen at her aunt's wake. One thing was sure: Whether they were kids, adults, or phantoms, someone was trying to frighten her and doing a damn good job of it. That's where Buster came in handy. He might not be the brightest dog, but he had a bark fierce enough to peel paint from a picket.

She pulled the covers up over her and turned onto her left side, favoring her right shoulder. It had been a long, strange day, and it didn't seem to want to end. She remembered that her shoulder hadn't hurt so much when she was by the grave, and that worried her. Her shoulder. . . .

Judith *Brightman*?

Jane sat bolt upright in her bed and Buster lifted his head, alert for he didn't know what. *How did McKenzie know Judith's last name was Brightman?* He'd tossed it off so casually that it hadn't sunk in at the time. The woman couldn't possibly have been a friend of his; the stone was too old. An ancestor, then? That'd be logical, except that if the burying ground were a family plot, there should have been a McKenzie tucked here or there—unless McKenzie's mother was an only heir, and his father had married into the family. Or maybe . . .

She slumped forward, hair drooping over her eyes. Who cared, anyway? Why was it so important to know who Judith—Brightman, Schmightman, whatever—was?

Because she wants me to know, Jane told herself tiredly. She hunkered back down and pulled the comforter over her aching shoulder. *She won't let me forget.*

Jane awakened the next morning to the sound of heavy breathing. She opened her eyes to see Buster sitting next to her bed and panting happily, waiting to be fed for a job well done.

"Okay, okay," she said, swinging her legs over the side of the bed and running her fingers sleepily through her thick straight hair. "What does something like you eat for breakfast? A roast pig?"

She padded out to the kitchen and searched through her

cupboards and fridge for something suitable, but the pickings were slim. Now that she looked at Buster, she wasn't even sure it was food he wanted. Maybe his morning constitutional? Was that why he was sitting by the door? Dogs were another subject she didn't know much about; her father had kept his family on the move too much for her ever to own anything more demanding than a turtle.

She dressed in jeans and a hooded sweatshirt and hauled Buster over to Bing's house. If Cissy wasn't up yet—too damn bad. She remembered McKenzie's black mood the day she met him and sympathized belatedly.

After a little detour Jane got the dog to sit alongside her on the front steps. She rang the bell and waited. It was Bing who opened the door, rubbing sleep from his eyes.

"Hey hey!" he said with a surprised grin. "Treats on my doorstep!"

"*Dog* on your doorstep," Jane said, trying to maintain her fine sense of outrage. "Buster got loose and woke me up in the middle of the night. Here. He's all yours." She let the dog go and he went loping off to the kitchen. "What time did you get back?" she asked, a little hurt that Bing hadn't stopped by, since he claimed to be so all-fired anxious to see her again.

"Oh . . . late," he said vaguely. "Cissy's dead to the world; I don't know when she got in. Did you know she has a beau?" he asked with a wry look. "She won't tell me who he is. I gather he's no kid: she keeps referring to him as 'quite mature' and 'very manly.' "

From out of nowhere the image of Mac McKenzie came rocketing into Jane's consciousness. *McKenzie*—with Cissy? Was it possible? Surely not. And yet it certainly was one way to solve his easement problem: seduce a relative of the grantor. But he wouldn't . . . he couldn't. . . . But who knew? For McKenzie the stakes were unbelievably high.

"Earth to Jane . . . earth to Jane," Bing said, tugging

at a lock of her barely combed hair. "Dinner tonight? At last?"

Jane shook herself free of the speculation—it was too absurd, too calculated a thing for anyone to do—and said in a lighter mood, "I thought you'd never ask."

"Great. I'll pick you up at seven. You know, of course," he added in a softer, more serious voice, "that you have no right to look so pretty at this ungodly hour."

Jane colored and said, "I'll bet you say that to all the dogcatchers on the island," and then she left, with his compliment still hovering sweetly in her ears. What was it about Bing? If any other man had said that, she'd have thought it was a line. But she believed Bing implicitly, even if he *was* a bachelor.

The morning was very fine, the warmest since her arrival on the island. A bird was singing some brand new song; Jane convinced herself that it was a harbinger of spring, even though the season had just begun. She'd heard that spring on Nantucket was a season of despair because it took so long to arrive, but today, at least, it was ahead of itself. Reluctant to go inside, she detoured to the burying ground, retracing her path through the downtrod grass from the day before, to visit Judith's grave.

Somewhere she remembered reading that if a person was being harassed by a spirit, then all he had to do was confront the spirit and he, she, or it would be civil about the whole thing and go away. That would be easier to try now that Judith had a surname; Jane felt as though they'd been formally introduced at last.

She stood alongside the grave as if she and Judith were chatting in front of church on a Sunday morning and said, "Judith Brightman. I don't know what's going on. But you have my attention. Here I am. What is it you want?"

Jane had no idea whether she was addressing the rose or the remains beneath it. She reached out and touched, ever so gingerly, the tip of the longest cane. Then she stood there for a long time, waiting for some sign.

"All right," she said at last, "if you don't want to tell me."

She turned to go. But as she did she became aware that the dull ache in her shoulder had eased, just as it had the day before. *Brother. This is just too weird,* she thought. *Obviously I'm having a psychosomatic response to this rosebush.*

She lifted her arm as if she were hailing a cab; for the first time since she'd suffered the scratch, her shoulder felt free of pain. She flapped her arm up and down half a dozen times, testing it, all the while keeping a self-conscious eye for the green pickup. There was no pain at all.

The sense of relief she felt was extraordinary. Apparently she'd given herself a psychosomatic disease; and now, she'd pulled off a psychosomatic cure. She thought of confiding her thoughts to another person, but who? Her sister would laugh, her mother would worry, her father would scold. Bing? Bing might be sympathetic. He'd only smiled, after all, and hadn't hooted outright when she told him about the bookcase and the spoon.

The bookcase and the spoon—and last night, the bulkhead doors. Those three events made up another mystery altogether. She felt sure of it. They were too . . . *worldly,* somehow. They didn't seem related to the pain in her shoulder. Anyway, she could live with the occasional loud crash or bark in the night. What she couldn't live with was being incapacitated.

As she turned away, mulling over her separate-but-not-equal mysteries, she heard the sound of a tractor. It came from beyond the row of towering arborvitae that she knew separated McKenzie's land from Phillip's. So McKenzie was up. Of course he would be. She decided to walk over and see McKenzie's property. She'd never been back there, and Bing had told her to be sure to see the place. Why not?

The part of the lane where Jane began her trek belonged to McKenzie. To the left was the row of arborvitae, tall and green and quivering in the light southwest wind. To the right was a field of fir trees between four and eight feet tall: for the Christmas trade, she assumed. There were other evergreens being cultivated too, although she did not know their names.

The lane turned muddier, and Jane had to pick her way around all the low spots that were pooled with water, but by now she was very curious about what was back there. The property seemed a perfect metaphor for the man: remote and forbidding. Jane was impressed by the vast amount of land McKenzie owned; it seemed almost tragic to her that he had no direct access to a road.

Her running shoes were thick with mud by the time she emerged from the trees into a clearing where an old shingled farmhouse stood, surrounded by several smaller, equally weathered outbuildings. The whole place had a sad, not-quite-hopeless look to it. Jane walked up to the closest outbuilding and peeked through the dirty window.

It was being used as an office: the walls were papered chaotically with slips and invoices, and the beat-up oak desk was buried under nursery catalogs and more papers. She walked around to the door. A small, handwritten sign taped to the inside of its window said WHOLESALE ONLY.

A plastic-covered hoop house blocked Jane's view of the tractor, which she could hear moving back and forth. She headed for it with every intention of picking McKenzie's brain about Judith Brightman. How she was going to do this discreetly, she had no idea. She was busy trying out different openers in her mind when the tractor emerged. But the driver wasn't McKenzie; it was a young boy about ten or so—Mac McKenzie in a smaller package.

He had the same thick, half-wild hair his father had, and as he drove the tractor toward her, she saw that he also had his father's calm and inscrutable hazel eyes. "Hello," she said, madly trying to remember the boy's name. "I'm looking for Mac McKenzie."

The boy put the tractor in neutral and gazed down at her from his metal perch with a look of quiet pride. *I'm driving this machine,* his look said, *because I'm a guy and that's what guys do.* "Dad? He's over in the house, making chowder," said the boy, jerking his head in that direction. Jeremy—that was his name.

Jeremy put the tractor back in gear and rumbled off at three miles an hour or so, sneaking a look back at Jane to see if she was admiring his driving skill. Jane was standing there, paralyzed, thinking, *Now what? I can't barge into a man's kitchen and demand to learn all he knows about some dead person. Mother would say it just isn't done.*

"Hey!" the boy yelled back over his shoulder. "It's okay. Just knock on the door. Go through the wart—the little lean-to on the side," he explained when she hesitated.

Now she felt stupid. Left with no choice but to follow through, Jane decided to knock and just, oh, double-check about when McKenzie was taking the holly. *Tomorrow, right? Fine.* Then she'd get the heck out of there. She fluffed up the few brain cells that were still working and stepped through the lean-to and knocked on the tongue-in-groove door with its single diamond-paned window.

"C'mon in, it's open," came his shout from inside.

She pressed down on the door latch and stepped back in time two hundred years, into one of the most delightful country kitchens she'd ever seen, from the exposed beams laden with drying herbs, to the cavernous brick fireplace at one end.

McKenzie was in jeans and a plaid shirt, standing in his stockinged feet on wide-board floors at an enormous black stove, where he was frying up a batch of onions in salt pork. He looked up, not at all surprised, as if it were her habit to drop in at seven-thirty in the morning on a weekend.

"Hi," she said. "Smells good." She didn't want him to think she was inviting herself to a breakfast of onions and salt pork, so she added, "Jeremy said you were making chowder." *That* sounded as if she was trying to weasel her way into his son's affections, so she said, "He looks just like you." Since *that* sounded as if she was trying to score points with McKenzie, she just stopped talking altogether, gliding to a bumpy halt like a single-engine plane that's lost power.

But McKenzie seemed not to notice her babbling. He was in a wonderfully mellow mood—for him—and actually seemed to want to chat. "Jerry's a good kid," he said as he crisscrossed a cleaver over stacked-up onion slices on a board. "This is the first time I've let him run the tractor himself. Without hovering, I mean," he said with a smile. "It's killing me not to run to the window every ten seconds. Has he plowed through the hoop house yet?"

He looked up at her with a good-humored grin and Jane caught her breath: the man was transformed, completely transformed, by his love for his son. His hazel eyes shone with a kind of luminous goodwill and his mouth, normally so set, so unyielding, suggested that he was capable of gentler, sweeter language than she had heard so far.

"N-no-o," she stammered, "he's being very careful. I don't think he'll be breaking through any sound barriers quite yet."

"He'd better not," McKenzie said, plowing the onion slices into the soup pot with his cleaver. "My neighbors out back would love an excuse to haul me before the Zoning Board."

"Are they the same ones who don't like your rooster?" she asked. When he nodded she said, "*I* never hear him crow."

"Of course not. I ate him," McKenzie said, stirring the onions. "Had to."

"Oh." She didn't know what to say, so she said, "That was considerate of you."

He gave her a wry look and went back to his onions. "So," he said without looking up, "what brings you here?"

"Well, first of all, I'm here to thank you for the hand drill." She saw he didn't want to be thanked. "And to just make sure about the holly. You're coming tomorrow?"

"Oh, hell," he said, slapping his forehead. "I forgot about the holly. Jerry flew in early this morning for the three-day weekend. It was a last-minute thing; his mother was called out of town. I don't think—"

"Of course; you'll be making other plans," she said quickly.

"On Nantucket, in March?" He snorted. "Not likely." He thought about it a moment and then said, more to himself than to her, "maybe I'll have him help me move it. It'd be something he'd remember. . . ."

He seemed to stop himself from sounding too keen on trees by making a big deal of stirring a bowlful of clam liquid into the onions and salt pork. The mixture hissed and bubbled, then settled down. He kept on stirring while it thickened.

"Well, look," Jane said, "just play it by ear. I may or may not be at home myself," she added, implying that her calendar was completely penciled in.

"All right," he said with a noncommittal glance. "We'll leave it at that. Did you want to sit down?"

It was the merest formality. She was aware that the air between them was cooling again, and she wondered why. Was it the talk of hollies? The talk of ex-wives? She shook her head, not wanting to stay on sufferance, and said, "Thanks, but my shoes are muddy. And I do have to be going. This is a wonderful kitchen, by the way," she said, genuinely impressed. She took in one last sweep of the sunny, homey room with its multipaned windows and sim-

ple Shaker and Mission furnishings. It was a superb restoration.

McKenzie took a bowl of potato chunks and began shov-
eling them into the brew. "Yeah, well, my ex had a thing
about everything being original. She and her interior deco-
rator had at least three false ceilings taken down from this
room alone. We spent four years camping out in one corner or another while they took away every memory I'd ever
had of the place—at least, on the first floor," he muttered
with a dark look.

It was a look Jane knew well. *Uh-oh*, she thought. Best
to avoid the subject of change. Still, she did risk saying, "It
turned out beautifully."

He turned to her with an almost baffled look on his face,
as if he didn't understand how he could resist a room so
warm and charming. "Yes. Celeste was a perfectionist," he
said quietly.

Jane had had her hand on the door latch for the past five
minutes, despite the fact that her mother had taught her
that lingering in the hall was the worst possible form. She
said, "See you later, then."

Just then a kind of send-off committee sauntered in
from the room beyond: an old, big gray cat with huge yellow eyes that narrowed when he saw her. *Beat it*, he
seemed to say. *You're on* our *turf now.* He threw himself
down on the braided wool rug and began grooming his
belly.

"*That's* Wicky," McKenzie said, by way of an introduc-
tion. "Is he your beast in the basement?"

"Maybe . . . no . . . I'm not sure," said Jane, crouching down to give Wicky her fingertips to smell. The cat
sniffed her hand regally, then bared his fangs in a nasty
hiss. "Whoa!" she said, drawing her hand back. "Yes, that's
him, all right." She stood up, embarrassed by the rejection,
until she remembered that her hands smelled like Buster.

She remembered something else. "Cissy said that my

aunt was supposed to have had a three-legged cat at one time. Do you know how it got that way?"

"Yep. Someone shot out a foreleg," McKenzie said in a flat, controlled voice.

"Oh, no," Jane said, dismayed. "Is the cat still living?"

"No. She never would stay inside for Sylvia. Eventually something caught her. Dog, probably."

"That's sickening. Who would shoot a cat?"

McKenzie put a lid over the pot and turned down the heat. "He knows who he is," he said cryptically.

"I suppose I should be grateful that Cissy's version isn't true," Jane said dryly. "Someone told her that my aunt needed the paw for a spell."

McKenzie grimaced. "That'd be *my* aunt. She lived in Bing's house with my uncle before they . . . up and sold it," he said, the muscles in his jaw working. "Aunt Lucille saw a witch under every toadstool. No one took her seriously."

"Cissy did."

"Cissy would."

She felt a nudge on the other side of the door; in came Jerry, his cheeks flushed with accomplishment.

"I checked the oil, Dad," he said triumphantly, as if he'd actually discovered some instead. "You're down about a quarter of a quart. Or maybe a fifth. But you're definitely down."

"Go to it, Jer. You know where we keep it," McKenzie said in a carefully offhand way.

Jerry turned and skipped away. McKenzie watched him with a look impossible for a nonfather to understand. Jane felt like an intruder.

Time's up, she thought, and this time she meant it. She left without being any the wiser about Judith Brightman.

CHAPTER 9

When Jane got back to Lilac Cottage, she saw a white Toyota pickup in her drive with a license plate on it that read BILLYB. Billy B. himself, a man in his early twenties at most, was prowling around the house with a clipboard in his hand, madly taking notes. Jane could see in his face that he thought he was looking at a year's supply of Pampers and Gerber's, at *least*.

Jane waved and they introduced themselves. She said, "I don't think I'll be doing much to the outside of the house besides patching the roof—"

"I can do that," Billy B. said eagerly.

"And replacing the two bad steps—"

"I can do that."

"And of course I'll have the house painted when the weather turns warmer."

"I can do that, too."

"Gee. You sound pretty versatile," she said vaguely. How much experience could he have? Two years? Three?

They went inside and it was the same thing in every room. Move a wall? Install cabinets? Replace the plumbing? New flooring? Billy B. insisted he could do it all and more besides.

He *sounded* like he knew what he was talking about. But so had everyone else she'd talked to. The people that Bing recommended were absolute pros. The difference was that Billy B. was not a buy-it-all-new maniac. Jane liked that in him, that willingness to compromise and patch when possible. The kitchen cabinets, for instance. Billy B. said they

were perfectly usable; all she had to buy were new fronts.
When they were in the basement, he even found the old
fronts: glass-paned doors that Jane hadn't noticed, hidden
in the clutter.

She trusted him, despite his threadbare jeans and strag-
gly hair. In the end, it all came down to price. "How much
do you charge an hour?" she asked him bluntly.

When he told her, she was amazed; kids in Connecticut
got almost that much for flipping hamburgers.

"If I got a lot of work out of this, that price would be
negotiable," he quickly added.

Jane folded her arms across her chest and leaned against
the ancient Frigidaire. "That's less than anyone else has
quoted me," she said, studying him with a sideways tilt of
her head. "How come?"

"Well, my wife just had a baby and had to quit her job at
the liquor store," he said, pulling nervously on his baseball
cap. He added, "And business ain't exactly been coming
my way. I'll be honest with you," he said after some hesitation. "You'll hear it anyway. I got into some trouble a couple of years ago. With the law."

Let me guess, she thought. *Car theft.*

"I stole a car and took it for a joyride."

Jane shook her head wonderingly. "What is it—some
kind of rite of passage around here?"

He shrugged. "Not much else to do off-season. It was
only a misdemeanor—they can't get you for nothin' more
than that unless they can prove you stole the car to sell it
for parts, and that ain't possible on an island like this."

"Is that true? Has the law always been that way?" she
asked, thinking of McKenzie and the stolen Porsche.

"Dunno. I think it used to be tougher. Anyway, the
owner was really mad—even though I didn't damage
nothin'. Right after that, I got married and settled down,
but people have long memories, y' know. I really could use
the break, Miss Drew. I'm good. That's no bullshit. I've

been doin' general contracting almost since I could lift a hammer. My dad was in the business."

How could she say no? She'd feel like the villain in a Frank Capra movie. So they struck a deal, work to begin midweek, and Billy B. walked away with a new spring to his step. Despite some misgivings, Jane was feeling upbeat. McKenzie was going to remove a holly for free, and a contractor was going to put her house in order at a wage she could afford. The work she was doing was moving along at a reasonable pace. And best of all, her shoulder had stopped hurting, at least for now.

That night Bing pulled out all the stops. He took Jane to Le Petit Pois, a tiny, elegant restaurant located in the heavily beamed basement of an art gallery on Centre Street. Le Petit Pois was new and didn't know it couldn't make a living in the off-season; but judging from the nearly empty dining room, it was learning fast.

Bing ordered a bottle of Dom Perignon to celebrate the passing of winter, while Jane tried to keep him in perspective. But that wasn't easy, not by candlelight, so she reminded herself that he was thirty-eight, and he was a bachelor. *Bachelor*—dread word; she and her single friends all had a healthy fear of it.

"The worst is over," Bing said, lifting his glass to hers. "Before you know it, it'll be July."

"I know you don't believe me, Bing," she said with a rueful smile, "but I won't be here that long. Once Lilac Cottage gets fixed up, I'm hanging a For Sale sign in the window and heading back to Connecticut to look for work. I may or may not find it there, but I *know* I won't find it here."

In the soft ambience of the room her words sounded jarring and defeatist, even to her. Feeling like a wet noodle, she picked up her menu and opened it. Bing folded the menu back up for her, then wrapped his hand around her wrist and gave her a beseeching look. Oh, he had it down cold, that Robert Redford sincerity.

"Isn't there *anything* else you can do besides graphic design?" he asked with gentle irony.

"You sound like my mother," she quipped, trying her best to fight the seduction of his gaze. *Bachelor. Bachelor.* She repeated the word to herself, like an incantation.

"Your degree is in fine arts, isn't it?" he pursued. "What about oil painting?"

"Unless it's the side of a house, I doubt that there's any money in it," she said, trying not to wilt under the heat of his touch.

"Okay, okay. Let's think about this. You have a great eye for color—that peach silk thing you're wearing looks terrific with your hair and green eyes. Have you considered interior design?"

She laughed at that one. "Just what Nantucket needs, another interior designer," she said, rolling her eyes. "Bing, don't think I don't appreciate this," she said in a softer voice, turning her hand up in an almost imploring way.

"But," she continued, "I have a plan of my own. If I sell Lilac Cottage, I'll be able to set up my own business in Connecticut. It has to be in Connecticut," she added when he looked stricken. "My contacts are there; my old accounts are there. My professional future is there. I can do the job better and cheaper than the firm that fired me, and I *will.*"

"You sound like someone with something to prove," he said shrewdly, trailing his fingertips across the palm of her hand. "Could it be you're still smarting from having been let go?"

Jane dropped her gaze away from his. "I suppose I am," she admitted. "No one likes rejection." She opened the menu and buried her nose in the dazzling selection of fine French cuisine. "Let's order, shall we? I'm starved."

The plain truth was, being fired had been the single worst humiliation of her life. Jane was Phi Beta Kappa, clever and intuitive and hard-working, a woman on the fast track to fame and fortune. She'd spent the booming eighties moving steadily upward, courted by one firm after another—and then, somehow, suddenly, she was out. Just like that: boom. Rejected.

She'd learned the hard way that there was no such thing as company loyalty, not anymore. With a flick of a pink slip, her whole value system had come crashing down. And yet she still had all this unspent . . . she didn't know what. Passion? She hesitated to call it that, and yet there it was: a feeling as deep and wide as the ocean around her that there must be *some*thing still worth striving for in life. *Some*thing had to be worth all the hard work, all the devotion, all the intensity. There had to be more to life than dull bottom lines and empty profit margins. There *had* to.

"Or . . . perhaps you'd rather I made a choice for you?" It was Bing, embarrassed. The waiter had approached the table discreetly to be of service, and Jane had left them both twisting in the wind.

"Mmn? Oh, I'm sorry . . . everything just looks so wonderful."

They could have been offering Hamburger Helper, for all she knew; she hadn't read a word. "Yes, why don't you choose for me?" she said, covering her lapse.

The waiter was sent on his way to rustle up some escargots and a rack of lamb. "I'm sorry for trancing out like that," she said, reaching her hand across the table to Bing. "So tell me, did you manage to nail down that Edward Hopper painting for your museum?" she asked with a warm smile.

"It's ours," Bing said. A look of unmistakable satisfaction lit up his face. "I'm on a roll, come to think of it. I've also nailed down a landscape by Thomas Cole and a series of sketches by Thomas Eakins—and I have a shot at an early Georgia O'Keeffe."

Jane conjured images of each artist's work, from Cole's lush Catskills to O'Keeffe's rich red poppies. It was so good to be with someone who cared about real art, someone who'd never had to swim in the shark-infested waters of commercial advertising. Bing Andrews was the dream date from heaven.

But his obvious joy in his work made Jane even more depressed that she herself had chosen so badly. For the first time, she wanted to discuss it with someone. With him.

"I haven't talked about being let go with anyone up until now," she said with startling abruptness. "I never even went to see the psychologist they provided for us, even though everyone else who . . . who got the ax, went to him for counseling."

Bing switched gears with ease. "Good lord, Jane, why not? There's no stigma to being let go; every company in the country is downsizing, from GM to IBM. It's a fact of life. It will be a fact of life for the next decade, especially in New England."

"So they say," she said with a sad little grimace. She took another sip of champagne. Maybe it was the bubbles; maybe it was finally admitting she resented being downsized. But the words were coming more easily now.

"The problem is, my family is very stiff-upper-lip. You know what I mean: bad form to blubber at funerals, that sort of thing. If life isn't going so well, just keep it to yourself, thank you very much. So I've been . . . *reeling* now, for months—and even as I tell you all this, I feel guilty for admitting it. It sounds so whiny."

"Don't feel guilty, dope."

"It's also true that I haven't had . . ."

She stared at the bubbles rising from the tulip of her glass with a rather fierce expression. *I'm tipsy,* she realized, amazed by the fact. *I almost told him I have no love life.*

"So . . . are you seeing anyone in Connecticut?" Bing asked softly.

"No," she said, suppressing a hiccup. "I have no love life."

That made him smile. "We can change all that," he said. He cocked his head at her. "Are you okay?"

The hiccup came out anyway. "Oh, sure," she said breezily. "It's been a while, that's all."

"Since you've had a love life?"

"Since I've had *champagne,*" she said and began giggling uncontrollably.

The escargots, thank God, made their appearance and Jane brought herself back under control. With a wary expression the waiter laid the plate of snails before her.

"I just forgot I remembered to eat lunch," she said, looking up at the waiter in abject apology. "I mean . . . I just remember I forgot to eat lunch."

The waiter pretended his eardrums were shattered and left. Jane took a deep breath and plowed on. "Champagne always hits me hard. Hits my stomach hard. Hits us both hard. I'll be fine. I just need some"—she put the palms of both hands on the table and studied her plate—"of these things."

Bing was doing a very poor job of not smiling, which she thoroughly resented. She was not a child, after all. Just because she had no job and just because she had no love life did not mean she could not hold her liquor.

"Did the dish ever come back with the spoon?" Bing asked her pleasantly.

Jane stared blankly at her table setting. "What? They're both here."

"No, I meant, did you ever find the missing spoon from your aunt's display rack?"

Jane shook her head, which made her see little starry bubbles sweeping back and forth across the snails.

Bing said, "There haven't been any more mysteries at

Lilac Cottage, have there?" He took his pick and inserted it with a surgeon's precision into the snail shell. A stab, a twist, and out came the rubbery contents.

"Uh-h-hn. Maybe I'll just pass for now," she said, nudging her escargots ever so slightly away. She closed her eyes for a moment and took a deep breath to knock back her queasiness. Really, she was being absurd. Her mother would *not* approve. What was the question? "Oh. Mysteries at Lilac," she said aloud. "Yes, there's been one . . . other. Someone opened the storm doors to the basement last night."

"Are you sure you didn't leave the doors open yourself?"

"Pretty sure. But don't worry. The steps up to the kitchen are gone; the intruders couldn't get very far. Unless they're ghosts, of course," she added in a studiedly cheerful voice. "I'm not sure how ghosts get around on Nantucket. I read somewhere that they travel in great big bubbles."

"Let's be rational about this," Bing said, smiling. "With all due respect, there's absolutely nothing worth stealing in Lilac Cottage. That leaves you. Now, granted, you're the kind of woman who might tempt a man to a criminal act, but that's not Nantucket. So what're we left with?" He answered his own question: "Mischief makers. Doesn't that seem more logical?"

For the first time since she'd known him, Jane saw him step back from her emotionally. *He thinks I'm a nut,* she realized. *He thinks I'm making this up.* Her cheeks flamed. There was no way, in that case, that she'd tell him about the strange phenomena she'd experienced at Judith Brightman's grave. She herself was unsure of that part. But not about the bookcase, the spoon, and the bulkhead doors.

"I agree," she said guardedly, "that someone wants me out of there." She placed her hand over the stemmed glass he was trying to fill and said darkly, "We both know that off-islanders aren't that welcome here. Haven't you felt that?"

"Not very much," he admitted. "But you're in a different category from me. I suppose you're seen almost as a real estate speculator. Don't expect any sympathy from me," he added in a lighter tone. "All you have to do is stay, and the problem's solved."

She stared at him blankly. "*Wa-a-ait* a minute. Let's run that through one more time. Someone's trying to drive me out because I don't want to stay. But if I stay, they'll stop trying to drive me out? Is that what you're saying?"

"I know it sounds crazy."

"Sheesh."

They drifted off the topic of mischief makers without reaching any conclusion and went on, during the course of dinner, to talk about a lot of things: politics (Bing was a liberal, she a moderate); sex (Bing was a liberal, she a moderate); and even sports (neither had a position).

By the time they drove back to Lilac Cottage, Jane felt as if she'd known Bing half her life. The man was charming her socks off; she began to feel he might not stop there. He was so easy to talk to; he understood her thoughts almost before she spoke them.

The subject of siblings came up. Bing told Jane what she already knew: that his parents had died in a car accident, and that he'd assumed complete responsibility for raising his little sister. It hadn't been easy, he said—not because Cissy was so headstrong, but because she was so very submissive. She was forever letting men assume control over her.

"Sometimes I wonder if I'm one of them," he said thoughtfully. "Maybe it's inevitable. I'm sixteen years older; she looks on me as a father figure." His voice trailed off into a sigh. "How about your sister? Is she older, or younger?"

"Lisa's younger than I am," Jane said. "I'm anything but

the guiding light in *her* life. Unlike me, Lisa knew what she wanted from day one, and now she's got it all: perfect husband, big house, and a bright-eyed prodigy with another prodigy on the way. All, I might add, within an easy commute of the doting grandparents."

"Hmm," said Bing. "I suppose your sister the princess is married to a heart surgeon in San Francisco?"

"Plastic; in Sausalito."

"Hmm. You jealous?"

Jane laughed. "You betcha. Sometimes, anyway. I mean, her life is so settled. There's never any question of, will things turn out? Will I be happy? Things *have* turned out. She *is* happy. She made it look so easy."

"Hey, different strokes for different folks. The only standard you have to measure up to is your own. Besides, I don't think you're ready to settle down yet."

Oh, sure, she thought with a sideways glance at him as he expertly downshifted his little red sports car. *You hope.* It had to be so much more convenient for bachelors like him when the women they dated were dead set on independence.

They were at Lilac Cottage now. Bing reached out to stroke her cheek with a feathery touch. "The only question you have to answer is, 'Am I doing what I want to be doing?' Besides, I don't want you moving out to the West Coast," he admitted with his boyish grin. "Connecticut is far enough. If you're going to please someone else besides yourself, I'd rather it was me."

"I didn't say—"

Bing slipped his hand behind her neck, pulling her toward him in a deep, silencing kiss. The whole evening had been leading up to this moment: his glancing caresses, the warmth in his voice, the innuendo. And yet, when the moment came, she was surprised. Maybe she expected to be able to resist him; after all, she knew what he was.

But when he released her with a low murmur, she kissed

him back. She did it without thinking, without wondering
how he'd take it or what it meant. She just . . . kissed him
back. His mouth was silvery-sweet and delicious, and she
wanted to taste it again. It seemed reason enough.

"Jane . . . I . . . you're irresistible to me, you know
that," he murmured into her hair. "What do I do now?"

"I don't know," she whispered, because she wasn't sure
how he meant it. Her eyes were closed, her breath a little
ragged. It was hard to think.

He kissed her very gently on her lips and then got out of
the car and walked around to her side. The brace of night
air that wafted in and around her seemed to restore her,
but only briefly, because when he helped her out of the
low-slung seat, the gesture became an embrace, the embrace a kiss, the kiss a return kiss, and she was left even
more dazed than after their first embrace.

They strolled hand in hand to the front door, up the
battered steps that she'd stood on the day before with Mac
McKenzie, arguing about the oversized hollies. She could
hear Mac's voice now, serious and condescending. "A holly
grows very slowly," Mac had said.

And then it becomes irreplaceable.

Should it be the same with a relationship? If you invest
time in it, and nurture it along, and try not to rush things,
will it end up having a value that's irreplaceable? Did the
rules of gardening apply to the dating game?

Bing stood at the door, tall and lanky and beguilingly
handsome, waiting for her to open it. Jane reached into the
pocket of her coat for her key and slipped it in the lock. *It's
been so long,* she heard an inner voice whimper. *I want this
relationship. I want it now. Don't worry about whether it's
irreplaceable or not. This is the age of Bic pens and dispos-
able cameras; everything's replaceable. Nothing lasts.*

But something—guilt, maybe, or a compulsion to second-guess—made Jane turn to him with an apologetic
smile.

"I think . . . maybe . . . it's been a wonderful evening," she said, falling back on a well-used phrase of dis-
missal.

She could see that he was caught off guard by her turnabout. "Something I said?" he asked mildly; but his look
was troubled.

She raked back the hair that had fallen over her forehead. "No, not at all. I think I've had a bit too much to
drink, that's all. I don't trust myself."

"*Woman*," he groaned. "Why don't you just smear Krazy
Glue on my shoes? Do you really think I'll be able to walk
away after a confession like that?"

"I know you can," she said with a relieved grin. This was
a man she could grow fond of fast. "That's why I told you."

He sucked in a lungful of air, raised his eyes heaven-
ward, and sent it whistling through his nose. "Don't you
dare start having a good opinion of me, Jane Drew. It
won't work, I'm telling you. It won't work." He smiled
helplessly, a lopsided, goofy smile, and then he held her
face in both his hands and kissed her tenderly good night.

He left and Jane turned the key and let herself in, still
smiling at the thought of him. "Okay, so he's never been
married," she found herself saying aloud. "There's always
a first time."

The next morning, her shoulder ached. Jane had assumed that that chapter of her life was over; she was bitterly disappointed to see that she hadn't turned the last
page on it. She got out of bed, rubbing her shoulder with a
viciousness that only the infirm and arthritic can understand, and wandered out to her kitchen-in-progress to
make coffee. It was just past dawn, but she knew from
recent experience that when her shoulder was on the fritz,
sleep would not come.

The hot water was halfway through the Melitta filter
when she idled over to the window to see what kind of day

it was going to be. That's when she remembered that she had to take in the laundry, and that's when she saw that it was no longer on the clothesline. It was on the ground, all of it: the sheets, the pillowcases, the towels. Shocked, Jane ran out in her robe and pajamas for a closer look.

She couldn't believe it. Every piece was on the ground, damp and muddy. Clothespins were scattered everywhere. And yet the clothesline itself was intact; even the forked clothesline pole she'd used to keep the line from sagging was still in place. She walked around the pieces of laundry, studying them. The sheets looked as though they'd been rubbed in the muddy grass deliberately; a sense almost of violation hung over the scene. It was a vindictive, furious thing for someone to do, and it frightened her in a way that the bookcase, the spoon, and the bulkhead doors had not.

She began scooping up the linens in her arms, ashamed somehow that she'd slept right through the attack on her laundry. She had no real idea what to do. Report it all to the police? Jane could see the crime log now: *transient reports missing spoon and dirty laundry.* Hire a detective? Even funnier, considering the state of her wallet. Alert the neighbors? She *had* alerted the one neighbor who could've seen it, and look where it got her: He'd slept through it, too.

Unless Bing Andrews himself was the perpetrator.

No. Jane slammed the door on *that* closet right after she opened it. She refused even to think back whether he'd been on the island for each of the other occurrences. It was absurd to suspect Bing, who was no more likely than . . . than McKenzie, or Phillip, or Dorothy Crate, for that matter. But there was one thing Jane felt sure of now: It wasn't the work of kids. There was something too adult—too *symbolic* almost—in this last act.

Shivering from the cold, she brought in her bundle and threw it almost feverishly into the washing machine; she wanted to erase any trace of the fury that someone—or something—was feeling for her. She turned the setting to hot wash, hot rinse, and poured half a box of Tide into the machine. Then she closed the cover and leaned on it with both arms while the washer filled, as if whatever evil was in there might still seep out, might still blight her with its malevolence.

And yet, despite her efforts, the malevolence seemed to have escaped anyway: the stabbing pain in her shoulder suddenly became a white-hot sword through her flesh.

"Why are you doing this, why are you doing this?" she began mumbling, over and over. She was hovering on the edge of hysteria; her thought processes were a jumble of memory fragments and irrational fears. When the fill cycle ended and the washing machine clunked into its agitation cycle, her mind clunked with it, and she broke into sudden, heaving sobs. She stayed bent over her aunt's washing machine, her head buried in her crossed arms, for a long time.

She lifted her head when she heard the heavy pounding of the brass door knocker. It was Sunday, too early for anyone on a civil mission; it must be an emergency. Jane grabbed a dishtowel to blow her nose in, then went to answer the door.

Mac McKenzie, dressed in workclothes, narrowed his eyes when he saw her. "Mornin'," he said laconically. "Thought I saw you outside earlier when I was headed out. I must've been wrong," he said, eyeing her getup.

"No; no you weren't." She glanced at the dishtowel in her hand, then wiped her nose on her sleeve instead. "I was taking in the laundry." She said it almost defiantly, as a kind of test, and waited for his reaction.

"It's probably not a bad idea to hang it in the night," he said in his dry way. "Some of the neighbors think it's unseemly to clutter up their view with longjohns."

"Ha! Well, maybe that explains it, then," she said ambiguously.

She didn't explain, and he didn't ask. It continued to

amaze her how difficult it was for them to communicate. *I suppose it's because we come from different backgrounds,* she told herself. She found the thought depressing somehow.

"So what's up?" she asked, no longer dazzled by the fact that he could outwait her every time in these little wars of silence.

"I thought we'd get an early start on the holly, Jerry and I. Unless you're doing brunch in bed. I'd hate to wreck your concentration for the Sunday *Times* crossword," he said with a thin smile.

"I'm not the type who spends Sunday in bed," she answered, retying the belt of her robe with great dignity. "And I'm certainly not the type to tell you what type I'm not."

The smile flickered at one end of his mouth, and then it died. "Good. Jerry's on his way with the machinery. Don't mind us. Just do whatever it is," he said evenly, "that you were doing."

Jane pictured her red nose, her unkempt hair, her flannel gown and ratty robe. What did he think she'd been doing? Watching Jim and Tammy Bakker reruns on TV?

She had to resist slamming the door on his impertinence. She forced herself to smile, and to close the door gently. Then she leaned back on it with her arms folded, her face a study in concentrated annoyance. He was so *damnably* provoking. She kicked a slippered heel into the door, frustrated beyond measure. How long was he going to punish her for being an heiress and having a career? Couldn't he see that her inheritance was modest and her career was erstwhile?

Ah, the hell with it. Why should she care anyway?

CHAPTER 10

A shower went a long way toward rinsing away the morning's hysteria. The hot water seemed to ease the hurt in her shoulder, suggesting that maybe there was nothing supernatural about the pain after all. But if that was true, if there was no spirit working its malevolence on and around her, then Bing was right: The nasty tricks could only be the work of someone creeping around Lilac Cottage in the dark.

Some choice, Jane thought grimly as she stirred her coffee. *A ghost named Judith or some homegrown pervert.*

It occurred to her that she was feeling as tight as an overwound clock. *I need to get out more, to do something more aerobic than stripping wallpaper.*

Jane was a jogger and had kept it up even after she got fired; but that all stopped the day she stepped off the ferry on Nantucket. She forced herself into a do-it-now mood and went back to her closet and changed into a jogging suit and her running shoes. She'd take a run first, and then come back for breakfast. Maybe by that time Mac and his noisy tractor would be done and gone.

She slipped on a headband, then hesitated on her side of the front door, feeling amazingly inappropriate in her pink and silver jogging tights. The tractor was idling quietly now; Jane wondered whether Mac and Jerry had gone back to the house. But no. Peeking out the window, she saw them tinkering with some big metal contraption, apparently the tree spade, that was attached to the tractor.

"How come she's getting rid of it, Dad?" the boy asked,

glancing up at the hollies. "Doesn't she know how much they're worth?"

Jane jumped away from the window, then crept over to the closer one, curious to hear Mac's answer.

"Don't know that she cares, Jer," Mac said quietly. "She has a blind spot or two. That's okay. We know what they're worth."

"A *lot*," Jerry said, although Jane had the impression that Mac didn't mean it literally. "You could sell this for a thousand dollars, couldn't you, Dad?"

"I suppose," Mac said absently. He was tightening a little silver clamp around a thin black rubber hose; Jane was frankly surprised that he could adapt his big, powerful hands to such finicky work. She was also surprised by the value of her hollies.

"But you'd never sell it, would you, Dad?"

Mac shook his head. "Nope."

Jerry went on. "Mom says you wouldn't sell an inch of land or a blade of grass if your life depended on it. She says you'll never leave Nantucket."

"No secret there, son," Mac said mildly, picking over a set of wrenches for one the right size. "I guess that's why your mom and I aren't together anymore."

"Yeah." The word drifted through the window to Jane— a sad, single note of comprehension. There was a silence, and then Jerry said, "She has a new boyfriend. He's a lawyer too."

"That makes a lot of sense," Mac answered. Jane thought she heard a kind of hardness creep into his voice.

Almost as an afterthought, she realized she was eavesdropping. *I have no business here,* she told herself. *I should just go.* She reached for the doorknob, then had second thoughts. What if Jerry was reaching out in some way to his father; should she blunder in on their heart-to-heart? Absolutely not.

Jerry was saying, "Two lawyers in one house is too many.

You don't know what it's like, Dad. They talk about their cases all the time. I don't like him. He's always trying to take me to a Celts game, or the Bruins—except you know how Mom feels about hockey—and I think he's just, I don't know, trying too *hard*," he said plaintively.

"Well . . . at least he's trying," Mac said quietly. "Some of the other ones didn't."

"He knows I don't like him," the boy boasted. "He doesn't know *anything* about sports, not really. He called Michael Jordan *Matthew* Jordan the other day. How dumb can you get?"

"Hey, pal, c'mon. Give the guy a break," Mac said. But Jane thought it cost him something to say it. Again she tried to move away from the window, but Jerry's next question kept her glued to the spot.

"Dad? I was wondering . . . would you still be with Mom if she didn't leave first?"

There was a pause, painfully long, before Mac let out his breath in a deep sigh and said, "I don't know, son."

Now she was ashamed for eavesdropping. She backed away and knocked over a galvanized bucket that had been left inside near the door, setting off a crash that could be heard on Martha's Vineyard. So she picked up the bucket and walked brazenly out with it, intending to make a business of taking it around to the back.

McKenzie looked up and took in her Lycra outfit in one withering glance. "Off to milk the cows?" he asked pleasantly.

Jerry was still crouching with his back to Jane. He swung his head around and said, "Hi again."

Jane shifted the bucket from her right hand to her left and walked up to the boy and said in her most cordial voice, "Hi again to you too. I'm Jane."

"I'm Jerry." That seemed to be all he had to say to her, so he went back to working on the tree spade.

A regular chip off the old block, she thought, stepping

over and around their tools. "I thought I'd go for a jog," she volunteered to no one in particular. When no one in particular responded, she walked smartly away from the scene to the potting shed, where she got rid of the damn bucket. She hadn't bothered to stretch and wasn't about to, not with McKenzie directly in her line of sight. So she just set off cold and passed them at a brisk pace, just as she would have done at her peak of fitness.

That lasted about a block. *My God, I'm out of shape,* she realized, pausing to wheeze and bend her back belatedly. She decided to walk briskly for a while instead, her thoughts on the sad and poignant conversation she'd just overheard.

Why do people marry when they're so clearly opposite? It wasn't the first time she'd wondered. Couldn't they see it would never work? Although Jane did not agree with her father on many things, she did agree with him on one thing: A couple had to be *compatible.* If nothing matched —experience, education, age, interests—how could they hope to stay in love? How could they hope to spare their children the pain of separation?

She walked on, her pace slowing as her reverie deepened. McKenzie, although not her type, was undoubtedly a terrific catch for someone. He was even stronger—not to mention, silenter—than the proverbial strong, silent type. If that was some woman's cup of tea, she could hardly do better than Mac McKenzie.

But for him to marry an ambitious urbanite who'd probably end up Attorney General of Massachusetts? Jane shook her head. No, it was as unsuitable a match as . . . as McKenzie and *her.* No wonder he never had anything except a sneer and a snotty word for Jane: he was taking all the hostility he felt for his ex-wife, and dumping it on her.

The sad thing was, this Celeste of his was probably just as good a catch for the right someone as he was. She sounded very directed, very purposeful, which was not a bad thing. But Celeste had one set of values, and Mac had another, and poor Jerry was caught in the middle. She wondered what the custody arrangements were, and whether they'd changed in the past three years.

She turned to go back home. The southwest wind had begun to pick up, bringing with it the instant ocean chill that day by day she was becoming accustomed to. The only way to stay warm would be to jog, so she cranked up her determination and broke into a trot. With the wind at her back it wasn't so bad. And she had a view of the ocean, brooding and magnificent, all to herself.

Jane jogged along the empty road past empty houses, wondering anew how anyone could abandon this wild and charming isle in the off-season. She wasn't far from home when she spied a little clump of blue tucked in front of a large rock that marked the corner of someone's drive. Suddenly, jogging seemed irrelevant. Jane stopped at once and crouched down before the pale blue clump for a closer look.

It was a small cluster of flowers, tiny and insignificant and without even a redeeming fragrance. But they were flowers—in *bloom*—and that made them more valuable to her than a pocket of amber. The house they belonged to was, of course, shuttered up for the winter. Jane plucked one of the pale blue blooms with its short stem and ambled homeward with it, cradling it in the palm of her gloved hand and marveling at its delicate resilience. She thought of Shelley's immortal question, the one everyone asks at the first proof that winter is packing it in at last: *Can Spring be far behind?*

When she got back to Lilac Cottage, she was surprised to see that the holly was still in place; the tree spade had looked powerful enough to rip it out in a single scoop. Instead, she found Mac and Jerry probing gingerly with old-fashioned shovels around the roots of the male holly, the one without berries.

When she asked them about it, McKenzie paused and leaned on his shovel, like a soldier resting on his sword. "It'd be better to cut through everything but the root ball and leave it to recover in place, and then move it next fall. Any chance you'll agree?"

He said it with such a pessimistic look on his face that she had to smile. "You're making me the meanie again, Mr. McKenzie. I think the sooner the four of us put this trauma behind us," she said, nodding at the hollies, "the better off we'll be." To deflect yet another argument, she held up the little blue flower for his inspection. "What's this called?"

"Scilla," he said briefly.

Jane slipped away to shower and change. When she went out to check on their progress, she found McKenzie sipping coffee from a thermos and Jerry huddled over a bag of Doritos, exactly as if they were at a work site in downtown Cleveland.

She thought of Bing and his neighborly invitation to breakfast. "Hey, why don't you come on in and warm up?" she suggested. "I've got some of Mrs. Adamont's coffee cake defrosted . . . and I can make you some hot chocolate, Jerry."

It was a one-two punch and it worked; father and son exchanged a silent signal, then McKenzie shrugged and said, "All right."

"You've been busy," he noted politely as they walked through the disassembled rooms to the kitchen. Every one of them was in some stage of progress except for the fireplace room, which Jane was oddly reluctant to change.

"I took your advice about Billy B.," she said, pleased that McKenzie had more or less complimented her, maybe. "He starts midweek. He seems like a nice guy; I hope he's as good as he says he is."

"He is. We reroofed my house together." McKenzie squeezed himself behind Jane's little oak table while Jane brought out serving things and the apricot cake and put a pot of milk on to boil. At Jane's prodding, McKenzie helped himself to a thick slice of the loaf cake. Jerry stuck with his Doritos.

This was a mistake, was Jane's first thought. The moment had none of the free and easy spontaneity of the breakfast on the morning of the snowstorm. When McKenzie hadn't felt like talking in Bing's kitchen—most of the time—both Bing and Cissy had been there to help carry the conversational ball. But here? Jane was on her own. She whisked chocolate mix into a mug of steaming milk for Jerry and set it before him.

The subject of Billy B. wound down to a close. McKenzie, predictably, did not offer another in its place. *Okay, fine,* Jane decided. *We'll just cut to the chase.*

"You talked the other day about the rugosa rose on Judith Brightman's grave," she said. "I've been meaning to ask you: How did you know the last name was Brightman? That part of the headstone is missing."

"Now it is; but it didn't used to be," McKenzie said. "I grew up next door to that grave. Years ago the stone was in one piece, even though there wasn't much on it: JUDITH BRIGHTMAN, 1802–1852." He added thoughtfully, "When I was a kid, I used to wonder why there were no words of comfort on it, the way there were on the other gravestones."

"You mean, like on Gramma's, Dad? HOLD FAST THE GOOD?"

"That's the kind of thing I mean, right."

"That's called an epitaph," the boy said proudly, jamming his fist in his cellophane bag for the last of the crumbs.

"So that's all you know about Judith Brightman?" Jane asked McKenzie, disappointed.

He gave her a wry smile. "Yeah, well, we weren't all that close."

"I'm sorry. I was just . . . curious. I'd like to know more about her. And the rose."

McKenzie glanced at his son, then back at Jane. "I think I've mentioned that the rugosa rose is *not* the rose you're looking for," he said meaningfully.

Plainly, he did not want this conversation to be happening in front of his son. Fine. All he had to do was answer her next question and she'd change the subject to Ninja Turtles. Call it conversational blackmail; she didn't care. She needed that information. If nothing else—bizarre as it seemed—Jane wanted to be able to eliminate Judith Brightman as a suspect.

"You remember Phillip's dinner party a few weeks ago?" she asked casually. "All those different versions of the legend of the, ah, rose?" In deference to Jerry, she dropped the word "cursed."

"Well, I was wondering . . ." She saw McKenzie's chin lower, a bad sign, but she swallowed and went on. "Do you know which legend was the true one?"

"Legends aren't necessarily true."

"All right, then—the original one."

"What legend, Dad?"

"I repeat. The rugosa on Judith Brightman's grave is *not* the rose of the legend."

"Dad? What legend?"

"*That* rose . . ." McKenzie seemed to consider whether to go on. His look was pure hard steel. "That rose was in the Quaker Burial Ground."

"Oh."

Well, at least it was an answer. Jane didn't know whether she was happy about the information, or disappointed. She hunkered down and shot off one more question. "Is it still there?"

"I'd say to go and see for yourself," McKenzie suggested through clenched teeth. He stood up abruptly. "Jer? You finished? Daylight's burnin'."

Whether he was finished or not, Jerry knew enough to say yes. He slugged the rest of his hot chocolate and said, "Thank you, ma'am," and they left. Jane was left staring at the crumbly remains of the apricot cake and wondering why McKenzie was so anxious that his son not hear his version of the Legend of the Cursed Rose.

How horrible could the legend be? Certainly not enough to frighten a ten-year-old. Every boy nowadays knew and probably loved Freddy Kreuger; could the story be any worse than *Nightmare on Elm Street*? She sighed and picked off a corner of the coffee cake to nibble. At least she had an end date for poor old Judith, and the apparent location of the actual Cursed Rose. Two brand-new facts.

It had been like pulling two brand-new teeth.

Jane spent the next hour or so spackling walls, amazed at how free of pain her shoulder was. Maybe it was because of the earlier long, hot shower. Then again, maybe it was because she was moving ahead on the Judith Brightman investigation. She wasn't being very scientific about controlling her variables.

She took a little break and, on her way to the kitchen, peeked out the front window. Just as she thought: Holly still in the ground, tree spade still to the side. McKenzie and Jerry, shovels in hand, were continuing their slow probe to China. But since he wasn't charging her for it, it was none of her business how he moved it.

In the kitchen Jane discovered she was out of coffee. She grabbed her car keys and threw on a jacket, intending to run out to the A&P for a few groceries. After a polite "Howzitgoin'?" to McKenzie, she headed for her car, then paused and turned.

"I'm off to the A&P. Can I get you anything?"

McKenzie said no thanks, but Jerry had other ideas. "Snickers! That's what I want," he said, throwing down his shovel. "I have money in my jacket pocket. It's on the tractor seat; I'll get it."

"Hold your horses, Jer," said his father. "Aren't you over your quota for junk food today? Your mother's given strict orders—"

"Aw, Dad," the boy said, embarrassed to be treated like a ten-year-old. "I'm working as hard as any grown-up."

"Yeah . . . well . . . okay." Then McKenzie gave Jane a hapless look that said: *Kids.*

Jane waited, then watched in horror as Jerry, sprinting for his jacket on the tractor, tripped on his shovel and went flying headlong into the metal tree spade. She saw it so clearly, almost in slow motion, as his face came down on the side of the sharp metal brace. His father sprang to intervene but was too late. After that it was chaos: cries and tears and blood, an unbelievable amount of it, gushing from Jerry's cheek while his father tried simultaneously to soothe the boy's panic and assess the wound.

Jane stood over them both, feeling faint, while Mac whipped out a clean hanky from his back pocket and began wiping away some of the blood from Jerry's face.

"Hold on . . . let's see what we've got . . . here we go . . . well . . . I know . . . I know . . . that's not so bad . . . a coupla stitches, maybe not even . . . you'll be like new."

"Should I call Rescue?" Jane asked, bending over them. It never occurred to her that she didn't have a phone.

"No, I can get him to the emergency room faster . . . oh, *shit,* the truck's back at the house—"

"Here. Take my keys," she said quickly. "Do you want me to drive you?"

"No, that's all right . . . thanks," he said, grabbing the keys from her.

The anguish in his eyes as he looked up at Jane stunned her. She'd never seen it before, the deep controlled panic of a parent whose child is in crisis. Not in her mother; not in her father. *Were we never hurt?* she wondered as Mac helped Jerry to his feet. He began to scoop the boy up in his arms, but Jerry was mortified by the thought and insisted on walking to Jane's car.

They drove off. Jane watched until she could see them no more. She was shaking; there was so much blood. She wanted to talk to someone, to say, "Did you see that? Did you see that?" even though it was obvious that no one else had. Bing's car was gone, and so was Cissy's Jeep. She felt impossibly alone. It seemed as if there must be something she could do. She went inside, her concentration completely destroyed. What had she been doing? She had no idea.

It's not that Jerry was going to die or lose a limb or be told he had a terminal disease; she knew that perfectly well. It was just that, one minute he was excited about a candy bar, and the next, he was rushing to be stapled shut or sewn up or whatever it was they did. One misstep . . . one false move . . . and his life, or at least this one day of it, had been forever altered. He would have the scar, no matter how tiny, to remember this Sunday on Nantucket.

She tried to put a positive spin on things. *By Tuesday he'll be showing off his war wound at school.* And good or bad, at least he'd been doing *something,* not sitting around and watching TV. But she felt restless and upset and was still watching the clock when Bing arrived.

"I didn't see your car; I assumed you were in town," Bing said after she hailed him over.

They stood beside the tree spade, hovering over the dark spots of blood on the grass, as Jane filled him in on the accident. Bing looked concerned, but not overly so. He told Jane he'd had his share of stitches when he was growing up; all boys did.

"We do it on purpose, split ourselves open and get sewn up again. Later on, when women ask us about the scars—

and they always do—we make up exotic stories about how we got them, usually in duels."

It was impossible not to smile. When she did, Bing stole a glancing kiss, claiming the smile, he said, for his own. "Don't worry about Jerry. It's part of growing up."

But Jane was still unconvinced. "That's easy for us to say; neither of us has children." She stood there in the cold April air, morose and shivering.

Bing put his arm around her to warm her and started nudging her back into the house. "C'mon; I'll make us both some tea."

They were walking up the stairs together when Jane heard the sound of her car and swung her head around. "They're back!" she cried, her heart lifting at the sight of them both in her front seat. She waved at them happily; McKenzie drove on by.

"I think they're both a little dazed," Bing said softly, apologizing for his neighbor.

"Well, sure, I'd expect them to be," Jane said, flushing. She felt incredibly foolish, presuming to be part of their family intimacy just because she'd happened to witness the accident.

They went inside and Bing, true to his word, brewed both of them tea. He helped himself to what was left of Mrs. Adamont's cake. "I ran into Lucy and Hank McKenzie in town," he said, obviously trying to distract Jane. "They're the ones who used to own my place." He added, "Don't expect to see them around here, though."

Jane remembered the name. "Mac mentioned an Aunt Lucille. He told me she saw a witch under every toadstool," she said, wrapping the string around her tea bag, squeezing out the last of the liquid. "He didn't sound like he liked her very much."

"No; why should he? A few years ago Hank McKenzie got into a blood feud with his brother—Mac's father—and after Mac's father died, he continued to take it out on

Mac. It's a pretty vindictive thing to sell your house to a perfect stranger—me—and leave your own nephew land-locked. As far as I can tell, Mac was an innocent caught in the crossfire."

"I still don't understand how he can be landlocked if the family's been driving back and forth over your property forever. Isn't there some law—adverse possession, some-thing like that—that gives him an automatic right by now to come and go?"

"Not if the owners of my property gave the owners of his property permission in writing over the years, which they did. Historically, Nantucket land deals have a reputation for legal correctness."

"What was the feud about?"

Bing shrugged. "Who knows? A lamp, a snow shovel, someone's recipe for shepherd's pie. By the time the dust settles, most people don't even remember."

"How did the house fall into your hands? You'd think Mac would have moved heaven and earth to buy your place. He could've made a blind offer or something; his uncle didn't have to know he was the buyer."

"He didn't have the money, for one thing. He'd just bought out his brother's and sister's shares of the tree farm —the mortgage for it has got to be crippling. I'm also will-ing to bet that that's what precipitated Mac's divorce.

"As for how *I* ended up with the place—that was pure serendipity. I was driving around one weekend, totally in-fatuated with the island and looking for a place to rent year-round. Hank McKenzie was out in front fixing his mailbox. I stopped, we chatted, and the next thing I knew I was in his kitchen, making an offer.

"I wasn't really planning to buy," Bing explained, "and he wasn't really planning to sell. I don't know who was the most surprised: Hank, me, Mac—or Phillip Harrow," he added. "Phillip told me later that he'd always had an eye on the place. He also told me I paid half again what it was worth. Which is why Phillip's in real estate and I'm not," Bing said with a rueful laugh.

"I get the impression Phillip would rather not be in real estate anymore," Jane said thoughtfully. "He sounded pretty disillusioned the last time I spoke with him."

"Maybe you're right," Bing admitted. "In any case, I'm not backing off the serendipity part—especially considering who it is who's inherited the cottage next door." His voice dropped into the seductively charming tone she knew so well. "Today, I figure my house would be cheap at twice the price."

They were sitting on either side of the corner of her little oak table, close enough to one another that she could see the light reflecting off his blond eyelashes. His eyes were so incredibly blue, his voice so incredibly soothing and kind and reassuring. She had wanted to tell him about the laundry episode, but this was not the time.

When he leaned over to kiss her, gently, tentatively, she did not resist. Sometime, after he left, she would try to sort out the flattery, if that's all it was, from the sincerity. But not yet. Not now.

The kiss was interrupted by the sharp rap of the front door knocker. Only one person on Nantucket knocked that way—as though he'd already been kept waiting too long. She jumped, remembering poor Jerry—and feeling a rush of guilt that she'd been able to forget—and said, "That's Mac, with my car keys."

"So? He's delivering your car keys, not a subpoena," Bing said with a chuckle, pulling her close to him for one more kiss.

Jane broke away with a dizzy smile and went to answer the door. It was Mac, all right. The color had returned to his face and his eyes, under the shaggy brown hair, still burned bright with emotion. He handed over the keys.

"Thanks for the car. I'm afraid we got a little blood on

the front upholstery. I got it out, but your seat will smell like ammonia for the next few hours."

"Don't worry about that," Jane said. "How's Jerry?"

"Not too bad. They think he may have a mild concussion. He's supposed to stay quiet for a while. Look, you won't mind if—"

Jane smiled reassuringly. "The holly's been there all your life, as I recall," she said, anticipating him. "It can stay there awhile longer. And the tractor too."

Bing ambled out behind Jane and leaned his forearm against the doorway. "Hey, Mac," he said in a friendly way. "How is he?"

Mac, who'd stiffened when Bing appeared, answered tersely, even for him. "Mild concussion, four stitches."

"Four! How'd he do?"

"About like you'd expect."

"Yeah."

Jane listened to their exchange feeling completely left out. They were talking man to man about a boy; no girls allowed. But there seemed to be more going on than that. Bing was especially relaxed, and Mac, more ill at ease than ever. She had the sense that one man was asserting power while the other was questioning it—some strangely male dynamic that she didn't understand at all.

"That's a nice car you have," McKenzie said to Jane, suddenly inclined to chat. "What kind of mileage does a Volvo get, anyway?"

Since Nantucket didn't have any highways, Jane couldn't imagine why he cared; but she answered his question anyway.

Mac nodded thoughtfully. Somehow that put the ball back in Jane's court. She felt obliged to return it. "I've decided to sell the car," she surprised herself by saying. "So if you know anyone, please keep it in mind." Up until that moment, she hadn't yet made that decision. But she was running out of money fast, and *some*thing had to go.

"Is that so?" Mac answered genially. His hands were in his pockets as he rocked back and forth on the soles of his feet. He looked exactly like a car dealer. "I'll mention it around. What're you going to get instead?"

"I was thinking a pickup is a handy thing," she admitted, although her mother might not agree. "I could use it to haul stuff back and forth."

"Is that so?" Mac said again. He rubbed the back of his neck thoughtfully as he stared at his shoes, considering. When he looked up again, the look in his hazel eyes was offhand, shrewd, and pure Yankee. "I know of a pickup that might suit you. It belongs to my uncle. He's getting on, and his driving years are probably behind him. The truck's old but sturdy enough. It might suit."

"I'd like to see it," Jane said with far more enthusiasm than she could afford, since she hadn't exactly sold the Volvo yet.

"All right. This week sometime. Count on it," he said, and then he turned to Bing. "I expect you're off for New York, then?" he asked blandly.

Bing, who'd been set carefully to one side during their conversation, glanced at his watch. "Hell. I guess I am."

Mac smiled lazily. "Have a good trip."

CHAPTER *11*

Without Bing to distract her, Jane fell to brooding about her part in Jerry's accident. *If I hadn't got him thinking about a Snickers bar . . . if I hadn't waited for him to get the money . . . if I hadn't stood where I did . . .*

Jane was taking far too much credit for determining Jerry's fate; she knew that. But she wanted to make amends anyway, so she whipped up a batch of her famous Cheater's Spaghetti Sauce and poured it into a Tupperware vat, then put the vat into a shopping bag with a box of spaghetti and half a loaf of Italian bread. It would be more than enough for their dinner.

She changed turtlenecks, tied her hair into a ponytail, and headed for Mac's house. It was six o'clock and still light out when she knocked on the door to his kitchen. No one answered at first and Jane considered leaving her care package on the doorstep; but eventually the door opened. It was Jerry, dressed in Nike sweats and with a dramatic bandage covering his left cheek. He didn't seem to know whether to blush or swagger.

"Hi, Jer," Jane said, holding up her AnnTaylor bag by its string handles. "I don't know if your dad's had time to make dinner yet, but here's some spaghetti fixings just in case."

"Dad's gone off to get me my Snickers bar," Jerry said with his father's ironic smile. "He says stitches are like having my tonsils out, so I get to have a treat. . . . Do you want to come in?" he suddenly offered, his voice reverting to a little boy's.

Jane thought he might be bothered by being alone, so she smiled and said, "Just for a minute."

She hung her jacket on a peg and they went into the keeping room adjoining the kitchen. It was a captivating room, with heavy-beamed ceilings and a massive hearth, and nice old furnishings which, though not valuable antiques, were in keeping with the spirit of the place. Mac had set the boy up on the sofa with two pillows, a down comforter, and a pine worktable that held prescription bottles, a half-empty glass of milk, a few comics, a book or two, and the remote control to the television.

Jerry settled under the comforter and politely zapped the television into silence. Jane took a seat in a slipcovered wing chair and, after a few discreet questions about Jerry's hospital adventure, wondered where to move the talk next.

He's more civil than his father, she thought, *but he doesn't trust me either. I suppose it's because I'm stupid enough not to know or care what my hollies are worth.* The funny thing was—just as with his father—she really did want the boy to approve of her. She looked around the keeping room, as beautifully restored as the kitchen, and said, "That's a wonderful fireplace. Do—did—you have fires in it very often?"

"Not very much," Jerry said, pulling his knees up to his chin and gathering the comforter around them. "It was the last thing to be fixed up. We moved right after. But our townhouse in Boston has three fireplaces and we use *them* a lot," he volunteered, trying to be helpful.

Jane wondered what paid for all of it—the Boston townhouse, the pre-prep boarding school, the planes back and forth to the island. Some trust fund? Celeste's job? Or was the money coming from the guy who couldn't afford to buy a permanent right of way across any of his neighbors' properties?

Jerry was watching her with a certain calm and appraising glance that seemed to run in the family. *When he fin-*

ishes growing up, this kid's gonna be one heck of a poker player, Jane decided. *Pity the poor girl who sets her sights on him and has to figure him out.* She smiled and asked Jerry how he liked school, and what he was planning to be when he got older. She thought he'd say, "Oh, most likely an astronaut," but his answer showed surprising depth.

He said, "I want to have my own business, I'm sure of that, but I don't want to be a lawyer. And I don't want to be a doctor, even though they get to have their own office. Something *like* a doctor, maybe, because they do good things for the world. But I don't like hospitals, I really don't," he said, shuddering. "I'd rather be outside where the air smells better."

"Maybe a tree surgeon," Jane suggested, amused by his earnestness. He seemed both older and younger than ten.

Jerry stared at her in amazement. "Are you kidding? Mom would never let me do that," he said.

They heard a truck door slam, which saved Jane the awkwardness of a response. And then they heard another door slam. And voices—loud, angry. First Mac's, abrupt; then a woman's.

"Twenty-four hours! I can't believe it! You have my son for twenty-four hours and he lands in a hospital! I asked you to watch him. I *warned* you he was at that awkward age—"

"That's my *mom*," Jerry whispered, his face paling under the bandage. "She's not supposed to be here. . . ."

"*Will* you lower your voice, Celeste?" It was Mac, obviously trying his best to lower his own.

"Who's going to hear me, the cab driver? For God's sake, Mac," his wife said contemptuously.

Jane sat wide-eyed and frozen in her chair. Should she flee, signaling that she'd heard them, or should she stay and pretend she hadn't? When the kitchen door slammed, she bolted up from her chair. *Flee,* something said. But she didn't—couldn't—move.

"If you think Jeremy's ever coming back to this island, think again! Last summer it was a broken toe, the summer before that, a sprained ankle! He'd be safer in—in Central Park at midnight than he is with you! Damn you, Mac!"

"Jesus, will you calm down? He's in the other room—"

"Jeremy!" Jane heard his mother cry.

She watched unobserved as the short-haired, chic brunette rushed into the room and threw her arms around her son. "Darling . . . oh . . . you poor *sweet*heart . . . oh, dear God . . . what have they done to your face. . . ."

She swept his hair away from his cheek with manicured fingers, then cradled his chin in both her hands while she moved his face up and down, back and forth, staring at the bandage as if she had X-ray vision. Jerry submitted to her twists and tweaks with a woeful expression on his face. He didn't have a clue what to do about Jane, that was obvious.

Who do I introduce first? seemed to be the question. *The ranting mother or the lurking stranger?*

He said nothing but continued to stare over his mother's shoulder at Jane, who stared back. Suddenly Celeste McKenzie turned sharply and saw Jane behind the wing chair at about the same time that Mac himself realized she was standing there.

Poor Jerry found his voice at last. "Mom, this is Jane."

"Jane!" It was the first time Mac had ever used her name—that, she remembered afterward. "What the *hell* are you doing here?"

"S-spaghetti," she stammered. "I brought some."

Celeste gave Jane a look of pure, cold contempt and flipped the comforter off her son. "Let's go, Jeremy. The cab is waiting."

"Celeste! Are you crazy? He's supposed to take it easy."

"Fine. He can do it at home. Get your things, Jeremy."

"Mom," the boy said in an agony of feeling. "Do I have to?"

"At least stay the night, Celeste. You can fly out tomorrow. I'll make up a room—"

"Never!" Celeste said, turning on him with irrational rage. "I will never, ever spend a night on Nantucket again!" Her face, so beautifully made up, was hard with fury.

As for Jane, she was edging toward the door when Mac caught a glimpse of her out of the corner of his eye. "What the hell are *you* doing? Stay right there, goddammit!"

Like a deer panicked by the headlights of a car, Jane became deathly still. Mac spun around to his ex-wife, all patience gone, his anger erupting with snow-white heat.

"Who the *hell* do you think you are, coming in here and snatching our son! He's *our* son—yours *and* mine! If he got hurt on your watch, do you think I'd rip into *you* that way? Do you think I'd do anything except grieve for his pain— and yours? What's the *matter* with you, Celeste? You're getting worse, more possessive—more paranoid—about every one of his visits—"

"That's *right,* that's *exactly* what I'm getting," Celeste said, throwing her ex-husband's fury back in his face. "Every time he comes back, I have to work to undo all the damage this place does. *Obviously* I blame you—you and your attitude! He won't study, he wants to run wild all day —after last summer he demanded his own *horse,* for God's sake. He mopes in class for weeks and his grades suffer. And each time it gets worse."

She whirled around to her son, who was standing in front of the sofa clutching the comforter against him like a bulletproof vest. "Jeremy! Did you tell your father your grades in math and language after your Christmas vacation here?" She swung back around on Mac with a look almost of triumph. "C's! He got C's in both! How will he ever amount to anything if he won't apply himself? How will he ever—"

She stopped herself mid-tirade. "Oh, God," she said

wearily. "We've been all through this. Come on, Jeremy."
Her voice became as gentle as a ripple on a beach. "It
really is time to go home. I'll wait in the cab."

She walked past Mac without looking at him. Then, at
the door, she turned and gave her ex-husband a look so
sorrowful, so poignant, that Jane caught her breath: When
she was not raging, Celeste McKenzie was an extremely
beautiful woman.

Mac turned away with a kind of smothered groan and
said, "I'll help you pack, Jer."

Celeste walked out. Jane murmured, "I have to go now."

But Mac wouldn't let her. He put his hand on her forearm, encircling it. "No. Not yet."

Now that he mentioned it, Jane had no great desire to
walk past Celeste as she sat brooding in the cab. So she
nodded silently and went back to her seat in the wing chair
while Mac collected Jerry's medicine and followed him up
the stairs to retrieve his things.

Jane sat in a state bordering on shock, staring at the
restored brick fireplace. Her own parents had pretty much
agreed on how to raise their two daughters; if they'd ever
argued over Lisa and her, they must have done it in the
privacy of their bedroom. Jane couldn't remember anything between her parents resembling the hostility she'd
just witnessed. And they'd never battled like that in front
of strangers, of that she was certain.

Still, it wasn't the first time that a mother and father had
fought over a child—certainly not in *this* house. Two hundred years' worth of parents had come and gone through
it, had courted and wed and given birth to children they
later agonized over in one way or another. Jane stared at
the cold and unused hearth, with its crumbling, powdery
bricks and centuries of soot stains. If only it could talk;
surely it would have an answer to the McKenzies' impasse.

Jane heard a heavy tread and a light one on the creaking
wood steps but did not turn to watch Mac and Jerry pass

through. It was only after she heard a faint and demoralized, "Bye, Jane," that she peeked out from behind one of the wings of the chair and said, "Bye, Jerry."

But by then the boy was out of sight.

Jane stayed where she was and prayed that Mac wouldn't get into another shouting match; she'd done enough eavesdropping and overhearing for a lifetime. But she heard nothing, only a low exchange of voices, then the slam of car doors. The cab drove off, and she got up to leave. She met Mac just inside his kitchen door.

"That wasn't pretty," he said bluntly. "I'm sorry you were here to see it."

If he was in pain, he was doing a good job of masking it. Or maybe he was just emotionally exhausted; Jane was. She smiled wanly and said, "Pretend I didn't see it."

"How the *hell* can I do that? Celeste and I were going at it like a couple of stevedores, and I'm supposed to pretend you didn't see it?"

"Okay! Pretend I did see it, and don't do it again," Jane said, more sharply than she meant to. "Anyway, it's Jerry you should be worried about, not me." She turned to go.

"I know, I know. Do you think I don't know that? Sit down! You're always so jumpy. You drive me crazy with that nervous energy of yours. I'm making us coffee," he said in exasperation.

She turned and snapped, "Perfect. I'm jumpy and you're irritable. Who the hell needs coffee?"

Mac was standing at the stove indecisively, one hand still on the coffeepot, when he noticed Jane's shopping bag on the butcher block table next to it. "What's this? Oh, right: food. Fine. You can have some with me. Is it hot?"

"I didn't make that for me," she said quickly. "I made that for you and your son."

He took it the way he would a blow to the stomach. She watched his expression contract with pain, then heard the pain trickle out on a sigh: "Oh, Christ . . . Jerry."

"But actually, I *am* kind of hungry," she volunteered hastily. She could see that he was reliving the scene in his mind, that he'd be doing it again and again. "Do you want me to start water boiling for the pasta?"

"Pasta?" he said vaguely. "Oh. The noodles. Yeah, use the pot on that shelf. Wait, you can't reach it," he said as Jane tried to snatch it by a handle. He came up behind her and reached up for it, his arm stretched alongside hers, his body looming behind hers.

It was as if she'd backed into a furnace. Immediately she felt the heat, felt encompassed by him, by his size. She stiffened and Mac moved deliberately away before he slapped the pot on the counter for her. She didn't dare look at him, didn't dare acknowledge the mocking look in his eyes. He knew that she felt threatened by him. Knew it, and despised her for it.

The question was, *why* did she always feel so threatened? She never reacted to Bing that way, and Bing was a lot more free and easy about touching—accidental or otherwise. So whose fault was it, Mac's or hers? She took the pot over to the sink to fill it, feeling as self-conscious about using his kitchen as she would about using another man's shower.

Mac was dumping the sauce into a pan for reheating. "Celeste is doing a great job with Jerry and his education," he said without looking at her. "Just a great job—he's in a day school," Mac added, his voice low with a kind of rueful pride. "After that it'll be prep school—Exeter, or Andover."

"Oh yes; your boy is very bright," Jane said with feeling, grateful that Mac was calming down.

He stopped to give her an ironic look. "Naturally you would recognize academic potential." He was silent for a moment, then tried again. "Despite what Celeste says, I'm not trying to sabotage Jerry's education—"

"Of course not, I realize that."

"If I might just finish," he said stiffly. "I try to encourage my son, try to set myself as an example of the way *not* to go," he said, flushing.

He seemed determined to make a full confession. "No one wants Jerry to get a college degree more than I do," he said. "No one knows more than I do what it means not to have one nowadays."

"No, that's not true," she said, interrupting him. "You can do great things without one and you can be useless *with* one—"

"*Will* you let me finish?" He gripped a slat of the ladder-back chair and stared at the little cracked sugarbowl on the table, choosing his next words. "For all the value I place on a good education—and that's a great, great deal—I still think there's more to life than a hotshot job and a big salary; more to life than a mad scramble for power and control.

"Let me put it another way," he said, struggling to make himself clear. "There's a T-shirt they sell in town—for all I know, it's sold everywhere. It says, HE WHO DIES WITH THE MOST TOYS WINS."

He lifted his head. His hazel eyes were shining with emotion. "I don't want my son winning that contest."

"N-no, I can see that," she said quite honestly. "But just because he graduates from college doesn't mean he'll turn into Donald Trump."

Mac made an impatient gesture with his hand, sweeping away her objection. "It's not just the schooling, it's everything. I think Celeste just . . . controls him too much. She wants to protect him from any influence that could possibly be harmful. *Any* influence—physical, psychological, you name it."

Now that he had begun to confide in her, it poured out in a torrent. "I gave Jerry a jackknife for his birthday," he said. "Celeste threw it in the trash can. Some bully in school kept cornering him, so I bought him a pair of gloves

and taught him how to defend himself. She made noises
about child abuse. And why do you think I tried to stop
you when you went on and on about the Legend of the
Cursed Rose? Because if it got back to her that I was filling
his head up with stories like that . . .”

He grimaced and shook his head. It was over, as quickly
as it had begun. He was done spilling out his frustrations.
He took out two plates and some flatware and began setting the table.

“I’m sorry I put you on the spot like that about the rose,
I really am,” Jane murmured. “If it’s any consolation, my
parents yanked me off Nantucket permanently once they
found out Aunt Sylvia had been telling me ghost stories,
and I’m still feeling deprived about it. Everybody needs a
supply of ghost stories.”

He gave her a look that was quick, wry, and sympathetic.
And then he smiled. It was the first time he’d ever come
close to sharing an emotion with her, and it threw her for a
loop. How could he be so appealing? How could he be so
warm? The surprise must have shown in her face, because
he turned off the smile almost as soon as he had turned it
on.

He pulled a wooden spoon out of a crock and plunged it
into the pot of boiling water, swirling the spaghetti with a
vengeance. “What’ll you have to drink?” he said gruffly.

“Sparkling water will be fine,” she said. She didn’t dare
ask for Perrier; probably he bought A&P’s house brand.

Mac took down a glass, went over to the sink, and
turned on the tap. He filled the glass and set it down next
to one of the plates. “Water it is,” he said with a derisive
look.

Here we go again, she thought, biting her lip. No matter
how hard she tried to keep the peace, he managed to turn
her good intentions into yet another skirmish in their class
war. She could see it in his eyes: Snob. Snob. Snob. *Okay,
fine.*

"On second thought, gimme a beer," she said in a belly-up-to-the-bar tone.

He rubbed his chin, hard-pressed not to smile. "Perhaps you'd prefer wine," he said in a smooth turnabout. "I have a very nice Beaujolais—robust, rich, and well balanced."

She looked startled, then burst into laughter. "Just give me the goddamned beer, McKenzie, and let's stop playing games. Yes, I've had all the—quote—advantages. And no, I'm not sorry about it. That's no reason to shoot me.

"And if you care to know what I thought about that little scene I witnessed between you and your ex-wife," she added recklessly, "I think you were *both* grandstanding for Jerry's benefit. It was a lousy thing to do, but I probably would have done the same damn thing. All's fair in love and war."

She flipped her ponytail back in a small defiant gesture, then held her breath while her little speech sank in. Mac was standing with a potholder in each hand, getting ready to lift the pot of boiling water from the stove. She thought he looked endearingly quaint: powerfully built, in tight-fitting jeans and a blue flannel shirt, his hair curling wildly over his forehead, clutching two little country-theme potholders, one with ducks, the other with bunnies, in his massive hands.

He stared at her with an impenetrable look. Then he said, "I like that in you. You're very fair." And he lifted the pot of spaghetti and dumped it into a colander in the sink.

The last time Jane felt that good about getting someone's approval was when she was sixteen and the Motor Vehicles Bureau granted her a driver's license. She stared at Mac's broad back as he shook the colander free of water and thought, *Why do I feel this need for his approval?* Was it because if he accepted her, it would prove she wasn't a snob?

Mac turned and said casually, "Help yourself." No appetizer, no salad, definitely no candles. She brought her plate to the sink and speared a little spaghetti, then went over to the stove for the meat sauce. Mac popped open two beers and joined her at the table. "Cheers," he said, tapping her can with his.

Two days, two men, two meals. They couldn't be more different. She'd adored her time with Bing; it was filled with charm and romance and free-flowing confidences. But tonight? Up, down, and everywhere between. Even now she hadn't a clue what Mac McKenzie was thinking. It occurred to her that with a man like him, you never *would* have a clue.

"A penny for your thoughts," she ventured, partly to provoke him.

He took a slug of beer and surprised her by saying, "I was thinking I didn't handle my divorce very well. You're right; it really was a war. The thing is, I'm the only one in my family who's had to go through one. In our family," he added grimly, "we tend to stick it out." He heaved his fork into the spaghetti like a pitchfork into a haystack. End of discussion.

They began eating in silence. Jane found herself sneaking glances at his face. After a lifetime of exposure to the sun, it was etched and lined, well beyond his years. He had none of Bing's prime-of-life glow or Phillip Harrow's smooth indoor looks. He was like most of the homes on Nantucket, she decided: weathered and a little beat up, but full of character and strength.

"What's wrong? Sauce on my chin?" He picked up a paper napkin and dabbed elaborately at the lower half of his face.

Jane blushed, ignoring the sarcasm. "Do you have much family still living on Nantucket?"

He shrugged. "Not many; they can't afford it. Scattered cousins, a couple of aunts, and the uncle I told you about, the one too old to drive anymore. My brother and my sister both bailed out of the farm after my father died; they've

BELOVED **165**

gone to live on the mainland. In case you're wondering: I'll be paying them off until I die."

"I wasn't wondering at all," she said, but of course she was. She added, "It must be hard, trying to squeeze a profit from a nursery when you have big mortgages hanging over your head."

"Hard, I can handle," he said grimly, twirling spaghetti around his fork. "It's the impossible that scares me."

"I know what you mean. . . . Sometimes my plan to start my own agency terrifies me, too."

He looked up, surprised. "I didn't know you planned to go solo. Well . . . good luck." After a pause he added casually, "Any nibbles on Lilac Cottage?"

"No, but Phillip Harrow dropped by recently and he thinks he may have someone in the offing. He told me not to sign on with a realtor quite yet; he may be able to save me the commission," she said, feeling vaguely indiscreet.

She saw Mac stop his fork mid-twirl, then resume. "Phillip Harrow is a licensed broker," he said coldly. "It's a violation of their code of ethics for him to try to skirt around a formal contract."

"Oh . . . I didn't know that. Please don't say anything around town," she said, distressed. "He was trying to do me a favor; I wouldn't want him to get in any trouble."

Mac snorted. "Phillip Harrow is very good at not getting into trouble," he said cryptically. "I wouldn't worry about him."

Jane felt uncomfortable with the way the talk was going, so she said nothing.

They ate in silence until Mac put down his fork. *His* repast, at least, was over.

As for Jane, she'd hardly eaten a thing and wasn't hungry. When she was around the man, her stomach invariably rearranged itself into a tight little knot. Suddenly she wanted to go home and maybe have an Alka-Seltzer.

"Well, I think it's time for me to head on home," she said, almost timidly. "It's been a heckuva long day."

He looked startled, but stood up and said politely, "Can I give you a lift?"

She declined with a smile, and he saw her to the kitchen door. Obviously a farm family's habit was never to use the front door; she wondered how that sat with Celeste when she'd been living in the house. They stepped outside together and stood in the dull halo of the porch light. The night was very fine.

"I can't get over how many stars there are out here," she said wonderingly. "Even the moon can't dim them. It's like being on a ship at sea, away from the highways . . . the sirens . . . all the din and clatter. What a wonderful little speck of the universe this island is."

"Have you ever been to sea?" he asked her. He was standing beside her, scanning the skies, his hands in his pockets, oblivious to the chill night air.

"Well, yes, once," she answered vaguely. With her parents, on the *QE II*, in the South Pacific. Probably it wouldn't be smart to go into detail. "What about you?"

"I did a hitch in the Navy during 'Nam. But I'm not all that keen on the sea, despite being born on an island. A lot of my friends are fishermen; I guess they're more masochistic than I am." He looked around at his land, so cruelly cut off from the road, and laughed under his breath. "But not *much* more." He turned back to her. "Well . . ."

It was her cue. She stuck out her hand. "Today was a bumpy day; tomorrow will be better."

Again she felt the surprisingly rough texture of his callused palm around hers. "First thing, I'll take out the holly."

Jane pulled out her mittens from her pocket, dropping one. She went down, and he went down, to retrieve it. Her cheek brushed close to his, so close that she could smell a faint, faint whiff of his aftershave. A wave of poignant nos-

talgia washed over her, mixed with an almost shaking
awareness of his nearness. The combination left her light-
headed and off balance as she rose to her feet. He handed
her the mitten. She thanked him and wished him good
night again and turned away, striking out down the dark
and potholed lane that led past the row of tall, brooding
arborvitae and on to her house.

Old Spice. That's what Mac was wearing. When Jane was
a little girl she'd bought it for her father, Christmas after
Christmas. She was a teenager before she learned the awful truth: her father never wore aftershave. Even now, she
occasionally wondered what he did with all those bottles.
Old Spice. How touching that Mac wore every little girl's
affordable idea of a Christmas present. She smiled to herself. Too bad he'd never had a daughter.

Jane was halfway between Mac's house and hers now,
abreast of the burying ground. It seemed much darker in
this part of the lane. She began slowing her pace, not only
to feel her way around the potholes, but to keep all her
senses alert. It was comforting to know that the Cursed
Rose was in the Quaker Burial Ground and not in this one
—but not very. Jane cursed her fearfulness under her
breath, knowing that once she gave in to a sense of dread,
it would be impossible to drive it away.

Maybe I should try whistling past the graveyard.

She pursed her lips in an arbitrary collection of notes;
for the life of her, she could not think of a tune. The qua-
vering sounds seemed to do nothing more than call attention to her presence. She dropped the idea; it seemed
pretty dumb. Eventually she got past the trees and into a
clearing. With the help of the moon, she was able to make
her way with greater ease—until a cloud came slouching
along, plunging her back into an eerie, creepy darkness.

Bing would've insisted *on driving me home,* she told herself petulantly.

Without realizing it, she'd slipped her mittens off and

balled her right hand around her keys in the classic urbanite's grip, with one key protruding between the third and fourth fingers.

My God. I'm preparing for a possible attack. It was an appalling realization: She was slipping back into the hypervigilant state of a city dweller. *This is* Nantucket, she insisted to herself. *Anyway, what good are keys against a ghost?*

She thought she heard a rustle behind her. She stopped and swung sharply around; but there was nothing. She thought she saw something in her peripheral vision, but there, too, she came up empty. She quickened her pace, forcing herself not to break into a panicky run, and that's when she heard the sound, even over the pattern of her own labored breath: a kind of ghastly, sickening snuffle.

Terrified, Jane gave in to the panic and ran, driven utterly by fear. Her heart seemed to constrict; her breath felt sucked from her chest. She was running blindly, in danger with every step of tripping into a muddy pothole. She hadn't got very far down the rutted lane when she felt a heavy sideways force on her thigh; it threw her off balance, forcing her to stumble to a stop.

It turned out to be—who else?—Buster, curious to know whether she was after racoon or other, bigger game. He looked up at her with that semi-intelligent face of his. *Where we goin'? Where we goin'?*

"Oh, God, Buster, you scared the living . . ." Jane bent down and gave him some rubs behind his ears, less angry than relieved; right now, he was looking like pretty decent company.

She kept him close by her for the rest of the way, calling his name softly and petting him indulgently whenever he trotted back to her side. So shaken was she by her night walk that she brought the dog into the house with her again. Earlier she'd picked up some Alpo at the A&P, because that's the brand she remembered Lorne Greene had told her to buy, and now she put out a bowl of it. Buster slurped down the food while Jane cleaned up the dishes from earlier in the day.

She decided she wanted a bath, so she went into the bathroom and began running bath water. Buster followed her in and helped himself to a long drink from the toilet bowl. Jane headed for the bedroom to get her pajamas and robe, with Buster tagging loyally behind her.

Until she actually went into the bedroom.

Buster refused to go in after her. His steps became tentative, then stopped altogether at the doorway. His ears flattened on his lowered head and a low, ominous sound came from somewhere deep in his throat. Jane had never heard the sound before from him; it made the hair on the back of her neck stand on end. His whole body seemed to skulk and cower, as if he wanted to run but didn't dare turn his back on what he saw.

And he did see something: he was staring at the rocking chair in the corner of Jane's bedroom. It was a pretty chair, very old; Jane would sit in it once in a while, with a cup of tea.

"Buster, come here," she beckoned softly. But Buster did not move; he continued to stare intently at the rocker with flattened ears and what Jane could only describe as a teeth-clenched howl. She stood there a long moment, poised between him and the rocking chair. She herself felt nothing; no presence, no sense of . . . anything. She walked slowly over to the rocker and gingerly lowered herself into it. Nothing.

"Come here, Buster," she coaxed.

But Buster would not come in.

CHAPTER *12*

Jane knew a thing or two about apparitions. She knew that people who saw them claimed they were accompanied by a sour smell . . . or a chill movement of air . . . or a deep sense of unease. She'd felt something of that sense of unease whenever she was in, or even around, the burying ground; but no such feelings were bothering her now. The air in the bedroom was cozy and warm, and smelled of nothing more sinister than potpourri. Buster, of course, was scaring her plenty; but Buster was the only one.

She left the chair and called repeatedly to the dog, but he kept staring at the empty rocker, ignoring her. Eventually he stopped his moaning howl and turned cautiously away, head held low, tail between his legs, glancing behind him until he was safely down the hall and down the stairs. Jane remembered that she was running bath water and dashed into the bathroom before the inevitable flood. She took her bath, went to bed, slept unusually soundly, and didn't wake up until she heard the rumble of the John Deere in front of the house.

In a moment Jane was up and getting dressed. She was very aware that she'd said nothing so far to Mac of the creepy series of events that had become part of life in Lilac Cottage. She wanted to tell him about last night. After all, he was a man of the earth; he'd know if Buster was just baying at the moon or not.

But something held her back. For one thing, she still didn't—quite—trust Mac. He was so full of hostility; who knew where it might lead him? Anyway, even assuming that none of the pranks was his doing, he simply wasn't the kind of man who'd accept some weird interpretation of ordinary events—she found *that* out after being scratched by the rose. Mac McKenzie would demand proof of a perpetrator: photos, tape recordings, eyewitness accounts by sober groups of ten or more. No, Jane was not yet ready to confide to him her bizarre little tales.

Mac was sitting in the tractor seat. The morning was mild and he wore no hat. He greeted her as he always did, with a slightly ironic, squinty hello. He'd already positioned the tractor so that the spade was encircling the male holly, ready for lifting. Jane went up to him and asked him if he needed any help.

He nodded. "Keep an eye on the house; make sure I don't bang it up getting the holly out. Watch for buried wires or pipes, although we should be okay there." He showed her two or three hand signals to use, and Jane took up her position.

Mac set to work on the hydraulic controls, lowering the huge steel spades into the ground to a depth of several feet. The spades sliced through the damp earth like butter, cutting through whatever roots lay in their path. Jane stood alongside, watching for problems, awed by the mechanical ruthlessness of the machine.

By the time Mac got down from the tractor to take a closer look, Jane was having serious misgivings.

"Can a tree really survive this kind of thing? Do you think we ought to have waited for a better time? What if something goes wrong? I'd never forgive myself."

"Neither would I," he said.

He got back on the tractor and began to control the process of lifting the holly from the patch of earth that had protected and nourished it for the past half century. Jane listened in agony to the sound of the last of its roots tearing and breaking and understood, at last, what Mac had

been trying so hard to make her see: that some things in
life are irreplaceable.

And inseparable. The two hollies had grown old together, had slowly reached out over the years to one another across the expanse of her front porch. Together
they'd sloughed off rain and snow and fog. Together they'd
watched Mac grow up. And now, because she said so, the
male holly was going to be torn away from its mate and
forced to exist in dreary isolation, out of sight, out of har-
mony with its universe.

"I'll move the door!" Jane cried over the chugging din of
the tractor. She was wringing her hands with remorse. "I'll
move it, I promise, I'll move it."

Mac turned off the engine. The uprooting of the holly
was now a fait accompli; anyone could see that. The root
ball had been cut completely away from its larger root system and the holly lifted a foot or so out of the ground. She
was too late.

Mac walked over to her and stared at the uprooted tree.
"So now you want to move the door." He said it completely without emotion, which made Jane extremely uneasy. She edged away from him an extra foot or so.

"I should have done it in the first place," she said in a
tremulous voice. "It's not a big-deal doorway. It has no
pediment, no sidelights. I should have done it in the first
place. I'm so sorry, Mac," she said, biting her lower lip. "I
wasn't thinking."

"You were thinking, all right," he said in the same lifeless tone. "You just weren't feeling."

It hurt, the way a slap across her face would hurt. The
one thing in life she never wanted to be accused of was not
feeling. "Can we put it back?" she asked in an impossibly
tiny voice.

"Of course we can put it back. We can put it anywhere
. . . now. It doesn't make any difference. Now."

"It does make a difference! It will mend better here. It's

used to being here. Used to the exposure . . . the soil
. . . used to *her,*" Jane said, pointing to its berry-laden
mate. She sounded like an idiot, projecting human feelings
onto the holly that way. But she didn't care. All she cared
about was putting things back the way they were, before
she'd come and turned them upside-down.

"This is so typical," Mac said tiredly, more to himself
than to her. He climbed back onto the seat of his tractor.

"I . . . what do you mean?"

He folded his forearms across the steering wheel the way
a cowboy would fold them over the horn of his saddle.
"You people can't sit still, and you can't seem to let anything else sit still, either. If something's in your way, hell,
knock it down. Tear it out. So what if it's been around
longer than you have. You have a *vision,*" he said deri-
sively. "And nothing can get in the way of your vision."

"I said I was sorry," she said humbly.

"Right." He pushed a button and the diesel sprang back
to life.

Jane wanted to run and hide under a bushel basket, but
she forced herself to stay and watch while Mac lowered the
holly carefully back into its hole. That done, he used the
spade to tamp down the earth around the replanted root
ball. He was finished. The holly was on its own.

"Is there anything I can do to help it live?" she asked,
feeling miserable.

"Water. Plenty of it. Then leave it alone. You can do
more harm than good at this point."

He backed the tractor away from her house and headed
back to his nursery. Jane ran to her aunt's potting shed
with all the urgency of a surgeon in triage and emerged
with an old galvanized sprinkling can. She made half a
dozen trips to the bathtub to fill the can before she realized
there was an outside spigot on the side of the cottage.
Presumably there was a hose around, too.

Gawd. A gardener I'm not, she thought morosely. Really,

it amazed her how little she'd learned in life. Ten-year-old Jerry knew more about nature and survival than she did. Part of the problem was that, like Cissy, she was a city girl thrown into a semirural setting on a remote island. There were no building supers to call when the faucets leaked; no all-night drugstores around to buy Robitussin from when she was sick. No discos, no Wal-Marts, no Dunkin' Donuts. It was disorienting.

Still, she was learning, even if slowly. She sat on the steps next to the holly as if she were sitting next to a hospital bed comforting a patient in intensive care. "I'll make a deal with you," she whispered, leaning close to the glossy green leaves. "Promise not to die, and I'll promise to decorate both of you with white lights this Christmas."

As soon as she made the promise, she realized that she wouldn't *be* on the island this Christmas. "No problem," she added. "I'll make it a condition of the sale."

The next morning Jane went wandering through the lanes of town again. Her walks past the colonial houses and their picket-fenced gardens were becoming a habit, almost an addiction. The old "runner's high" was being replaced by the new stroller's contentment.

Today Jane had a specific goal in mind: to find the Quaker Burial Ground and, with any luck, the Cursed Rose itself. She wondered what a Cursed Rose looked like. Did it grow gnarled and crooked? Was it massive and intimidating? Was there something that would make it stand out from the pack? Hopefully the caretaker at the Quaker Burial Ground would have some clues.

She started out for the cemetery with clear directions in her head, but after detouring down Fair Street past the old Quaker Meeting House (which was closed), and then meandering across Lucretia Mott and down Pleasant, then across Candle House Lane, up New Dollar Lane and across Milk Street, she ended up, at last, on Vesper, one of the streets which she remembered bordered the cemetery.

She walked a fair distance out of town before deciding she'd got it wrong after all. Disheartened, she was about to turn around when Mac McKenzie pulled up in his dark green truck.

"You look lost," he said, rolling down his window.

Jane reluctantly explained her problem.

"You're looking for Vestal Street, not Vesper," he said. He reached over and opened the door to the passenger side. "Get in; I'll take you there."

Jane climbed into the cab of his truck feeling less competent than ever. Mac didn't allude to the holly fiasco, but after a little neutral chitchat about the weather, she felt obliged to bring it up herself.

"I owe you some money for your time lifting and replanting my holly," she said in a businesslike voice. "Please send me a bill." She thought of Jerry's four stitches and Mac's fight with Celeste, all for nothing. She wanted to ask Mac how his son was doing but didn't dare.

"What's doing at the Quaker Burial Ground?" Mac asked, not unpleasantly.

He honestly didn't seem to guess why she wanted to go there. "I, ah, thought I'd just look around . . . see what the rose situation was . . . whether there was . . . ah . . . one that looked like the one on Judith's grave."

Mac turned to her and laughed out loud; the surprise in his face was genuine. "Well, here we are," he said, pulling up alongside a stile-fenced meadow. "See for yourself."

It was a lovely spot, on high ground the way cemeteries often are. The view was rural and expansive, marred only occasionally by new construction. As for the cemetery itself, there didn't seem to be any: only a big grassy field, dotted by a couple of lonely headstones. Well over to one side, there were several dozen more headstones squeezed together. But mostly it was plain, mowed grass. All that was missing were the picnic tables.

"I don't get it," Jane said, her voice a blank. "Where is everybody? This is supposed to be a major burial ground for the Quakers."

Mac was leaning against the front fender of his pickup, with his arms folded across his chest and a glint in his eye, watching her confusion. He was wearing his heavy canvas work jacket, which made her wonder whether she was keeping him from a job somewhere. "They're there," he said at last. "Ten thousand Quakers—all the movers and shakers of old Nantucket.

"It's a funny thing," he said, his voice becoming pensive. "The Quakers made Nantucket rich, made it a household name around the world. And in the end, they willed themselves into oblivion. What you see is almost symbolic."

"But . . . but I don't see *any*thing," she said, as baffled as ever. "Including any roses—cursed *or* blessed." There was nothing growing in the field except a few shrubs along one section of the stile fence. As for there being an actual caretaker on the premises—well, Cissy wasn't the only naïf on the island.

"Can we go in?" she asked.

Mac nodded, and they climbed over the fence together and began walking toward the cluster of headstones at one end. A candy wrapper and a crumpled sheet of paper littered the field; Mac picked them up and stuffed them in his pocket.

"Will you tell me about the Cursed Rose now?" she asked him softly.

He answered her question with a question. "And your shoulder?"

She stooped down to pick up a bit of litter on her own. "I have to admit, it's better." If only she knew why.

He paused and scanned the horizon, then pointed out a newly built and rather pompous house nearby. "So. It's finished," he said with obvious distaste. "What a piece of . . ."

They walked on, and Mac got around, finally, to the Legend of the Cursed Rose. "All the versions you heard the night of Phillip's dinner party were malarkey. Do you know anything at all about Quaker history?" he asked, throwing her one of his *you've*-been-to-college looks.

She shrugged. "I know the usual amount: that the Friends were nonviolent, had no formal creed, heeded an 'inner light,' and were all for equal rights. Oh, and they spoke in *thee*s and *thou*s." She added, "I do know that the Quakers were a major force on Nantucket."

"You can see why. They put a premium on hard work, simple living, education, and equality. How could Nantucket go wrong with a value system like that? During the Revolution half the islanders were Quakers—that's why Nantucket stayed neutral in the war—and their influence on island life was profound. After that their popularity continued, but by then things were going very wrong—am I boring you?" he asked self-consciously.

"No! No, please continue," she said, intrigued as much by his enthusiasm for the subject as by the history itself. He was speaking in whole paragraphs; it was a breakthrough of sorts. "I want to know."

"Good. The point is, disownment—ejection from the Society of Friends—was the only penalty these people had for an offense, no matter how big or how small. Of course, anyone would agree that disownment was justifiable for the serious violations. For example, forty-seven Nantucket Quakers fought in the Revolution; under their strict code of nonviolence, all forty-seven were disowned. Or say someone married outside the Society, which happened. You could argue that that was a serious breach as well, and worthy of disownment.

"But somewhere along the line, the Elders got caught up in going after the trivial stuff, all in the name of simple living. If you wore a fancy little buckle, for instance—disowned. If you went dancing, disowned. Furniture too fancy? Disowned. Drunk? Disowned.

"It got to the point that for every one new member born into the Society, five were disowned. It doesn't take a genius to figure out that those numbers can't work for long. The Society kept on petering out, and by the middle of the nineteenth century there were only about three hundred practicing Quakers on Nantucket."

They paused to read a headstone: EMILY W. HUSSEY, WIDOW OF JOSEPH W. HUSSEY, DIED SEPTEMBER 1859, AGED 63 YEARS, 9 MONTHS.

"She would've been one of them," he commented. "The last formal Meeting of the Friends on the island wasn't long after that," he said. "By 1900, when the island's population had dropped from ten thousand to three thousand, there were no Quakers left at all. An enlightened and wildly successful movement—finished. And why? Because they lost their way. The quest for simplicity became a corruption of power."

"Is that why there are no headstones?" Jane ventured. "Because they were considered a vanity?"

He shot an appreciative glance at her. "Exactly. The few headstones you see were from the reform movements that came too late for Nantucket. There were the Hicksites, and later the Gurnyites. It was the Gurnyites who began using headstones, around 1837. You'll find no stone here that predates that time."

"But where does the Cursed Rose fit in?" Jane asked, although even as she said it, she thought she knew. It's as if the answer was stored in some locked box in her mind, and all she needed was the key. Mac had the key.

"Ah, that Cursed Rose." He smiled to himself and pressed an upturned clod of earth back into the ground with his heel. "That part's a little tricky. Sometime around 1830, a man was buried here. His widow, distraught by the notion that there would be no marker on his grave, dared to plant a rose on it."

His voice became low and thoughtful, as if he were reaching back to the moment a century and a half earlier. "You have to understand that while the Friends permitted the planting of herbs and vegetables in their kitchen gardens, they disapproved of flowers. Like music and art and literature, flowers were frivolous. So the widow's deed was doubly offensive: she committed an act of defiance with a thing of beauty."

An act of defiance with a thing of beauty. It simply amazed Jane that Mac McKenzie was capable of such eloquence and sympathy. She did not know the man at all. "What happened to her?" Jane asked, although of course she knew.

"Disowned. She's not buried here, you can count on that. But the question you should be asking is, what happened to the rose? I have no answer to that. What I've told you so far is fairly common knowledge to anyone who bothers picking up a history of Nantucket.

"But there's also a story, less well known, that an outraged Elder personally yanked out the rose, and that he died immediately afterward. That, I assume, is where the Legend of the Cursed Rose began. You can safely forget the brain fever, forget the gangrene." Mac let out a soft, rueful laugh. "What he probably died of was hypertension."

Jane plunged her hands deep in her pockets as they continued their stroll among the headstones. The wind whipped her auburn hair in long, snaking tendrils around her face. She wished she'd worn a sweater under her light jacket; it was a gray, penetrating day, and she felt it keenly on the hill. "I don't suppose it was a rugosa rose," she said without much hope.

"Don't know that either; but I'd guess not. The Quakers would have found the *Rosa rugosa* too useful to be so offended by it: it had medicinal value, after all. I suspect the so-called Cursed Rose was pleasing to the senses, and that was all."

Jane sighed deeply. "So this is it; a dead end."

"As far as I know."

He seemed to share her sadness; she couldn't imagine why. Or maybe it was the sweet and simple melancholy of the place affecting them both. They walked among the few dozen gravestones, a roll call of names familiar to the island and around the world: Chase and Hussey and Coffin and Mitchell and Folger.

After they looked at them all, they began heading back to the truck. Mac said, "I suppose when you consider the fortune in shipping the Quakers made—in coffee and dry goods and whale oil—it's not hard to see why the Society of Friends died out on Nantucket. These were wealthy men; they wanted their mansions. And yet they couldn't put a second story on their lean-to houses without being disowned by the Overseers for extravagance."

And they couldn't mark the graves of the ones they loved. "How is it you know so much of Nantucket's history?" she asked.

"I do know how to read," he said with his usual irony. But he seemed not to want to break the mood of friendliness between them, because he added with a smile, "The winters are quiet here, and I don't have cable."

She liked that smile. The truth is, she'd pay big money to see it more often. It softened the lines of his face and added even more depth and richness to his voice. What was it about him? He could be so defensive and so completely open at the same time. She'd never known anyone like him.

They were at his truck. He said, "I'm headed out to Cisco, but if you need a lift back to town . . ."

She thought about the way he'd phrased his offer. He specifically wanted her to know he was headed in the opposite direction. God forbid he should spend an extra five minutes with her. "Oh, no thanks," she said, hurt. "It's a short walk back, now that I know where I am." She smiled and waved good-bye as he took off.

I wish to hell I knew where I was, she thought with a sigh, staring after his truck.

CHAPTER 13

The first phone call Jane received on her newly installed phone was from her father.

"Dad! Hi! Gee! How did you know I had a phone?"

"Not from you, Robinson Crusoe. I have a meeting in five minutes, so I'll make this quick. There's an associate of mine whose company is looking to open a branch in Connecticut. He needs a place to stay for six weeks, and I thought of your condo. It'll pay your mortgage for a couple of months. Interested?"

"You bet! I can't possibly finish Lilac Cottage in less than a month, and probably more. The timing couldn't be better. Will the guy need a car?" she added, fired with enthusiasm. "I'll be taking the Volvo back to Connecticut to be sold."

"What's wrong with the Volvo?"

"Nothing, Dad; it's just more car than I need."

"It's a good, safe car."

"Never mind; I shouldn't have brought it up."

"That's a top-rated car, dammit. Sell it now and you'll take the whole hit on depreciation. What's wrong with the Volvo?"

"Dad, I *told* you—"

"I don't want you selling that car. I've got to run. Your mother will call you. Kiss."

And that was that. Neal Drew had managed to find time for another pit stop in his daughter's life, and now he was roaring back onto the race course of his career. Jane wondered whether, deep down, he ever got tired of it. He didn't seem to. Every once in a while he stopped long enough for an engine overhaul—the cruise on the *QE II*, for example—but by and large he seemed to thrive on speed. He wouldn't think much of Nantucket.

Jane's mother called late that night to fill in the blanks on her father's proposal and to get a rundown on Jane's progress so far. Jane lied through her teeth about the progress and then was sorry, because her mother ended up offering to take the Volvo back to Connecticut for Jane the next time she visited, which was going to be in a couple of weeks.

Perfect, Jane thought as she hung up. *If I don't sleep between now and then and I hire a dozen good men, maybe, just maybe, I can bring Lilac Cottage up to her expectations.*

But Jane didn't have a dozen good men. All she had was Billy B., who showed up the next morning as he had promised. It was a rotten day out, raw and rainy and "typical," as he said. They decided he should work on the kitchen first. After giving Jane a gentle lecture on the futility of knocking down a wall to save part of a contractor's fee, Billy B. began trying to put the place together again.

In general, Jane was pleased. Billy B. wasn't gabby and he kept on working while he drank his coffee. So things settled down into a kind of friendly domesticity. Jane worked her room and Billy B. worked his, and when they met in the kitchen for lunch, the conversation flowed easily. Billy B. was crazy about his new little girl Sarah, crazy about his son, crazy about his wife. If Jane really was headed for the poorhouse, she couldn't imagine a nicer person sending her there.

On Friday the weather improved and Billy B., armed with metal flashing and a bundle of asphalt shingles, climbed up onto the roof for some selective patching and repair. As for Jane, she had decided to do just what Phillip Harrow warned her not to do: wallpaper.

She had nothing against white walls; she loved them in

her condo. But for Lilac Cottage, nothing less than rich floral prints would do. It would cost her more, and it would take more time, and if it killed a sale, she had only herself to blame—but as far as Jane was concerned, painting the walls of Lilac Cottage in up-to-date white was like dressing Queen Victoria in a miniskirt.

Jane had managed to find a wonderful bird-of-paradise pattern in the same rich ivory, rose, and green as the antique paper in the fireplace room and was standing back, admiring the first laid strip of her handiwork, when she heard Mac shouting a greeting to Billy B. Jane stayed where she was, uncertain whether Mac had come to see Billy B. or her. When she heard the heavy rap of the brass door knocker, her heart did a completely unexpected and uncalled for cartwheel in her breast.

"I'm on my way over to my uncle's place," Mac said when she opened the door. "Were you serious about wanting to see his pickup?"

No hello; no how's things. Certainly no friendly smile. Disappointed, she said deliberately, "I'm fine. How're *you*?"

"Yeah."

Yeah? What kind of pleasantry was that? *Yeah.* He was impossible, always running hot and cold—well, warm and cool. She thought they'd begun to find common ground in the Quaker Burial Ground—where else, if not there?—but apparently she was wrong. Mac McKenzie had a bias against her, and nothing she could do on earth would change that. Well, nuts to him.

"I was *quite* serious about looking at it, actually," she said in a laughably snooty voice. She never talked that way. Why was she talking that way?

"Well, then, if you're *quite* serious—shall we go?"

He gave her that look, the look that made her want to hit him over the head with a broom. God, he was infuriating! After a word or two with Billy B., she climbed into the truck with Mac and they drove off. For a while, no one spoke.

"Was it something I said?" she finally demanded to know.

"Excuse me?"

"You seem particularly distant lately. In fact, I'd assumed this excursion was off. You never called to make arrangements."

"I didn't know you had a phone," he said reasonably.

"Bing knew. He called 411."

"Bing's a man of the world. I'm just a humble islander."

"Stop it! Stoppit stoppit!" she cried, her patience snapping like a little dry twig. "I'm sick of this bumpkin routine! Where do you get off with such arrogance? Who do you think you are?"

"I'm just a humble—"

"*Stop it!* You can just start acting like the rest of us and brag and make a fool of yourself and just—be normal, dammit! You're a thoughtful, smart, well-read man and what you're doing is the worst form of reverse snobbism, and I for one am just—tired of it! Spare me! Please!"

Jane leaned her head back and closed her eyes. Let him stop the truck if he wanted and boot her into a ditch. She really didn't care anymore.

Mac was broodingly silent. Then, as he turned onto a well-traveled road dotted with surprisingly humble houses, he allowed himself a very small, very private chuckle.

"I do wonder what the hell to do with you," he murmured.

Jane looked up sharply from her purse. Mac was looking straight ahead, so she couldn't read his eyes. Not that it mattered: his look was impenetrable anyway. As a result, her feelings went into a kind of free float: first rising, then falling, then settling on some vague middle ground.

Mac pulled up in front of a plain little ranch house clad —like everything else on Nantucket—in weathered gray shingles. A plastic Season's Greetings wreath still hung in the picture window. Two flat-topped yews, one on each side of the stoop, were the only concessions to landscaping. *Probably Mac doesn't offer a family discount,* Jane thought wryly as she waited with Mac for his uncle to answer the door.

When his uncle finally opened it for them, Jane was surprised to see that he looked nothing like Mac. After seeing Jerry, she'd assumed all the males came from the same cookie cutter. But this man was thin, frail and bald, and as outgoing as Mac was reserved.

"C'min, c'min. Well, Mac, if you're gonna sell my truck out from under me, at least it's to a looker." He winked at Jane, found out her name, and introduced himself before Mac had the chance. "Ebeneezer Zingg. You call me Uncle Easy. Can't think of anyone who don't."

"E-Z?" she repeated.

"He'll say it's because of his initials, but don't believe it," Mac said with an affectionate shake of his head. "We started calling him Uncle Easy when we were kids, because he was so easy to shake down for a dime whenever we came around."

"That was just to make 'em go away," Uncle Easy said with another wink. "Buncha pests."

"Don't believe that, either," Mac said with a grin. "Uncle Easy rigged a big swing set out back for us, and bought us a pool; it was a real status symbol back then."

"You're talkin' about the *old* place," he said with an instant faraway look. "Yeah. But it was only a twelve-foot pool." He ran his hand over his bald head, as if he was wondering, still, where all his hair went.

"Listen, Mac, I gotta problem," he said. "You remember when that nor'easter knocked down O'Riley's tree next door. I never noticed but yesterday that it took out a gutter bracket when it went down. Do me a favor and drive the damn thing back in. On the southeast corner of the house. Then we'll look at the truck."

Mac glanced at Jane, and Uncle Easy said with another of his winks, "Don't you worry about her. She's all set."

Jane smiled politely and Mac went out in search of the ladder. Uncle Easy shuffled with quick, stiff steps into the kitchen and put a pot of water on for instant coffee. "He's a good kid," he said. "Always a handful, though. Defiant. Never would take 'Because I said so' for an answer. Drove his mother crazy that way. I suppose that's how it is when you're the last one through the gate. Don't know; never had kids of my own. That I know of."

His hands shook badly while he spooned Sanka into two stoneware mugs. Jane wondered how old Uncle Easy really was.

"Mac's divorced, you know," he went on without looking up. Jane heard him make a tisking sound as he shook his head, obviously reliving the scandal of it all.

"That marriage never shoulda happened," he added bluntly. "Me, I never took to the gal myself. She didn't want to share him with any of us, was the problem. But Mac, well, he don't forget family. When my furnace went out last month, he kept my wood stove goin' for me night and day 'til the new burner finally come in. I coulda done it myself," he added, "despite what Mac says."

Jane remembered Mac's repeated forays in and out during her first days on the island. *So much for my Colombian cartel theory,* she thought, marveling at her simplemindedness.

"Mac wanted me over his place while my heat was out," Uncle Easy explained, "but it's hard finding your way to a new bathroom in the dark. You know?"

He poured from the full teapot with some effort, then put the teapot back on the burner, still on "high." Jane hesitated whether to say anything as, with an unsteady grip on the mugs, Uncle Easy began making his way to the table.

"Uh . . . the burner?" she finally ventured.

Flustered, Uncle Easy wheeled around, spilling some of the coffee. "Gawdamighty, I *do* that nowadays." He shuffled back to the stove and turned off the burner. When he turned back around to Jane, the cheerful good humor was gone from his ashen face. "We don't have to say nothin' about this, do we? It's mighty embarrassin'."

But he looked more than embarrassed. Jane's heart went out to him. She thought of Aunt Sylvia and her losing battle against entering a nursing home. She thought of her grandmother, and her grandfather. No one got to grow old at home anymore. Their kids were all gone, off in other cities, even other countries. . . .

"Oh, I do that all the time," she said cheerfully as she peeled off a paper towel and mopped up the spilled coffee. "Once I left the oven on for three whole days before I noticed."

He was grateful to her for that. An irresistible smile set off a road map of wrinkles on his face; his blue eyes shone with renewed life. They settled down with the coffee, and Uncle Easy said, "So. Whaddya think of my nephew?"

When she acted blank, he said, "Don't tell me you ain't interested. I know he's got somethin' that appeals deep down to women like you. Lookit Celeste. Who'da guessed they'd marry? Course, it was a disaster—but all the same, I'm curious. What is it about 'im?"

Jane flushed and said, "If you mean, why would he be considered . . . attractive, yes, I suppose that would be the word . . . to some women, I suppose it's because he cares for his family . . . he's hard-working . . . he cares about the environment. . . ."

"Yeah, yeah. Besides that. What *is* it about him?"

He asked the question with a kind of wide-eyed innocence that Jane assumed came only with age. There was certainly nothing indecent in it. In fact, if anyone was feeling indecent about anything just now, it was Jane. About Mac. And it was new. And shocking.

Oh no. Oh nuts. Oh damn. Is that what it was all this time, that feeling of being threatened? Nothing but simple, sexual desire? Impossible. She wasn't stupid. She'd been turned on before. She'd had men before. She knew what simple, sexual desire felt like. What she felt around Mac was *nothing* like that. It was scarier.

"Well, you know how intrigued women get when they're around quiet men," Jane said with a nervous laugh. "They always want to know what the guy's thinking."

"They won't find out from Mac McKenzie. Guaranteed. That boy knows how to keep his own counsel."

Uncle Easy leaned over his coffee cup and tapped the table with the middle finger of his liver-spotted hand. "Lemme give you an example. When Mac was a kid, he got in some trouble over a car. He took the rap for it all by himself—but he wasn't alone. I know that for a fact."

He sat back in his chrome-legged chair. "How do I know? Because he come by before supper on the night he sunk the Porsche. He was all excited, I remember it like it was yesterday. He told me, 'We're gonna test-drive Elway's new car tonight.' Course, he never said nothin' about stealing it first, but that ain't the point. He had an *accomplice* is the point, and whoever it was let Mac take the blame, and Mac never said nothin'."

Uncle Easy folded one arm over the other. "*That's* the kind of boy he is."

"But . . . but his whole life might have turned out differently!" Jane said, dismayed by Mac's outlaw code of honor. "Maybe it was the other kid who actually did the thing . . . maybe Mac just went along for the ride."

"Now you're talkin'," Uncle Easy said, nodding sagely. "And I don't mind tellin' you I got a fair idea who it was. Local snot-nosed kid, his parents no better'n anyone else, but they inherited waterfront, sold some of it, put on airs and sent the little twerp off-island to some fancy-pants school in Andover."

Something began moving in Jane's memory, like ice breaking up in a harbor in spring. She knew who the old man was alluding to, even though she couldn't possibly have known.

"You're talking about Phillip Harrow," she said, shocked.

"He's your neighbor," Uncle Easy said quietly. "You ought to know what kind of man you got for a neighbor."

"*Phillip*. But he had so much to lose!"

"Exactly. He had so much to lose. So he run like a dog. Him and Mac was palling around all during that week. It was Phil's spring break—Phil went to grammar school on the island, so they were still friends of sorts. Who else could it've been?"

"Did you ever tell this to anyone?" Jane asked.

"Nope. Except to Mac. He said to mind my own business, which I done. But now I'm old and I don't care anymore. Besides, I *didn't* tell you," he added slyly. "You figured it out yourself."

"This is awful! Mac's reputation has been ruined, if you're right . . . but if you're not . . . but you must be right. . . ."

"Ruined? Hell, it was only a car. . . ."

They heard the front door and Uncle Easy made a silencing gesture with his hand. "Shush. Water under the bridge," he said in a hiss.

Mac came in and of course realized that the two conspirators had been gossiping about him. He looked from one to the other with a fine sense of irony and said blandly, "I cleaned out the leaves from the gutter while I was up there. Anything else before we go out to look at the truck?"

"Nothin' at all. The place is runnin' like a clock. My

thanks to you, lad. Now: Let's go sell the girl some wheels."

They went out to the garage, tucked partly behind the house on the narrow lot. The truck was a true island vehicle: old and heavily rusted, but with low mileage. There was some talk of whether or not it would pass the next inspection, but that was almost a year away. It had been handpainted in camouflage rust, which the men considered a plus. The price was right, in the hundreds rather than in the thousands. Jane agreed on the spot to buy it. Virtually everyone on the island drove either a pickup truck or a four-wheel drive. Jane was pleased; she felt like one of the crowd.

She wrote out a check and Uncle Easy gave her a laboriously written bill of sale and directions to the Motor Vehicles Registry in town. When she and Mac were settled back in his own pickup, which looked pretty spiffy by comparison, Jane said, "How will your uncle get around without a car?"

"He'll manage. Those of us who're left on the island will chip in on the chores and shopping. I hate to see him lose his wheels, but . . . he's been a little forgetful lately," Mac admitted with a sigh. "We're all taking this one day at a time," he added.

"I like him; he's a straight shooter."

"He talks too much."

"Oh, sure; *you'd* think so."

They exchanged tentative, ironic smiles. Jane drew a long, discreet breath, scrambling for oxygen. This was not on the agenda, this light-headedness she was feeling.

It was Uncle Easy's fault. He'd put a ridiculous bee in her bonnet, and now she'd probably spend the rest of her stay on Nantucket second-guessing her—and Mac's—every look, every smile, every pregnant pause. Heck, she liked it better the old way, when all she wanted was for Mac not to despise her.

"Have you heard from Jerry?" she ventured to ask, driving all such speculations from her mind.

"Yeah, he's fine. The bandage is off and the stitches are on their way out. I think he's a little disappointed. *Sic transit gloria mundi.*"

"He'll have other shots at glory," she said, surprised once more by this thoroughly mystifying neighbor of hers. What did he do? Study Latin in reform school?

"That was the damnedest accident," she added thoughtfully. "I still can't believe it was . . ."

"Was what?"

She heard the warning in his voice: whatever it was she was going to say, he did not want to hear it. But Jane plowed on anyway.

"An accident," she said.

"He tripped," Mac said evenly. "That's called an accident."

"But *why* did he trip?"

"Because he wasn't looking where he was going." Irritation was beginning to seep into Mac's voice.

"That's true; but what made him so inattentive?"

"For God's sake, the thought of a Snickers bar, what else?" He turned his head sharply to study her. "What're you getting at?"

Jane took a deep breath and plunged. "Okay, well, here's the thing: A lot of weird, unexplainable . . . happenings . . . have been . . . happening. You already know about my shoulder—"

"Which you said yourself is fine—"

"But I haven't told you about all the other things."

She related in spare detail the events of the fallen bookcase, the missing spoon, the open bulkhead doors, and the muddy laundry. She expected Mac to laugh, but he didn't, and it frightened her. All in all, she would've preferred hilarity.

"Have you changed the locks on your doors? Put locks on all your windows?" he asked her sharply.

"Well, no. Bing said Nantucket was safe as gold bullion," she said, with a sinking, sickening feeling.

"Do you believe everything Bing tells you? For Chrissake, you've got a handyman right there! He can install the locks. What're you waiting for?"

"I don't know; for . . . nothing, I suppose," she said stupidly. "But what good are locks?" she blurted. "Locks are for people, not for . . ."

"Not for *what*?"

"Spirits?" she whispered. "I know; I know how you feel about this, but I'm not kidding. When I got back from your house on the day of the accident, Buster refused to go into the bedroom. He hunkered down into some kind of groaning howl; it was . . . hideous," she said, closing her eyes at the remembrance.

"And you think—"

"I think there's some kind of curse on Lilac Cottage. That's what I think. I don't know how it all sorts out," she said quickly before he could interrupt, "but too many things have happened for them to be coincidence. And that includes Jerry's fall over the shovel," she said defiantly. "This all ties in to Judith Brightman. I *know* it."

They'd driven back through town and were heading out on North Water Street toward Lilac Cottage. Mac slammed on the brakes so forcefully that Jane's seat belt locked. He swung hard onto a short, muddy lane that connected to South Beach Street and began heading back to the center of town.

"What *is* it with you and this curse?" he said angrily as they went bumping over the cobblestones. "Every time I see you, you're prowling some graveyard . . . and now you're looking for ghosts behind every missing teaspoon. You're like my Aunt Lucille, for Chrissake! What's next? Cutting open a chicken and reading the entrails?"

Mac made a right turn so sharp that Jane ended up with
a rib full of door handle; he was hopping mad. "Don't you
get it? Someone must be stalking you—someone you've
brought with you from off-island, I suppose. . . ."

He shot her a glance of pure fury. "No," he said through
a clenched jaw, "you *don't* get it, do you? You came to
Nantucket fully prepared to find ghosts, and by God, it's
ghosts you're finding. Well, congratulations. When Nantucket starts up a haunted-house tour I'll put your name in
for hostess. Jesus! What *did* they teach you in finishing
school?"

Jane stared at him, agape, as he pulled up in front of the
brick Town Building on Broad Street, leaned over in front
of her, and threw open the door for her to leave. One part
of her was saying, yes, it's definitely Old Spice, and another
was quaking before the full brunt of his fury. She had expected cynicism and feared his sarcasm, but nothing she
knew about the man had prepared her for *this*.

"Why are you throwing me out *here*?" she said, her own
anger starting to displace her astonishment.

"You want to know about Judith Brightman? You start
with the death record. Have fun!"

He slammed the door on her and roared off. Jane was
left to dust herself off, so to speak, and continue on her
way. Muttering under her breath, she walked into the Town
Clerk's Office and asked for the death record of Judith
Brightman, died 1852. In two and a half seconds she was
handed a large, black, leather-bound book that said,
"Deaths, 1850–1889, Town of Nantucket." Among the hundred and sixty-five deaths recorded in the year 1852 she
found a simple, handwritten summary of Judith Brightman's life.

Her "condition" at the time of her death was: widow.
Her place of birth: unknown. Her age: just as the gravestone said. The name of her parents: unknown as well,
dammit. The place of internment: Nantucket, big help.

And the informant: an undertaker by the name of William
Calder. Judith died not of dropsy or croup or pot ash
(whatever that was) or bilious fever, nor did she die by
burning or drowning or in childbirth as some others had.
No, Judith Brightman died of fits.

Fits. What in heaven's name were fits? Was she an epi-
leptic? Was she insane, or hysterical? Or was she—*could
she have been*—possessed in some way? If Judith had died,
say, of consumption or influenza, then that would be that.
A not abnormal end to a not abnormal life span. But *fits.*
"Fits" had more than a touch of the supernatural about it.

There was one other intriguing bit of information in the
record: Judith Brightman's occupation was listed as "merchant." Jane had read that the nineteenth-century Nantucket woman was unusually career-oriented, and that
merchandising was one of the socially acceptable ways for
her to earn money while her husband was off whaling.
Nonetheless, among the mariners, fishermen, coopers,
sailmakers, laborers, farmers, and lawyers who'd died in
1852, Judith Brightman, female businessman, stood almost
alone. She had to have been a woman of great determination.

Jane's next stop was at the Atheneum, Nantucket's library. The Greek Revival structure, with its lofty columned
facade, soared above her as she read with disappointment
that winter hours were in effect. She'd have to come back
later. So she trekked on home, fired with curiosity over this
Judith Brightman, this merchant woman who died of fits.
Suddenly Judith had become so . . . legitimate. Up until
a few minutes ago she'd been officially no more than half a
gravestone. But now Jane knew she was real. She lived, she
died. And she had some unfinished business on Nantucket.

It was up to Jane to finish it for her.

As she was walking up to Lilac Cottage, Jane saw Billy
B. charging out of the driveway.

"Where you off to?" she asked when he stopped the truck.

"Hardy's. For some window locks and a barrel bolt," he said, pleased that Jane saw he was on top of things.

"Says who?"

"Says Mac. He stopped by a little while ago. I have to say, his mood was blacker'n hell."

Her fists came up and since Mac wasn't around, they landed on her hips. "What did he say?"

"Um . . . let me think. 'If I can get so much as a flea's butt through this door tonight, I'll cut you in two and feed you to the wolves.' He didn't really mean it. We don't have any wolves on Nantucket."

"Turn around, Billy. Locks are *not* on today's worklist," she said, turning on her heel for the cottage.

Incredible. She'd opened herself completely to Mac, risked being treated like a fool, and he was treating her like . . . a fool! As if she were some child, afraid of the bogeyman!

She stomped inside, looked up Mac's telephone number, began punching it in, stopped, slammed the receiver down, picked it up, got halfway through the number again, slammed the receiver down again.

No. He wasn't worth it. He was too earthbound to see the possibility of another dimension, too cynical to believe in it if someone else pointed it out to him. She'd tried and she'd failed and the hell with him. *Haunted house tour hostess.* That jerk!

She was pacing through the house, trying to regroup, when she came upon the single strip of wallpaper she'd hung in the front parlor. It was a sudden and charming surprise to her, like stumbling on the little clump of blue scilla along the road, and it had an instant effect on her overheated temper. She made herself a soothing cup of tea, avoided Billy B.—who was avoiding *her* like crazy— and spent the rest of the afternoon hanging wallpaper. It was wonderful, watching the room come vibrantly alive strip by strip.

When she heard the brass door knocker later in the evening, she was reluctant to answer it; she wanted nothing to break her mood of enchantment. But it couldn't be Mac—the door wasn't rattling from the force of his banging—so she risked opening it.

Bing. She hadn't expected him until the next day, Saturday, and to see him standing there with that irresistible grin on his face was like being handed four dozen yellow roses wrapped in a tissue of sunshine.

"Bing! I thought you were—"

He caught her in his arms. "Nothing could have kept me away—nothing!—for another day. I've been counting hours, minutes, seconds," he said elatedly, lifting her from her feet and swinging her round. "Your getting a phone was a disaster for me. I was okay until I heard your voice, but after that . . ."

She laughed giddily as he lifted her above his head. "After that?"

"After that," he said softly as he lowered her slowly to the ground, "after that I began to wonder how I'd make it through the week without you."

He lowered his mouth to hers in a kiss of silvery sweetness that traveled like a kind of lazy lightning along her nerve endings. When he released her she said breathlessly, "Can you stay awhile?"

"I was afraid I'd have to beg," he murmured, nuzzling the curve of her neck.

He released her and she noticed, for the first time, a business envelope that had been slipped through the mail slot and lay on the floor underneath it. She picked it up; the logo said J & J NURSERY AND LANDSCAPING, NANTUCKET. From Mac—no doubt an apology. She opened the flap and read the contents.

It was a bill:

> Lift holly.
> Plant holly.
> Time and equipment: $300.

CHAPTER 14

"What is it?" Bing asked. "You look surprised."

"It's a bill. From Mac."

"For what?"

"Moving the holly tree."

"Moving it where?"

"Where it *was*, obviously." Immediately Jane was sorry. She was letting Mac destroy a perfectly romantic moment without even having to be there to do it. "I'm sorry, Bing. This is . . . nothing," she said, tossing the bill on the nearest table. "Just Mac being Mac. Let's have a drink, shall we?"

Bing made rum and tonics while Jane peeled back the bedsheet she'd been using to protect the Empire sofa from work dust. She turned down the lamps to throw a soft golden glow over the worn reds of the tattered Bokhara, and tucked a couple of kilim pillows in the corners of the sofa. She loved the room, loved its romantic, exotic, ambience. What a pity that her aunt had spent the greater part of her life in it alone.

Bing came back with their drinks and they settled in on the sofa together. Buster, who was visiting, settled on the floor alongside, happy for the company. Jane took off her shoes and tucked her stockinged feet under her legs, Indian style, aware that trying to appear sexy and seductive in jeans and a sweatshirt was pretty much a waste of time. The wonderful thing about Bing was that he seemed to be dazzled by her no matter what she was wearing.

He was looking pretty dazzling himself tonight. There

was something about him that made her think along the lines of Greek gods. His hair was as bright as spun brass, his eyes the color of the Caribbean Sea. His teeth—so white, so straight—were as perfect as his profile. Yes: Apollo, the Sun God. Patron of the arts. Lover of nymphs, goddesses, and daughters of kings.

And—as she recalled—husband to not a darn one of 'em.

"You have a very dreamy expression on your face," Bing said softly. "I wonder what you're thinking."

"Oh . . . I don't think you want to know," she said with a wry smile, fluttering her lashes. There was a silence, very pregnant, before she raised her head and said, "And New York? How goes the battle of the new wing?"

It was a deliberate change of subject, and Bing knew it. With a smile and a shrug he obliged Jane with an amusing account of the trials and perils of building in Manhattan.

When he finished there was a thoughtful pause, and then he said, "Did you know that Cissy's been spending the last couple of days buying out Fifth Avenue?"

"Yes, she told me she was going shopping in the city. I must say, this sudden desire for a makeover surprises me; she's turned into a clotheshorse overnight. What's going on?"

"That's what I'd like to know," Bing said with a thoughtful shake of his head. "Obviously she's going all out to please her Mr. X. But she's so damn secretive about the guy. I've never seen her like this, so devotedly in love. It's like he has some Svengali hold on her. She was nothing like this when she married Dave—although it's true she was even more of a child then."

Bing got up and began pacing the room, clearly uneasy. "And that's the other problem—Dave. My Nantucket number's unlisted, so Cissy's been safe from his calls here. But he was able to reach her this week at my co-op. It was pure rotten luck that she picked up the phone.

"He's called me in the city before, drunk and wheedling, trying to get me to intervene on his behalf. I've managed to keep things cool, but I guess when Cissy answered the phone he lost it. She told me he got pretty ugly. He always was a mean drunk."

"Can you put the police on notice?" Jane asked, concerned for Cissy. She'd read too many stories of estranged husbands to be comfortable with what Bing was telling her.

"What can I tell them? That they had an acrimonious conversation on the phone? What divorcing couple hasn't? It's not grounds for a restraining order. No, she'll be safe enough on the island, if I can just coax her out of Bergdorf Goodman and onto a plane. She's supposed to be here tomorrow evening, as soon as she's finished with her fittings at Saks."

"You'll breathe more easily then," Jane agreed.

"You think I'm an alarmist," he said. Jane denied it.

"Dave's never hurt Cissy physically," Bing admitted. "Never even threatened her. But when she finally mustered the resolve to walk out on him and his escapades . . . well, Dave's too macho to take something like that without lashing out. Can you blame me for worrying?"

He had his hands in his pockets and was staring without seeing at the slant-top desk and its leaded-glass bookcase. "I wish to God our parents were here!" he burst out bitterly. "She's too much responsibility for me. *Damn* it to hell!"

Surprised by his vehemence, Jane said thoughtfully, "I had a college chum who was a lot like you. She wanted everything to be perfect, from her boyfriend to her master's thesis."

Bing turned and cocked one eyebrow at Jane. "Come again?"

"Well, for instance: She could never walk into a stereo shop and say, 'That sounds good. I can afford it. I'll take it.' Oh, no; she knew too well what the best equipment was. But it cost too much. So she sat in silence.

"My friend wanted a garden filled with exotic delphiniums and tender calla lilies; no easy-care daisies for *her*. But she didn't have the time; she couldn't take the trouble. So she ended up with weeds."

Jane smiled ruefully to herself. "Needless to say, she never finished her thesis; she was always researching one more aspect of it. For all I know, she's still in the RISD library."

"So what're you saying? That I don't have a green thumb? That I'm poor material for graduate school?"

He was being deliberately dense; Jane ignored it. "I'm saying that you cannot create a perfect life for your sister, no matter how hard you try. I'm saying your sister herself will not be perfect, no matter how much you want her to be. That doesn't mean you should resent the commitment —or walk away from the responsibility."

"Am I really such a coward?" he asked with disarming candor.

"You're an emotional idealist," Jane said carefully. She unwrapped herself from the lotus position she was in and went over to Bing. "And you're beating yourself up for no reason. I won't say Cissy's a big girl now—in many ways, she's not—but I don't think you can put her in a pumpkin, either. She won't let you. So far Dave is nothing more than a nuisance. As for her Mr. X, if she wants to date someone who likes fine clothing . . ."

It was as if two light bulbs went on at the same time. *"Phillip?"* they both ventured at once.

It was such a startling thought that they both burst out laughing. Phillip and Cissy? Phillip—who could name every wine district, parish, and chateau in Burgundy—with Cissy, who thought Burgundy was a shade of nail polish? And yet, Jane could see the match. Phillip was older, commanding, knowledgeable—everything that Cissy wasn't. As for Cissy, she brought youth, beauty, and an eagerness to please. That was enough for many a middle-aged man.

"I guess it proves that opposites attract," Jane mused. "Were we the last ones to figure it out?"

" 'Mistress of Edgehill,' " Bing murmured with a wry smile as he led Jane back to the sofa. "It does have a certain ring to it."

"At least we know that Phillip's the marrying kind," Jane quipped, and immediately she blushed.

Bing never even noticed. It was so obvious he was relieved about his sister. For once, Cissy was involved with someone responsible. That left Bing off the hook for other distractions, and Jane clearly was one of them.

Smiling, he slipped his hands under her heavy auburn hair, drew her toward him, and kissed her. It was a bantering caress, filled with sweetness and light. Jane loved that about him, that his kisses were like nectar; she could hover there forever, sipping and tasting.

A low sound of poignant yearning escaped her throat. Bing's response was instantaneous: his kisses became harder, deeper, an elemental reply to an elemental sound. He murmured her name, and other endearments, as he kissed her. His hands circled the back of her head, holding her lips close to his, making her need him.

It was hard not to. She'd gone so long, had been so disappointed, in other sexual encounters. Bing would be an exciting lover, attentive and considerate—Apollo himself. She was certain of it. They had everything in common, everything. . . .

"Jane?"

"Hmmm?" She half opened her eyes, still dazed, when he held her a little away from him. "Yes?"

His brows were drawn together in a disappointed frown. "It's not really 'yes,' is it?" he said in a husky voice.

"I . . . why do you say that?"

"Because you're hesitating; I can feel it in you. Jane, I

won't push you into this," he whispered, caressing her cheek with his fingertips. "You mean too much. . . ."

"But that's why I'm . . . hesitating," she admitted, putting her arms around his neck. "Because *you* mean too much."

"Oh, great," he said in a groan. "What a team."

She smiled wanly. "I don't want to rush into this, Bing. Men have come and then they've gone, throughout my life." She looked away, her forehead creased by pain. "I'm not sure I want you to be one of them."

"I know. I know," he said softly, drawing her head to his shoulder, stroking her hair. "I'm not sure I want to be one of them, either." He laughed softly in her hair. "God. I never thought I'd say that to any woman."

He cradled her chin in his hand and lowered his face to hers in a kiss. Then he stood up. "Yep. Gotta go," he said, tight-lipped.

She looked up at him, surprised, but then she understood. She'd been pushing his self-control to the limit. "I'm sorry, Bing," she whispered. "I never meant to play games over this."

He stood over her, sad, pensive, resigned. "I know, darling. Good night."

He let himself out and Jane was left alone, wondering whether she should seek psychiatric help.

What is wrong *with me? The man rates a ten on any desirability scale. He's even hinting that maybe, just maybe, he's finally ready for a meaningful relationship. He's rich, well educated, charming, handsome, interested. So, I send him packing. Why did I do that? Mother would have a conniption if she knew.*

Ah.

Could that be it? She was being perverse to spite her mother? It wouldn't be the first time. She remembered, almost with affection, the times her mother had tried to pair her with someone "suitable"—from James in dancing school (no spark) to Paul at the country club (something missing). Jane used to say that her mother was pushy; Gwendolyn used to say that her daughter was picky. The standoff had lasted most of her life, and now Jane was still single and thinking maybe her mother was right.

With a sigh, Jane picked up the two half-empty glasses and walked across the room to turn off the wrought-iron floor lamp with its muslin shade. She peered through the darkness in the direction of Bing's house. The side that faced her was unlit. She was about to turn away when she caught a movement near some towering shrubs across the drive, just to the north. Someone was standing in the shadows.

She sucked in her breath. Bing had no reason to be lurking there; it wasn't on the way to his house. *No one* had a reason to be lurking there. She pulled back from the open window and flattened herself against the wall with a silent shudder. It was both terrifying and infuriating not to know what to expect, not to know who the enemy was.

This is stupid—stupid, she told herself over the pounding of her heart. She felt a wave of regret for having refused to let Billy B. put locks on the windows. Mac had been right about that, just as he'd been right about there being a stalker. But whoever this was couldn't be from the mainland. She had no enemies on the mainland. This terror was island-based. But she had no enemies on the island, either. Maybe it had nothing to do with her at all, but with Lilac Cottage. . . .

Expecting anything from gunfire to baseballs, she peeked through the window again. Nothing. She dropped to all fours and came up alongside the next window. Yes: definitely someone was still there. It seemed to her that his arms were folded across his chest; that he'd been there for a while. She resented it thoroughly and somehow that gave her a crazy kind of courage. She stepped boldly in front of the window, then reached over to the nearby lamp and switched it on, throwing herself into full illumination.

Here I am, she thought. *Who the hell are* you?

The light from the lamp affected her night vision, but she was able to make out that the figure had stepped almost casually away from the shrubs and was sauntering down the lane toward Mac's place.

Mac. It had to be. She raced for the phone and dialed his number. It rang a dozen times without an answer. Hardly conclusive proof, but it was good enough for her. What was he up to? Trying to scare her into installing window locks? Or had he happened to pause during a stroll for a little late-night voyeurism? She shivered, then closed up the inside shutters and left a light on in that room and every other room in the house. In a few minutes she tried Mac's number again. This time he answered the phone.

She placed the receiver carefully in its cradle.

The dream came again, more frightening than before. She was back on the edge of the precipice, but this time there was no driving rain—only fog, thick and damp and cold, wrapping itself around her long gray skirts. She could scarcely see five feet in front of her. If it was to be today, he would surely perish. She never should have let him go. The money wasn't worth it.

She gripped the splintery wood railing with both hands and leaned into the fog, furious that she did not have it in her power to dispel its thickness once and for all. The sharp sea air, once so pleasing to her, smelled rank and insidious. Somewhere above her was a nearly full moon, but it was of no more use tonight than a lighthouse without a lamp.

She hated this place, this desolate island. She hated everyone on it. How could they be so fatalistic, so accepting? They had wealth enough to live anywhere they chose, and yet they chose this rock. Worse, their women gave up their lovers and husbands with hardly a murmur, because that's the way their mothers did it, and *their* mothers, and their mothers before that.

But she was not from Nantucket. She would *not* give up her man, not without a fight. She loved him more than life itself.

"Damn thy traditions!" she cried. "Damn thy hidebound ways!"

She pushed furiously at the wooden rail, spurning everything it stood for. Suddenly the rail gave way and plunged over the precipice while in the same split second she herself went lurching forward.

"No!" Jane screamed, waking herself from the dream.

She lay in bed supporting herself on one elbow, half in and half out of sleep, breathing heavily, her heart thundering. "No," she murmured in her muddled state. *No.* She did not want to die. More than that, she did not want *him* to die.

Whoever he was.

The dream stayed with her all through the next morning. To call it a dream seemed completely inadequate. It was closer to a possession. This one was not like the first dream, where Jane kept part of herself sitting in the front row, watching the drama. This time the woman's agony was completely her own, and so was the near-plunge over the precipice. If Jane hadn't awakened herself from the dream, she was certain that she'd be dead now.

It was an intensely disturbing experience and it left her shaken—shaken, and deeply intrigued. After all, she herself was nothing like the woman in gray. Jane *loved* Nantucket; clearly the woman in gray hated it. On the other hand, the woman in gray loved someone with a depth and fury that left Jane with an aching hole where her heart should be.

Was the woman in her dream the one in Aunt Sylvia's

sketch? Jane wandered over to the drawing of the young woman in the coal-skuttle bonnet and stared at it while she plaited her auburn hair into a single braid. Jane had had the usual number of weird dreams in her life, but she'd never used the word "thy" in any of them. Obviously the woman in her dream was a Quaker. Was she *this* Quaker?

And was *this* Quaker Judith Brightman?

Jane wanted so badly to believe it was. It made a certain amount of sense. Maybe Aunt Sylvia had scratched herself on the rugosa rose and suffered the same troubling symptoms as Jane; maybe the sketch was as close as her aunt had ever got to identifying Judith Brightman. If only her aunt had said something about it during those last two years in the nursing home.

Maybe she had. She did tend to ramble, and sometimes she didn't make sense. Jane hadn't wanted to accept that her aunt's mind was failing, and so she used to interrupt, or change the subject. . . .

The metallic thunk of the brass door knocker sent her to the front door. It was Billy B., with a grin on his face and a box in his arms.

"Window locks," he explained when she gave him a puzzled look. "Mac says you changed your mind."

"*Did* he. Well, you tell Mac—"

Tell him what? That she preferred cowering under windows and running up her electric bill?

"You tell Mac 'thank you' when you see him," she said with a tight smile.

"That I will. I'll install 'em right after I finish flashing the chimney. That's first; we don't get May mornings in April very often."

Billy was right; it was a fabulous morning. Mild, seductive air wafted into the room from outside, promising bliss. Jane decided on the spot to rake up the grounds and perk up the cottage's "curb appeal," as the realtors so quaintly put it. By the time she changed into her heavy shoes, Billy

was up on the roof, pounding away. Jane rummaged
through the potting shed and came out with a couple of
rakes and some trash bags. Her heart felt light and eager;
right now, right here, she was utterly happy.

She began by raking the border in front of the house.
The wet leaves were old, rotted, well on their way to being
compost. She stuffed them into the bag. Panicking earth-
worms scrambled in every direction. Flowers—surely those
green straps were flowers and not weeds popping through
the earth—flowers were bursting out all over. She raked
away more leaves, gently now, and found hundreds of little
white pendant bells. And tiny violet crocuses; she recognized those. And blue scilla! She had her own! Jane fell to
her knees for a closer look, awed by the very old, very
predictable, very astonishing rite of spring.

"Thank you, Aunt Sylvia," she whispered with her head
bowed. "I wish you were here to teach me."

"Hey! Jane! Up here!"

Billy was hailing her from the rooftop. Jane backed away
from the house to see him better.

"Ever see the view from up here?" he shouted down to
her. "Come on up."

She eyed the two-story-high roof with its steep pitch. "I
don't think so. I'm not big on heights. Besides, your wood
ladder looks like it's seen better years."

"Don't be silly; you're lighter than I am. Keep to the side
of the rungs if you're worried about it. Once you get up
here, it's easy. Someone's nailed in toeholds, probably for
the chimney sweep." He added the clincher: "You'll never
know what a great view you have, otherwise."

"I don't know if my insurance policy has a clause for
Stupid Homeowner Tricks," she called up with a nervous
laugh.

But she ended up giving it a try. The house was a small
house, after all, on a low foundation. Climbing the ladder
was easy. Getting onto the roof and inching up the wood

slats toward the chimney was not. Just because Billy had suction cups for feet didn't mean everyone else was blessed that way. But the prospect of being at the peak was strangely compelling; and besides, she didn't dare turn around to enjoy the view until she had something solid, like bricks, to hold on to.

Billy's steady grip was there for her as she inched her way into an upright position alongside the chimney. Jane had absolutely no desire to look out at the ocean or anywhere else. *How the hell do I get back down?* was the only thing on her mind.

"Well? What do you think?"

Jane forced herself to lift her gaze from the bowels of the chimney. *"Oh."*

The view was spectacular. From their spot on the hill, the island tumbled gradually to a long white strip of beach that in turn was washed by the no-nonsense blue of New England water, as far as the eye could see. She could see the harbor entrance, and the long, low jetty, and Brant Point Light, and fishing trawlers on the distant horizon. The whole scene was washed in brilliant, shimmering sunlight. It took her breath away.

Billy was babbling happily on, pointing out the local landmarks, trying hard to nail down more work. "So I'm thinking, how about a deck? It don't have to be a big deal. A few steps in the attic and you're—"

"A deck . . . you mean, a widow's walk?" She remembered reading that the wives of whalers used such banistered platforms as lookout posts, to watch for their husbands' ships to make landfall. Something lurched in Jane's breast, a sickening sense of unease. . . .

Billy chuckled and said, "Well, technically they're *roof* walks, not widows' walks. Like they say, the women wouldn't be up there if they were widows."

The dream came roaring back, like a river that's burst its dam, overwhelming Jane. The woman in gray, the Quaker:

she was a whaler's wife, watching for her husband's ship from the roof walk of his captain's house. The ship was overdue. A small mail packet from the Vineyard had sailed in with the news that the *Chelsea* had been sighted at sea over forty-eight hours earlier. Oh, God. After three years at sea, the *Chelsea* was overdue.

Everyone knows that Nantucket is the Siren of the Atlantic . . . that she wrecks her own ships, and drowns her own men. Humane Houses! What good are they in December? If the Chelsea *strikes a bar . . . and Ben has to swim ashore . . . he will perish, he will surely perish . . . in this, the most joyous of seasons . . . and my life shall have no meaning. Oh, God, Thou art a cruel Thing, and Nantucket is Thy handmaid in evil.*

"Whoa there, kiddo!" Billy's voice was alarmed as he grabbed Jane by her arm to steady her. "You got a touch of vertigo, it looks like. Just stand still a moment. Focus on something that's off in the distance. It'll pass."

Jane held on to the chimney for dear life, trembling from the shock of her experience. The woman in gray . . . the Quaker . . . Judith . . . whoever it was, was here— *here,* in full possession of Jane, as she stood on this roof-walk-to-be. Testing the view had triggered the dream, and triggering the dream had somehow called the Quaker woman forth.

Oh God, this is new misery, Jane thought. *What will I do? What will I do?*

"You okay now?"

"I'm . . . not sure."

How could I know all those things? That a ship was named Chelsea; *that it was overdue?*

"Billy," she said in a faint and tremulous voice. "What's a 'Humane House'?"

"Geez, I dunno," he said, startled by the question. "An animal shelter, maybe?"

"No . . . no, that can't be it," Jane said distractedly. "Billy—I can't do it. I can't climb down. I can't."

"Sure you can," he said nervously. "You got to. I can't throw you over my shoulder like a bundle of roof shingles. You ain't *that* light," he said, trying to make a joke of it all. "Just take it one step at a time."

But like a swimmer frozen on the high dive, Jane just stood there, clutching the chimney. Was it mere coincidence that she was up here, on a roof, the morning after the dream? She'd never been on a roof in her life.

In her dream she'd been standing on the edge of a *roof walk*, not the edge of a precipice. How had she not known? When the banister gave way in her dream, she'd saved herself by waking herself up. But there was no banister now, and Jane could hardly be more fully awake. What if the dream was a premonition? Worse, what if she herself was some sort of instrument—if some hideous fate had to be played out every so often, and she just happened to be the one caught in the wrong place at the wrong time?

She'd been looking out at the sea, at the straight blue horizon, struggling to calm her turmoil. Apparently Billy had been making small talk. She hadn't heard a word of it. The impulse to hysteria had passed, but the immobility remained.

"Pray for a high tide, Billy," she said with an edgy laugh. "Maybe I can swim off."

"Y'see, your problem is you're *thinking* too much about it. You have to think about something else—"

"Ahoy up there! Is that a private party, or can anyone join in?"

It was Mac, standing on the front lawn, hands on his hips. Even from the rooftop she could see that he was amused. More than amused; he actually looked impressed. How could he know that she was clinging to the chimney like a barn swallow?

"Good morning," she called down in a falsely casual

voice. "I was just coming down. You don't have to come up."

Even if you can *leap over tall buildings,* she thought.

She took a deep breath and began assessing the best way down. Maybe she'd fall on her head and maybe she wouldn't. One thing she knew: If she didn't go down now, she'd have to be airlifted by helicopter. The damnable sea breeze had started to pick up and the air felt thirty degrees colder. Her hands were already white-knuckled; she didn't need frostbite to boot.

She waved away Billy's offer to assist. Very, very gingerly she lowered herself into a totally undignified squatting position and began picking her way backward down the roof. Each little toehold comprised a new and separate battle in her war of nerves. All she could think of—besides the fact that Mac was judging her both on style and technical merit —was that she was there to reenact some horrible, ghostly event.

She paused at the gutter to plan her next move and was dismayed to see that Mac was at the foot of the ladder, steadying it. No doubt it was the neighborly thing to do, but it had the effect of rattling what was left of Jane's nerves. She completely forgot Billy's advice to step on the outside of the rungs, and came down the centers instead.

The ladder held her fine—until she slipped on a rung about two-thirds of the way down, then lost her footing and came down hard on the next rung, which broke, sending her flying backward through midair and knocking Mac to the ground underneath her.

She ended up in a sitting position across his midsection. "Thank you," she said with as much dignity as she could muster.

"My pleasure," he drawled, propping himself on his forearms. "Any broken bones?"

"I'm afraid not. Sorry."

They were very, very close. Close enough so that she

could see brown flecks in the rich hazel of his eyes. Close enough so that she could see that his lashes were thick and brown, and that he had three small freckles on the side of his temple. Close enough so that she could feel him stir beneath her, could feel the heat.

She scrambled to her feet, scalded by his nearness once again. Maybe she was overreacting, but if so, it was his fault. He could have had the decency to be embarrassed.

"Yo, Jane!" It was Billy on the roof, looking relieved. "I guess you were right about the ladder!"

Only now, as she stared up the formidable height of the ladder, did it occur to Jane that she might've broken her neck. She might've been the perfect ritual victim, if it hadn't been for Mac. Apparently she owed him; she found the notion ironic.

"I saw you in the lane outside my house last night," she said coldly as Mac rose to his feet and brushed off his khakis. "What were you doing there?"

"Wa-a-ll, I was in the area—"

"I *know* you were in the area. What I'd like to know is why." She folded her arms across her chest like a nineteenth-century schoolmistress. Prim. That's what she felt. Prim.

Her body language seemed to strike a nerve with him. The cautiously friendly expression on his face turned dark. "God, you want to know why. I would've thought it was obvious. Someone has an interest in you that's not what I'd call healthy—"

"Because they threw my laundry in the mud? Believe me, mister, that's the least of my problems right now."

She considered telling him about the paranormal experience that she'd had on the roof. But how could she possibly describe it to him? That was the problem with the paranormal—it wasn't normal.

She settled for saying, "I appreciate your keeping an eye out for me, but I think the window locks and barrel bolts will do just fine. Billy's putting in a yard light, too. All I'll have left to do is sign up for the handgun course," she added sarcastically.

She jammed her hands in her pockets and said in a sulky voice, "But I would like to add that all of this is just whistling in the wind. It won't solve *anything*." She looked away from him and up at Billy, driving nails with an expert hand.

"I take it you're still on your Judith kick," Mac said perceptively. "Did you find anything useful in the death record?"

"Only the bare bones of her life," Jane admitted. "She was a merchant and she died of fits."

Mac raised his eyebrows in an ironic grimace. "Not much, but you can build on it, I'm sure."

"You bet I can," Jane said, her chin coming up defiantly. "I can tell you that Judith Brightman was married to a whaler named Ben; that she was friendly with, or even related to, the wife of the captain of a ship named the *Chelsea*; that the ship ran up on a bar somewhere near the island; and—I'm not positive about this part—that Ben may have drowned trying to make it ashore."

When Mac gave her a puzzled look, she said, "I have not made this story up, nor have I read an account of it anywhere."

When he still didn't say anything, she said, "I can add, with complete confidence, my belief that Judith Brightman is far and away the fiercest, most singleminded and devoted woman ever to have lived on this island."

That got him. "What do you mean, 'is'?" he said under his breath. His attention was divided between Jane and Billy, who was coming down from the roof. "What the *hell* are you saying, Jane?"

"I'm saying I've made contact with her," Jane answered, with far more triumph than she felt.

Mac simply stared at her.

"At least, I'm assuming it was Judith Brightman," she said less confidently. "I'll be able to verify it Monday when I go back to the town clerk's office."

Like a sailboat that's been knocked down by a gust of wind, Mac struggled to right himself. "Your ghost keeps office hours at the Town Clerk's Office?"

"Very funny. I just need to be sure of my facts."

"Facts! You call those facts? I've seen more facts in the graffiti on a subway car!" His eyes were blazing, his voice a strained growl. "You naive little twit! There's nothing funny about this. You've got to stop—"

Suddenly he pointed to her pile of leaves. "If you're going to put them on the curb for pickup, don't," he said in a complete change of tone. "I'll throw them on my compost pile."

"What? Oh. Sure," Jane said, turning around. Billy was walking past, an amiable smile on his good-natured face. She wondered how much he'd heard.

Billy tossed a scrap of leftover flashing into the back of his pickup. "Did you ask Mac what a Humane House was?" he said to Jane. "Maybe he'd know."

"Humane Houses? That's what they called the lifesaving stations that used to be located around the island." Mac turned to Jane and said, "Why do you want to know?"

Jane sighed and shook her head. "Ben Brightman was trying to reach a Humane House after the *Chelsea* went up on the bar," she said quietly. "He was coming home from a three-year voyage; he didn't want to die within sight of Nantucket's shore."

"You read about this somewhere," Mac said, almost angrily. "In a tourist brochure. In a history of the island."

Jane answered him with a sad and forlorn smile, as the pieces to the mystery continued falling quietly into place for her.

She wrapped her arms around herself. It was very chilly. Low gray clouds had crept in from the southwest, and an energetic sea breeze was whipping loose strands of auburn hair across her cheek. She had no desire for this argument. Mac didn't believe a word of her story, and of course he never would. How could he? He'd put all of his faith in rich, brown earth, and deep roots, and green leafy things. There was no room in that doctrine for something as evanescent as a ghost.

Mac was looking off in the distance, to where a view of the sea would be if it weren't blocked by scrub trees and brush across the road. His jaw was set in the way she was learning so well. It depressed her, more than she was willing to admit; he was so unyielding. He zipped his canvas jacket and flipped up its collar, then turned to her, his back to the chilling wind.

"Don't pursue this, Jane," he said in deadly earnest. "Don't. You're stepping where angels will not tread."

Again she shrugged. "I have no choice, Mac. Can't you see that? Anyway, I'll try to go on tiptoe." She said it with a lightness she did not feel.

It was another one of their standoffs. Afterward Jane thought that they might have grown old and died on the spot where they stood if it hadn't been for Billy.

"Hey, Mac," he said, driving a playful fist into his mentor's solid biceps. "Carol tells me you're throwin' a shindig for Uncle Easy. Eighty, that's a big one. We'll be there for sure."

"Great," said Mac without much enthusiasm. "And bring the kids. It's a family affair."

At the mention of the words "family affair," Jane did the polite thing and began to take her leave.

"Just a minute," Mac commanded, stopping her in her tracks. "Uncle Easy specifically asked for you. A week from next Saturday. If you can't come, of course we'll understand," he added with typical irony.

It was an invitation, an honest-to-goodness invitation.

Sort of. Jane couldn't have been more impressed if she'd been asked to a state dinner.

She smiled graciously and said, "I love birthday parties. When and where would you like me?"

CHAPTER **15**

As it turned out, Uncle Easy had "specifically requested" just about everyone around for his birthday party, since most of his own friends had "gone off-island once and for all," as he put it. So Bing was invited, and Cissy too, for no other reason than that they were there, and they were alive.

"I met the old guy exactly once," Bing said, laughing, as he, Cissy, and Jane lingered over hashbrowns in town on Sunday. "He's a real piece of work—I remember he tried like hell to sell me some broken-down truck he had no use for. Brother. He must think I have 'City Slicker' written all over me."

Jane, new proud owner of the truck in question, smiled weakly and changed the subject. "So, Cissy, how's your Mr. X? Not on the island, I guess, since you're here with us. Whatever the reason, it's nice to have you back."

And it was. Cissy was wonderful therapy. Unlike Jane, she seemed incapable of feeling tense, anxious, or depressed. Having an estranged and angry husband in the wings didn't seem to bother her a whit. Cissy could face down anything, including Judith Brightman; if Cissy ever bumped into *her,* she'd probably offer to take her downtown for a new wardrobe.

One thing was sure: Cissy knew all about new wardrobes. Gone were the studded denim jackets and duct-tape skirts. Gone were the spiky hair and black funky boots. In their place was a young woman right out of *Town and Country,* in a softly cowled cashmere sweater, plain gold

earrings, and a skirt neither too long nor too short. Her
hairstyle was subtle, her shoes correct, her Coach handbag
just big enough to hold the minimal makeup she wore.

"I can't believe how more . . . mature you look," Jane
said, choosing her words.

"D'you think so really? I mean, do you really? It was so
weird, throwing out everything I owned. I mean, it's possible I *might* have worn this sweater, y'know, or the earrings,
or even the skirt, but, like, never all *together*. And never the
shoes," she added, sticking out her foot to display a low-
heeled shoe of supple leather.

She studied her foot, then sighed. "I'm just not sure it's
me." But then she brightened, as she always did. "On the
other hand, I've always dressed the way I felt and this
really is how I *feel* now. I think. Y'know?"

Bing exchanged an amused look with Jane and went
back to the Arts and Leisure section of *The New York
Times*. Jane wondered, not for the first time, whether Phillip ever permitted Cissy to open her mouth. *Phillip Harrow.*
She shook her head. *He* can't *be the one.*

She decided to try to find out. "So where is Phillip, anyway? Still in New York?"

"Oh, no; he had to fly to Palm—" Cissy caught herself
and stopped, blushing furiously.

Bing lowered his newspaper and said gravely, "You may
as well tell us, Ciss. It's Phillip, of course."

"When did you find out?" she asked, biting her lip.

Bing couldn't suppress a grin. "Just about now."

Cissy looked like a child whose ice cream has fallen out
of its cone. Jane tried to comfort her. "We won't say
anything, Cissy, don't worry. But why is Phillip being so
secretive?" *Why indeed, unless his intentions were completely
dishonorable.*

"Well . . . he never did like to be the center of attention . . . you know how developers are . . . and then his
wife drowned. . . . And then he ended up right back on

the front page. Can you blame him for trying to keep a low profile?"

"Cissy, you know I worship the ground you walk on," said her brother. "But even *I* don't think Phillip Harrow's dating you is newsworthy."

"Well . . ." Cissy had been tearing her napkin into thin shreds and piling them up on her plate. She studied the little mound of paper and said uncomfortably, "That's what he told me."

"I don't like this at all," Bing said, now that the subject of Phillip was finally out in the open. "You're both entitled to your privacy, but Christ. He acts ashamed of you."

"No, no, he's not ashamed—well, maybe of the way I used to dress. But can you blame him? I looked like a hooker."

"You looked like every other twenty-two-year-old," Bing said wryly. "Who does this guy think he is? Pygmalion?"

Cissy smiled dreamily. "He's just like Rex Harrison in *My Fair Lady*," she said, completely missing the connection. "Rex Harrison really *cared* for Eliza. And Phillip really cares for *me.*"

She plopped her chin on the palm of her hands with an injured, disappointed expression that her brother had no doubt seen before. "I wish you wouldn't be like this, Bing. Phillip isn't Dave."

Relenting, Bing sighed and said, "All right. But it's damn awkward. I'll see this guy and not know whether to welcome him into the fold or punch his lights out."

Somehow Jane was convinced that Bing would be doing neither. Her guess was that Phillip was very good at leaving people holding the bag—whether it was Mac with a sunken Porsche, or Cissy with a broken heart. And yet, who knew for sure? Phillip had been really kind to Jane, going out of his way to send her a potential buyer. True, the buyer had seemed to have very little interest in Lilac Cottage; but that wasn't Phillip's fault. He'd even promised to send her another prospect.

Before the three of them broke up—Cissy to catch up on her sleep, her brother to fly back to New York—Bing took Jane aside.

His expression was hesitant. "Look . . . are we all right with one another? After Friday night?"

"Of course we are," she said, giving him a kiss right there on the street to prove it.

"That's great," he said softly. "We're going to need some time to sort things out. I suppose it's a good thing that I have to get back to the City early. Still, the thought of being away for two weeks . . ."

He hesitated, then said, "Jane, there's something I think I should tell you before I go. After I left your place on Friday, I stayed up and read. When I finally turned in about three in the morning, I looked out and saw . . ."

He took a deep breath. "Well, I saw Mac. He was leaning up against a tree, watching your house. Naturally I went out and confronted him about it. He told me you'd had some trouble—which was no secret—and that he was just keeping an eye out. So I suppose it's all right; but I'd rather you knew. I told Mac I was going to mention this to you," he added scrupulously. "He wasn't very happy about it."

Jane realized that Mac must've returned after she saw him leave. She was amazed. "You two were carrying on under my window at three in the morning, and I never even heard it? I don't believe this. No wonder someone's getting away with murder around here."

"I don't like anything about this," Bing said quietly. He left Jane reluctantly, with a troubled good-bye.

The next morning, Jane saw Mac's dark green pickup parked by the Town Building on Broad Street. So! He was trying to beat her to Ben Brightman's death record! It was

BELOVED 223

incredible nerve, to call her a naive twit and then sneak in ahead of her to find out if he was right. She stormed the building, ready to do battle.

On her march down the long, narrow hall to the Town Clerk's Office, she nearly ran him down. But Mac was coming out of the Registry of Deeds, not the office of the Town Clerk. Momentum-wise, Jane felt as if she'd tripped and fallen on her nose.

"You're supposed to be in the Town Clerk's Office," she said indignantly.

"I can't imagine why. The plot maps I was looking at are in the Registry of Deeds."

"But—"

A man in a suit and tie walked past and said, "Mornin', Mac."

"Hey, Pete. How's it goin?"

"But what about Ben Brightman?" Jane demanded to know.

A young woman, neatly dressed, had her child in tow. "Hello, Mac," she said with a friendly smile. The boy smiled too.

"So, Jimmy—you taking good care of your mom?" Mac asked, tousling the boy's hair. They toddled off, and he turned back to Jane. "Ben Brightman is your problem, not mine."

"Okay, fine," she said stiffly. "Will you believe my story if I come up with proof that he died around 1830?"

"You won't find that proof in the death record."

"Mac, my main man! Big game Sunday, don't forget."

"Gotcha, Ned."

"You know what your problem is?" she said, annoyed that people seemed to like him. "You've got an *attitude*."

"Mac."

"Bill."

Almost as an afterthought, Mac turned back to Jane and said gently, "I know what you want to believe: that Ben

Brightman was buried without a gravestone, and that Judith Brightman wants you somehow, some way, to make it right. It's a lovely, romantic idea. But unless this Judith Brightman of yours has become more than a pain in the shoulder and is actually at the chitchat stage, or unless she's left behind a diary of her grievances tucked between your floorboards, I can't see how you're going to figure out her problem, much less a solution to it. Have you considered—"

He interrupted himself to shake the hand, in mysterious silence, of a bearded man who'd come up to him.

"Have you considered a séance?" he asked her.

Was he serious?

"You're outrageous, you know that?" she said quietly, and she turned on her heel and left him, presumably holding court for the small remainder of the forty-three hundred registered voters he hadn't greeted so far this morning.

Once again Mac had been able to read her like a book. Yes, she *did* think Judith and Ben were the star-crossed lovers behind the Legend of the Cursed Rose. And yes, she *was* willing to consider a séance, maybe, if it wasn't too expensive. She walked into the Town Clerk's Office in a complete snit, determined to track down the facts of Ben Brightman's death and rub them in Mac's face.

But—it was not to be. Nantucket's formal death records dated only to 1843, too late for Ben, if her theory was correct that Ben's death was behind the furor over the rosebush. To trace a death in 1830, she'd have to pore through the clerk's genealogy records. Jane did that, but soon discovered that they were filled exclusively with the family trees of the rich and famous of Nantucket: Coffins and Gardners, Folgers and Swains, Husseys and Macys. Obviously the Brightmans didn't rate.

All of which Mac, a keen historian, must have known.

He might have saved her the trouble, dammit, instead of making easy predictions that she would fail.

The hell with him.

Jane vowed to keep looking.

She left the new and plain Town Building and walked through a moody fog over to the closed Atheneum to check the library's hours. Staring up at the facade's soaring white columns, all muted in gray mist, Jane was convinced that the old library held secrets that the new Clerk's office did not. After all, Nantucket was fiercely proud of its history. Much of it was out there for all the world to see—the captains' houses, the cobbled streets—but most of it was tucked away on dusty shelves in out-of-print books and monographs and ships' logs.

And also, as Jane found out that afternoon, on microfilm. The Atheneum had copies of every issue of the Nantucket *Inquirer,* the island's newspaper, beginning with the first one published in 1821.

The microfilm viewer was at one end of the downstairs conference room. It was a room of gracious proportions, with large six-over-six windows that let in light even on a foggy day like today. The painted half-paneled walls, the ivory and green drapes, the rose and pale green Oriental rug, and the long mahogany table edged in a rope twist pattern would not have looked out of place in some whaling captain's dining room. Over it all hung a stately bronze chandelier, each of its lamps surrounded by a small linen shade.

Even the desk that held the microfilm viewer—a nicely turned-out piece of mahogany with heavy brass pulls on its drawers—possessed unusual dignity. Jane settled into the deep cushion of the bamboo-style armchair in front of the viewer, determined to search all day if she had to. It was comforting to know that upstairs tea and homey Fig Newtons were set out for anyone who wanted refreshment. The library was nothing—nothing—like the impersonal urban versions she was used to.

She began her search for news of Ben and his ship earlier than she needed to, in January of 1828. The first two pages of the four-page weekly format were disappointing, filled with travel sketches, poems, and excerpts from other papers in the region. But on page three Jane found a feature column called "Ship News." It contained a list of the week's ship departures and arrivals, and was followed by a kind of nautical gossip column under the heading "Memoranda."

It was the "Memoranda" part that intrigued her. Nantucket ships sighted all over the world were reported in this section, along with the number of barrels of oil on board so far—a kind of stock market report for the islanders, Jane figured. But there was more: Local sightings of ships were noted here, whether the ship was anchored around the corner waiting for a fair tide, or whether it was wrecked on some nearby rocks and offloading its cargo.

Yes. This was it, the kind of forum she was looking for. She read through issue after issue, straining to read the fine, crabbed print, focusing with an effort on the sometimes blurry reproduced pages. In a way the search became a journey in itself, as she retraced the routes of the whaling captains who sailed their ships—without electronics, without engines—anywhere they chose: to Oahu and Japan, to Portland and to Lima, and to all points between.

Finally, in the December 26 issue of 1829, she found a small mention at the bottom of the "Memoranda" that sent her heart racing.

> *Two ships were seen on Tuesday south of the Vineyard, one a whale ship. They took pilots a little before sunset, and stood westward by Noman's Land. It could not be determined from Edgar-*

town, whether the other was a whale ship
or not.

Jane was absolutely sure that the other *was* a whaling
ship—the ship *Chelsea.* Trembling from the shock of recog-
nition, she was thrown back into the seizure—there was no
other word for it—that she'd experienced on the roof of
Lilac Cottage.

In this most joyous of seasons . . . Yes, she remembered
now. Whatever had happened to the *Chelsea,* it had happened in December, around Christmas. The unknown ship
spotted from Edgartown was the *Chelsea;* it had to be.
Logic confirmed it, and intuition, and the sharp throb in
her shoulder that was now spreading to her heart.

She pressed her hands over her heart, trying to ease the
pain there. She wondered if she was having a heart attack,
except that the path of the pain was headed backward. She
thought of crying out for help, but it was such a quiet
place; she shrank from making a scene.

Is this *how Judith died, then?* she asked herself in a panic.
*She didn't have fits and die of convulsions; she simply died of
a broken heart?*

She sat there for an eternity, clutching her breast, her
pain releasing itself in long, ragged breaths. Eventually the
pain eased. Finally it went away and with it, her terror. Her
mind heard only the distant sound of rolling thunder, the
way it does after a squall has passed.

Jane waited a moment longer, and then with a kind of
dreadful, awestruck curiosity, she started the microfilm
inching forward again. Page one . . . page two . . . page
three.

She shuddered and let out a deep sigh. It was as she
thought. The *Chelsea,* loaded with twenty-three hundred
barrels of oil, had run up on a bar off Nantucket in heavy
weather. The cargo had been offloaded, the paper an-
nounced, and salvage operations were underway. In the

immediate aftermath of the grounding, several members of
the crew were known to be lost. It was not explained how
they were lost—or who they were.

Dismayed, Jane searched frantically for the obituary column. Under the simple heading "Died" were listed several
names of people who'd died either on the island or off, but
there was nothing at all about a Ben Brightman. Nothing
at all.

"I suppose you could call it a good-news, bad-news kind
of thing," Jane confessed to Cissy over pizza and beer that
night. (She had to tell someone. She knew that Cissy, of
everybody, would believe her.)

"The good news is that I don't seem to be insane. The
bad news is that I may die of fits at any time." Jane tried to
laugh off her fear, but the truth was, she was as frightened
as she'd ever been in her life. All of what had happened so
far—the nasty tricks around the house, her frightening
dreams, even the "presence" that had set off Buster—was
nothing compared to these possessions of her by Judith.

"I don't know, maybe I'm developing multiple personali-
ties," she confessed, pressing a loose piece of pepperoni
onto her slice of pizza. "Maybe I *am* losing it. Maybe it's
the stress of not having a job."

"That's crazy," Cissy argued, refilling her glass. "*I've*
never had a job. Do I look stressed?"

Jane looked across Bing's breakfast counter at his sister
and snorted good-naturedly. "The other bad news—and it
is bad news—is that I don't actually have proof that Ben
Brightman died in the grounding of the *Chelsea*. The paper
never mentioned his name."

"Oh, you'll find it. Maybe someone kept a diary back
then."

"Cissy, it's not as though there's a Diary Mart on Nantucket," Jane explained patiently. "Working through any
archives and private collections could be a monumental

task. Scholars get awarded Ph.D.s for tracking down stupid little details like this. I couldn't possibly—"

"Did you check the following week?" Cissy suggested, brightening. "Maybe they were late getting his name in."

"Um. Well. Actually . . . no. I was so rattled. . . . Hmm. I'll have to do that."

"Isn't this great? We're like a team or something," Cissy said, beaming. She nibbled her way through a long piece of stringy cheese and added, "I'm really, really glad you confided in me, Jane. I mean, what you're going through is just so cool."

"Oh, absolutely," Jane said dryly. "That's what I was thinking." Jane eyed the last slice of pizza, then thought better of it. She didn't want any dreams of any kind tonight, and that included those induced by heartburn.

"We have to have a plan," said Cissy. She reached around the counter to a side shelf and brought out Nantucket's very slim phone book. "We'll hire a professional, and *she'll* get Judith to tell us what to do." She turned to the yellow pages under "Mediums" and then under "Spiritualists" with no luck.

"Try 'Psychologists,' " Jane suggested with a wry smile. "Times are tough; maybe they do séances on the side."

Cissy took her seriously, of course, expecting to find a discreet little ad that said, "Spirits Summoned—Reasonable." When she came up empty again, she was very disappointed; she wanted so badly to help. So she chewed on the problem for a bit, like a puppy with a sock, until she came up with another idea.

"We'll do an all-nighter! I'll bring Bing's camcorder, and I'll hide in your closet. That's what these experts do; they bring tape recorders and cameras and things and sometimes they get lucky."

"Gee. Maybe we can pitch it to 'America's Funniest Home Videos,' " Jane said. She thought it was an incredibly dumb idea.

"I've seen actual photos, Jane," Cissy insisted. "No one can explain the images that sometimes show up. A tourist took a photo of a ghost once and he wasn't even trying! He was walking down the stairs of some castle in England."

"The tourist?"

"The *ghost*. Okay, I can see you don't want my help," Cissy said, hurt. She closed up the pizza box and began folding it down to manageable size.

"No, no," Jane answered. "I really appreciate what you're trying to do. I suppose we could give it a try. What the heck."

"We have to do *some*thing."

By the time Cissy came over at ten with the camcorder and a tripod, Jane's misgivings were great. Except for the time that Buster had seemed to see something in the rocking chair of her bedroom, there had been no evidence so far of any kind of apparition. Why should Kodak be able to capture what the human eye could not? Besides, Judith had done all of her communicating through Jane, which would seem to make Jane herself the medium in this affair. Logically, the camera should be aimed at Jane all night, an idea which made her skin crawl.

"It's bad enough to be videotaped when you're asleep and vulnerable," Jane complained to Cissy as they discussed strategy. "But if Judith comes tonight, do I really want to be able to watch myself as she . . . does whatever it is she does to me? Mac is right. There are some things," she said with a shudder, "that go too far."

So the two of them walked round and round with the tripod, trying to locate it in an optimal spot. They tried the bottom of the stairs, and the top, and the hall. But there was absolutely no evidence that Lilac Cottage was haunted —only that Jane was—so in the end they set up the tripod in the bedroom closet, with the door partly opened, and put a chair inside for Cissy. Jane stood behind the lens, focusing it on the white eyelet-trimmed pillowcases of her bed, and thought, *I must be mad. How have I let things get this far?*

If someone had told her two months ago that she'd be sharing nervous giggles with a gullible child-woman at midnight in the closet of her bedroom while they tried to catch some apparition on videotape, she'd have edged away from him and called the police. Instead, she was cracking ghostbuster jokes that weren't very funny and trying hard to ignore the fact that it was midnight and time, at last, to go to bed.

The plan was simple. Cissy would stay up and Jane would sleep. Jane didn't think it was fair, but there didn't seem to be any alternative, and Cissy claimed, after all, to be a night owl. So Jane slipped into a set of lightweight sweats, while Cissy dressed in a ruffled cotton gown in keeping with a girls' sleepover. She had her supply of caffeine—a six-pack of Coke—beside her and looked ready to party all night.

As for Jane: Despite her trepidations she was exhausted. She slipped self-consciously under her white down comforter, let out a nervous sigh, and said, "Okay. Roll 'em."

It became very quiet. Cissy, suddenly deadly serious, didn't talk, didn't sneeze, didn't clear her throat. There was only the rise and fall of Jane's own breathing, which sounded unnaturally loud to her. She lay there in a kind of terrified calm, feeling like some sacrificial victim. Her emotions were at war. On the one hand, she had an irresistible urge to bolt from her bed. On the other hand, she knew now that she couldn't escape Judith, not until Judith's mission was done. If Jane was the victim in this ritual drama, then she was also its high priestess.

So she lay there, unsure of her power, uncertain of her resolve, until a deep, steadying heaviness crept into her limbs and then, at Judith's mercy, she fell asleep.

*   *   *

When Jane woke up, enormously refreshed, bright sun was pouring through the deep-set window of the east dormer. She opened one eye sleepily and took in the pale yellow walls with their cabbage-rose borders and thought how very pretty the room was. She liked everything about it, from the way her old steamer trunk fit perfectly under the sloping eave, to the needlepoint rug that lay over the scarred and golden pine floor.

Easing onto her back and stretching luxuriously, Jane opened the other eye. And found herself staring into the baleful eye of a camcorder.

Jeez!

She'd forgotten completely about the videotape. She jumped out of bed, wondering where Cissy'd gone off to and swung open the closet door. There she was on the floor, curled up in a nest of spare blankets and surrounded by six empty Coke cans. The last videotape was still on the floor beside the tripod, unused. So much for the scientific method.

Smiling, Jane crouched down and shook Cissy gently awake. "Rise and shine, kiddo."

Cissy started from her sleep. "I'm awake! I'm awake!" she cried. When she saw that the sun was up and the second tape had run out, she winced. "I blew it, didn't I?"

Jane pointed to the empty Coke cans. "Hey, you tried."

"I did go downstairs to pee twice," Cissy admitted. "But other than that I sat right here for four whole hours, honest. And I didn't see anything, not a damn thing." Disappointed, she got to her feet and began stretching her obviously stiff limbs.

"Never mind," said Jane, more relieved than not that the night had passed without incident. "Who's to say Judith had plans to be here in any case? Come on, I'll make us pancakes. We'll play the tape anyway; I want to see if I snore."

"You don't," Cissy was able to confirm. "You slept like a baby. That's how I know no one came."

The two of them trotted downstairs, with Cissy already planning the next vigil and Jane thinking how much easier this all was with someone to share it with—even if that someone was a naïf like Cissy.

Jane thought of Bing, who, despite his love for Nantucket, could only give it bits and snatches of his time. He was far too busy prying artwork from the walls of bored collectors, and doing something really nice for an art-starved public besides. Could she honestly expect him to stay on the island and devote himself to her utterly bizarre quest?

And then, of course, there was Mac—brooding, cynical, filled with contempt for her and everything she stood for. Oh, Mac was willing to keep an eye on her, all right, just as he'd kept an eye on her Aunt Sylvia when she was his neighbor. It was the commonest of courtesies. Besides, Mac was enough of a chauvinist to think that sooner or later every single woman needed a strong man. Maybe it was to nail down a gutter; maybe it was, who knows, to take her to bed. But chasing down ghosts? Uh-uh. Mac had the time to help Jane, but not the inclination.

That left Cissy clearly as the best man for the job.

So Jane and Cissy hooked up the camcorder to the television and popped in the first of the two tapes while Jane whipped up some pancake batter in her half-redone kitchen. The record of her falling asleep was amazingly boring; the novelty of watching herself sleep wore off after about sixty seconds.

Jane rolled her eyes and flipped the first half-dozen pancakes on the griddle. "Cissy, you deserve a medal for staying up through this."

"I think adrenaline kept me going through the first tape," Cissy said. She had settled into a sunny spot in the kitchen; sunbeams bounced off her long blond hair while, still in her nightgown, she sipped coffee and watched the tape fixedly. After a while, even Cissy's attention began to wander.

"I slept better last night than I have in weeks," Jane mused, stacking the first load of pancakes onto a heated platter and slipping them into the oven to stay warm. "It must be a plot to throw us off guard."

"That's the thing about apparitions," Cissy said, sounding like an expert. "Nothing is as it seems."

"That's the thing about this whole *island*," Jane muttered. "Not to mention the people living on it. Take Mac, for instance," she said, shaking her spatula at Cissy. "Look at him. I've never seen him smile. No one ever visits him. He's your typical curmudgeon, right? So how come everyone who sees him lights up like a roman candle? I don't know . . . I feel like there's something real, something genuine going on out here . . . but I just can't figure out how to become part of it. . . . I catch glimpses, and then they're gone. . . ."

Jane's lament was interrupted by the sound of her own voice: a quiet, almost petulant moan came from the sleeping figure on videotape. Both women jerked their heads toward the camcorder in time to see the recorded Jane frown slightly in concentration and then shift her position on the pillow. Jane ran to the recorder and rewound a few feet of the tape, then pressed the "Play" button.

They watched in silence as the little gesture repeated itself. "See anything?" whispered Jane as the tape continued to roll.

"Doesn't it look maybe a little fuzzy above your head?"

Jane didn't think so. Cissy said, "Maybe Judith got scared off by the camcorder."

"She wouldn't know what it was," Jane answered, as if they were having a perfectly reasonable conversation.

They let the tape play on while they talked and drank coffee and ate pancakes in the pleasant, sun-filled room.

Finally Jane stood up and said gently, "This isn't going anywhere, Cissy. If Judith had been here, I would have known." She stopped the tape.

But Cissy, showing an amazing amount of grit for a dilettante, refused to give up. "I'll take the second tape and play it on the player in my room," she said. "If I see something, I'll run right over."

The girl hesitated, then put her arms around Jane in a shy hug. In her ruffle-edged nightgown, with her hair lying straight and unstyled, Cissy looked and acted like a teenager; she could've been Jane's much younger sister. Touched by Cissy's timid little gesture of affection, Jane gave her a big, reassuring hug back.

She's never had any women close to her, Jane suddenly realized. *Only men.*

But that was more than Jane had.

CHAPTER 16

Cissy never came back with her evidence, and when Jane walked out to go to town the next morning, she saw that Cissy's Jeep was gone. Nine chances out of ten Phillip was back and snapping his fingers. It bothered Jane that the girl had fallen so completely under his spell. Not that there was anything wrong with spells, but Phillip was far too jaded for Cissy's sweet innocence. They were a tricky combination as a couple.

Jane held up the pale yellow sleeve of her sweater against the peeling clapboard of the cottage and speculated about that shade of paint. Too yellow for Nantucket? Was white the best? She sighed, pleasantly obsessed by the homeowner's ultimate dilemma—what color to paint the house—and realized again how good life could be on Nantucket year round. True, she hadn't been tested through an entire long and empty winter; but she knew instinctively that she'd fit in. Books, a crackling fire—no ghosts—and a man who truly loved her; that was the formula for making it through the cruel months.

Too bad I can't get the formula quite right, she thought wistfully. *I have one ghost too many and one man too few.* She paused and listened to herself. This fretting over ghosts was new, obviously. But so was this fretting about not having a mate. After all, Jane was the one who'd always been comfortable about being single. Her friends used to be very impressed by her cool independence—the same friends who were now all married with children.

Jane Drew—having second thoughts?

Oh, what the hell. Chalk it up to spring.

Besides, her love life wasn't *completely* without hope at the moment. Sooner or later Bing would be, if ever so briefly, back on Nantucket. She laughed a resigned little laugh and struck out on foot for Cliff Road and the town center, pausing every little while to admire the yellow forsythia still in bloom, or to stick her nose in the sweet waxy flowers drooping from the branches of an Andromeda bordering the road.

Jane was still ambling along when she heard someone behind her. She turned to see Mac McKenzie coming up fast. It caught her unaware; he seemed to appear out of nowhere. He was wearing town clothes and walking with long, powerful strides, completely in his element on this stretch of near-country road. She couldn't help remembering him as he was at Phillip Harrow's dinner party, when he'd seemed so hemmed in by Phillip's fine antiques and crystal.

At the time she thought he was shy, or possibly just plain sullen. Now she saw that he'd been biding his time all evening like some cornered lion, waiting to leap over their gentility and savor his freedom again. He couldn't survive for long in the drawing room, not without hurting himself or someone else. He needed *this*—the land, the sky, the ocean—the way Jane's mother needed theater and the opera.

As he drew nearer to her, Jane saw a look on his face that she'd never seen before, a mix of contentment and anticipation. He looked far younger than his forty years. *Of course!* she realized. *He feels it even more than I, this surge of spring. His whole life has oriented him to this season. He doesn't just* witness *the miracle of rebirth. He lives it; he's part of it.* She could see it in his eyes, in his bearing, in the ruggedly handsome lines of his face.

And it took her breath away.

She stopped and waited for him. "Good morning," she

said rather shyly, aware that their last exchange had been a typically caustic one. She wished, quite suddenly, that she could erase her memory of it. It was too perfect a day to go on sniping at one another—and anyway, she was wearing a skirt. Skirts made her feel feminine and winsome and not like fighting.

Mac picked up right away on the fact that she wasn't in jeans and a sweatshirt. His gaze swept over her skirt, her lemon yellow sweater, her pinned-back auburn hair. "You finally get a job?" he quipped as he fell in alongside her. But there was an appreciative softness in his voice that was new, and it made her heart beat faster.

"Nothing so radical as that," she said lightly, suddenly hoping against hope that it would matter to him. "It just feels good to dress up a little now and then."

Mac slipped his hands in the pockets of his corduroys and slowed his pace to match hers. "Well, you'll be wearing power suits soon enough, back in Connecticut," he said without looking at her.

For Mac it was a pretty blatant feeler, and it showed: a dark telltale flush began creeping up his neck.

"All my plans are on hold right now," she confessed, giving him the information he seemed to be after. "I may never get off the island. Someone's living in my condo, my mother's taking my car, and no one wants to buy Lilac Cottage."

"No one? That's hard to believe; you're doing a good job with that house," Mac said. "I'm glad to see you're not tarting it up."

She savored the compliment, such as it was, before she disillusioned him. "Yeah, but you weren't there when Phillip's first buyer went through. 'Rough as a corncob' was all he said. The second one said even less—he just paced it off, muttered 'No land,' and left."

Mac laughed under his breath and said, "That's the oldest one in the books: Send over a couple of so-called buyers to bad-mouth the property and drive down your hopes."

"What're you talking about?" she asked, at a loss. "Why would Phillip do that?"

"Obviously, because he wants to buy your property himself," Mac said in a voice that was suddenly low and grim and bitter.

"What? Phillip isn't interested in Lilac! I had to force him just to take a polite look around. He doesn't want *any* more property on the island, Mac. He's told Cissy that he thanks his lucky stars he didn't get stuck with Bing's place. I assume Phillip has a cash-flow problem just like everyone else."

"Naturally you continue to defend him," Mac said as they walked side by side. The more annoyed he got, the faster he walked. The faster he walked, the more annoyed Jane became.

She decided that Mac was too biased ever to be fair to Phillip. "Mac, I know all about what happened when you and Phillip were in high school," she blurted. "I can see why you don't trust the man. But give me a little credit, won't you? I work with all kinds of people—"

"And I don't, you mean?" he shot back. "I spend the day swinging from the tree limbs I'm paid to saw off?"

She flushed, then halted and retreated in the face of his anger. "Okay, I agree, Phillip's not the best. But that doesn't mean he goes around twirling his mustache and plotting evil all day long," she said stubbornly.

There they were, standing in the middle of Cliff Road, exchanging blows again. And meanwhile the sun was just as warm and bright and the daffodils were just as beguiling. Heartsick that they were destroying a perfectly magical walk, Jane sighed and said, "Why do we always do this? Why do we always fight?" She fell back to walking, but her heart wasn't in it.

"Wait!" Mac said, reaching out for her arm. Electrified,

she stopped and turned, and he released her. His look was intense, determined. "We fight because we can't communicate. Then we get frustrated. Then we get mad. Isn't it obvious?"

"Not to me it isn't," she said, still burning from his touch. "This has never happened to me before. People in advertising don't usually have problems communicating."

"It's happened to *me* before," he said in a voice of black calm. "With my ex-wife." He turned away from Jane and started heading alone to town, leaving her standing there.

"Oh. Well—*well, I'm not your ex-wife, dammit!*" she yelled as he walked on ahead. "And I wish you'd stop treating me as if I were!" She listened in amazement to herself screaming.

Mac stopped—again—and turned in time to see her throw up her hands in frustration. "All right," he said with an ironic smile. "We'll start over." He bowed and held out his hand in a gallant gesture for her to join him. "What do you want to try to talk about?"

It was as close to a truce as she was ever going to get. Mollified, she fell in beside him again and said, "This is how we'll handle it: If one of us doesn't want to discuss something, we'll just say 'pass.' And the other will respect that. Do you agree?"

He nodded, humoring her earnestness with a grin, and she noticed for the first time how really handsome he was in profile. He had a dimple in his right cheek. Now she wanted to know if he had one in his left.

"For . . . for instance," she stammered, still distracted, "I've been meaning to ask you about that sign in your office—WHOLESALE ONLY. How come you don't sell retail? Is there a zoning problem?"

"No; I'm grandfathered for retail business. I don't know," he said with a shrug, "I used to do it, but it's a hassle. I can't be in a shop and in the field at the same time, and I'd rather be in the field." He broke off a twig of

spicebush and stripped its leaves absentmindedly, crushing
them in his hands. He took a deep whiff and held out his
cupped palm for her to smell.

"Nice," she said, inhaling the sweet scent. "But wouldn't
it pay for you to hire someone to work that side of the
business?"

"They'd have to work for next to nothing, and the only
one who'd do that would be a wife," he explained laconically.

"I understand. Whereas your wife Celeste—"

"Pass."

"Right. But it does seem a shame that you can't cash in
on the seasons more than you do. I know I sound merce-
nary, but there's money to be made from events like Daffodil Weekend. And you just missed Easter. Mother's Day is
coming up . . . June weddings . . . and Christmas! If
you could just see your way to expanding from trees and
shrubs to flowers and wreaths—"

"I think I've explained why I'm not interested," he said
with surprising patience.

"Yes, because you can't afford to pay for full-time help.
What if you started small? Your advertising could be minimal, just some flyers around town and a two-line classified.
You don't need much inventory. Can you heat the hoop
house? Oh, and an answering machine, that would definitely help. Someone could come in for you, say, just on
weekends—"

"Pass, I said."

She had an inspiration. "*I* could come in, just on weekends! I wouldn't mind. It'd be fun!"

"Pass. *Pass,* for Chrissake!" he shouted, clapping his
palms to his forehead. "What is it with you? You get me to
agree to this . . . this rule of civility, and then you run
roughshod over it!"

"Oh." Jane stopped on the sidewalk—they were in town
now—and blushed a shade of red as deep as the bricks

under her feet. Of course if he didn't *want* her free help—
the damn ingrate—then *fine*. He could just hide back there
and lick his wounds until the bank foreclosed.

She was rounding on him, ready to fire into him for his
defeatist ways, when she spied a small rabbit across the
street on the front lawn of one of the grand prewar summer houses that lay at the edge of town. The rabbit was on
its hind legs, watching them with an expression that said,
"People, *people!* This is a residential neighborhood!"

It all took less than five seconds. Jane realized—really
for the first time, since she'd had no experience—that it
took two to do battle. To maintain peace, all she had to do
was hold her fire. She took a deep breath, threw a smile at
the bunny rabbit, and said to Mac, "You're right. I did
break my rule, and I was butting in where it was none of
my business. Friends?"

She held out her hand to Mac, who shook it suspiciously.
They walked a little way together, their conversation more
awkward than their silences, until Mac suddenly stopped,
bent down, and snapped off a daffodil that was growing at
the base of an enormous maple.

He presented it to her. "You don't need a designated
weekend to enjoy a daffodil," he said with a look as complex as anything she'd seen from him.

This was new for her. In her lifetime she'd been presented many times with roses by the boxful, all swathed in
tissue and highlighted with Baby's Breath. But to be given
this single, humble, naturalized flower . . . She was over-
come by a surge of emotion that lifted her like a moon
tide, snapping the single thread that held her to her moor-
ings. She was adrift; she didn't know what to do or say.

"I can see why you chose it," she said, trying to sound
lighthearted. "It's definitely the prettiest one on the island."

"I think so, too."

She was hearing his tone more than his words. "N-no, I meant the flower," she stammered, blushing furiously.

"So did I," he said with a smile.

That, of course, made her blush still more. Maybe he was right, after all; maybe they couldn't communicate. And yet, she was holding his keepsake in her hand, and they were strolling side by side, and now that she thought about it, she *wasn't* mistaken about the tone in his voice.

They came to the corner of Lily Street and Mac paused and said, "This is my turnoff."

"You're not going into town?" she asked, surprised.

"Actually, a very nice lady has asked me to lunch."

Young? Pretty? Good cook? The questions lined up on the back of Jane's tongue, but she beat them back and said, "I'll be seeing you, then."

"Where're *you* off to?"

Jane considered lying, but she answered, "The Atheneum."

"And what's at—"

"Pass," she said tersely.

"Ah."

There was no denying the disappointment in his face. He seemed almost hostile, as if this were an inconvenient time for her mad obsession about Judith to surface. Jane sighed and shrugged, the disappointment in her face mirroring his own.

She went the rest of the way alone, absently twirling the flower in her hand, wondering how they were going to get around this last and biggest impasse of all. Maybe they could skirt around the subjects of his wife, his financial straits, and his business methods; maybe they could come up with a way to pretend she didn't have a master's degree and a staggering number of frequent-flyer miles with three different airlines. But they sure as hell were not going to get around the fact that she believed in ghosts—well, *one* ghost—and he didn't.

Jane wanted so much not to believe. Take right now, for instance. The thought that the spirit of Judith Brightman was using her to complete some unfinished business seemed ludicrous. This was *Nantucket,* not Salem. This was the nineties; the only thing appearing and disappearing nowadays was the peace dividend.

Dammit! She'd never live in a historic zone again; give her a nice new suburb anytime.

Jane had time before the Atheneum opened, so she lingered over a simple but hearty calzone at the year-round waterfront café, then wandered aimlessly around the wharf area. Some of the shops, housed in tiny neat shacks with still-empty windowboxes, hadn't yet opened for the season, but here and there a determined shopkeeper or gallery owner had turned on the lights and the heat.

There were no yachts, there were no shoppers to speak of, and yet the wharves had a cheerful, never-say-die air about them, probably because they were vibrant with spring bulbs: tulips and daffodils and grape hyacinths, all enjoying their all-too-brief time out of the ground.

Jane had no real desire to go to the library, not after her experience there the day before, but at two o'clock she turned dutifully in the direction of Federal Street. She walked up the steps and stood under the library's columns, clutching the daffodil, which she'd wrapped in a wet paper napkin, and tried to think of reasons not to go in.

If you find Ben's name in there, then what? And if you don't find his name—then what?

Then what. The question had hung over her from the start like a cold, foggy shroud. It was pointless to speculate; who could possibly say what Judith had in mind next? Jane took a deep breath and went in, praying that whatever happened, she would be spared the pain and fright she'd suffered the day before. In a minute she was in the micro-

film room, spooling through the last week of 1829 and into
the first of 1830.

And there it was. The bodies of three sailors—Ben
Brightman, Francis Sylvia, and Ned Quick—had been discovered thrown up on the beach within a few hundred
yards of the Humane House. Jane found herself actually
disappointed that she hadn't come up with the names of
the other two sailors on her own. It was a little like being at
bat and hitting only one for three—a decent performance,
but not good enough for Most Valuable Player.

Shocked by her cool detachment, Jane rewound the
spool and hurried from the library. The one thing she
didn't want to do was to lose sympathy for Judith's cause.
She knew, instinctively, that that would be fatal.

Billy was at Lilac Cottage, putting up the last of the
repainted glass-front cabinet doors. The kitchen was looking wonderful in an old-fashioned cheery way. Somehow,
without installing Corian counters, designer faucets, or a
Jenn-Aire cooktop, Billy had managed to bring out the
best in the sweet old room. The new window over the sink
invited twice as much sunlight, and with the pantry wall
knocked down, the light was able to reach every corner.
Best of all, everything was original, from the stripped-down
pine floors and white wainscotting to the homey porcelain
sink, newly adorned with a blue gingham skirt.

"Billy, you did really, really well," Jane said with quiet
satisfaction as she turned slowly around the room. "I'm
glad you talked me out of the linoleum."

"Hey, whaddya need it for? You don't have kids crawling
around on their hands and knees all day."

It was like taking an unexpected blow. "That's for sure,"
she murmured, catching her breath. She handed him a
screwdriver, thinking, *It's happening. I'm starting to panic.
I'll be going to a sperm bank next.*

Billy looked down at her from his stepladder. "Did I say something wrong?"

"No, not at all," she lied. "I think I must be a little blue over . . . over funds, that's all. I'll be fine as soon as my mother pays me for my car this week. I have to admit, I thought I'd be back in Connecticut by now, having new business cards printed; but out here, one week seems to fade into another. . . ."

"Yeah. That's life, I guess."

That evening the fickle month of April, like an ill-bred mistress, turned from temptress to banshee. A solid bank of clouds had been approaching the island all afternoon, and when it arrived, it came with a howling wind and pounding rain. The effect on Jane was profound. The last of the optimism she'd been feeling that morning was washed away in a wave of misgivings. The cold, hard facts were these: She was going through her money like a drunken sailor; Bing was never around long enough for them to develop a meaningful relationship; and Mac seemed on and off to hate her guts.

And then there was Judith. Judith, like Cissy, apparently had gone into hiding. Cissy might be with her Phillip, but Judith was definitely not with her Ben. So where was she? Was Jane supposed to sit around in some melancholy funk, waiting for Judith to make her next move? Jane wandered from window to window, paralyzed by a brooding sense of expectation, watching the driving rain turn the night into a sodden, muddy mess.

Okay. Enough is enough. I'll build a fire and read a fun book; anything to take my mind off this.

She threw on her oilslicker and plunged into the wild, windy night for some of the firewood that Billy had stacked neatly under a canvas tarp. She had to make three trips and got soaked in the process, but the very act of building a fire seemed to rally her. It was Jane's first fire in the house, and it took on ritualistic importance. Carefully she stacked the kindling, crisscrossed the logs, and bundled crushed paper under it all. She fully expected it to light with one match.

And it did. A roaring, crackling, oversized fire began almost at once to warm the room and her spirits. Jane wrapped a towel around her rain-soaked hair, slipped into pajamas, brought out a bottle of apricot liqueur, and cracked into Grisham's latest hit. It was the perfect escape, and she was absorbed for several hours.

After that, her attention began to wander. Whether the fault was hers or the author's, Jane just couldn't concentrate. She felt restless, almost itchy. She threw another log on the fire, then circled the camcorder as if it were a crystal ball.

Cissy was convinced she saw something fuzzy there, hovering over Jane. True, Cissy was a flake, but she was a *young* flake, with sharper eyes than Jane's. Feeling self-conscious, Jane turned down the already dim lamp and fast-forwarded the tape to the scene in question . . . freeze-framed it . . . adjusted the contrast . . . and gasped. Her heart went rocketing through her breast; her head felt trapped in a vise of fear.

How had she missed it before? Granted, the sun in the kitchen had been very bright, but *still.* . . . She peered more closely at the tape. There, above her sleeping body, was a kind of a *shape,* a decided *shape,* not as clear as a vapor, yet more substantial, somehow, than fog. She rubbed her eyes ferociously, which only made everything blurry. After a while she was able to focus again, and there it was again, that pale promise of another world.

She ran the tape a little ahead, but there was nothing. So she decided to start from the beginning, searching for other images of Judith. For two hours Jane sat there, strained to the breaking point. Outside the storm raged; she was hardly aware of it. And then, when she was nearly at the end of the tape, a particularly violent gust shook the house and the electricity went out.

It was as if someone threw a switch in Jane's soul. She felt cast into oblivion without any warning. For a while she sat there, numb, bereft, completely at a loss. Eventually, when the electricity didn't come back on, she stumbled over to the window. There were no lights on anywhere that she could see—which around there proved nothing. For the first time in her life, Jane understood the meaning of the word "desolation." Nantucket had been a mistake for her, and now, finally, she was willing to admit it.

She threw another log on the fire and sat huddled in a blanket, staring at the darkened camcorder, waiting for dawn. But the all-night vigil was not to be. Almost at once she fell into a troubled, disjointed sleep.

It was a cold, rainy day. She was in the sitting room of her house, hers and Ben's, with her coal-skuttle bonnet still in her lap. Her shawl, of an exquisite pale gray weave, was folded across the rocking chair in which she sat. She loved the shawl because it was Ben's favorite. It was part of a shipment she had ordered from New York, the only one that wasn't black. She'd been advertising the black ones at a very good price, and they were nearly gone. But the gray one she kept, because it set off her blue-black hair.

She felt quite calm. Today was First Day, and she should have gone to meeting. But there seemed no point, and at the last minute she decided to stay home. The Overseers had warned her sharply and ordered her to remove the rose from the mound that, after the recent rains, was scarcely recognizable as Ben's grave.

She had refused.

It was only a matter of time before they came. She had been under dealings from them before: when she'd bought the spinet, for example, and begun to teach herself to play; and when she'd planted the moon garden, so that she could wander among white flowers on a warm summer night; and when she'd come back from Boston with a tasseled vermilion chair for the sitting room.

And each time, at Ben's urging, she had yielded to the Overseers' puritanical ultimatums. She sold the spinet and uprooted her perennials and tore the tassels off the chair, covering it in a drab and sickly green. Ben had kissed her and petted her and said that none of it mattered; that their love for one another brought all the music, light, and color to their lives that they needed. But each time it had been harder for her to conform, harder for her to comprehend why the orthodox Friends on Nantucket had twisted the lessons of simplicity taught by the original Quakers.

And now, she didn't care. Ben was dead. The one man on earth who had the power to make her bend to the dour, petty demands of a group of oppressive old men was dead. Let them come. Let them expel her. She didn't care. Ben was dead.

When she heard the knock on the door, she almost didn't bother to answer it, so loathesome had the thought of facing them become. But she wanted to put them behind her, and so she opened her home and her heart to their uncharitable scrutiny one last time.

"I pray thee, gentlemen, come in," she said, her voice stripped of emotion.

The four of them filed in one by one, led by Jabez Coffin. He was the group's senior, an unbending work of steel tempered by decades of self-denial. He paused in front of the fire and glanced around her pleasant sitting room with distaste, fixing his disapproval on an intricate silver frame adorning a small silhouette of Ben that sat on the mantle.

She went up to the mantle, picked up the frame, and pressed the silhouette to her breast. If the innocently indulgent frame annoyed Jabez Coffin, so much the better.

"Thee has something to say?" she said, sweeping them

all up in one proud glance. The three who were with Jabez Coffin avoided her look.

"Judith Brightman," said Jabez, "there is a concern upon our minds, and thou art fully aware what it be. On the twenty-sixth of twelfth month, thy husband's ship foundered and Benjamin Brightman perished seeking the safety of our shore. On the second of first month, thy husband was buried in the Friends' Burial Ground. Eight days ago this day, thou engaged in an act of ill-considered defiance: marking thy husband's grave in the manner of the world's people."

Jabez paused and looked at the others to see whether they had any cause to challenge the facts so far. The three men, all of them past the half-century mark, seemed to wilt under his fiery gaze like schoolboys, as if the devil himself had dared them to contradict him. When no one spoke, he continued.

"Is it the truth I have spoken thus far?" he said, focusing his fire-and-brimstone gaze directly on her now. When she said nothing, he said in a severe tone, *"Thou wilt answer me . . . Friend."*

"I planted a rose on Ben's grave, yes," she said, raising her chin. "So that I would know where to find him when I am old."

"A rose. Thou didst plant a rose." Jabez glanced at his cohorts again, an unpleasant grin assuming control of his face. It seemed odd to her that for all his abstinent ways, he had bad teeth.

"There are thousands of souls who have cast off their bodies and left them behind in the burial ground," Jabez said. "Is it not fair to say that they have left behind many thousands more who have loved and mourned them?"

She nodded.

"And of all the thousands who have mourned, has there been a *single other one* who has chosen to mark the gravesite of a loved one?"

"Perhaps they never thought to do it," she said ironically.

"Do not toy with me, child! I ask thee one last time: Wilt thou own to thy vanity and repent? Wilt thou remove the rose?"

"I will not," she answered in a clear and calm voice. "I loved Ben, and I want to be able to visit his grave and to reflect on the life we shared, and to say a prayer for his soul. There is no vanity in that, only simple, human emotion."

Jabez drew his white, bushy brows together in a searing scowl. His blue eyes burned bright with terrifying self-righteousness as he said, "Then, child, thou hast lost that which thou holdest most dear."

He threw an imperious look at the other Overseers, willing them into a show of support. "We have much discussed this among us." They nodded timidly.

Then he turned to her and intoned, "For this and other disregards of the way of truth, thou art to be set aside from the Society of Friends. Thou mayest no longer be present at Meeting, and thou mayest not set thy foot on the burial ground."

Stunned, she watched the play of muscles in his jaw as he added, "*We* will remove the rose for thee."

She had expected to be disowned, had accepted the fact that she would have to come to terms with her Maker on her own; but she was not prepared for this. To be forbidden even to walk over the general ground where Ben lay— it was not to be borne.

For one crushing moment, her spirit collapsed completely. She was overwhelmed with a sense of deprivation. "*No!*" she cried, her face contorted with grief. "How can you? Have you no heart? Have you no kindness?" Tears rolled down her cheeks as she clutched her hands in supplication.

But she could see, even as she begged Jabez Coffin, that

it was a waste of time. He was enjoying her distress, just as he would doubtless enjoy tearing out the rose from Ben's grave.

Something died inside her then. She could feel it go, just as she could feel something else begin to stir, a superhuman determination not to let this withered soul come between Ben and her.

"Go, then!" she cried. "Leave my house. Thee has made a mockery of Christ's teaching. There is no love in thy heart, only envy and meanness. Is it any wonder that the Society is splintered, that Elias Hicks draws away Friends from thy rigid, uncaring ways? *Go!*"

She watched, trembling with fury, as Jabez Coffin drew in a sharp breath and held it. The veins in his temple pounded; his cheeks flamed. She thought that the heart in this hard-hearted man might be about to fail at last, but Jabez was stronger than that.

He took one last, sweeping look around the little sitting room with its cheery rag rug, and its yellow export vase filled with pussy willows, and its bright curtains thrown open to the day's gray light, and in a low and deadly growl he quoted a passage from Scripture. " 'Set thine house in order,' " he said with vicious irony. " 'For thou shalt die, and not live.' "

He swept out of her house with his deputies in tow. She slammed the door on their backs and only then did she understand that she had slammed the door forever on any possibility of being buried next to Ben. She had slammed the door on eternity.

She let out a long, agonized scream and collapsed onto the floor. It was a cry of despair, a cry from the deepest part of her heart, a cry from hell.

A horrible, shrill sound, the sound of harpies shrieking and tearing at entrails, jolted Jane awake from her agony. She opened her eyes, and she saw flames.

CHAPTER 17

The edge of the Oriental rug nearest the fireplace was covered with embers and on fire. Bounced into action by the din of the smoke detector, Jane ran for the fire extinguisher in the kitchen. But the lights were still out and she stumbled, first into a stool, then into Billy's stepladder, which crashed to the floor. She groped in the corner where the fire extinguisher was supposed to be—it wasn't there. She ended up crawling around on her hands and knees, feeling for the metal cylinder.

It was on the floor beside the stove; she snatched it up and ran back to the fireplace room. Fighting panic, she sprayed a blanket of white chemicals on the aged and burning rug until the fire was extinguished. Then she took down the shrieking smoke alarm and collapsed on the Empire sofa, where she sat clutching the empty cylinder and staring at the mess by the fading light of the fireplace, watching for flareups. But it was over.

For now. The thought bubbled up from some hidden depth, unnerving her. *This was no accident, no renegade ember popping out of the flames and creating havoc.* There were a whole bunch of embers on the floor, hurled there by —by what? Certainly not by any human being: the windows were locked, and so were the doors.

Judith.

The dream began coming back in fractured, incoherent pieces. Something about an Overseer . . . and a picture frame. . . . And a door; a door figured prominently in it.

Jane went straight to the phone—which was still working, despite the power outage—and dialed Mac's number. "He's so s-smart," she said through chattering lips. "Let *h-him* figure it out."

A sleepy voice answered at the other end. By now the reaction had set in; Jane was shivering violently, unable to control the chattering. "I j-just wanted you to know that we were b-*both* wrong. I thought she didn't mean me any h-harm. F-f-fat chance. And as f-for *you*—wake up and s-smell the coffee, would you?"

She slammed the receiver down before Mac had a chance to say a word, then dragged herself back to the Empire sofa, where she wrapped herself in the blanket and prepared again to wait for dawn. It occurred to her that she should've done a better job explaining things to Mac. It just didn't occur to her how.

Why did I bother at all? she wondered morosely, pulling the blanket up under her chin in an effort to warm up. *He's no different from the rest of us: he sees what he wants to see.* And he did not want to see Judith.

She sat there shivering violently, wondering why it was she'd never read the instructions on the portable kerosene heater that was in the house when she arrived. A minute later she saw headlights flashing in the lane alongside. Almost before she could identify the truck as Mac's, she heard banging on the back door. She ran to open it and was pelted by the slashing torrent of rain that drove Mac inside into the darkness of her kitchen.

"What." His voice was taut, anxious, illogically angry.

He had a flashlight with him. He flipped it on and kept it trained on the floor to avoid blinding her. She saw his rain-spattered, beltless slacks, and his sweatshirt, but she could scarcely see his face. The scene was eerie—ghostly—and it set her off again.

"She's back. She's back. I thought she was gone but . . . first the ladder, now the fire. The ladder breaking, okay, that could've been an accident like Jeremy's gash, but the fire . . . the fire's different, Mac, she's angry with me—"

"Jane. *Stop*. Don't tell me about Judith. Tell me about the fire."

"Yes, yes, the fire, that's what I mean. She's not what I thought, Mac. She's no grieving lover, she's, she's demented, she wants me to fix this thing with Ben but what can I do, I can't dig her up and put her next to him, I don't even know where he's buried and it, I don't know, it's probably illegal . . . oh, God . . . oh, God. . . ."

She broke down into a series of bone-racking sobs, undone by the long and endless torment of her stay on Nantucket, unwilling and unable to hold herself together any longer simply out of pride.

Mac laid the flashlight on the counter, with its light facing the wall. Then he turned and gathered her into the rock-solid security of his arms and held her while she sobbed away some of the night's terror.

"Shhh . . . it's over now," he whispered into her hair. "All over . . . shhh. . . . Hey now. . . ."

Through it all she was piercingly aware of his warmth, his hand cradling her head close to him, his simple words of comfort, even the barely perceptible and still endearing scent of Old Spice. It seemed incredible to her that she was in the arms of the one man on earth she could not talk to for more than eleven seconds without coming to blows. And yet here he was, and here she was, and she felt absolutely, inviolably *safe*. No one—not even Judith—could touch her now. Not while she was in his arms.

He held her for what seemed like a passing lifetime, until her sobs calmed down and she was able to hear the storm outside over the storm within. She drew in a deep lungful of air and let it out in a long, shuddering sigh. "I'm better now," she said at last, but she lifted her head from the sanctuary of his breast with reluctance. "You must think I'm an awful jerk."

He didn't say yes, he didn't say no. But there was something in the way he let her go, some ever-so-slight hesitation on his part, that made her wonder whether he didn't need to protect her right now just as much as she needed his protection.

He brushed back a heavy lock of her hair that had fallen over her cheek and said in a husky voice, "I . . . ah . . . the fire . . . was in the library, it smells like. Let's take a look."

He took up the flashlight again and led the way for her, pausing to stand the stepladder back up as they passed out of the kitchen. The embers in the fireplace were out. Mac swept his light across the floor of the room, highlighting the sticky white mess of chemicals on Aunt Sylvia's fragile, worn-out Oriental rug. There were burns in the wood floor, too; those looked permanent.

"See?" Jane said, her voice unnaturally high and excited. "Look! Look at it!"

"Yes, I see it. That's why people use fire screens, Jane," Mac said gently as he closed the flue.

"Fire screens!" she said with a bitter laugh. "They're to protect against the odd ember, not a volcano!" She began shivering again, as if she knew there'd be a hard fight ahead to prove that Judith was behind this.

"The chimney hasn't been used in years," Mac said slowly, as if Jane had only a middling grasp of English. "Did you have a chimney sweep clean it out?"

"What am I, Mary P-Poppins? *No,* I didn't have a chimney sweep clean it out. Anyway, it worked fine at first."

"But the wind's been picking up all evening—listen to it, Jane. It's blowing a full gale." He tried again, with infinite, infuriating patience. "Do you know what a backdraft is?"

"This wasn't a backdraft, this was Judith." She nearly spat the word: *"Judith!"*

A thought occurred to her. "I can prove her to you! I have her on tape," she said, rushing to the camcorder.

There was, of course, no electricity to run it. Frustrated by the failure of everyone, including Mother Nature, to cooperate, Jane slammed her hand down on the machine. "Son of a bitch. Son of a *bitch,* son of a bitch."

Mac flashed the light briefly over her face and said, "Hey, hey, Miss Drew. That's no way for a lady to talk."

It was obvious that he was worried about her, despite his light tone. But she wanted him to admit it. "Why did you shine that light in my face, Mac?" she asked in a dangerously still voice. "Reality check?"

"Maybe," he said quietly.

"Do you think I'm hysterical?"

"Not clinically, no."

"You infuriating—give me that!" she said, snatching the flashlight from his hand. "Look at this sketch. *Look!*"

She flashed the light on Aunt Sylvia's charcoal drawing of the young Quaker woman—it was Judith, of course—who was pictured exactly as she'd appeared in Jane's dream. The same imploring pose, the same thick, dark hair. And the coal-skuttle bonnet on the floor beside her: It must have fallen from her lap when she went to answer Jabez Coffin's knock.

"That's Judith Brightman," Jane whispered, holding the beam of light unsteadily on the sketch. "She's just been set aside from the Society of Friends . . . and forbidden to enter the Burial Ground. . . . Jabez Coffin did this to her. My God. There's nothing I can do about it now . . . nothing."

She turned slowly to Mac in the darkness and flicked the light over his face. He winced, but whether because of the bright light or her state of mind, she could not say. "Do you believe me?"

"Can you think of a reason why I shouldn't?"

"Yes," she admitted sadly, letting the flashlight droop by her side. "You can point out to me that I had the dream *after* I'd studied the sketch. And you can add that a lot of what I know, I could have learned subliminally as I scanned through issues of the *Inquirer,* or from what you told me when we walked that day in the Burial Ground. But Mac—oh, please—believe me anyway," she whispered.

"Am I to believe your Aunt Sylvia as well?" he asked her gently.

"Aunt Sylvia? What has—oh. I see. She had to have had the same dream that I did, to be able to do that sketch." Jane laughed—a small, hopeless sound. "Boy. It's not looking too good for me, is it?"

She handed him back his flashlight as if she were handing over the scepter of command. "What do they call people like me? Delusional?" It was a measure of her respect for him that she assumed he would know precisely which psychotic category she belonged in.

"I'd call someone like you damned tired," he said gruffly. "You should be in bed."

"No!" she said in a panic, thinking of the videotape. "*She* might be there." She felt her cheeks glow with embarrassment; it all sounded so absurd. "I know I sound like a kid afraid of the dark, but—"

"I'd ask you to my place," Mac interrupted in a strained voice, "but somehow I don't think that's such a hot idea."

She had no idea what he meant by that, so she agreed with him politely. "N-no, of course not. I'd be fine, if only I knew how to use the kerosene heater. I could sleep right here."

Mac seemed relieved to shift the talk to things mechanical. Before long he'd located the old heater, verified that it was filled with kerosene and not something dumb like gasoline, cleaned the wick with his knife blade, and had a nice clean blue flame going. He showed Jane how to turn down the wick and blow it out if she needed to, and then it was time to go.

She thanked him profusely while she stood wrapped in the cocoon of her blanket, as close to the heater as she could get. She was thanking him all over again when the unmistakable smell of singed polyester reached her nose and Mac's at the same time. Mortified, she yanked the blanket off the heater.

"We're going to have to get you flameproof Dr. Denton's to sleep in," Mac said wryly. "Just how accident-prone are you?"

"Can you possibly think this is f-funny?" she snapped, beginning to shiver violently again. She'd had one too many near-misses in a row; she was becoming unraveled.

He didn't bother answering her question, but he said, "I'll sit with you awhile." It wasn't an offer, it wasn't a request. It was a simple statement of fact.

They sat down on the Empire sofa, with the blanket pulled loosely over Jane's lap. She was reminded of the practice of bundling, peculiar to old Nantucket, that allowed a male suitor, fully clothed, to climb into bed with the object of his affections, also fully clothed, so that they could court without wasting precious island firewood. A board placed lengthwise between the couple was supposed to keep things from getting too cozy.

Not that we'd need the damn board, she thought with a sigh. Mac's willpower amazed her. Any man—she thought of Bing—who found himself in the company of an attractive woman, in the dark, with no heat, would think he'd died and gone to heaven. That much she'd learned in her dealings with the opposite sex.

But not this man. In the dim light of the kerosene heater she could see Mac clearly, leaning back on the sofa, his hands locked behind his head, his long legs stretched out in front of him. He looked maddeningly relaxed. He wanted her to be at ease; she understood that. But he didn't have to be so good at it.

"I was wondering," she ventured, "how you manage to be so content to live alone. *I* thought the isolation was charming—at first. But look at me now. I'm a basket case."

He laughed softly and then added, "Who says I'm content to live alone?"

The question sent a kind of sweet chill of hope rippling through her. She said, "I guess it just looks that way to someone like me."

"Because I'm not living with someone, you mean?"

"Well, yes. That *has* to be by choice." She was as much as admitting he was irresistible.

"I suppose it's true that I'm not at the frantic stage yet," he said thoughtfully, oblivious to the compliment.

" 'Frantic.' I can't imagine you frantic," she said dryly.

He laughed out loud at that, the most good-natured, seductive sound she'd ever heard. "You think I'm too deliberate," he said. "Yeah . . . you're probably right," he said, leaning forward pensively, resting his arms on his thighs. "Chalk it up to my misspent youth. It's made me think twice before I act on some bright idea."

She wanted so much to ask him about that misspent youth, but now was not the time. Still, she took heart from the fact that they were at least talking comfortably to one another. In a strange way she thought that Judith deserved some of the credit, and she was grateful.

"I've been meaning to ask you," she said softly. "Did you know my Aunt Sylvia well?" She'd asked him once before, and he'd brushed aside the question with one of his evasions.

"Pretty well. I liked Sylvia," he said this time. "She was very much her own woman. Sharp as a tack, well informed . . . a CNN junkie, in fact. We didn't see eye to eye on politics, of course, especially local politics," he said, chuckling at the memory. "She wanted more laws, I wanted fewer."

"That sounds about right," Jane said, smiling. "I remember the day I first saw you," she added. *How could she possibly forget?* "It was at Aunt Sylvia's funeral, and it was pouring out."

"That was your mother with you, right? A striking woman; I'd recognize her again."

"I bet she'd be able to pick *you* out of a li—a crowd—too."

She went back to the subject of the funeral. "You tossed a tiny red rose in Aunt Sylvia's grave."

"Yeah. Before she moved into the home off-island, she gave me Wicky to take care of, and also a miniature rose she'd bought for herself years earlier. I asked her why she wasn't taking the rose to the nursing home. She told me it'd be pointless. I've wondered what she meant by that; everyone else there had a plant in his room."

"You were there?"

"Of course," he said, surprised that she would ask. "I'd go whenever I got off the island—which as you know isn't very often."

Jane *did* know. Lately she'd been locked onto the comings and goings of his truck like a radar scope; but of course she couldn't tell him that.

"She never told me about you."

"She never told me about *you.*"

"She was good at keeping secrets," Jane said, thinking of the sketch on the wall. "She never said a word about Phillip either, even though Phillip told me they were great friends."

"Phillip lied."

Mac said it with such finality; for a moment Jane almost believed him, even though it made no sense.

"Why would Phillip lie about his friendship with my aunt?"

"He wants to buy your place."

"Mac! I've already *told* you—"

"Let me rephrase that. He wants to buy *my* place. But first he has to get his hands on your place. That'll tighten the noose around my neck nicely."

His mood was turning black, as it always did when the

subject of Phillip Harrow came up. Mac's grudge ran deep, and Jane couldn't blame him; there was bad blood between the two men. But it would be so much better if Mac could put it behind him instead of letting it affect his judgment this way.

She tried to draw him away from his anger. "If Phillip really wanted your property, surely he'd go after Bing's place first. But we know from Cissy—"

"Damn Cissy!" Mac said angrily, jumping up from the sofa. "What does a little peanut like Cissy know about anything? *Look.* Phillip got Bing to grant him first refusal on his property, all right?" he said bitterly. "Now you know."

He balled his right hand into a fist and punched it into his left palm. *"And I have to live with that knowledge every goddamned day of my life."*

Slowly it began to dawn on her. "So if Bing decides to sell his property, he has to offer it first to Phillip. And if Phillip buys the place—"

"I'm at his mercy," Mac said in a grim voice. "I may have to get in and out by helicopter."

The image was all too plausibly clear. If Mac was right, he was in a horrible position. His beloved homestead and two hundred years of family history would be completely in the control of his worst enemy.

If Phillip was as hostile as Mac said he was. And *if* Phillip really did have first refusal. "Are you absolutely sure Bing and Phillip have an arrangement?" she asked.

Mac was staring out the window at the storm, which seemed at last to be abating. "I can't swear to it, no. Once I forced myself to ask Bing outright about it. His answer? 'I'd rather not say, but you have nothing to worry about, old boy.' "

She saw that it must have cost him dearly to ask Bing. As for Bing's refusing to charge him for the right to traipse back and forth across his land—she knew already that Mac considered it an act of charity and resented it as such. And yet, what were his options? He couldn't afford to buy Bing out, and even if he could, he'd have to get in line behind Phillip.

She threw off her blanket and went over to him. She wanted to comfort him. She wanted to put her arms around him as he had around her, and say, "The hell with 'em. You'll work it out." But there was something about the set of his back that made her murmur lamely, "Still and all, you aren't *positive* that Bing granted Phillip first refusal."

Mac stiffened, if possible, still further. "Ah, yes—the communication thing," he said caustically. "I forgot I don't speak or understand English."

"Dammit, you *know* that's not what I mean," she said, dismayed that they were sliding down that slippery slope again.

He spun around angrily. "Maybe. But I know god-damned well what Phillip Harrow means," he growled. *"The son of a bitch means to have my land."*

He's paranoid, Jane decided. *In his own way he's more deluded than I am. He has no hard facts, nothing, only a gut hatred for Phillip Harrow.*

"Hey, hey, Mr. McKenzie," she said, trying to mimic his earlier tone. "That's no way for a gentleman to talk."

He grabbed her by her arms. "But isn't it what you expect from me? Good vulgar, savage behavior?" He yanked her toward his chest; his breath fell hot on her cheek. She hadn't seen it coming, was overwhelmed by the raw, sexual power in him, left breathless by the force with which he held her against his broad, hard body.

She didn't know what to say. She should be angry—she *was* angry—but somehow it wasn't working out that way. Somehow her lips were parting, her eyelids lowering, in anticipation of his kiss. Somehow her breath was on hold and all her nerve endings on tiptoe, waiting.

He held her pinned to him as they stood in the dark, their lips half a breath away from one another.

"God."

The single syllable was wrenched from him with obvious pain; she knew he would not yield another.

He released her, then turned on his heel and walked out, leaving her to wonder which of them was more tormented in his own particular hell.

If it weren't for the strange, swishing sound, Jane might have slept around the clock. But the noise was subtle and different, more distracting than a jackhammer. It wasn't Billy; he had a small job to do for his mother this morning. It wasn't squirrels in the attic; by now Jane knew exactly what squirrels in attics sounded like. She thought it might be bats—she'd had two or three of those up there, too—but no, it wasn't bats.

She got out of bed, the bed she'd crawled into just after dawn, and began tracing the sound: it seemed to come from between the walls. Sleepy but curious, she put on jeans and a heavy sweater and raked the tangles from her hair with her fingers, then made her way down the stairs. She caught a glimpse of herself in the hall mirror: *oh well.*

She forced herself to go into the fireplace room, where the mess on the rug came as a brutal reminder of the night before. The smell of burnt wool was unmistakable. She threw open the windows to air the place out. The sound was definitely louder in that room; it was coming from inside the chimney. Puzzled, Jane went outside. Perched on top of her roof like a large crow was a man dressed all in black and wearing a soft peaked hat—obviously a chimney sweep. He had his broom and he had his vacuum, and apparently he had his orders.

"Hey, you up there!" she called, cupping her hands around her mouth. "What're you doing in my chimney?"

"Heard you had some problems, and lady, I can see

why," the fellow yelled down. "You have enough birds' nests in here to start your own aviary."

"Who—?" But it was obvious who. For an aloof neighbor who hated anyone butting into his own business, Mac McKenzie seemed to have very few compunctions about butting into hers.

"Could the nests have caused a bad backdraft?"

"Sure could," he yelled down.

Ha, she thought. What did *he* know?

"How much is this going to cost me?" she yelled, on her guard.

"Don't worry about it; Mac and I worked something out."

Worked something out. She shook her head and began walking back to the house. Didn't *any*one use American currency on this island? And what the hell was Mac up to, anyway? She was getting deeper and deeper in his debt. The only bill she'd ever got from him was for moving the holly up and down, and she'd had to beg for that. And he hadn't cashed her check anyway. Since then he'd mowed and cleared her grass when she was in town; thrown her trash in the back of his pickup for carting off to the dump; and hauled away a massive limb that had been lying behind the house probably for years.

And every time, he had an excuse for refusing payment. Either he happened to have the riding mower out anyway, or he was headed for the dump anyway, or he could really use the firewood anyway—he was an expert at maintaining the upper hand over her. It had to stop. She would've loved to have been on equal terms with him, to give and to take as friends and neighbors do. But this give, give, give on his part . . . it was a form of rebuffing her, of keeping her at arm's length.

Of course, there are some who'd say I was being a little weird about this, she decided with a rueful smile. And anyway, was he really trying to keep her at arm's length? Last night . . . *last night.* . . .

Two loud beeps of a horn sent Jane jumping out of her reverie. She turned to see a car she didn't recognize pull into the drive. It was Mrs. Adamont's; she was delivering Gwendolyn Drew to Lilac Cottage, four days early.

Mrs. Adamont rolled down her window and greeted Jane. "I was just getting off work at the A&P when I overheard Mrs. Drew directing a cab to your place. 'Well, why should she pay good money?' I said to myself. So here you are. Cheerio, Jane. I'll see you Saturday night."

She and Jane's mother exchanged good-bye pleasantries and then the elderly woman backed her Dodge out of the drive, leaving Jane standing there in a state that best could be described as psychologically naked. Jane always liked to have some warning before her mother's arrivals so that she could put on the best linens and set out flowers in the guest room, lay in some decent wine and good cheese, clean up the place, clean up her self, and have something from the *New York Times* nonfiction bestseller list sitting on the coffee table.

She wasn't ready—she'd never be ready—for a visit from her mother.

CHAPTER 18

"Mother! What a surprise this is!"

"Darling, what a mess you are!" Gwendolyn said, brushing her daughter's cheek with her lips. "Your hair has grown absolutely wild."

"I've been awfully busy," Jane said, rearranging the tangles.

Her mother added, "And your nails!"

"Mother, I'm rehabbing a house, not writing poetry," Jane said testily. "It's very physical work."

"The only thing that needs rehabbing around here is you, dear heart," said her mother, squeezing her affectionately as they walked back toward the cottage. "How've you been? I've missed your calls."

Jane took her suitcase and said, "I'm sorry I haven't done more. But this whole Nantucket thing has turned very . . . well . . . intense. *You* look wonderful, Mother," Jane added, and it was true: as usual, not a hair was out of place. "What brings you to Nantucket early?"

Her mother caught the gentle reproach. "I should've called you, I know, when I found myself in New York. But I didn't want you fussing at the last minute; no notice seemed better than short notice."

Jane laughed at her mother's whimsical logic. "Why were you in New York?"

"Another funeral. Do you remember Earl Simton? We used to belong to the same club. He keeled over; just like that. Your father is devastated. After all, Earl was five years younger than he is."

"I'm sorry to hear that. Where's Dad now?"

"He's determined not to waste the trip East; he's lined up meetings right through the weekend."

"Oh. So he won't be coming to Nantucket, of course," Jane said, trying not to sound as if it mattered.

A look of sudden sympathy crossed her mother's face. "Oh, sweetheart, you know he would if he could. But he's been so busy; the company's restructuring—"

"Sure. I understand. Well, anyway—close your eyes," Jane said, wanting to get off the subject. She flung open the relocated but not yet repainted front door and led her mother into the house by the hand. Gwendolyn Drew opened her eyes. A look of surprised delight washed over her face, the look a mother has when her daughter gets all her lines right in her first school play.

"Jane! It's wonderful!"

Her mother walked slowly around the room, soaking up its light and airy presence. Jane wanted the look of a Victorian conservatory, and she had succeeded. Bright tulips in vases set off the bird-of-paradise pattern on the ivory wallpaper, lending them their own real fragrance. Old but solid wicker furniture that Jane had tracked down through an *Inquirer* ad and sprayed deep green looked as if it had been there from the start. Jane had sewn cushion covers in complementary colors, then added a big rag rug and potted palms to tie it all together. The room wasn't finished yet— the long, sparkling clean windows were unadorned—but it was on its way.

"I didn't mean to buy any furnishings, but once I got the wicker so cheap—well, one thing led to another. I just thought the place might sell better if it looked lived in," Jane said guiltily. And then she thought, *Why am I apologizing?*

"I must say, this is nothing like your Connecticut condo," Gwendolyn mused, looking at her daughter curiously.

"*I'm* nothing like my Connecticut condo—not anymore. I can't imagine living in that chic, stark . . . box. I'm not a study in trendy off-whites anymore, Mother. I want a little more softness in my life; I want a little more charm."

"You're being too hard on the condo, I think. It was elegant, sophisticated, and yes, it did suggest a woman on the way up. Does this new look have something to do with your abandoning your career?" her mother asked shrewdly.

"I haven't abandoned my career," Jane said, irritated. "My career has abandoned me. Anyway, I *will* be going back into advertising—but it'll be on my own terms. Once I've sold Lilac Cottage, I'll have the money to finance my own agency. I've explained all that."

"And yet you don't seem in any particular hurry," Gwendolyn couldn't help remarking. She trailed a manicured nail across a pillow of polished sea cotton. "Sewing cushion covers?"

"Okay, okay, I got a little distracted there," Jane admitted. "But I almost can't help myself. I haven't enjoyed anything this much since my watercolor classes at RISD. Maybe Bing is right; maybe I ought to go into interior design," she said on their way to the kitchen.

"Bing? The man next door? Will I be meeting this Bing?"

"Probably," Jane said vaguely. She wasn't ready to get into Bing with her mother, not until she'd sorted out her own mixed feelings about him. "He'll be back on the island Friday or early Saturday."

"Good. Oh! Darling, *what* a difference!" her mother said as they entered the sun-drenched kitchen. "It's the same, and yet it's not the same at all. Really. How very nice. The only misstep that I can see," she said, "is keeping that old porcelain sink. You'll never sell the place without a dishwasher and twin basins."

"Maybe; but I enjoy washing dishes in the same sink that

Aunt Sylvia used. It gives me a sense of—I don't know—
continuity."

Gwendolyn laughed and said, "Well, you haven't had
much of *that.* Many sinks ago I thought your father and I
might actually live our lives in Delaware; that was before
you were born. We had a nice old house with an apple tree
and lots of land. We were so young then, and life was so
. . . simple," she said wistfully. "*But,* that was then and
this is now. So," she said, shaking off the memory, "what
did you do to the bathroom?"

They surveyed the white-on-white bathroom, which was
unchanged except for paint and bright towels, and then
moved on to the scene of last night's traumas. The room
clearly was not at its best. The tired old wallpaper and
dark, eccentric furnishings—and the gooey mess on the rug
—were a shocking contrast to the pristine airiness of the
rest of the downstairs.

"Jane! You haven't touched this room!" her mother
said, surprised. She walked around it slowly, pausing at the
mess for an explanation.

"A little chimney flare-up, that's all," Jane mumbled. "I
should've used a screen."

Gwendolyn spied the tarot cards still arranged on the
little gaming table exactly as she and Jane had seen them
the day of the funeral. She went up to the table and said,
"My God. You haven't changed a thing, have you? You've
turned this room into a . . . a shrine."

"Really, Mother, you make me sound like Miss Haver-
sham. I just haven't . . . got around to it yet."

Jane was still convinced that the tarot cards held some
kind of clue to Judith's dilemma. With a little more time
and a little more study, she might be able to break the
code.

"This isn't right, Jane," her mother said, upset. "This
really isn't." To Jane's horror, she scooped up the cards

and dropped the deck into her handbag. "Sylvia's dead, and what she was or wasn't isn't your concern."

"*Mother!*" Jane cried, appalled. "I'm not eight years old this time! I'm an adult, and what I do or don't do isn't *your* concern!"

Gwendolyn Drew looked as if she'd been slapped across the face. Her high, fine cheekbones flushed a bright pink as she lifted her chin in a gesture Jane knew well. Her mother adjusted the designer scarf she wore around her shoulders a fraction of a millimeter, and waited. Whether she was counting to ten or expecting an apology, Jane had no idea. But Gwendolyn Drew had crossed a line, and Jane had to let her know it.

After a brief eternity, her mother dropped her imperious gaze. Her face, so exquisitely made up, became older and troubled; it became every mother's face. The look in her eyes, so blue, so bright, said, *This is how you treat your mother?*

Jane held her ground.

Finally Gwendolyn reached into her handbag, pulled out the tarot cards, and handed them over to her daughter. "You're right," she said with a sigh. "You're *not* eight years old anymore, and there's not a damn thing I can do about it." Her smile was stiff and rueful and something else: resigned. She had begun, at last, to let go.

Jane dropped the deck of tarot cards on the mantel and said, "Let me show you to your room. Then I'll shower, and I'll take you out to lunch."

"No, I'll take *you*—"

"Mother."

Gwendolyn sighed and said, "All right; why not? I've brought a check from your father for the Volvo. You're rich. For now."

When they got back, Billy B. was in the kitchen, having a good laugh with the chimney sweep. Jane didn't need her master's degree to know that she was the butt of their good humor; presumably the most simple-minded islander knew to look up his chimney once in a while.

Still, Billy took full responsibility for the incident. "I shoulda warned you," he insisted after introductions were made. "After all, you're new to owning a real home. Anyway, I cleaned it all up, no charge. I'll be able to sand most of the scorch marks out when we finally do that room. Well, back to the salt mines." He went outside to work on the new front steps.

The chimney sweep took off, leaving Jane with her mother and three more days in which to amuse her. They'd already walked around town after lunch, and together they'd admired the historic houses on Main Street, and poked into two or three antique shops along the way.

"That's pretty much *it* for things to do," Jane warned her mother as she brewed them a pot of tea. "Daffodil Weekend is over, and the first yachting event isn't until the end of May. It gets pretty quiet," she added, hoping her mother would suffer culture withdrawal and head back to the Big Apple. The thought that she might be in the house during a Judith episode struck terror in Jane's heart. "It's really quite boring," Jane repeated.

"Funny," her mother said. "You don't look bored. You look the opposite, in fact; almost harried. Are you all right?"

That was another point about mothers; they noticed every little thing.

"Maybe I've just been inside too much," Jane said quickly. "After tea I'll show you around the house. Aunt Sylvia has stuff growing everywhere. You've missed the crocuses and glory-in-the-snow, but the heath and groundcovers have come into their own."

Jane guided the talk toward safe things like color schemes and poor old Buster, who had no idea who his owner was anymore, and afterward the two women changed into outdoor clothes and stepped over Billy and his new stairs into a cool spring evening.

"Feels like we'll have fog tonight," Jane remarked, zipping up her jacket.

Her mother laughed and accused her of sniffing the air like a farmer, and Jane flushed. They walked out toward the property's boundary and inevitably they found themselves at the small, forgotten burying ground. Jane tried to steer her mother away, but Gwendolyn would not be budged.

"I love these old gravesites," she said, bending over to read the weathered stones in the slanting light. "Have you taken any rubbings? It'd be nice to bring a memento of the place with you when you leave the island."

"Somehow I haven't felt the need," Jane said without irony.

"And look at this one with the broken stone—how neatly tended it is," Gwendolyn said, stooping down for a closer look.

" 'Judith' something, born 1802. I suppose she's someone's relative. Still, it's surprising that anyone still cares, after nearly two centuries."

"Just because she's dead doesn't mean she's gone," Jane said laconically. "Why shouldn't someone care?"

As she phrased the question, Jane realized that she did care, and deeply, about this tormented woman. Despite the fear, despite the agony, she felt a deep connection with Judith, just as she felt a connection with her Aunt Sylvia. *We're all women, and we all want to love and be loved, and not one of us has been able to get it right.* On one level it was as simple as that.

Her mother, crouching at the gravestone, gave Jane another thoughtful, troubled look. At the same time, Jane heard the sound of Mac's pickup in the lane behind her. She turned, her heart bounding at her ribcage, in time to see him slam on his brakes. They exchanged a look as intense, as burning, as unresolved as silent speech could be, and then Mac spotted Gwendolyn Drew and immediately threw the pickup into gear. He roared off just as Jane's mother came up alongside her.

"Him," Gwendolyn said, her voice low with apprehension. "Has he been bothering you?"

Jane laughed weakly. She'd done everything to get Mac McKenzie's attention except maybe the dance of the seven veils. "No, Mother, he hasn't been bothering me. I don't think I'm his type."

"I'm glad to hear it. The last thing you need is someone like that—well, you know."

"No, Mother. I *don't* know." Her mother's well-intentioned snobbery suddenly had become insufferable.

They walked in strained silence in the direction of Phillip's house and came to the little wooden footbridge over the narrow gully, now swollen from recent rains, that ran through his property. Gwendolyn balked at using the footbridge; she would not follow her daughter over it.

"Come on! It's old but it's solid," said Jane, surprised by her mother's timidity. "And the water's not exactly deep," she added with good-natured irony. "Maybe six inches."

"It's not drowning I'm afraid of; it's my ankle going through one of the boards and breaking. Anyway, it's getting damp and cold; can we go back?"

"Sure," said Jane, not all that surprised. Her mother was an indoor plant, not a wildflower. August on Nantucket would be rough enough for her. "We can build a fire in my nice clean fireplace," Jane promised.

When they got back, there was a note on the table from Billy, who'd left for the day.

> *Mac came by for the tape in your camcorder. He said you wanted him to see it. And if you want to bring some kind of noodle thing, that's okay with him.*

"What tape?" her mother asked, glancing at the note over Jane's shoulder. "And what noodle thing? I thought you said he wasn't interested in you."

"The tape is just some old . . . tape," Jane answered inadequately. "And the noodle dish must be for Uncle Easy's potluck birthday on Saturday. Half the island will be there; it's not exactly an intimate dinner for two. And even if it *were*," she added acidly, "I thought you and I had reached an agreement."

"Yes. I suppose we have," her mother agreed through compressed lips.

That evening, despite the damp and penetrating fog, Jane and her mother sat without a fire and read in the wicker chairs in the newly decorated front room. Her mother seemed to have an aversion for the fireplace room, as if the spirit of Sylvia Merchant was too much in it. Still, the arrangement had an advantage: the only phone was in the fireplace room, and Jane could use it privately there.

With heart hammering, she dialed Mac's number. For the last hour she'd been staring at the same damn novel she couldn't finish the night before, turning the pages for her mother's benefit while she relived every second of her time with Mac McKenzie. This man had held her, calmed her, caressed her; had kept her literally from falling apart. Step by step he'd led her out of one hell—and step by step, he'd led her straight into another.

Things used to be so simple between them. Mac hated everything Jane stood for, and Jane couldn't stand Mac's obstinate ways. He was here for the long haul; she was strictly hit-and-run. He said noodles; she said pasta. But now he seemed not to despise her anymore, and she seemed not to want to take the money and run anymore. It was all incredibly muddled.

And, he was willing to take a look at the videotape, which astonished her.

He answered his phone and she said stiffly, "Is this a bad time?"

His laugh was tense. "I've had better."

The remark meant nothing, of course, and yet Jane felt her cheeks begin to flame. It was never *what* he said; it was always *how* he said it.

"I wanted to let you know that I have an unexpected house guest," she said, "so I won't be able to come on Saturday after all. You probably noticed that my mother is here."

"It'd be hard to miss the daggers that went whizzing through my truck window this afternoon."

"You're wrong about her," Jane lied, "just as you're wrong about me."

"Is that so? Hell, then bring 'er along," he taunted. "The more the merrier."

"Oh, well, I wouldn't want to . . . although it's kind of you to . . . all right. I will. Mother would be delighted. Thanks *soo* much for asking," Jane said, furious with his ability to throw ice water on whatever warmth of feelings she had for him. "I'll bring lasagna."

"Fine. You never asked about the tape."

"I nearly forgot," she said breezily. "What did you think?"

"It's nothing. I know what you *think* is on the tape; I even know where you think it is. But it's nothing."

"It's her. You know it and I know it. Last night you had me convinced I was wrong. But in the clear light of day, thinking of what I know and when I knew it—it's her, Mac."

They said good-bye with more sadness than anything else. Jane was about to force-feed Mac's invitation to her mother when the phone rang. It was Bing, in the city. He didn't start out with his usual charming banter; his voice was nearly as tense as Mac's had been.

"I've been trying to reach Cissy," Bing said without preamble. "Any sign of her?"

"I saw her car tucked behind Phillip's house when I was out walking earlier; she must be holed up over there. What's wrong?"

"It's Dave again. He was over here a little while ago, telling me he'd sworn off alcohol and insisting that I intercede for him. Eventually I tried to nudge him to the door; it turned into a shoving match. Maybe I should've brought charges, but I didn't. Now I'm wondering from something Dave said whether he might be on his way to Nantucket."

"You want me to walk over and warn her?"

"We're not supposed to know she's there, remember? I'd rather you kept an eye out for Dave. Big guy, tacky dresser, black hair—you can't miss him. If he shows up, let me know."

"Bing—what did he say that makes you think he's on his way?"

Bing hesitated. "He said, 'She may be getting it from someone else, but the bitch is still my wife.' "

Jane winced and said, "I'll watch for him."

She hung up and rejoined her mother, who looked up from her book and said, "Was it something serious?"

Jane forced a carefree laugh. "On Nantucket? Never. That was Mac again; we were comparing lasagna recipes, that's all. Which brings me to an interesting proposal. . . ."

CHAPTER **19**

U ncle Easy's party was nothing like the ones Jane had ever thrown. Jane's parties were like her parents' parties: she invited people who shared similar backgrounds, tastes, and career levels, then sat back as they all had a predictably pleasant time.

Uncle Easy's party, on the other hand, was closer to social anarchy. The variety of cars parked all around Mac's grounds was amazing—everything from a Mercedes to a battered VW bug. The old house itself seemed energized. Maybe it was the hand-lettered bedsheets proclaiming, "Easy's Eighty!" and "Eighty's Easy!" Or the exuberant balloons (mixed colors, no theme) and tulips (mixed colors, no theme) that marked the way to the back door. Whatever the reason, the McKenzie homestead looked alive and kicking and ready for just about anything.

Jane's mother, dressed with casual elegance in pale blue, stepped out of the Volvo and, ignoring the balloons and flowers by the back door, began walking around to the front.

"That's the company door, Mother," Jane said, tugging her back with her free arm.

"Aren't we company?" her mother asked with a bland expression.

"Maybe; but I'd rather be family." The words were out before Jane knew it. But it was true. She was so deathly tired of being treated like a temporary resident; all she wanted was to be part of things.

They went through the little wart and knocked and

waited at the diamond-paned door. Jane was beginning to
wonder whether there was some secret password; but eventually someone noticed them and waved them in. She and
her mother stepped inside to a scene of good-natured
chaos, with potluck dishes being passed and stored and
heated and covered and uncovered and assembled and re-
frigerated, all without an apparent system. There was, after
all, no woman of the house.

Still, Mrs. Adamont wasn't a bad pinch hitter. She was
there, twinkle-eyed and in her element, to take Jane's pan
of lasagna from her and put it somewhere logical. Mrs.
Adamont was the only one who seemed to know intuitively
where the potlids, big spoons, and wine openers were. She
gave Gwendolyn Drew a cheerful "how-do-you-do-again";
handed their gift to a couple of kids to put on the gift table
in the keeping room; advised Jane with a wink that Mac
and Billy were moving the beer tub out of the kitchen and
into the keeping room; and greeted the next incoming
guests, all without missing a beat.

Jane and her mother made their way through the crush,
looking for the guest of honor, introducing themselves as
they went. It hardly seemed necessary; just about everyone
knew who they were.

Uncle Easy's younger cousin Doris sure did. She button-
holed Jane's mother and said, "Look around. Now this is
how it's *supposed* to be. That boy has never once had us
over, not since his wedding reception. First the excuse was,
she was too busy fixing up the place. Then the excuse
was, she was gone and who'd do the cooking? And you
know, she never *did* like this house; it was set too far back
from the road for showing off. But don't it look nice? Too
bad it didn't work out."

Gwendolyn agreed completely, even with the parts she
didn't understand, and she and her daughter moved on.

They bumped into the two elderly sisters from the back
row at Aunt Sylvia's wake. "We think it's so much better,"

the sisters said pleasantly, "to tell someone what you think of him *before* he's six feet under. Have you tried our cucumber sandwiches?"

Dorothy Crate was there, too, looking down her long, aquiline nose. "Mother couldn't be here today. She isn't well, despite the fine weather we're having. It was so kind of Mac to ask us to Mr. Zingg's party. Such a . . . surprise."

And Jane finally got to meet Billy's wife, Carol, complete with a fat and pretty Sarah in a pink baby sling. "Boy, am I glad you gave Billy the work," Carol said, shaking Jane's hand warmly. "We were two months behind in the rent . . . my folks were all tapped out. . . . I didn't know what we were gonna do. Doesn't Bill do fine work, though? I hope you'll pass his name around. Maybe it'll make up for the car the dope took."

Jane's mother smiled when she was supposed to, and nodded when she had to, and generally was the gracious trooper she'd always been. But it was obvious that she was looking for the man next door, and the man next door hadn't yet arrived.

Jane was surprised to see that Mac's son Jerry was there, playing Nintendo with what were apparently a couple of his Nantucket cousins. But she was even more surprised—shocked, really—to see that Jerry's mother was at the party. Celeste McKenzie was standing at the mantel, a little preoccupied and aloof, although her smile was friendly enough for anyone who stopped to chat.

God, she's a knockout, Jane realized anew. In her subtly textured sweater and her beautifully tailored skirt, Celeste was definitely in the running for best dressed. Jane herself had worn a soft, simple white blouse and a denim skirt because she knew the company would be mostly casual. Now she regretted it.

"Who is *that*?" her mother murmured into her ear.

"That's Celeste McKenzie, Mac's ex. She's a Boston attorney."

"And looks it. My *goodness*. She married our host? Where *is* our host?"

Their host was apparently done with his hosting and moving like a steam locomotive across the room to be with Celeste. Jane watched with dismay as Mac, oblivious to the merrymaking, fell into an intense discussion with his ex-wife.

"I thought you said he didn't talk much," her mother remarked.

"I guess he does, when he has something to say."

He doesn't see anyone else in the room, Jane realized with a sinking heart. *And that definitely includes me.* So she'd been wrong, after all, to think she'd seen nuances. Actions spoke louder than nuances—and so far, she herself had seen precious little action from this guy.

She watched mesmerized as Celeste suddenly flushed and dropped her voice and looked away. Mac seemed to be pleading with her, trying to force her around to his way of thinking. Whatever it was he was selling, she wasn't buying.

It could be about something as routine as whether Jerry can take karate lessons, or who gets all that Calphalon in the kitchen, Jane insisted to herself.

"Jane, for goodness' sake. You're staring."

I'm jealous. God help me, I'm jealous of her. Jane blinked, trying to break out of the spell she was in. "I am not staring," she lied. "I was just trying to remember if I turned off the oven. Yes. I'm pretty sure I did. Ah, there he is—the guest of honor himself, interrupting the McKenzies."

"Shall we wish him many happy returns?" Gwendolyn asked politely.

They went up to the trio and Jane introduced her mother first to Uncle Easy, and then, with a certain amount of dread, to Celeste McKenzie. Almost as an after-thought she remembered that her mother had never met Mac.

Uncle Easy pumped Gwendolyn Drew's hand and said gallantly, "So you're the visiting mum. You're even better looking than they say—and the reports have been pretty good." And then he winked.

Celeste McKenzie said wearily, "Uncle Easy—behave yourself."

Mac's look was droll. He, too, shook Gwendolyn's hand. "Welcome to Nantucket," he said to her, giving Jane the briefest of glances. "I trust you're enjoying your brief so-journ."

He was using that snotty, yacht-club tone Jane knew so well.

Celeste knew it, too. She gave her ex-husband a look that blew the chip right off his shoulder. "No one loves Nantucket as much as Mac does," she explained to Jane's mother, "and he won't forgive us for being so unfeeling."

Celeste turned her attention to Jane. She gave no hint that Jane had been there for the bitter confrontation be-tween Mac and her. "So you've inherited Sylvia's old place. Tell me what you've done with it so far," Celeste said, slip-ping her arm through Jane's and leading her over near a table filled with chips and dips.

Uncle Easy took off again, leaving Jane's mother—oh, boy—with Mac. Jane kept an eye on the pair while she rattled on to Celeste about Lilac Cottage. She couldn't imagine what the two of them could be talking about.

"We still have to paint the outside," Jane finished up. "We're waiting for warm weather, but spring is dragging its feet."

"Spring *always* drags its feet on Nantucket. It sounds as if you've been working hard. You should be careful, Jane," Celeste added with a pained look at her ex-husband. "Re-doing a house is a great way to destroy a relationship."

It was candid advice; Jane wondered why Celeste hadn't taken it herself.

"I'm not getting into renovations all that deeply. And besides," Jane added with a self-conscious glance at Mac, "I don't have a relationship *to* destroy."

"Don't you?" Celeste took a sip from her wine. "It doesn't look that way to me."

Mac was trying not to look their way and not succeeding. And in the meantime Jane's mother was tracking who was looking at whom and just how longingly. *Well, good,* Jane thought, suddenly tired of it all. *Maybe she can tell me later what the heck was going on here.*

She was about to say something noncommittal when Celeste interrupted her. "I'm glad we had this chance to meet again. When I was here last . . ." She laughed softly. "When I was here last I put on quite a show. I've had time to think over the way I deal with Jeremy, and I guess Mac is right. Partly. Do you have kids?"

Jane shook her head and Celeste continued. "Then you don't know the pressures on a single mother." She rubbed a red-tipped finger across her sculpted eyebrow as if she were struggling to understand those pressures herself.

"It's—I don't know—you want to give the child everything, *everything,* to make up for what you've done to his world. You want him never to feel any pain, of any kind, ever again."

Even as she smiled apologetically, Celeste was searching out her son. When she found him, still huddled with his friends in front of the TV screen, a look both tender and fierce came over her.

She said, "So that's why you run the risk of taking a perfectly normal ten-year-old and turning him into what Mac would call a sissy. It's not a case of too much love, as Mac thinks it is. It's a case of too much guilt."

"Celeste, you don't owe me an explanation," Jane said,

embarrassed. "That was a rough afternoon for everyone. Words were bound to be said that—"

"Oh, but I *wanted* to explain. I'm an attorney; I know that every situation has two sides. I wanted you to hear mine," she said simply. "Whups, I think you're being paged."

Jane looked up to see Cissy across the room, frantically waving the back of her hand at her and pointing to a ring on it. Bing was with her, looking bemused by his sister's manic behavior. Instantly Jane felt less tense. Bing was a warm bath, a box of chocolates, and a good book, all rolled into one relaxed and easygoing smile.

Celeste excused herself as Cissy rushed ahead of her brother and flashed a sapphire in front of Jane, saying, "See? I *told* you he loved me!"

"Cissy! Does this mean you're engaged?" Jane asked, amazed that Phillip had made the commitment.

Cissy looked crestfallen. "Who said anything about being engaged?"

"Well, *that* was dumb of me," Jane said, trying to laugh it off. "So it's a friendship ring?"

"Those are for preteens!" Cissy said indignantly. "No, this is a ring that . . . expresses . . . a depth . . . well, I'm not sure exactly how Phillip worded it, but it means he really loves me."

Bing, who'd caught up to his sister by now, paused behind her and rolled his eyes. He slipped an arm around Jane's waist and dropped a light kiss on her lips. "Missed you, damn you," he murmured, brushing his lips against the lobe of her ear. It was a first, public display of his feelings for Jane, and she had to admit to feeling a thrill.

Aloud, Bing said to Cissy, "So we can assume that Phillip is finally coming out of the closet about you?"

"Yes you can!" Cissy said triumphantly. "Probably. He never really said. But—yes!"

"Will he be here later?" Jane asked innocently as Bing went off in search of wine.

The sunny expression on Cissy's pretty face clouded over. "I don't think Mac even invited him. Phillip never said a thing about coming, and I was afraid to ask. I think it's really crummy of Mac. Look at this place; the whole island is squeezed in here. What is Mac's problem, anyway?"

Jane just shook her head. "I was getting worried about you," she said, thinking of Bing's warning about Dave. "You just dropped out of sight. What do you *do* all day over there?" Obviously Phillip didn't hole up with her; Jane had seen his Mercedes periodically come and go.

Cissy went all dreamy-eyed. "Oh . . . I don't know . . . I play music . . . think about him . . . look at magazines . . . watch TV . . . wait."

"A prisoner of love?" Jane said it in the kindest possible way, but the truth was, she thought Cissy was insane. The girl was putting her whole life on hold, while some man tried to make up his mind what to do with her.

"Yeah . . . you could say that," Cissy admitted with a slow, sensuous smile.

Bing returned, juggling three plastic glasses, and they talked about what a great house Mac had. To Cissy it was just another perfectly restored piece of Nantucket history; she wandered off in search of more interesting topics. When she was out of earshot, Bing said to Jane in a low voice, "No sign of Dave, I take it?"

"None, and I watched your place like a hawk."

Bing frowned and said, "I told her about him; do you think she cares? This morning I caught a glimpse of a white Trans Am driving past; I couldn't see if it had a New York plate. *Dave* has a white something-or-other."

"It's a pretty common car," Jane said. She was thinking, *God. Another paranoic. There must be something in the water.*

"All Cissy can think of is that she got a ring today. She can't seem to remember that it's also the anniversary of her wedding to Dave," Bing said, scowling.

"Ah." That could complicate things.

"Jane?"

Jane turned to see her mother waiting to be introduced to "her Bing." She made the introductions and Bing, courteous to a fault, asked whether Gwendolyn would like a glass of wine. She said yes, Bing went off again, and Jane said, "Well, what do you think?"

"I think he's an amazingly attractive man, and he has excellent manners," Jane's mother replied, delighted.

"I mean, about *Mac.*"

"He impressed me as a man with a lot of anger," Gwendolyn said thoughtfully. "That's all very well when you're young or an artist—but he's at least forty and runs a business."

"I take it you two didn't hit it off, then."

"We didn't *not* hit it off. I would never give him the satisfaction. Anyway, he likes Bach and so do I. There was some common ground."

Jane sized up her mother with her short, perfect hair, her clear, untroubled gaze, and her cool and articulate manner, and thought: *No* way *is there common ground*.

She was scanning the room for Mac, who had disappeared again, when she saw Jeremy coming up for air from Nintendo. Their eyes met; the boy looked pleased to see her. He flashed her a V-for-victory sign which she didn't understand, and then he went back to his Nintendo. Bing returned with a glass—made of real glass—of wine for Gwendolyn.

"I want to learn everything I can about your daughter, Mrs. Drew," Bing said. "She's as tight-lipped about her past as a Gothic heroine—at least, she has been lately," he added with a mournful look at Jane. "And her modesty can be exasperating. I figure the best way to learn anything about her is to go straight to the source."

He took Jane's amused mother by the elbow and said, "I see a quiet corner." Then he turned to Jane with his rascal's smile and added, "I've abducted your mother; go find someone else to play with, darlin'."

They went off and Jane decided to see how life was treating Mac's son. The boy certainly looked happy—younger and more carefree than on his last visit to the island. The scar on his forehead was nothing more than a tiny pink reminder; and that, too, would someday disappear.

They exchanged greetings. "What was *this* for?" Jane asked him, flashing him his victory sign.

Jerry grinned and said, "I'm staying over for spring break, and Dad says it's partly thanks to you."

"He *did*? Did he say why?"

"Yeah. He said you read him the riot act."

"Jer, come *on!* Your turn!"

His cousin slapped him on the back of his head and Jerry elbowed him in his ribs while the third boy grabbed the Nintendo control and tried to steal a turn. The boys were busy being boys, and Jane left them to it. She decided to see whether she could be any help in the kitchen and got drafted immediately into carrying out cold salads and hot dishes.

The activity in the kitchen was at a fever pitch. This was it, the serving of everything at once, the moment of truth at any buffet. Mrs. Adamont was barking orders like a company sergeant, making grown men hop and their women laugh. Billy was running around like a chicken without a head, looking for a pitcher. Mac came in at some point and began a frantic rummage for extra serving spoons.

Jane was wondering how Celeste was managing the willpower to stay out of her own kitchen when Celeste did walk in, a three-year-old in her arms, and said, "Give Un-

cle Mac a good-bye hug." The toddler threw her arms
open wide and fell forward into Mac for the hug. With a
huge grin the child said, "Rub noses, rub noses." Mac, a
spoon in each hand, laughed and held her little shoulders
and rubbed her little nose and Jane felt a stab as deep and
as sharp as she'd ever felt in her life.

"Della's taking them home," Celeste said to Mac.
"Jimmy's a little feverish; he's sitting around like a bump
on a log."

"Geez—he *must* be sick," Mac agreed. "Are these the
only spoons we had?"

Celeste said yes and suddenly they both looked sad, and
Celeste turned away and left the room. Then the whirlwind
passed over Mac again, sucking him back into it, and he
began the next frantic search for the next needed object.

And all the while Jane was thinking, *This is a real family
in a real community where people care. Time and the outside
world have taken their toll, and the ties are a little frayed, but
everyone cares about everyone else. Even the divorced ones
care.*

"Hey! Daydreamer! Are you gonna fish or cut bait?"
Jane shook herself free to see Mrs. Adamont brandishing a
wooden spoon at her. "Can you carry this crockpot of
baked beans? It's heavy."

"Sure," said Jane; but Mac intercepted the cargo. "I'll
take it. You can have the next load." His smile was unlike
any of the half dozen he'd allowed her to see so far. It was
. . . affectionate. And the timbre in his voice—also new;
also affectionate.

"Don't forget to plug it in!" Mrs. Adamont shouted after
him. "Here, dollink, take out another batch of paper
plates. People are going to want to double them up. Why
Mac bought the cheap ones I'll never know. Take some
more napkins, too. These are awful. The man's been shopping for himself for three years; you'd think he'd learn."

Jane took the stuff out to the small oak table piled high

with eating tools. Mac was crawling around under the big dining table, plugging in the crockpot cord. When he came back out, he smiled and said, "I don't know why I bothered. Doris's beans will be gone in five seconds."

He stood next to Jane, hands on his hips, and looked around. "That should do it, then," he said, looking every inch like the lord of his manor.

The dining table was groaning under the weight of the food. From the chourico and peppers to the teriyaki chicken wings, from the Swedish meatballs to the New England cornbread, everything looked delicious. There was no rhyme or reason to the meal; it was as thrown together as the red, yellow, pink, and blue streamers spiraling the room, as diverse as the guest list itself.

The kids, obviously near death by starvation, were lined up by the table with paper plates flattened against their chests. There was some, but not too much, pushing and shoving as they waited for Mac, who waited for Mrs. Adamont, to give The Signal. When she finally said, "Okay, people, let's eat," there was a quiet but intense scramble for the marshmallow ambrosia, the little hot dogs on toothpicks, and the nachos, in that order. Mrs. Adamont scolded the first three kids for being pigs and encouraged the others to at least *look* at the spinach pie.

The buffet, it seemed, was going to be a success.

Relaxing, Mac said, "I think while everyone's out here I'll give Mrs. Adamont a hand cleaning up the kitchen."

"No, you don't," Jane said firmly. "You should be looking after your guests. I'll do it."

He looked surprised. "Thanks," he said softly.

One syllable: *Thanks*. And yet it set every hair tingling.

She left him and reported for duty to Mrs. Adamont, who handed her two trash bags and said, "Recycles in this one, the rest in this one." Billy's wife Carol was there, filling up the dishwasher, while her baby was screaming for a fillup herself.

"I'm going to have to feed her again," Carol said with a sigh. "She must know there's a buffet going on." She sat discreetly to one side, unbuttoned her blouse, and began nursing Sarah.

Jane went around picking up loose plastic and paper, then finished loading the dishwasher while Mrs. Adamont refilled some of the casseroles. All the while, she was replaying the way Mac looked and sounded when he said "Thanks." Somehow, in some way, she'd broken through some barrier. It was the first time Mac had let her do something for *him*, the first time he wasn't keeping her at arm's length.

She felt ridiculously happy. All her suspicions about him, all her careful reasoning—gone. All her fears and all her worries about Judith Brightman—gone. In their place was a warm, glowing feeling—*because he's let me do the dishes*. Jane had considered many careers in her life, but scullery maid wasn't one of them.

She laughed under her breath and shook her head. *I'm as bonkers as Cissy.*

There was a knock on the kitchen door and Jane went to answer it. She was extremely embarrassed to have to greet Phillip Harrow, the only man on Nantucket not invited to Uncle Easy's birthday party. As carefully dressed as ever, Phillip stepped inside and meticulously wiped his muddy feet on the mat. He seemed to be dragging out the awkwardness of the situation, and she disliked him intensely for that.

Carol, still nursing, adjusted her position away from him; it could have been taken as a snub. Mrs. Adamont, however, saved the day. "Don't just stand there like a little lost sheep, Phillip. Supper's on in the other room."

"Ah, but not for me," Phillip said ironically. "I'm here because I have an urgent message for Cissy Hanlin."

Nothing in Cissy's life was urgent, but Mrs. Adamont said, "Go on in and tell her, then."

"I think not," he said, turning to Jane. "Would you mind?" he asked her coldly.

"Yes, of course; I'll get her," Jane answered, beating a quick retreat into the keeping room. She didn't know who was being more gauche, Mac for not inviting him, or Phillip for coming over instead of picking up the phone. They were a hell of a pair.

She found Cissy sitting with her mother and Bing, who were equally dismayed by Jane's disappearance. Jane made her excuses and took Cissy aside. When Cissy went out to the kitchen to Phillip, Jane busied herself gathering empty plastic cups. Seeing her hang back, Mac broke away from the company and came up to her.

"What's up? Why did Cissy leave?"

Jane had to explain that Phillip Harrow was standing like a little matchstick boy on his kitchen mat, then watch Mac's relaxed and expansive mood dissolve into the cold, brooding one she knew so well.

"Maybe he's conveying a message from Cissy's husband," she said, mostly to give Mac someone else to think about. She filled Mac in on Cissy's situation, then was relieved when he shrugged and said, "That's none of my business."

Mac returned to the company, and when Jane peeked into the kitchen, Phillip was gone and Cissy was looking ecstatic; so the message must not have been about Dave. It turned out that Phillip had to fly the next afternoon to Grand Cayman on business. He wanted Cissy with him.

"Didn't I tell you?" she said jubilantly. "First the ring, now this! I have to leave now."

"Cissy! You can stay to sing happy birthday, at least."

After some arm-twisting, Cissy agreed to stay for the cake, but only if the gifts weren't opened first. Jane sent her back to her half-eaten meal, pleased that she'd thwarted Phillip's attempt to be a spoiler. She was taking sides, and she knew it. And she liked it.

She dragged Mrs. Adamont and Carol away from the kitchen, assuring them that the dishwasher would go on without them, then sat them down with her mother and Bing, got a plate of food for Carol, and burped Sarah while her mother ate. Bing Andrews and Gwendolyn Drew had become thick as thieves while Jane was gone; her mother's tone was gay, even flirtatious, with him. As for Jane's little mix of islanders and off-islanders, it was a good one. Bing knew how to charm women, and it didn't matter if they were young or old, rich or poor, married or single.

And yet . . .

From across the room Jane could see Mac holding court with a group of his own. Jane recognized Mac's gorgeous cousin Miriam from the church bazaar, and one of the men from the Town Building, and two or three others she didn't know—and Celeste. There were no bursts of scandalized laughter over there, of course; but what laughter there was, was easy and intimate, as if these people had laughed together before.

Jane was still finishing her own hasty meal when the dishes were cleared away and the cake rolled out. Uncle Easy, who'd been table-hopping all evening, sat down with a toddler on each knee and led the crowd in a lusty rendition of "Happy Birthday," then got all eleven kids to help him blow out all eighty candles on the sheet cake. After that he took a knife and sliced off a yellow frosting rose for each of them for their services, and ate the twelfth one himself. What was left of the cake was cut up and passed out with coffee and tea to the stuffed, contented company.

Before Uncle Easy began opening his gifts, Cissy went up to him and wished him a wonderful, wonderful life, as happy a life as she was having. Radiant with joy, she went up to Jane and said, "I'm off to pack. *Finally* I'll get to wear some of the resort wear that would've got me laughed off the island. Oh, and Mac will be watching Buster for me."

Jane hugged her and wished her a safe trip, and Cissy
floated out of the house into the dark May night. The
sounds of laughter brought Jane back to the keeping room;
Uncle Easy was wisecracking his way through the opening
of the gifts. Jane took the seat Bing had been saving for
her.

"If you jump up one more time, I'll tie you to that
chair," Bing threatened in a low voice. "As a matter of
fact, I may tie you to it anyway." He took her hand in his
and held it down in mock captivity, then leaned over and
brushed his lips against hers again.

But something was different for Jane. This kiss wasn't
like the earlier kiss. She felt no particular joy in having
Bing claim her publicly; quite the opposite, in fact. Something had changed in the course of the evening, and she
thought it had to do with the word "thanks." She glanced
across the room where Mac was sitting, just in time to see
him register a certain amount of disapproval over guests
making out during gift opening.

Jane watched as Mac leaned over and whispered something in his ex-wife's ear. Celeste nodded and reached
down for her purse, then got up and, blowing a kiss first to
Uncle Easy and then to her son, left the room.

Mac followed her.

CHAPTER **20**

It was as if all the air had gone out of all the balloons at the same time. Without Mac, the party wasn't the same. Even Uncle Easy seemed to feel it; his one-liners lost some of their punch. Or maybe it just seemed that way to Jane. She sat there with a poor excuse of a smile on her face, waiting for Mac to come back from what she hoped would be a quick walk to Celeste's car.

The pile of torn wrapping paper and undone ribbons got higher. No Mac. Uncle Easy opened Jane's gift—a collection of jams and jellies and half a dozen of his favorite cigars—and complimented Jane's interesting split personality. Everyone laughed. Ignoring the knot in her stomach, Jane laughed too. Still no Mac.

So this is what it's come to, she thought miserably. *Pining away like a teenager because the boy I like sneaked out early from the party with the prom queen. I hate this.*

Uncle Easy, sensing that the company was getting restless, whipped through the rest of the presents quickly. The chairs got rearranged again into small groups; the early leavers left. The older girls were playing Pictionary, the boys Nintendo, but the smaller children were beginning to get bored and cranky. Uncle Easy surveyed the situation, then yanked Jane aside.

"I ain't ready for this party to end. Help me round up the troublemakers. We'll herd 'em into an upstairs room with a game."

Jane turned to Bing and her mother, who were deep in a

discussion of fund-raising techniques. "Would you mind?"
Jane asked her mother.

Her mother waved her away without looking at her.
Bing's blue eyes flickered unhappily, but he continued to
hang on to every word that Gwendolyn Drew uttered.

The son-in-law from heaven, Jane decided with a wry
smile as she left them with their coffee.

The game Uncle Easy had in mind was Pin the Tail on
the Donkey, and the cutoff age seemed to be six or seven.
Certainly Jerry and his pals weren't interested. "Too bad
for *them,*" said Uncle Easy.

Despite Jane's objections, Uncle Easy chose Mac's bedroom to hang the donkey poster in; it was the only room
that didn't have a chair rail in the way. "Mac won't care,"
the old man said breezily.

With great care he opened the tattered cardboard box
and unfolded the fragile poster. The game was now an
antique; Uncle Easy had paid fifteen cents for it on an
expedition to Boston half a century earlier. Although the
original brass tacks were in the box, Uncle Easy had made
a concession to modern technology and brought along
plastic pushpins, because they were easier for a young
hand to hold.

In the meantime, Jane tried not to notice Mac's pajama
bottoms hanging on the door, and tried not to wonder
whether he ever wore the tops. She tried not to imagine
him lying on the plain four-poster bed, and tried *very* hard
not to speculate whether someone lying next to him would
roll into his heavier weight. But most of all, Jane tried not
to breathe, because the bedroom smelled intimately, irresistibly like books and leather and Old Spice and Mac Mc-
Kenzie.

She helped Uncle Easy organize the group into a kind of
big-kid, little-kid pattern so that there would be a sense of
drama. The first one up was Doris's grandson Stinky, a
seven-year-old who was so sure he'd win that he asked to

be spun around five extra times. Uncle Easy blindfolded him, spun him, and let him go. He pinned the tail on the donkey's nose. James, his four-year-old cousin, got so excited that they had to take the blindfold back off so that he could go to the bathroom. Lucy, also four, pinned the tail deliberately on the wall because she didn't want to hurt the donkey.

And so it went, with the simple, old-fashioned game yielding more about each child's character than any Nintendo game ever could. When everyone had had a turn, Jenny, a shy and adorable three-year-old sitting in Jane's lap, looked up at her and said, "Now *you* do it."

Instantly there was a clamor. "Do it! Do it! We'll help you! Do it!"

Jane laughed and let Uncle Easy wrap his red bandanna around her eyes. She stood there, waiting to be spun around, but nothing happened. "Well? Isn't anyone going to make me dizzy?"

There was another pause, and then some giggling, and then Jane felt two powerful hands take hold of her shoulders and begin to spin her slowly, slowly around. A low sound escaped her throat, of surprise and a sense of pleasure so deep it bordered on fear. Around she went, with one of his hands trailing across her back, the other sliding onto her shoulder in slow, fluid repetition. She was caught in a lasso of heat, and the pleasure it gave was almost impossible for her to understand. She let herself be turned; turned; turned. She would gladly have continued until the end of time.

But he let her go, amid squeals of anticipation from the children surrounding them. "You're cold, you're cold!" they screamed as she groped the air ahead of her, feeling for the donkey poster. "You're warmer! Warmer!"

Her free hand touched his face. "Hot! Hot!" the children cried, laughing hysterically at her error. She let herself fall under the spell of play, lightly skimming his high cheekbone, the cleft in his strong chin, the pronounced bridge of his nose. He did not move under her touch as she raised her other hand and pretended to get ready to pin the tail on him. The children were in an uproar. "No, no, no!" they shrieked. "He's a *man*! He's a *man*!"

Jane whispered, "I know."

He took her by the shoulders again and adjusted her direction slightly. Jane stepped cautiously forward while the children cheered her on. She found the poster, made her best guess, and drove in the pin to loud laughter and cries of relief. When she lifted the bandanna from her eyes, she saw that the tail was hanging from the middle of the donkey's chest.

"Right about where the heart would be," said Mac from behind her.

Wrong heart, she thought, turning to him. "I missed," she said in a small, sad voice.

"Then you'll have to try again sometime." He stood there, relaxed and smiling, in no particular hurry. She'd never seen him like this before. His hands were in the pockets of his baggy khakis; the trendy red floral tie that dressed up his stonewashed denim shirt was loosened. She'd been staring at that tie all evening. For a man like Mac to buy a tie like that—well, he was wearing it for *some*one, that was for sure.

The children were expecting something amusing to happen between Mac and Jane. When it didn't, they instantly lost patience and demanded their prizes. Uncle Easy worked out a system based on age, height, tail number, and sportsmanship. Everybody got a cash prize; Jane won fifty cents.

"Don't spend it all on one man," said Uncle Easy, winking at Mac. "Was there plane trouble?" he added to his nephew.

"We needed some time; she had the plane wait."

Uncle Easy snorted. "She can afford it nowadays."

They all poured out of Mac's bedroom, Jane with little Jenny in her arms. Mac said, "Thanks for your help tonight."

"Don't mention it," Jane replied coolly. *I'm jealous. Jealous, jealous, jealous.*

Mac looked baffled by the lightning shift in her mood. "Something I said?"

"Very possibly," Jane answered. They descended the rest of the stairs in silence. Mac went off and Jane handed Jenny over to her mother, a clerk at the town post office. Then she rejoined her own mother, who was making noises about leaving.

"I'm sorry now that I booked the car on the six-thirty ferry," Gwendolyn said with genuine regret, smiling across the room in Bing's direction. "Bing wanted to take us both to breakfast. What a perfectly wonderful young man he is. Kind, attentive, considerate; he's practically raised his sister, you know."

"So I've been told," Jane answered, a bit snappishly. "I hope I haven't led you on about Bing, Mother. He is *not* the marrying kind."

"Be serious, Jane. What man is, anymore? You just have to convince him that you know better. You're halfway there already," she added, lowering her voice. "Bing spent the better part of the evening raving about you. I admit, he has a certain . . . elusiveness. But when a man like that finally does decide to make a commitment, he'll charge straight ahead. Mark my words."

"Must we talk about this *now*?" Jane asked, amazed at her mother's indiscretion.

Chastised, her mother said, "You're right. You're right. I'll take the car back to the house myself. You stay. Enjoy yourself. Bing can bring you back." Gwendolyn kissed her daughter happily, said good night to her new friends and acquaintances, and left.

Bing came up to Jane immediately afterward. "Is there

something going on around here that I should know?"
There was a dangerous depth to his blue eyes, a darkness
she'd never seen there before. "Your mother is giving me
one set of signals about you, but you seem to be giving me
another."

"My mother talks too much. All mothers talk too
much," Jane said lightly. But she was thinking, *Is this a
birthday party or an encounter group?*

"I think it's time to stop being coy with me, Jane," he
said quietly. "If you're not interested, say so."

"Bing! How can you ask me that here . . . now?"

"Evasive isn't any better than coy, Jane."

"I'm not being either!" she said hotly, then lowered her
voice in the steadily emptying room. "But this really isn't
the time or place. The truth is, I don't have a *clue* what's
going on around here," she admitted, distressed. "I wish
you would give me time to sort it out. If I could just get
some time to think . . ."

"Falling for someone isn't like buying a car, Jane," he
said, idly fingering a gold button on her blouse. "You can't
sit down with a cup of tea and the latest edition of *Con-
sumer Reports* and research the person. When it's right, you
know it. For me, it's right. I want you to know it."

He looked immensely appealing just then: tall and lanky
and just ill-used enough to make her feel she was being
pretty stupid to keep him at bay. And after all, what *did*
she want? On paper—and in the flesh—Bing Andrews
looked perfect. Everything her mother said was true, and
more besides. If there was anything wrong with what he
was telling her, she couldn't see it; not with him standing
there with that rueful, beguiling look of his.

"Maybe I—"

"I would've preferred a yes or a no." He leaned over and
kissed her gently on her lips. "But I can see I'm not going
to get either. Do you want a lift home?" he asked, disheartened.

"I'd better not," she said with a sigh. "I'll just say my good nights to everyone and walk back. It's a beautiful night."

"It could have been," he said shortly, and left. She felt as if she'd turned down her first marriage proposal. When she thought about it, though, she realized that there was nothing new in what Bing had said. It was odd how good men were at implying that they were in love with you and wanted to spend the rest of their days at your side, when all they really wanted was to take you to bed.

She went into the kitchen to say good night to Mrs. Adamont, who was packing up the last of the leftovers for the stragglers. Mac was there, as Jane knew he'd be, saying good night to his guests in the most normal, friendly way. It simply amazed her. *I'm not the* only *schizophrenic here tonight, dammit.*

"Honey, get me more aluminum foil," Mrs. Adamont said to her as Jane waited her turn to say good night. "I think I saw an extra roll under one of the cupboards."

Jane tracked down the foil, and after that the plastic wrap, and somehow ended up scrubbing the pots that were too big to fit in the dishwasher. All the while she kept telling herself, *Say good night and get out; you're just trying to prove how humble you are.* But she couldn't. He was only ten feet away, close enough for her to hear the rich, friendly laugh in his voice, and soak up his nearness, and understand the side of him he would not let her see. She wanted so badly to be able to slip her arm through his and say to the guests, "We loved having you, come again," and to be the one to turn off the lights in the kitchen.

Maybe he could use a cleaning woman, she thought, trying to laugh off the irony of the situation.

She and Mrs. Adamont finished cleaning up about the time the last guest left. Mrs. Adamont took off the apron she'd brought and stuffed it into her paper shopping bag. Mac slipped his arms around her and said, "Adele, you saved my life. This could've been a disaster. How'm I gonna pay you back?"

"Oh, and I suppose limbing MacGruder's tree that was blocking my roses isn't payment? Now stop fooling around and let me go; I'll be late for *Saturday Night Live*." She grabbed her purse and shopping bag, gave Mac a buss on his cheek, and dashed out.

Mac, still smiling, turned to Jane. "Thanks again."

Jane, the last one there, was wiping her hands in a green-checked dishtowel and thinking, *Nice going, girl. He'll be calling in a SWAT team to get you out.* "Somewhere I lost track of Uncle Easy," she said, although she hadn't thought about him in an hour. "He must've gone on home?"

"He's up in my bed, staying the night. He petered out quick at the end; but then he never did know how to pace himself."

"He seems like that kind of guy," she agreed. *One bedroom for Uncle Easy, one for Jerry. A makeshift office in the third.* "So where will *you*—" She stopped herself, too late. Now he'd know she'd counted beds.

He politely chose not to hear the question, which embarrassed her even more. "I'll walk you home," he said. "Buster needs the exercise." He let out a soft whistle. The big, black dog came trotting into the kitchen from somewhere, ready for business. Mac grabbed a sweater for himself, and one for Jane. "You'll want this."

She pulled the baggy soft wool over her head. Big mistake. The one thing she didn't need right now was more of Mac, and this was more of Mac. They stepped outside together. She thought of the last time they'd done that, after his emotional encounter with Celeste. Jane had been jealous then, too, though she'd never have admitted it at the time. But now she did, and freely. Presumably that was progress of some kind?

There was a moon, which was nice; Jane had no desire

to trip and fall into a pothole. They ambled along, with Mac throwing sticks for Buster to try to retrieve by moonlight, and talked about the turnout. "Everybody came," Mac said, obviously pleased. "No one wanted to disappoint Uncle Easy. And yet you could see it in his face: a lot of his old friends *had* disappointed him."

"You mean . . . by dying?"

"Yeah," Mac said, hurling a stick impossibly far. The dog didn't care; he roared off after it anyway. "And the younger ones, too, by moving off the island. I look at Uncle Easy and I think, 'That'll be me. I'm halfway there.'"

"But you have a son, and he was here tonight," Jane risked saying. "That must've felt good. I mean, compared to—"

"Compared to his not being here at all? Sure," Mac agreed. "I have you to thank for that," he added, stopping to pick up another stick.

He whistled for Buster, who was probably halfway to 'Sconset, to come back. "That little scene that Celeste and I played out in front of you shocked us both back to the bargaining table. We're going to try again," he said quietly. "We were still ironing out some of the wrinkles at the airport, in fact."

It came as a staggering, shocking blow, a direct hit to her heart. She should have seen it coming, of course . . . all evening long . . . together . . . and it explained Celeste's explanation; she and Jane were going to be *neighbors,* for pity's sake . . . it was unbearable . . . and it was all Jane's fault . . . her stupid spaghetti . . . her stupid timing . . . and they were compatible after all. . . .

Reeling, she forced herself to say, "I'm happy for you, Mac. It's not every couple that can pick up the threads of their marriage again."

"Are you kidding?" he said with an incredulous laugh. "You *are* kidding. Celeste and me?" Jane could see by moonlight that he was shaking his head. "You don't know me at all, then," he said softly. "Somehow, I thought you did. I thought you knew what I was all about."

"How *can* I know? You won't let me near you," she shot back. He stopped in his tracks and she added quickly, "If you and Celeste aren't getting together again, then what *are* you negotiating? Peace in the Middle East?"

"Visitation rights, of course," Mac said, obviously amazed that she could be so dense. "We've been keeping it to a verbal agreement. Celeste's a lawyer; she can tie me up in knots any time, and she knows it. We wanted things to be as loose and civil as possible, for Jerry's sake. You see how well we succeeded," he added dryly.

Buster came back, wanting more. Mac threw the stick, this time in the direction of the graveyard—Jane could see the gravestones leaning forlornly in the moonlight—and Buster went charging happily off again. But he didn't go far before he turned and came back, his tail low, his head down, a low and pitiful moan deep in his throat.

Mac looked quickly at Jane, but she had nothing to say about the dog's strange behavior. He commanded Buster sternly to fall in beside them as they walked on. Jane was hardly aware of any of it. Maybe Judith was somewhere near, maybe she wasn't. Maybe Mac believed in her, maybe he didn't. But one thing was clear now: Celeste, at least, was not a factor. Beauty, brains, and a brilliant career did not cut it with Mac McKenzie. Jane wondered briefly what *did* cut it with him; but mostly she felt a giddy, light-headed sense of relief.

"Did I mention that Celeste was engaged?" Mac asked.

Better yet! "No," Jane answered, breaking into a wide and happy grin. "That's *wonderful*."

"I don't see what's so wonderful about it," he grumbled. "She hardly knows the guy."

"Oh. How long have they been seeing one another?"

"On and off, a year or so. Maybe two altogether."

"I see your point," she said ironically. "A whirlwind romance." *Oh Lord,* she thought. *How do you hurry a guy who tells time by the passing of the seasons?*

"Celeste is a part of my life," Mac said quietly as they continued their walk down the potholed, moonlit lane. "That's how it is. She's Jerry's mother, and I care about what happens to her; I always will. Divorce doesn't undo that, Jane."

He was like no other divorced man she'd ever known. The ones who'd been left by their wives were bitter about them—just as the ones who'd done the leaving never gave them a second thought. Mac was that rare breed, an ex-husband who cared.

They were at her back door now, standing in the dim light of the porch lamp. "You're an unusual man, Mac McKenzie," Jane said thoughtfully. "Just when I think I have you . . ."

"Pigeonholed?" he suggested. "Under which category would that be? Insecure townie? Defiant poor man? Abandoned . . ."

"Stop," she begged in a whisper, putting her hand over his mouth. "No more."

It echoed her action earlier in the evening, when she'd traced the outlines of his face. But she wasn't blindfolded now; she could see the burning hunger in his eyes, and it shocked and thrilled her. He took her hand away from his mouth and lowered his lips to her open palm in a kiss. It was so tender, so restrained, that it shocked her even more. He let her hand go, and he closed his eyes, and for one desolate moment she thought that he was letting *her* go.

And then he shuddered, as though the battle was lost, and took her in his arms and kissed her in a kiss so deep, so longing, so completely, enchantingly masterful, that he had to keep her from falling when it was over.

"Is this what you wanted from me?" he asked in a hoarse voice, his breath coming in a long, ragged gasp.

"I . . . yes. Yes . . . it is," she said dizzily.

"What's the point, Jane—what's the *point*?" He let her go with such force that she felt thrown backward. He turned and took two steps, three steps, away from her.

"Mac," she cried.

He turned around and in two strides had her in his arms again, kissing her with the kind of abandoned fury she'd only read about—deep kisses that left her helpless, devastated in their wake. "Don't go . . . don't go," she begged in an anguished moan as he buried his face in her hair, breathing in the essence of her, arousing her with the sound of her own name.

He held her away from him and seemed to search her face for some sign of . . . of what? She didn't know; she could scarcely see through the glaze of tears in her own eyes.

"Don't you get it, Jane? Don't you *understand*?" he said fiercely. "It didn't work the first time. It won't work the second. The odds get longer, not shorter."

"But they say practice makes perfect," she quipped, though her lips trembled as she said it. She couldn't let him walk away without even trying. She couldn't.

"Is it so funny to you?" he asked in a stiff, barely audible voice. "I suppose it must be."

"No! I didn't mean—"

But he put his hand gently over *her* mouth this time, and shook his head. "No more. No more." He whistled softly for Buster, who came tearing around the corner expecting treats, and then man and dog walked off into the silver, moonlit night.

It was a dream, surely some kind of dream, and she'd rewrite the ending as soon as she fell asleep again. That was Jane's belief as she tried the back door and then got out her key. But the time between now and then, this cursed awake time without him—how long might that last? For as long as a cup of hot chocolate? For as long as she lived? How long, before she could rewrite the ending and

be in Mac's arms again, and hear a promise never to let her
go?

Downstairs there was only one dim light over the
kitchen stove. Her mother must have gone to bed. Jane
hardly bothered to wash up; she was exhausted, and she
wanted to go to bed herself, to rewrite the ending.

No more . . . no more.

The words echoed in her mind like the tolling of church
bells as she walked wearily up the stairs to her bedroom.
She turned off the small lamp in the hall, then—remembering that she had a guest—turned it on again, because
the bathroom was downstairs and the stairs were steep.
She'd plugged night-lights into each of the rooms as well,
mostly for her mother's sake, but also to combat the night,
which lately had become her enemy.

When she entered her bedroom, her mind was focused
completely on Mac. She emptied her watch, earrings, and
hair combs on her aunt's old oak bureau and studied herself briefly in the small swiveled mirror that stood atop it.
Thank God she hadn't worn mascara; it would've been a
smudgy mess by now. She caught a glimpse in the mirror of
Mac's sweater, soft and woolly and brown, and held up her
arm to her nose, breathing in his scent. She began to pull
the sweater off over her head, but it was cold; she left it on.

It was much colder than it should have been—cold and
clammy and penetrating, like the day of Aunt Sylvia's funeral. Her memory of the funeral became suddenly very
sharp. She could see the coffin and the rain beading on its
waxed surface. She could see Mac under his big black umbrella, and the tiny red rose in his hand. And her mother,
standing in the pouring rain alongside her, looking impossibly crisp.

Judith had been there too.

At the time Jane hadn't realized it; now, in retrospect,
she did. It wasn't the cold rain that had caused Jane to be
chilled to the bone then. It was Judith. Judith was there

then, and Judith was here now. In this room. Now. Jane held her breath as she turned slowly away from the mirror and—instinctively—in the direction of the rocking chair that sat in its customary corner of the room. The chair, old and worn and black, was pitching lightly back and forth on its rockers, as if someone had just stood up from it. A cold, hard fear touched Jane's heart. In many ways she was prepared for this moment—had both dreaded and looked forward to it. And yet it was all she could do not to run screaming from the room.

She forced herself to stand there motionless, as if she'd come across a wild thing in the woods. Despite the falling temperature in the room she felt as hot as a coal fire. She wanted desperately to rip off Mac's sweater, but she didn't dare. All she could do was wait; wait and watch. After a brief eternity, the kind of eternity an earthquake takes, a lambent presence began to appear in front of the rocking chair. Jane recognized it at once: it was the foggy, tallish column that Cissy had captured on tape with her camcorder.

But this time the process of substantiation did not stop there. The haziness continued to define itself, to assume depth and clarity and detail, until it became Judith.

CHAPTER 21

Judith Brightman was as tall as Jane, and her black hair was luxuriantly, untamably curled. Those were Jane's first impressions. The gown she wore was not the subdued gray garment of her Quaker years, but a flattering, full-skirted dress of deep blue. Her waist was absurdly small, the waist of a woman who has never borne a child. She was, in fact, past her childbearing years, though she was still very beautiful. Her eyes were very dark—either brown, or an enviable shade of violet.

This is a hologram, Jane thought as she stared at the shimmering, wavering figure before her. *This is a trick. Someone with a vicious sense of humor and lots of money is trying to drive me mad.* But was there anyone else who knew about Judith in such detail? She tried to think it through but couldn't. Hologram or not, the vision was utterly spellbinding.

Jane waited for a signal, for something—anything—to happen. But no sooner had the apparition reached a state of complete clarity than it began to fade, becoming a hazy column again, and finally disappearing altogether.

"Judith?" Jane whispered, feeling absurdly self-conscious. But Judith was gone. The room warmed back to room temperature. Jane tried to capture the image in her memory. What was the expression on the apparition's face? Tragic? Pleading? Threatening?

None of them, Jane decided. If anything, it was . . . composed. Resolute. As though Judith had made a decision of some kind.

Jane looked down at her own body: it was shaking un-controllably. She turned away from the rocking chair, then jumped back with a violent start: Aunt Sylvia's roving cat Wicky was curled up on Jane's pillows, oblivious to the whole drama. Jane remembered Buster as he cowered at the threshold and stared at the rocker on the night of Jerry's accident. She thought of tonight, when he ran whimpering from the graveyard area.

There are only two possibilities, she decided, pulling her-self under control and gingerly approaching the big gray cat. *Either Judith was never here, or Wicky is so used to her that he considers her one of the family.*

She eased Wicky off the bed and crawled into it, too overwhelmed to undress. Wicky jumped back on the bed immediately and, to Jane's amazement, curled up with his chin on her thigh. The last sound she heard as she fell off the edge into oblivion was the old cat's relaxed and rum-bling purr.

When the call came from Phillip early the next morning, Jane was just back from putting her mother and her Volvo on the six-thirty boat.

Phillip apologized for calling so early and said, "Is Cissy with you, by any chance? I expected her last night but she never showed. I've just talked with her brother; he said the last he saw, she was packing a suitcase. The bag is by their front door, but there's no sign of her."

"Good lord. No, I haven't—wait, there's someone at my back door. Hold on; maybe it's her," Jane said illogically.

It was Bing and he was anxious. "Is she here?"

She shook her head and motioned him back to the phone with her. "Phillip? We'll meet you at your house; we'll go the back way."

She hung up and they went out together, with Jane try-ing hard not to show the fear she felt. If Cissy had chosen to take the shortcut and go the back way, she'd have to go past the graveyard. "I don't understand why she didn't take the Jeep," Jane said, almost angrily.

Bing's voice was hollow with apprehension. "I wish I knew."

They tramped through the tall grass past the small graveyard, which looked quaintly desolate in the morning fog. Jane scanned the leaning stones, looking for bright clothing, appalled to realize what it was she was looking for. From where they walked, Jane could see the rugosa rose on Judith's grave quite well. It was fully leafed out; there would be flowers soon.

They walked farther along and heard themselves hailed. Through an opening in an evergreen windbreak they saw Phillip standing in the gray mist, waving to them. Phillip yelled, "Anything?" and Bing answered, "Nothing!"

But Jane had been scanning the grasses, looking for bright colors. Her heart plummeted when she saw a patch of floral on a background of white at the base of the footbridge. "Bing," she said, gripping his arm, "Something . . ."

They both broke into a run for the bridge. When they found her, Jane knew at once that there was nothing to be done. Cissy's face, always pale, was a ghastly gray. While they stood there for one paralyzed second, absorbing the blow, another face, another grayness, flashed through Jane's consciousness and disappeared.

"Oh God. Oh my God. Oh no." Bing fell to his knees in the wet grass and lifted his sister to his breast. "Call an ambulance," he said without turning around. He brushed back the wet hair from Cissy's face and repeated, "Call an ambulance."

It was obvious what had happened to her. The handrail had given way and she'd fallen off the footbridge and hit her head on one of the rocks in the gully. She may have drowned: her face was lying on its cheek in three inches of water.

Jane turned to run back to the house just as Phillip arrived breathless at the scene. The look on his face would stay with her forever; it was as if someone had ripped away the cold mask of indifference, leaving only raw horror and disbelief. Phillip, too, dropped to his knees in the gully, heedless of the standing water. Jane looked at the two men bending over Cissy's lifeless form and thought, *She's dead. Can't they tell? She's dead.* But she ran like the wind anyway, because that's what they wanted.

She had dialed 911 and was giving a brief description of the accident when she saw an ambulance turn off the road into the foggy lane alongside the house. "Wait," she said, confused, "it's here already."

The dispatcher said, "That one's for someone else. Stand outside the house if you can, and wave the ambulance in when it arrives. They're going to need help with directions."

Jane was absolutely traumatized. There was an emergency at Mac's, a death behind her house, and in the meantime she was expected to stand in front and direct traffic. She ran back through thickening fog almost to the footbridge before she could see them all. The two men were still bent over Cissy. *Mouth-to-mouth,* she thought. Her spirits soared. They must have seen something, some flicker of life that she'd missed. She turned and ran back toward Bing's house but stopped dead in the middle of the lane that led to Mac's place.

What about them? she thought wildly. What had happened to which generation under Mac McKenzie's roof? The sound of a siren cut short her speculation and sent her bolting for the road to intercept Cissy's ambulance. She waved it into the lane that ran between Bing's house and hers and ran after it, breathless with panic, her mind no more than a blur of disjointed thoughts.

By the time she caught up to the vehicle, which had pulled off the lane as far as it dared, Phillip was leading the ambulance team to the footbridge. Jane was tearing after them when she heard sirens again, whirled around, and saw the first ambulance racing away from Mac's place. It was impossible to tell who was inside. She prayed that it not be Mac, or Uncle Easy, or Jerry; but she knew that that prayer would go unanswered.

A short time later the medics stopped working on Cissy. Her body was wheeled into the ambulance and Bing, utterly in shock, climbed in after it. Phillip went home to get his car to drive to the hospital and Jane was left in a daze, standing at the footbridge. She wanted to go to the hospital, too, but not with Phillip or anyone else. She began to stumble back to Lilac Cottage, then on impulse detoured into the graveyard.

She went up to Judith's grave and stood there, her heart immeasurably heavy, her mind and spirit completely exhausted from the past twelve hours' events.

"Is this your work, Judith Brightman?" she asked in a low and angry voice. "Does it give you pleasure to punish the innocent?"

She kicked at the gravestone, furious that she could not rid herself, or the island, of the spirit that hounded them all. It was an unthinking thing to do; Jane let out a cry of sharp, awful pain.

Afterward she decided that it was the pain itself that had triggered the vision. It was the same vision that had flashed through her consciousness when she first saw Cissy in the gully, only this time it lingered, more brutally explicit: She saw, in perfect detail, a woman in a deep blue gown being dragged over the side of a small workboat by two strong-armed scallopers. The waterlogged gown made her heavy; Jane could hear the grunts of the fishermen as they strained to bring her body aboard.

"Oh, no, no, no," Jane said in a low wail. "Not that. Not that."

She fell to her knees beside the grave, bitterly disillusioned. *All that love . . . all that fierce passion . . . and that's where it led her. Did she really believe she could be reunited with Ben that way?* Jane remembered the calm and resolute look on the face of the apparition in her bedroom the night before. It was a strange kind of courage that had allowed Judith Brightman to walk into the sea; but it was courage, nonetheless.

So this is what they meant in 1852 by "fits": death by suicide—death, obviously, by reason of insanity.

That fierce will, so misdirected then—was it being misdirected once more? Jane rose quickly to her feet and sprinted home, in fear for everyone else's life now. She dialed Mac's number. Jerry answered. *It must be Uncle Easy, then,* she concluded. It couldn't be Mac; Jane believed completely that Mac himself was invincible.

"Uncle Easy had a *stroke,*" the boy said excitedly, obviously unaware of what that meant. "It was all the stimulation from last night, Dad thinks. *I* think it was blowing out all those candles. They're at the hospital now."

Jane offered to take the boy with her, and before long they were joining his haggard and disheveled father in the waiting room. Mac was sitting in an armchair with his head in his hands when they walked in. He looked up and started; Jane flushed, remembering his impassioned embrace from the night before. She'd hardly allowed herself to think of it at all. She'd hardly had *time* to think of it at all.

He stood up when she walked in the room, which seemed endearingly old-fashioned of him. It seemed incredible to her that part of her could actually be charmed by part of him at a time like this. *I'm in love with him,* she thought, amazed that she was picking now of all times to admit it.

"How is he?" she asked, flushing more deeply than before.

"Unconscious—but that's not unusual," Mac added quickly when her face fell. "We have to wait and see. They can't tell us anything now."

"Jer," he said, turning to his son, "be a pal and bring us coffee." He gave Jerry directions to the coffee machine; when the boy left, Mac said quietly, "Harrow told me about Cissy. I'm sorry it was you who found her."

"We were all there," Jane said. "If I *had* been alone . . ." Repressing a shudder, she shook her head. "I don't know."

"Harrow said she slipped off the bridge? How?"

"Phillip didn't tell you?" *But then, you'd never ask him,* she realized. "A handrail gave way."

"A handrail? There was nothing wrong with the handrails."

"Yes there was. I saw the one myself, lying underneath her. . . ." Jane stopped, closing her eyes, reliving it again, then pushed it away. "Is Bing okay?"

Mac shook his head. "He's taking it hard. He's convinced that Cissy's estranged husband is involved, and he's been going on about it. Apparently she left behind a suitcase, as if maybe she got called outside unexpectedly. I tried to slow him down, but . . . there's going to be an autopsy, I'm pretty sure."

"This is unbelievable," Jane said, collapsing into a chair. "Last night everyone was so happy. . . ."

"Not everyone," Mac said in a low voice. His hands were in his pockets, his back to her, as he stared out the window at the thickening fog. "Obviously not everyone."

As usual, he was being ambiguous. She *thought* he was talking about himself and her, but she couldn't be sure. This time she decided to ask. "What exactly do you mean, Mac?"

"About last night . . ."

She was right.

He turned to her, his eyes dark with emotion. "I . . . look, I got carried away, all right? I said things—"

"*Said* things! *What* things? You *never* say things!" she said, exploding with tension. "That's the whole problem! A person has to be psychic around you! If you just *once* said how you really feel—"

"I'm *telling* you how I feel," he said, taken aback by her fury. His cheeks flushed with anger as he said, "I feel that that was the dumbest thing I've ever done."

"I mean how you *really* feel," she said, rejecting his answer. Whatever else it was, the kiss he gave her wasn't dumb.

She wasn't finished with him. "I can't *imagine* how those who love you can survive," she went on, frustrated beyond measure with him. "You're like a sun that won't shine, a fire that won't burn. Don't you see? A . . . a boy needs to hear his father say he loves him!" she said, veering off and substituting shamelessly. "He needs it the way a tree needs water!"

"*My* dad tells me he loves me. All the time."

Jane whirled around to see Jerry, a cup of coffee in each hand, standing there with a look of deep offense in his young face. The look said that Jane had crossed a line, that she had stepped inside a circle she didn't belong. Oh, how she knew that face, knew that look.

Jane had shot from the hip many times in her life, but she'd never shot herself *through* the hip before. Truly mortified, she blurted, "I'm sorry. I shouldn't be here," and fled.

No heart can take such a pounding.

Jane was back at Lilac Cottage, nursing a massive headache along with her heartache. Still, she tried to put her pain in perspective. *She* hadn't lost the one she loved to sudden death or to a stroke. Heck, Mac wasn't even hers to lose. He'd looked her over and found her attractive, but

316 Antoinette Stockenberg

not enough to make the leap over the chasm that he thought divided them. *So that's that,* she told herself—over, and over, and over.

She dialed the number of the hospital reception desk another time and asked about Uncle Easy. When she wasn't calling the hospital, people were calling her; word had whipped around the island like the back end of a hurricane. In the meantime she watched for cars: Mac's, Bing's, even Phillip's. She never did see Mac return; but a little while after Bing pulled into his drive, she called him.

He was inconsolable, almost incoherent. "I'm going back to the City *tonight,*" he said in a tense, distracted voice. "I know the Chief of Police. *He'll* get me satisfaction. I'm not getting anywhere at this end. The least they can do here is shut down the airport and outgoing ferries for a few days. But no; all they're doing is watching for Dave and his car."

Considering the circumstances, that sounded reasonable. But Bing didn't want to hear it. He hung up angrily; tomorrow he probably wouldn't remember talking with her.

Jane sighed and called the hospital again. Still no change in the patient's status. It was late. She hadn't the energy—and when it came right down to it, she hadn't the heart—to call Phillip and console him for his loss.

Overnight the fog moved on, leaving the island bathed in bright May sun. It was impossible not to think that things would get better—they couldn't get much worse—and when Jane called the hospital first thing, the news was good. Uncle Easy was conscious and in stable condition. That was all she knew until Billy B. arrived for work.

"It just goes to show," Billy said, shaking his head thoughtfully. He didn't bother finishing the sentence; presumably Jane already knew what it went to show. "But Dr. Braun does seem pretty optimistic about Uncle Easy, at least," he added.

"How do *you* know? They won't tell me a thing."

"My cousin works at the hospital," he said with a shrug. "So that's the good news. The bad news, though . . . boy, she was young. Do you think there's something to this crazed-husband theory?"

"How do you know about *that*?"

He shrugged again. "Carol's uncle is a cop."

"I did see a squad car come through first thing," Jane mused. "They were back there a long time. They must be taking it seriously."

"Let's look around ourselves," Billy said with a gleam in his eye. "Who knows? We might find something."

"You can't go tramping through a possible scene of a crime," she reminded him.

"We can if it's not taped off."

It *was* taped off—at least, the immediate area around the bridge was. There were several possible reasons for it, but none of them mattered to Jane then. She was staring at the trampled wet grass where the two men had hovered over Cissy. She was seeing Cissy, reliving the horror. She started to walk away, then forced herself to come back. If this was Judith's work, then Jane needed to know.

She took off her shoes and socks and rolled up her pants so that she could walk the two giant steps through the gully to get to the other side of the bridge. Nothing looked criminal to her on that side, either. They waded back.

Billy stared over the tape at the fallen rail and said, "It looks like the bolt worked its way out of the upright. None of the bolts have nuts on 'em—probably never have had nuts. See how the bolts are rusted their whole length?"

"But you wouldn't use sideways force just to walk over the bridge," Jane said thoughtfully. "Someone would've had to *push* Cissy into the rail to make it come apart."

"A pissed-off husband, maybe," Billy suggested.

"Maybe." But Jane wasn't convinced. She'd never seen

this mysterious Dave; he was even more of a phantom than Judith. "Come on," she said, "before we get caught."

In the next week Bing got the satisfaction he was demanding—more or less. The New York police hauled Dave Hanlin in for questioning, and Dave gave them an unshakable alibi: he'd been at a party, making a fool of himself in front of at least two dozen people. The autopsy turned up no evidence of rough play, only the single, hideously unlucky bruise to the head. The crime-scene tape was taken down from around the footbridge, and life on Nantucket began returning to normal.

Jane talked with Bing briefly in New York at the funeral. Still shattered, still inconsolable, he told her he was extending an upcoming business trip to Europe by a couple of weeks. He had friends in Rome, and he needed to be away. Jane's heart went out to him. Bing had tried to be mother, father, and brother to Cissy; when she slipped through all the love and care anyway, he took it personally. Jane held Bing close to her. Their parting was unbearably sad.

Now that she was off the island, Jane decided to visit friends who lived an hour north of the City. Hillary was rich and bored, the mother of two kids away in school and mistress of a big Greek Revival overlooking the Hudson River. Spring came early, almost excessively, to Hillary's valley. Riots of apple trees in blossom, acres of greening woods, stands of red-kissed magnolias—Jane had forgotten how lush a land could be. In Nantucket's grudging climate, only the salt-resistant survived on their own. Everything else was coddled by master gardeners and maniacs.

"And even then, one good nor'easter will burn every rhododendron on the island," Jane told her friend as they lingered over sundowners on her brick terrace.

"*Enough* about horticulture," Hillary said, amused by

her urban friend's conversion to the green-thumb faith. "Will you sell, or will you stay?"

Jane sighed deeply. "A few days ago, I was hoping I could stay. I had the inspired notion that I'd help run this tree farm," she said, blushing at the presumptuousness of it. "But the owner's not interested."

"Have you had any offers on the house?"

"Right before I left the island, I got a call from a neighbor who's taken an interest in finding a buyer for me; I suppose he wants to make sure his new neighbor doesn't collect junk cars or anything. Anyway, he says he's putting together a deal I won't be able to refuse."

"Good!" said Hillary. "Then you can set yourself up in Connecticut, and we can go back to visiting one another without calling in the Coast Guard. You must be thrilled; you'll be your own woman at last."

"Yup. Just what I've always wanted."

Jane stayed less than a week, but by the end of that time she missed the island with an intensity that amazed her. She'd had enough of lazy, warm days in the valley. She longed for the moody, rugged side of Nantucket—the biting salt air; the cold and clammy fog; the pale, subtle hues of the heaths on the moors. She missed the reassuring intimacy of the walkaround town, and the flowers jammed into every windowbox and pot. She missed the mournful sound of the foghorn on Brant Point, and walking on the beach with gulls screaming overhead.

She missed Mac.

She couldn't think of the island without thinking of him; they were as woven together as honeysuckle through trellis. Not that it mattered. It was obvious that her time on Nantucket was winding down. So she packed her bags and took the train back to New York, and a plane to Nantucket, and a cab to Lilac Cottage. Billy was outside scraping down the east side of the house, getting it ready to paint. Jane was thrilled to see that he was alive and that the house hadn't burned down. Everything looked so normal; maybe that horrible morning had cleared the air once and for all of tragedy.

They went inside and had coffee, and Billy brought Jane up to date on events. The big news was good news.

"Uncle Easy'll be out of intensive care tomorrow. They've unhooked the tubes; he's eating on his own. He told Mac to bring in the cigars you gave him. His nurse overheard him and said no way. He told her to go to hell."

Billy chuckled and added, "He's a legend around here, you know. *Every*one played in his homemade pool. My *mother* played in his pool. The townies called his place 'The Easy Living Country Club.' "

He held up his coffee cup in a toast. "Here's to Uncle Easy. He's dodged a bullet, and I for one am glad."

Jane clinked her cup to his. "I for two am glad," she said softly. They talked for a while, and then Jane asked casually, "How's Mac?"

"Busy. This is his big season, and instead he's been parking himself at the hospital where he second-guesses the physical therapists all day. They've thrown him out twice. You know Mac."

She laughed, but the fact was, she *didn't* know Mac. Everything she knew about him she'd learned from others, or by watching him furtively out of the corner of her eye. Mac himself had told her almost nothing about himself, and yet they *had* connected, in a very real way, more than once. Too bad she couldn't get him to admit it. Of course, that would require actual speech.

Billy went back to scraping, and Jane put on her rattiest workclothes and joined him. It was time for the big push. She couldn't hold out forever, waiting for some fairy-tale ending to the saga of Lilac Cottage. The tenant in her condo had moved out, which meant no more help with the mortgage, and meanwhile the spring real estate market was peaking. Lilac Cottage had to be sold, and soon.

So she and Billy shared the staging he'd put up, she at her end, he at his; and all day long, sun or fog, they scraped. Sometimes they played Billy's radio, and sometimes they talked, but *all* the time, they scraped. The paint came off in chattering, brittle showers, right down to the wood. They kept on scraping. On foggy days she bundled up. On sunny days she stripped down to shorts and a halter. Her limbs became deeply tanned, and her stamina improved. After a week, she stopped whining to Billy about how hard the work was.

And all the while, Mac drove up and Mac drove down the narrow strip of land that was his lifeline to the outside world. Often he had an assistant in the truck with him. For a while he had Jerry. The back of his dark green pickup was always filled with balled-and-burlapped shrubs and evergreens when he left. When he came back, late in the day, it was empty. Occasionally some other pickup came through, filled up, and left, but that was rare. Jane wondered just how profitable Mac's business was, and spent a lot of her time daydreaming about ways to improve it.

Mac almost never stopped to talk. He'd speed up, in fact, to get past her house quickly. If they happened to make eye contact, he nodded stiffly, and she smiled even more stiffly. Once or twice Billy flagged him down and asked about Uncle Easy. Mac's answers were short and to the point. Soon Billy gave up. He could tell something was wrong. A ladybug could tell something was wrong.

One afternoon, Mac did stop. He leaned out of his truck window and said, "Billy! Any idea where Phillip Harrow is?"

"Not re—"

"Tell him Phillip is in Grand Cayman," Jane muttered under her breath.

Billy looked at her and looked at Mac. "He's in Grand Cayman," he yelled.

"Any idea when he'll be back?"

"Thursday," she murmured.

"Thursday!"

"Thursday? Thanks. Uncle Easy gets out of the hospital on Thursday," Mac called back.

Billy turned to Jane and said, "Uncle Easy gets out of the—"

"For God's sake, I heard the man; I'm not deaf," Jane said irritably.

"And, Jane?" Mac called softly from the seat of his pickup.

She caught her breath at the sound of her own name and turned to him, her eyes flashing with tears of arbitrary, pent-up emotion.

"Uncle Easy says thanks for the flowers and the bubble gum cigars."

"Tell him—tell him I'm glad he's coming home," she said.

"He'd rather hear it from you, I think. I'll be off-island tomorrow," he added meaningfully.

"Ah." No risk, then, of some awkward meeting between Mac and her; no danger of being forced to chitchat politely in front of Uncle Easy. "I'll be there," she said. Too bad Mac wouldn't be; she could blow him away in a chitchat contest.

CHAPTER 22

Lilac Cottage was scraped, sanded, and waiting for dry weather. It looked about as bad as a house can look. So Jane was stunned when Phillip Harrow came back from Grand Cayman and promptly offered her more than she thought she'd get for it in her wildest dreams.

"You've done a very nice job with it," he said, "given the limits of your budget." He smiled good-naturedly and added, "I've been cheering you on, you know; you remind me of me when I started out in real estate."

They had just completed a tour of the inside and were sitting in the front room, looking out at a rainy, foggy day. Billy hadn't come today; Jane and Phillip were alone.

"So *you're* the interested buyer?"

"Yes and no," he admitted. "I have an aunt and uncle who've just sold a big house in Minneapolis. It had become too much work—he's ailing—and nowadays they hate snow. They're a sweet old couple, but they have no children; I'm their closest relation. They need looking after, and if they were in Lilac Cottage I could do that. We walked around it while you were away and they were very taken by it."

"Just like that? But . . . the stairs are steep; and there's no upstairs bath," Jane confessed.

"I'd put in a small bath for my aunt. My uncle would stay downstairs, in the room you haven't redone."

It was implicit that Phillip's relations were putting up the money in some capacity. So there it was: no broker's fee, an easy transaction, good neighbors for everyone else, and

Phillip would be able to do someone a great kindness besides. Jane could hardly do better than this sale.

And yet she hated the thought of it. She didn't want *any* stranger in Aunt Sylvia's room, sweet or not. She didn't want anyone else digging around in Aunt Sylvia's crocuses, or building a fire in her fireplace, or chopping down the holly trees because they blocked the light. Even worse: Mac's prediction about Phillip going after Lilac Cottage was coming true. Of course, Phillip's interest in it seemed perfectly logical, but who was to say there wasn't some grand design, some ulterior motive. . . .

Phillip clearly could see the anguish in her face. "Jane, you don't look ready to sell," he said in a kindly voice. "Obviously you love this place. Is this going too fast for you?"

When she sighed and nodded, he said, "I have a confession to make. My aunt and uncle fell *irrationally* in love with Lilac Cottage. The price they're offering is too much, but I told them you were on the fence about selling, and I think they were hoping to just . . . dazzle you into it. Obviously their ploy didn't work." He stood up to leave. "Thanks for listening to the offer."

"I *am* dazzled," she blurted, since he himself was being so candid. "But I just don't—can you give me a couple of weeks to think it over, Phillip?"

"Of course. If they become enchanted with something else in the meantime, I'll let you know. Or would you prefer a written agreement?"

"Well . . . maybe a written agreement's not a bad idea," she said as she saw him to the door.

They agreed that he'd have his attorney put something simple together, then shook hands on it and Phillip left. Jane wandered around Lilac Cottage adrift for the rest of the day, the wind taken completely out of her sails by Phillip's unexpected offer. It was over, then. Her work here was done.

And yet it wasn't *all* done. What about Judith? Somewhere along the line Jane had accepted responsibility for Judith Brightman's spiritual destiny. Now Jane had two choices: She could jump back into that nightmare, or she could sell Lilac Cottage and sneak off the island, leaving Judith to fend for herself. That would mean handing over a probably haunted house to an aging, ailing couple. *Not a nice thing to do, unless I reduce the price drastically,* she decided with grim humor.

But she still had two weeks. *Anything* could happen in two weeks. It was Thursday night and the Atheneum was open late. The rain had retreated and left behind a layer of sulky fog. Jane needed to think things out, so she put on a jacket and headed downtown on foot, careful to step out of the way of the occasional car that passed her.

She missed Cissy. Cissy had the kind of blind faith that gave Jane the confidence she needed to work through her theories about Judith. Right now, in fact, Jane happened to be working on a doozie. She was remembering that the two times that Judith had appeared in the bedroom, the first time when Buster saw her and the second time when Jane did—those two times came after moments when she and Mac had connected in a very elemental, very physical way.

The theory wasn't perfect (it didn't explain Judith's appearance, if that's what it was, on the videotape) and there were other possible combinations than Mac and Jane (Celeste McKenzie had been around, dammit, before both apparitions). But it did seem as if Judith's spirit was able to draw some kind of strength from the sexual intensity between a man and a woman.

Jane thought about it and shook her head. *If that's what you're looking for, Judith Brightman, then you're in big, big trouble.* The only thing intense about Mac McKenzie lately was his desire to keep his distance from her.

Jane went into the Atheneum, waved to the librarian,

nipped a Fig Newton, and headed downstairs for the microfilm viewer. Back to 1852 she went, scanning through the classified ads. Judith Brightman had been a merchant, and merchants advertised in the *Inquirer*. It was worth a shot.

She scrolled her way through the ads hawking everything from white beans to dress silks, looking for Judith Brightman's name. The big advertisements were taken out by—who else?—the Macy and Starbuck and Gardner types. But there were little two-liners by small-time merchants for everything from crushed sugar to cheap gaiter boots; those were the ones Jane read carefully. Some had names, some addresses. The most promising one, the one that made the hair on the back of Jane's neck tingle, was the following one:

> *Long Shawls. Just received a new lot of fine quality black shawls to be sold low. Also, tasteful muslin and cambric trimmings.*

There was no proprietor's name, only an address on Pine Street.

Jane forced herself to keep reading through the classifieds until the Atheneum closed its doors for the night; but nothing moved her as the shawl ad did. *It has to be her ad,* Jane decided, almost out of desperation. *I don't have time for it not to be.*

Pine Street was not Main Street; obviously the dry goods shop had been operated out of a private home, which wasn't uncommon back then. Jane hurried along the glistening cobbled streets, anxious to see what the establishment looked like. One thing she could count on in Nantucket: The house would still be there. She walked away from the town's center down the dark and empty street, listening to the sound of her own footsteps. The houses on

Pine were typically Nantucket: plain, solid structures built originally for mariners and tradesmen.

The fog was thick, the numbers hard to read. Jane passed the house right by, then had to back up to it. *Not a good sign; I feel nothing at all,* she decided, reacting like some latter-day psychic.

It was no captain's mansion. The little frame cottage was built on a high brick basement and, like so many Nantucket houses, fronted directly on the street. It had very little land, just a twelve-foot strip alongside to accommodate a car that no doubt wouldn't be showing up until July. *Yet another pied-à-terre,* Jane thought, feeling some of the distaste that Mac felt for the hit-and-run visitor.

She tiptoed into the drive, wincing at the noisy crunching of crushed white shells underfoot, to see what she could see. Each of the house's side windows, like the front door, was shuttered tight. There was a small back yard with what might have been a large lilac overspreading it; it was too dark there to tell. Squeezed between the drive and the house were a mix of shrubs and rosebushes, all of them pruned back severely to allow room for the owner's car.

Once, this was a garden, Jane realized with sadness; but the parking shortage was a fact of life in town. She remembered reading that when cars were still a newfangled thing, people had tried and failed to get them banned on the island. Now there were fewer cabbages, fewer tomato plants as a result of their failure. *Ah, well; the owners wouldn't be around to tend them anyway.*

She went back out in front and stood under a street lantern, trying to pick up some sense of Judith in or out of the house.

Is that the house where she waited for Ben? Is that where she defied Jabez Coffin and the Elders? What about the gray shawl, the only gray one in the lot—did she fold it over a rocking chair inside that *house?*

The dream. It began to come back. Jane stood very still,

willing the forgotten dream of Jabez Coffin and the Elders to return. She remembered it all now. She remembered the rocking chair, the gray shawl, the little framed silhouette of Ben Brightman on the mantel. She remembered every word of Judith's final confrontation with the relentless and unyielding Overseer. It was as clear in her mind as a big-screen film.

And now she knew something else: It was Judith's rocking chair that was sitting in the corner of Jane's bedroom. Not that it was surprising: Nantucket recycled its furniture the way some communities did their milk bottles.

How odd, Jane thought, that there was no pain in her shoulder this time, no psychic whispers of "Warmer! Warmer!" from Judith. Jane felt nothing, nothing but a bedrock certainty that this was the house where Judith had lived with—and without—the man she had loved more than life itself.

When Bing returned from Europe he looked a little thinner, a little older, and a lot wiser. He no longer had the sparkle of a man who believes that life's a cabaret, and most of the good-natured mischief was gone from his eyes. But his embrace was as warm and comfortable as ever; and when he let her go, Jane felt as if someone had taken away her favorite bathrobe.

They were sitting in the fireplace room of Lilac Cottage, watching a whimpering Duraflame log do its thing. Despite the chimney sweep's reassurances, Jane hadn't had the courage to crank up a good wood fire since the night she nearly burned the house down.

"You've had the damndest luck since you moved into this place," Bing mused after she explained that to him. He swirled the brandy in his snifter, no doubt remembering the one who'd had the worst luck of all. "Any more mysteries since I've been gone?"

"Things have been quiet."

"Mmmn—for me too. Every other time I've been in Rome—well, I've enjoyed doing what the Romans do. It's a great city, a great place to party. I love Rome. It has breadth. It has depth. It has the most heartbreaking sunsets I've ever seen. It has everything," he said, staring into the snifter.

He put the glass down on the little gaming table and said, "But it didn't have you."

"Rome knows how to party without me," Jane said, smiling.

"Hear me out, Jane," Bing said edgily. "This is brand new territory for me. I don't want to get lost. What I'm trying to say is, losing Cissy left a big hole in my life, right where loved ones and commitment should be. If all of Rome couldn't fill that hole, then I'm doomed, unless . . ."

"Jane," he said, tilting her chin up to meet his gaze, "you know how I feel about you. Maybe losing Cissy has crystallized those feelings, but I would've made it to this stage anyway, I'm sure I would have."

"Bing—"

"No. Let me ask. *Will* you marry me? Will you consider it?" he said quickly when she began to shake her head.

"Bing, I haven't let myself think about—"

"No, no, of course not. You're ambitious; you have plans. I know that. And I can help you realize them. The children would have to wait. Or maybe you don't want children at all—I hope you do—but if you don't, I'll understand that too."

"Well, no, *I* want children, sooner or later," Jane said in confusion. "But we're putting the cart before the horse."

He took her by her shoulders and said, "Jane—don't you see? If we don't grab at life now, if we don't just take love when we find it and hold on to it, it'll be gone. *We'll be gone.*"

There was a look of fear in his eyes that made her say,

"Bing, don't. You're letting your sister's death stampede you—"

"I'm not being stampeded. I love you, darling. I love you. I want you to love *me*."

He was drowning; she had to reach out to him, to keep him from going under in grief and panic. "I *do* care for you, Bing; I do. It must be love. . . ."

His blue eyes lit up in triumphant relief as he pulled her to him and kissed her, hard. If Jane needed proof that Bing was not The One, the kiss was it. There was a time when she thought he made her hear bells ring. Now, after Mac, it was like listening to a compact disc after she'd stood in the bell tower itself.

"But it's not the love you mean," she said softly, taking his hands in her own.

And he knew it; he could tell by the kiss. Jane was afraid he might be angry, but he was mostly puzzled. "I don't get it," he confessed. "We're a perfect fit, completely in gear with one another."

"True. We make great pals. But maybe there need to be one or two sharp edges between a man and a woman. It creates some pretty good sparks as they rub one another smooth."

Bing laughed skeptically. "Tell *that* to a machinist."

He didn't give up right away. They went round and round and round, until one or so in the morning. The last thing Bing told Jane was that he considered his proposal to be still pending. The last thing Jane said to Bing was, "*Please* don't tell my mother that." He laughed, and she closed the door after him and leaned tiredly against it.

So. Bing Andrews wants to take me away from all this. Phillip Harrow wants to send me away from all this. And Mac McKenzie just wants us all to go away.

"Nantucket," she said with a sigh, "you're breaking my heart."

* * *

Early the next morning Jane struck out down the lane to Mac's place, his sweater draped over her arm. She would've returned it sooner but she had too much sense than to throw her body in front of his speeding truck, trying to get him to stop for her. Secretly she hoped it was his favorite sweater, and that he'd be forced to come begging for it; but trying to outlast Mac McKenzie was a fool's game, and Jane Drew knew it.

Her excuse was the sweater, but her mission was to tell Mac that she planned to accept Phillip's offer on the house. She had no choice; it was an offer most people would kill for. She felt obliged to let Mac know first, even though she still wasn't one hundred percent sure she'd accept. Funny, how she was able to decline the hand of a demigod without a second thought, and yet was still hemming and hawing over a house that made no sense to keep. Pretty funny.

She saw Mac before he saw her. He was on a backhoe, scooping a four-foot Austrian pine out of the earth. He'd already removed three others; each sat neatly with its root ball on an open square of burlap. Buster was lying nearby, paws stretched out in front of him, tongue heaving contentedly. It was impossible for Jane to look at the dog without thinking of Cissy chasing madly after him, an empty leash dangling from her hand. Maybe that was a good thing: Buster kept the memory of her alive.

The dog got to his feet and came toward her with his tail wagging, ready and willing to knock down small buildings with it. Mac, still seated, swung partway round on the seat of his backhoe. He was surprised to see Jane there; the muscles working in his jaw were a dead giveaway. Then he saw the sweater, and seemed relieved. *Okay, you have a socially correct reason for being here,* was how she read the sun-squint look under his baseball cap.

"You're up early," he said, turning off the noisy engine

of the backhoe. "And how was Rome? Still eternal?" Obviously he knew that Bing had been over and stayed late.

"I think Bing said something to that effect," she said. "I brought you your sweater," she added, holding it up for his inspection. "I'd forgotten all about it." *Except for all the times I buried my face in it as I passed it on the hook by the kitchen door.* "Would you like me to put it somewhere for you?" she asked, seeing that there was no place on the small backhoe for it.

Mac swung one leg over the seat and dismounted. "That's all right; I was just going in anyway." He accepted the sweater from her and tossed it over his shoulder. "It's looking like my help is a no-show; I've got to call my customer and warn them that I'll be late with the delivery. *Damn,*" he muttered, more to himself than to her.

"Why 'damn'? Is it critical?"

"Yeah, you could say that. A family has planned a big reunion around a mass planting on their property. All of 'em—kids, cousins, grandparents—are supposed to take up shovels and help. They've been planning this for a year. I've pruned the roots; everything's ready to lift out. I shouldn't have waited until the last day to do it, shouldn't have counted on someone else."

She knew he'd been running himself ragged with his Uncle Easy; the patient himself had told her that. "I could give you a hand."

He smiled. "Thanks, but it's—don't be offended—pretty much a man's job. Someone has to tie up the burlap, tag 'em—"

"Oh, my! Exhausting!"

"And then help load 'em in the truck."

"I could do that, too."

"You might break a nail."

With a withering look, she held up what was left of her fingernails after weeks of scraping paint.

"Okay," he said with a look that was half bemused and

clearly desperate. "You pass. Come in and I'll give you some coveralls," he added, casting an appraising look over her snug-fitting denims. "Thin designer jeans won't cut it in the field. And it would help things out if you could bend."

She blushed at that one, but decided she had it coming because it was true: She *couldn't* bend. In the house he handed her a workshirt and a pair of heavy bib overalls and she changed in the downstairs bath while he made the call to the customer. She studied herself in the mirror and didn't like what she saw: no curves, no tan, no *hint* that a woman was underneath it all. The maddening refrain from "Old MacDonald Had a Farm" dropped into her head and stayed there as she twisted her long auburn hair into a quick braid. *Ee-aye-ee-aye-oh.*

Nuts. This was no way to impress a man.

She walked into his kitchen with a sheepish smile. "This doesn't feel terribly feminine," she confessed.

Mac gave her a wry and utterly penetrating look. "If you'd rather run home for the little halter and shorts, feel free."

He *had* noticed her all those times. Somehow it made her feel almost as bad as if he'd driven past without seeing her. Coloring, she said, "No thanks. I wouldn't look any more feminine with bloody knees."

He liked her answer; she could see the hard-edged glint in his eyes soften to grudging approval. "We'll make a soldier of you yet," he said, taking her by the shoulders and marching her out of the house.

Mac was clearly in a hurry to get the job done. He showed her how to fold the burlap square around the rootball, then tie a series of rolling half-hitches around it with manila twine. He handed her a sod knife and a pair of gloves and said, "You're on your own."

Jane dropped to her knees in her nice, thick overalls and got to work. The first three pines seemed to take her forever to bundle; she tossed the gloves aside almost immediately, preferring to work barehanded with the rough manila and knowing she'd pay for it later. It was hot, hard work. The beads of sweat on her forehead soon became rivulets. The scratchy branches of the pines seemed bent on a search-and-destroy mission for bare skin.

Whenever she glanced up, Mac had popped another pine out of the ground. She was getting farther and farther behind. When he reached the end of the row, she breathed a sigh of relief. But no; on to the next row he went. She became increasingly embarrassed by her performance; the greenest migrant worker could have done a better job. Maybe that's what Mac was after. Maybe he wanted to show her once and for all what a lousy arborist she'd make.

She wished she had a hat. If she had a hat to shade her face, things would be different. Mac could have given her a hat. Or a visor. Even a sweatband. *Some*thing. She wiped her brow with her dusty shirtsleeve, dirtying her face. She didn't care how she looked; *that* mood was long gone. She glared at Mac's broad back, at those compact buns sitting comfortably on the seat of the backhoe. *Oh, sure. Sit-down work for the overseer, pick-and-shovel duty for the help. If that wasn't the way of the world.*

The sun climbed higher. She was desperately thirsty, and she would have liked to pee. But Mac wasn't offering to take a break, and she'd die before she asked for one. By now her hands were chafed and cut from the manila. She had no choice but to put the gloves on, though she dreaded being slowed down even more by the awkwardness of wearing them. It came as a complete and very pleasant surprise that she began working faster than before because her hands no longer hurt as much.

Eventually—finally!—Mac shut down the noisy little backhoe and got to work at the other end of the line, bagging the pines at about twice her speed. Jane picked up the pace, focusing on her task as if she were conducting a nuclear experiment. They got down to one pine between them. She lunged for the burlap ahead of him and began folding it over the rootball.

He watched her lasso the rootball like the drugstore cowboy she was, which made her intensely self-conscious. "Do you want to take a break?" he asked when she was done.

"Who, me?" she said, bounding up. "Not unless you do," she said offhandedly, trying not to wheeze.

The corner of his mouth turned up in a one-dimpled smile. Then he shrugged and turned away. "Nope. I'm fine."

Jane dropped her chin on her chest with a silent groan. But at least she could slow down now. Labeling the little critters would be downright fun.

"The next thing we have to do is get those half-dozen pines out of there," he said, pointing to a thicket of evergreens. "It's too tight for the forklift, or even the nursery truck. The trees are already bagged, but we'll have to carry them out to the forklift by hand. They're heavy. Are you sure you're up to this?" he asked blandly. "You don't have to—"

"Lead the way," she said in a voice that was utterly grim.

Mac got the shrub-caddy, a kind of metal stretcher for trees, and they squeezed their way through the densely planted area. "I overplanted," Mac said tersely. "I hadn't counted on the crash in new-home building. I have to just about give these away now." He was just ahead of her, picking the path through the dense branches, holding an occasional bough back for her.

"Why don't you just have a live Christmas tree sale this December?" Jane asked. "You could have people cut their own. It would be a nice family event; kids adore that kind of thing. *I* did."

"I told you," he said as they stopped in front of the first balled evergreen. "I only do wholesale."

"But your stock needs thinning. . . . You can see some of the trees are growing misshapen."

"That's not today's problem. Tomorrow's reunion is today's problem."

"I don't understand you." Jane was sitting on the ground now, pushing at the root ball with both feet to tip it so that Mac could slip the caddy under it. It was like pushing on a granite block. She rearranged her arms behind her to get better leverage. "You can be so . . . *oof*," she said, her foot slipping right over the top of the root ball.

She fell flat on her back. She was so tired that it felt good. She closed her eyes and sighed, and when she opened them Mac was on one knee alongside her, chuckling. He offered her his hand to pull her up.

"Thanks," she said, taking it. But something—the glint in his eye, the rich, piney scent of the fallen needles underneath her—made her reach out her other hand to him as well. She didn't want him to help her up. She knew he understood that, as surely as he understood that *she* wanted to be the one to run his Christmas tree sale, and every other sale besides. She was being so obvious about both.

"Oh, Mac . . ." she said, her voice breaking with desire.

He made a sound low in his throat. "Jesus, woman, don't do that . . . don't invite me. . . ."

In one fluid motion he was on the ground alongside her, cradling her head in his hands, pinning her to the ground in his embrace, his mouth invading hers with a kind of fierceness that would've frightened her if she hadn't been feeling the same fierce passion herself.

He kissed her mouth, her cheeks, her mouth again—hot, tortured kisses—and she kissed him back, her mouth dragging across the slippery surface of his work-heated skin. Everywhere, everywhere there was salt from the sweat of their hard labor. It was a potent aphrodisiac, utterly different from the perfumed encounters she'd had with other men.

Here, together, it was impossible to tell where the earth ended and where they began. She felt a natural overload of the senses, a confusion of human and wild: of pine needles and his scratchy beard; of loamy softness and the rough weave of their clothing; of acid soil and the rich, true smell of them both; and with it all, the taste of salt. She was reeling from it, from the uniqueness of it all.

He was struggling with the brass clips at the top of her overalls; it was plain that he'd never had to remove them from someone else's body before. "Ah, beloved, I've bundled you up too well," he said shakily, and she was lost in joy that he'd called her "beloved."

She wanted to help him, to hasten the undressing of her, because she'd waited so long for him already; all of her life. So she fumbled at the other brass clip, and succeeded just before he did.

If Jane had set off a car alarm, she could not have broken the mood more thoroughly.

Mac rolled away from her and sat up, a stunned look on his face. "My God. What're we doing? I'm taking you like some . . . some fieldhand in a cornpatch."

Something inside Jane—some tiny, green shoot of hope —began to wither and die when she saw his face. She knew that the next words she spoke would be absolutely critical; she was terrified that she would not choose them well.

"I love being here with you," she said, moved to inexpressible emotion. "I *want* to be."

"No good. No good," he murmured distractedly. He ran his hands through his sweat-damp hair. "God, this is a nightmare. Every promise I've ever made to myself . . ."

He turned back to her. She was still lying there, brass clips undone, hoping. He lifted some strands of hair that were caught on her damp skin as if he were lifting a butterfly from a flower petal, and wiped a dirt smudge from her cheek as if he were setting it back down again. Her eyes glazed over with tears; she wanted so much to hold him against her breast.

"It's never going to be you," he said in a voice that was low and rich and aching. "It just can't be." She could see the desire, see the tenderness in his eyes.

And she could see the strength, the willpower. She'd simply not known another man like him. He'd made up his mind that they weren't suitable for one another, and nothing on *earth* was going to change that.

"I can't force you to make love to me," she said, unable to keep the despair from her voice. She reached up for the brass clips on her overalls and slipped them over the buttons herself, trying to salvage what she could of her pride.

There was a dark flush of emotion in Mac's cheeks; he understood perfectly what he was putting her through. He stood up, and she stood up, and he said, "I'll take you home."

"I'm not going."

The words slipped out before Jane had time to think about them, but after she said them their meaning became clear enough to her. "This has nothing to do with . . . there," she said, pointing to the ground on which they both had lain. "But it has everything to do with keeping my end of a bargain. I'm not being a martyr," she said quickly when he began to object. "I'm not trying to make you feel guilty. I'm just finishing the job. The family is counting on us. Let's get to work."

She'd left absolutely no room for argument. With a nod, Mac said, "I'll push. You hold."

He tilted the root ball for Jane and she held it in position with her feet until they got the caddy underneath. Then they lifted it together, with Mac showing her how to use her legs and not her back, and they carried it to the nearest clearing, where the forklift waited. From there they loaded it onto the truck. Jane was more limber than Mac, although she lacked his raw strength. By sitting down and using her legs to push and prod the trees into place, she managed to do a creditable job of keeping things moving.

And all the while they exchanged hardly a word. It seemed inconceivable to Jane that after all this time, after all that had passed between them, they had less to say to one another than ever. And yet they seemed more aware of one another than ever. Every move he made, every glance he stole, she saw. As for Mac, he seemed to know her thoughts before she did: If she needed more labels, or couldn't find the sod knife, he was there for her. They worked so well together; it amazed her that he couldn't see it.

The truck was filled to capacity, but it was still only half the total load to be delivered. Jane assumed that they'd be making a second trip and went into the house to use the bathroom. When she came back outside she saw that Mac had stripped down to his pants and was hosing off his arms. She tried to look away, to pay attention instead to the beautiful waterview. But the view a few feet from her was far more riveting: a man with a smooth, powerful torso, deeply bronzed and Nautilus-free. Mac was so completely at ease with his body. It was obvious in every move he made that he'd got his strength the old-fashioned way: by earning it.

He threw the hose to the ground and dried his arms quickly with a towel that hung on an outside hook, then grabbed his shirt and shot his arms through it in that strangely efficient way men have with shirts. "All set?" he asked, buttoning it hurriedly. His mind seemed to be completely on the delivery now.

Jane wondered what he'd do if she walked up to him and tore the shirt off. But she wouldn't dream now of taking the risk, and so she climbed dutifully into the front seat for the delivery. It wasn't until Mac stopped the truck in front of her house that she realized he had other plans for her.

"There are four generations of men over there," he said. "I should be able to draft a couple of 'em for the second load. If I can't find any volunteers I'll give a holler—unless you've had all the fun you can stand by now," he added dryly.

"Sure," she said without looking at him. But she knew she didn't have a snowball's chance in hell of being needed by him.

And she was right. A couple of hours later she heard his truck go roaring by, and the sound of young men's laughter inside.

CHAPTER 23

They had three days of sun followed by three days of fog. On the good days Jane and Billy painted from dawn to dusk. On the bad days, Jane wandered around in a fog of her own.

Billy was winding down at Lilac Cottage. He'd lined up a nice renovation job which would pay his bills for the next ten weeks. As for Bing, he'd gone back to work in the City; he was giving her time to regroup. Phillip was off the island, too. He'd gone from Grand Cayman directly to Minneapolis, where he was helping his aunt and uncle clean up their affairs. When Phillip called to find out whether Jane had made a decision, she told him she'd accept the offer after all. Phillip said his aunt and uncle would be thrilled.

They weren't the only ones. Jane's mother was ecstatic when she heard the news. She ran to put Jane's father on an extension phone.

"Nice work, lambkins," Neal Drew said, thoroughly impressed. "That's a damn sight higher than they told me you could get. With that start, the world's your oyster. You'll be hanging out your own shingle in no time. I'm proud of you, honey."

Jane couldn't have asked for higher praise.

There was, however, one little thing: Jane never did tell Mac that she'd had an offer from Phillip, much less that she'd accepted it. Paranoid or not, Mac deserved to be told. The question was how. Jane tried doing it in a note. She tore it up. She tried calling Mac, but hung up at the sound of his voice. She got halfway down the lane to his

house, then turned around when she heard the tractor.
Phillip wasn't due back for two whole days. She had time.

In the meantime she wandered around the island,
brooding over her imminent departure, trying to absorb
the moors, the beaches, the cobbled streets, and the
crooked lanes into her permanent consciousness. It was
devastating to her to think she'd soon be leaving all of it.

She was leaving, but the summer colony was arriving, in
force. Like Mac, Jane wanted to send them all packing on
the first boat out. What did *they* know about Nantucket's
winter moods and rich history? She and Mac had shared
that, if nothing else. Mac had two centuries of Nantucket
in his blood; Jane, in her soul.

And yet her connection to it all was growing fainter.
Judith seemed to have abandoned Lilac Cottage. Not since
the night of Uncle Easy's party had Jane had any sign from
her. The gravesite was equally quiet. The buds on the
rugosa rose were bursting into fragrant bloom—Jane had
some of them in a vase in the fireplace room right now—
but that was all.

That left the house on Pine Street. Jane went back to it
several times. Whatever there was left for her to know,
Jane felt certain she would know it there. She became
something of a loiterer, admiring an arrangement in a
flower box, bending over a picket fence for a closer look at
a delphinium, pausing before a door painted an especially
subtle color.

The neighborhood began to wonder about her: Jane
heard a mother say sharply through an open window,
"Timothy, go play in the *back* yard, right now."

Through it all, no Judith. No anyone, in fact. The house
on Pine was still shuttered tight, despite the fact that its
south-facing roses, warmed and coddled by the house itself, were in full bloom. *What a waste,* Jane thought.
Granted, passersby like her could admire the colorful

blooms. But one or two of the shrubs were old-garden roses; undoubtedly, they would have a seductive fragrance.

The owner should be here, filling up his house with their scent, she told herself. *It's a sin not to.*

Which is how Jane rationalized the nipping of a dozen or so blooms with the pruning shears she just happened to have with her, and tucking them into a canvas shoulderbag she just happened to be carrying.

The next day it was foggy again. By now Jane was wild from the constraint of not having anything constructive to do. She wanted to finish painting the house so that she could begin distancing herself from it emotionally. But Jane wasn't deluding herself: She knew she was edgy because she hadn't yet told Mac about selling Lilac Cottage to his lifelong enemy. She knew it, but she seemed helpless to do anything about it. And in the meantime Phillip was due back that night, expecting to pick up the signed agreement waiting on the table near the new front door.

Late that afternoon Jane was rearranging her stolen roses into smaller vases for no other reason than to burn off excess energy. She was as jumpy as a cat; even Wicky was staying out of her way. When the knock on the door came, Jane let out a startled cry and promptly knocked over the vase she'd been setting up on the mantelpiece. She grabbed unthinkingly at the thorny stems at the same time that water from the vase went flying over the mantel's edge, landing on the brick hearth and scaring the cat, who ran scrambling from the room with his fur on end.

"Oh, for pity's sake!" she said angrily.

She'd pierced her middle finger. Annoyed, she squeezed a tiny droplet of blood from it as she went to answer the knock. She swung the door open sharply, as if it was the door's fault that she was smarting.

It was Mac. Standing there in the fog, dressed as he was in jeans, a dark blue turtleneck, and a dark blue windbreaker, he looked almost more sinister than brooding. She hesitated whether to ask him in; she'd never seen him look that way before.

He saw that she was rubbing the tip of her finger. "Thorn," she explained briefly, holding it up for his inspection. "I don't know why I can't just pick daisies like everyone else. I . . . would you like to come in?" she asked suddenly.

So much for hesitating. It was no use; she could no more act indifferent to him than she could ignore the act of breathing.

Mac nodded and walked in ahead of her, straight to the fireplace room. She couldn't begin to imagine why he'd come; that's how much of a mystery he still was to her. He went up to the window that looked out at Bing's house, the window from which she'd once seen him lurking in the shadows outside, and stared into the fog-darkened twilight. His hands were on his hips; she heard him sigh and saw his shoulders droop a little, as if he didn't have the heart for what he was about to do. It threw a perfect chill around her soul.

"I'd rather say this to almost anyone else on the island than to you," he began. "I know they'd understand."

Here they were at the eleventh hour and he was still at it, putting her in a separate box from his friends and relations. Anger rushed in, replacing the chill he'd made her feel.

"Suppose you try me, just this once," she said with obvious resentment.

Mac turned around, surprised by her tone. "I'm sorry," he said. "You think I'm patronizing you. I'm not. But you've laughed at my warnings so many times before—"

"Oh, for crying out loud. Is this about *Phillip* again?" she said, disappointed.

His cheeks, ruddy from the cold and fog, turned a deeper hue. "I hate to be a bore," he answered. "But yes.

It is. Harrow's due on the island late tonight. That's why I'm here . . . against my better judgment."

She wanted to say, "Your judgment *stinks.*" Instead she simply said, "Go ahead. I'm listening."

One thing about Mac McKenzie: He got straight to the point. "First of all, let me say I don't think your life's in danger—"

"What?"

"But then I didn't think Cissy's was, either."

"What?"

"Her death wasn't premeditated, but it wasn't exactly an accident," Mac said quietly. "The footbridge was sabotaged. The handrail was rigged to give way; I found the bolt for it a few feet away, in the gully. It couldn't have fallen there. *You* were meant to get a dousing, Jane; but that's all. It was just rotten luck that Cissy slipped and fell hard on the rock."

"Oh, this time you've taken your paranoia too far, Mac," Jane said seriously. "I saw Phillip's face; he was horrified when we found her."

"That doesn't mean he didn't pull the bolt."

"No," Jane had to admit. "It doesn't." A troubling image flickered in her memory, like a navigation buoy glimpsed and then lost again in the fog. "I don't say it's not possible," she said vaguely, going up to the mantel. "I just don't think it's probable."

The fact was, she had the power to turn Mac's suspicion upside-down with one short sentence: "I've accepted an offer from Phillip." Obviously no one would bother with dirty tricks when money could do the job so much more pleasantly.

But to tell that to Mac would take more courage than Jane currently possessed. She needed a moment to gather her wits. Stalling for time, she carefully lifted the pale pink roses from their spilled vase and began adding them, one by one, into the pitcher that held the darker rugosa roses.

"Isn't this pink one incredible?" she remarked, holding her nose close to one of the yellow-stamened roses. "Such a strange, exotic fragrance. It's called 'Belle Amour.' I swiped it from . . . in town. It's quite ancient; I looked it up. They say it was discovered in a German convent."

The scent really was remarkable: intensely fragrant, and yet faintly bitter. She'd never known anything like it. "Here. Smell," she said, offering Mac the one she was holding. In the meantime she was thinking, *I have to tell him. I have to tell him.*

He reacted with a daunting scowl. "What the hell is wrong with you? Have you heard anything I said? Do you understand that Harrow's undoubtedly the one behind the attempts to frighten the daylights out of you? That he's the one who threw your laundry in the mud?"

"What can I tell you? You're wrong," she said calmly. She looked down to see that she'd pricked her finger yet again on the Belle Amour rose, this time in two places. She stared at the drops of blood in amazement. She was reminded of a friend who'd once crumpled a wineglass in her hand as she washed dishes during an argument with her lover. The friend, too, thought she was being perfectly normal, perfectly calm.

"You're bleeding," Mac said in a low, tense voice.

"No I'm not," she answered stupidly. "Anyway," she added, popping a Kleenex out of a nearby box and wrapping it around her finger, "I'll think about what you said. Honestly I will. And thanks."

"It'd be nice if you believed me," Mac said with a dark look. "Phillip Harrow can be dangerous when it suits him."

"Good grief," she said gaily, trying to keep it light. "Next you'll be saying he murdered his wife."

"Her fall from the boat was very convenient," Mac agreed, astonishing Jane with his bluntness. "She was a wealthy woman."

He's obsessed, Jane realized with dismay. And yet something—maybe his sudden, surprising candor—drove her to provoke him. "Where has all the money gone, in that case?" she demanded to know. "Phillip is strapped for cash. Everyone on the island knows that."

"Everyone on the island knows what Harrow wants them to know."

"I've heard very nice things about him," she persisted, struggling to fit the last pink rose in the pitcher without pricking herself again. "And besides, why haven't you taken your suspicions to the police?"

"Because they're only that—suspicions. This is a small island. Reputation is everything. Trust me," he added caustically. "On a more cynical note, I can't afford a lawsuit for slander."

Jane turned away from her flower arrangement on the mantel and looked Mac straight in the eye. "Aren't you taking a risk in telling *me,* in that case?"

She saw a flash of the fire that she'd seen in his eyes the week before, under the Austrian pines. He turned away from her and leaned both hands into the mantel, pushing against it. He reminded her of a runner, stretching before he hit the road; she took it as a sign.

She was expecting some why-did-I-bother response from him. Instead Mac looked down at the brick hearth and shook his head and said, "If you don't know that I trust you, Jane Drew, then you don't know anything at all."

In its lefthanded way, it was a wonderful compliment. Jane was deeply moved. It was no small thing for a man like Mac McKenzie to admit he trusted an off-island female who was on record as being in a hurry to cash in her piece of his beloved homeland. How could she possibly betray that trust? Instantly Jane resolved not to sell, not to leave—not while there was still hope.

She fiddled with the pitcher of roses on the mantel, trying to think of the right thing to say. One wrong move and he'd bolt.

And yet Mac didn't seem inclined to bolt. He seemed inclined to stand on the hearth next to her, engulfed in the delicious, overpowering scent of the old-world roses. Even Jane, unconsciously aware that the faint bitterness of the Belle Amour rose had disappeared in the combined new scent of the two roses, was mesmerized.

"Well, if you trust me, and if you're worried about me," Jane said softly, "then why—"

"—do I steer so clear of you?" he asked, anticipating her question. He took a deep breath and held it, then exhaled. When he turned to her there was a surprised look in his eyes, as if someone had spiked the office punch.

"Why do you think? We're a complete mismatch, I . . . I've told you that," he said vaguely. He seemed to be struggling to remember exactly what constituted a mismatch. "You have a master's degree," he said at last, picking up the thread of his thought. "Whereas I have a high school equivalency. . . . You've circled the globe . . . I've hardly been off the island. . . . You have what my folks used to call expectations . . . I'm up to my ears in mortgage debt. . . . I don't know," he said, baffled and disoriented. "There must be other reasons. . . . You say *tomahto* . . . I say *tomayto*. . . ."

Something was happening between them. She could see it in his eyes; she could feel it coursing through her. He was smiling now, bemused and enchanted, sliding his hands into the thick silk tresses of her hair, wrapping them once around, lowering his mouth closer to hers. "Did I mention money . . . that I don't have any?" he asked in a dreamy, drunken voice.

"That's okay," she said with a dizzy, champagne smile of her own. "I don't have what you're calling expectations, either."

"And another thing . . . this urban thing," he said, his brows still drawn in reverie. "I'm a country boy; I don't think much of red lights. . . ."

She slipped her arms around his neck. "The light is green, Mac," she whispered.

He brought his mouth down on hers in an open kiss of piercing sweetness; it was like the time he gave her the daffodil, without the daffodil. It simply took her breath away, that he could be so tender and so overwhelming at the same time. Jane had been kissed by gentle men, and she'd been kissed by strong men, but she'd never been kissed by the perfect man before. *This is it,* she thought with a kind of panicky ecstasy. *He's ruined me for anyone else.*

He kissed her again, a long, lingering kiss that was light-years different from their torrid encounter in the pine grove. She rejoiced in it, because this time, he was taking his time. There would be no impulsive dash into mindless passion, no wrenching away with agonies of second thoughts. This time they were in perfect accord. This time they had forever.

She lifted her head and their eyes met. Mac said simply, "Are you sure?"

She threw her head back and chuckled, a rich sound of confidence that echoed deep in her throat. "Mac. My darling, deliberate Mac—does McDonald's have arches?"

"What's a McDonald's?" he said through his smile, his mouth trailing to her throat.

She laughed out loud, amazed at the change in him, wondering how and why he'd decided to open his heart to her. But her happiness got swept away in a new and deeper thrill when he began to undo the metal buttons of her shirt, sliding it just away from her shoulders.

He dropped a feathery kiss on the outside curve of her shoulder and said, "I've wanted to do this since I saw you on the staging, scraping paint with Billy B." He trailed a path of kisses from her shoulder to the hollow of her throat, murmuring, "It was all I could do . . . not to knock Billy off the staging . . . and take his place."

She moaned a delicious, vindicated moan. "Ah, Mac, I wish you had. It would've saved me so many sleepless nights."

"Yeah, but Billy might not paint so well in traction." Mac's laugh was as shaky as his touch, as he skimmed the outline of her breasts with his fingertips. "Ah, love . . . I've wanted you much further back than that," he said, sounding almost baffled by his own desire.

Her eyelids were heavy with passion, but she was afraid to close her eyes completely, afraid that when she opened them, he'd be gone. "How far; how far back have you wanted me?" she begged to know.

His laugh was bemused, unsure, as he unbuttoned the last of the metal buttons. "Since . . . I want to say, the funeral, but it must be . . . before that. I suppose, since I was fifteen, and you spent the summer here. . . . No, even that's not right."

He cradled her face in his hands and gave her a look so intense with longing that she felt *his* pain in addition to her own. "I've wanted you as long as memory itself," he said at last, struggling to express his thought. "It's a very strange thing."

Even more strange was the fact that she felt exactly the same way he did. She didn't understand it, any of it. It was all too much—the intoxication of the roses; his sudden, seductive candor; the addictive sound of his voice; and especially, the overwhelming sense that they'd been together before. That they'd been apart, and that now they were together again.

He lifted her up in his arms as if she weighed nothing at all. "Will you let me make love to you, Jane Drew?" he whispered, kissing her, leaving her dizzy with desire for him.

It was so typically endearing of him, this blend of courteous knight and lusty warrior. It made her drunk with power and crazy with love to know that if she said, "Fat chance,"

Mac McKenzie would put her back down and bite through steel before he'd push himself on her. She wondered whether he had any idea how erotic his self-control was.

"Mr. McKenzie," she said, returning his kiss with a taunting tenderness to match his own, "if you *don't* make love to me, and soon, I'm going to throw myself off Sankaty bluffs."

He gave her a sexy grin and carried her up the stairs, which delighted her. She thought—almost with pity—of the wife who'd divorced him, of what treasure she'd left behind on this enchanted isle. Jane had absolutely no doubt that Mac McKenzie was a perfect lover; she knew it, just as surely as she knew she was the one right woman in the world for him. In her heart, in her soul, it was that simple.

Mac pulled back the green-striped comforter and laid her on the white eyelet sheets of her great-aunt's bed. She didn't expect him to be self-conscious about his physicality, and she was right.

"We were taught no street clothes on the sheets," he said with a devilish sideways look before he yanked the turtleneck over his head. His jeans and underwear went next, and then he was sitting on the bed alongside her. Just like that, the mystery of Mac McKenzie was revealed to her.

She liked what she saw—liked it so much, that she clamped her mouth shut, afraid that she'd say something just a little too modern for his old-fashioned taste.

But of course he noticed. *"What,"* he said, cocking his head and looking at her through half-lidded eyes.

She shook her head, then touched the four-inch welt of an old scar on the lower part of his thigh. "You've been in a duel," she said with a sympathetic smile, remembering Bing's quip about men and their wounds.

Mac took her hand and traced it across the scar, as if he wanted her to know everything about him, starting with the damaged parts and working her way from there. "Billy B. worked for me when he was fourteen. I think it was his Texas-Chainsaw-Massacre period. You know what mimics kids are," he said with his deadpan look.

"And this?" she asked, tracing a triangle-shaped scar on his upper arm.

"Misdirected tree limb. I'm no better than Billy when it comes to chainsaws."

She tisked and said, "It could've been an eye," in a maternal kind of way. "And—this?" she asked, touching a small pink scar near the nipple of his left breast. It looked like a stab wound. "You really *were* in a duel."

"Ah, that one's newish," he said, looking down at it, his chin doubling with the effort. "That's where the arrow went that recently pierced my heart."

Startled, she looked up and instantly lost herself in the profound depths of his hazel eyes. "Really, Mac?" she whispered.

"Truly," he said, with a look that made her dizzy. He leaned over her and brushed his lips across her mouth. "Well, my fair one," he murmured. "We've had the worst. Now, it's my turn."

He unfolded both sides of her blouse as gently as he might the petals of a flower. She was wearing a bra that fastened in front; he unsnapped it and drew aside the fabric, leaving it nestled in the folds of the blouse. She'd never been undressed quite that way before, with such care and attention. He had the naive curiosity of a youth from a very small town, the experienced touch of a Paris rake. It was a breathtaking combination. Jane knew that her breasts were more shapely than earthy, and that her waist didn't tuck in like, well, like Judith's—but he was making her feel like Venus de Milo.

"You aren't fashionably thin," he said in his droll way.

Jane knew that coming from Mac McKenzie, it was the

highest of compliments. She batted her eyelashes and said, "Hauling trees around always gives me an appetite."

He smiled, remembering. "I wanted you so much that day," he said, leaning on one arm alongside her. He bent his head over her breast, cupping it in his free hand and caressing the pink tip with his tongue.

She closed her eyes and said, "Just . . . hold . . . that thought," between gasps of pleasure as he played light and magical games with her body. She brought her knee up and pressed the heel of her foot into the soft down of the comforter in a futile attempt to stay earthbound. But it was no use; no matter how she tried, she found herself spiraling upward, upward and outward, and bound for heaven.

His hand slid lower, over her smooth, warm flesh, and stopped at the heavy brass zipper of her jeans. He slid open the zipper, which made a funny little questioning sound, like a sentry surprised at its post: "Yes?" went the sound.

"Yes," she whispered in a shudder.

She lifted her hips and he slid away her jeans and panties in one deft movement, and then caught her in his arms so that she could slip out of the rest of her things. She remembered other undressings, groping and awkward. How different this was, how completely without fear. Again she had the uncanny sense that they'd been together before, and forever.

With a complex smile he let his gaze wander over her full length and back again. It was like setting her oven temperature to quick preheat. She wound her fingers through his and said, "Once you've opened the wrapper, you can't return it, you know."

The sound of his laugh was mixed with pain. "I wish you weren't so beautiful," he said in a wistful voice.

"Beautiful . . . I'm not beautiful," she said, surprised. Then she added, "Why do you say you wish I wasn't? Which I'm not. But if I were."

He climbed in bed and lay alongside her and raked his fingers gently through her long hair, fanning it on the pillow. "I want you, *not* because you're beautiful," he said, pressing his lips first to one temple, then to the other. "I want you because you're real. I love that you enjoy my people. I love that you could get excited about a rusty pickup truck. I love—I was amazed—that you moved your door and not the hollies."

He was lying across her breast, supporting his weight on one elbow, his wide shoulders overshadowing her smaller frame. He lowered his mouth on hers in a kiss of almost unbearable tenderness and said, "And I wish now that I hadn't eaten your Napoleon at the church bazaar; I know you wanted it."

It was the craziest, most whimsical declaration of—of what? Want? Love? She didn't know; all she knew was that she wanted—and loved—this man. She held his face between her hands and brought his mouth back down on hers and kissed him fiercely, not because she was impatient, but because he was *so* patient. If he wanted to make this last, he was doing a superb job of it.

"Ah, Jane," he said hoarsely between kisses, "I don't want to rush this. . . ."

"Mac McKenzie," she said with a giddy laugh as he buried his face in the curve of her neck, "you who watch trees grow for a living—there's no *way* you could rush this."

His voice was both wry and rich with emotion as he said, "Trust me; it's been a while. I think what we need . . . we need to give you a head start," he murmured, beginning a slow and wicked descent with his tongue across the sometimes uncharted terrain of her body.

Jane had no idea, she hadn't a *clue*, that a man could make a woman feel this way, this long, this well. She sucked in her breath sharply, then sucked it in again, forgetting to let go, until her mind was spinning from lack of oxygen, until some survival reflex let the air out again, in long, shuddering waves, and she began all over in sharp, staccato intakes, her blood pulsing the whole time, her heart ragged from the effort to keep up.

More than once she thought she had died; it seemed inconceivable to her that the human body, the female body, could survive such repeated plunges into near-oblivion and live to dream about it. She felt such incredibly intense, explosive *yearning* for him; she had nothing in her life to compare it to.

But she had her experience of Judith. The image of Judith, once it filtered through her consciousness, became stronger and more pervasive until she understood on some level that *she* was Judith, and Sylvia was Judith, and so was Cissy. All women were Judith, anyone who'd ever loved the way a woman can, with all her heart and soul.

And whether the love turned out well, or whether children followed, or long life, almost didn't matter, because the essential thing, the one essential thing, was to have opened oneself to the experience of loving someone without holding back.

She opened her eyes, drugged with love, and saw Mac alongside her again, his chin resting on one hand, a bemused half-smile softening the craggy features of his face. "You *are* beautiful," he said softly. "More than ever."

"It must be my feelings shining through," she whispered. She touched her fingertips to her lips, then pressed them gently to Mac's full, handsome mouth. "I think maybe you gave me too much of a head start," she said dreamily. "I seem to have got there before you."

"I can probably still catch up," he said with a sensuous, lazy smile. He had the bedrock confidence of his sex; there wasn't a doubt in her mind that he was right. She wondered what would happen *now* if she said, "Fat chance."

Fat chance that she'd ever say it.

He brought his mouth down over hers in a test-the-waters kiss. Jane knew—how could she not?—that he would give her all the time she needed. The waters seemed just fine: not too hot, not too cold. The silvery lightness of his kiss lingered until it became something more liquid and golden, and then something else again, hotter and molten.

And this, too, was new: this heat. She had wanted him before in an almost ineffable way, and he had more than satisfied that desire. But there was something else, an emptiness that needed to be filled, a mating ritual as old as time itself that needed to be consummated.

Her voice was barely a shudder, lost in the tangle of her senses, as she said, "Come into me . . . come into me now. . . ."

And when he did, in a slow slide into the melting recess of her self, she closed her eyes and breathed a sigh of exaltation because now, at last, she was whole.

Mac, who parceled out his words like gold coins, parceled out three more. "I . . . won't . . . last," he said, his brow beading up from the effort to do just that. He became very still.

She had to smile. "The general idea is, you don't have to," she answered, sliding her hands through his wild, sun-streaked hair. "Because there's more, you know."

His voice was tremulous, almost apologetic. "I pace myself much better than this . . . but with you, it's different. I . . . something . . . drives me to you. With you . . . I have no choice."

"It's the roses," she said with a soft, mysterious sigh. "We're bound by them."

She watched as he closed his eyes, savoring the moment, savoring her. "Bound," he repeated softly.

The word hung in the air between them, the simple sum of their destinies. Mac seemed to relax, as if the word had liberated him, freed him from the agony of having to make choices. She, too, felt that way. *Bound:* to the present, to one another, to the act of loving. *Bound:* to the past, to the memory of Judith and Ben Brightman, and all lovers during all ages. *Bound:* to a future together, a man, a woman.

They were bound, and somehow that made them free. Mac quickened his pace, and she opened herself to him, made it easy for him, until he shuddered, and she cried out, "I do love thee!"

CHAPTER 24

She lay on his breast, listening to the steady thump of his heart. After a while Mac said softly, "You called me 'thee.' "

"Thee has a problem with that?" Jane said lightly, tracing an aimless pattern on his chest. She remembered the "thee" very well; it came right after the I-do-love part.

He stroked her hair away from her face and said, "I wouldn't have, if I were two hundred years old. Are you trying to revive an old tradition? Or are you just trying out for the lead in *Friendly Persuasion?*"

She hesitated, then said, "I guess I was feeling just so . . . overwhelmed. I guess I was feeling . . . Judith."

For another long moment he was quiet. Then: "Tell me about her. What else, since the chimney fire?"

It didn't seem possible that Mac could want to hear about Judith; but his voice was low and kind and intimate, so Jane threw open this deepest, most secret part of her life to him. She described Judith's apparition on the night of Uncle Easy's party. She told Mac about her discovery of the house on Pine Street. And she confessed that that's where she'd found the Belle Amour rose.

At the end she said, not daring to look at him, "Couldn't the Belle Amour be the rose from Ben Brightman's grave? Ben's rose—or its offshoots—could have been around forever; there's a rose called the Tombstone Rose in Arizona that's supposed to be four hundred years old. The Belle Amour could have been brought from Europe on a ship to

Nantucket, just as so many trees and shrubs were. If the
house really was Judith's and Ben's—"

"*If.*"

"And if the rose really is from Ben's grave—"

"*If.*"

"If," she conceded softly. "Something happened to us
downstairs, Mac," she said. "I added the Belle Amour
roses to the pitcher with the rugosa roses, and the combined scents of the two—well, here we are," she said, propping herself on one elbow and giving him a whimsical,
helpless look. "Nothing else has been able to get us into
bed."

He slid his hand around her back and began idly rubbing
concentric circles into the base of her neck. "You don't
think we were headed here on our own?"

She closed her eyes, relishing the sensation. "I think we
got a little push."

"So the 'thee'—that was Judith speaking? Judith was
using you as a surrogate when we made love? And Ben was
making the most of me?"

"I don't know. It could be."

"And the part before the 'thee'?" he asked her softly.
"That was Judith too?"

She opened her eyes. He hadn't missed a thing. "That
part was me," she admitted with a steady look. "Because I
do."

He returned her look with a troubled one of his own.
"This is moving along, isn't it?"

Jane colored and said, "No obligation, sir, none at all. It
was just something . . . I needed to say." She hunkered
back down, with her cheek pressed against his heart. Wild
horses wouldn't drag another declaration of love out of her
now; not until he got a little further along in analyzing his
feelings for her. She sighed and wondered when that would
be.

"I wish . . ." She stopped, then began again. "By now

you think I'm completely mad, but . . . what if there were some way to combine those two roses? Permanently, I mean. Isn't there something horticulturalists do—stick one branch on the other or something to make a new hybrid? Grafting, isn't it called? Could we do that with two such dissimilar roses?"

He still seemed a little thrown for a loop by her admission that she loved him. "I—what? Graft them? I guess so. You could try budding the Belle Amour onto the roots of the rugosa. The new rose would flower next year. But why?"

Jane really wasn't sure why. She struggled with her reasons, then said, "You, of all the people I know, see first-hand how life—this is such a cliché, but it's true—how life goes on. Trees, flowers—people—grow old; they reach the end of their lifespan; they die. They decay, and turn into another form of life. Some of us hate to admit it," she said with a sigh. "But it's like the song says. Soldiers eventually go to flowers; every one."

"And our two lovers have gone to roses?" he asked, idly stroking her hair. "And the only way they can be together is if we do the job *for* them?"

"I truly believe it."

"Isn't that a little like playing God?"

"I don't think God would mind. It's spring. It's His busy season," Jane said, smiling. But she wouldn't look at Mac's face; she didn't want to see the skepticism that she could hear creeping into his voice. Not now. Not after today.

"Well, you should know," Mac said at last. "You're a closer relation to Sylvia than I am."

"Sylvia? What does my Aunt Sylvia—a *closer* relation! Are you telling me that you're *any* relation to her?" she asked in a scandalized voice, bolting up.

He laughed and pulled her back down to him. "She's probably my twentieth cousin six times removed. On Nantucket everyone's related to everyone else. Don't worry," he said, kissing her forehead, "we haven't violated any civil laws this afternoon. My point is that everyone around here knew Sylvia was empathic. You must have inherited some of her sensitivity to the paranormal."

"*Excuse* me? Why didn't you tell me this on the night of the chimney fire?"

He grimaced. "You really wanted to be told you were psychic?"

"No," she said, giving his hair a yank. "I'd much rather go on thinking I was insane." She sat up and reached for the robe that was lying over the footboard. "Is that why everyone on the island avoided my aunt?" she asked as she got out of bed and slipped the robe around her. "Because she was psychic?"

"Not at all. Sylvia was born off-island and out of wedlock. Her mother was an islander, but she hated Nantucket; people here remember stuff like that. Sylvia grew up, moved here, and married a local boy, but by then people's minds were set against her. By then it was a tradition."

"You people sure are hell on outsiders," Jane said, tying her robe and looking down at him with a rueful smile.

"Yeah, it's our one edge over you: We were here first." He caught one end of her bathrobe tie. There was a stirring in him, a glimmer of lazy interest. "Leaving?"

Jane slid the tie out of his hand with a knowing smile. "I'm starved. I thought I'd go downstairs and bring back some milk and Oreos on a tray. And, what the heck, maybe the pitcher of roses. I think we ought to test my theory again."

"I've always been a believer in the scientific method," Mac said, folding his arms contentedly behind his head. "Want any help down there?"

She shook her head and said, "Stay right where you are." He was so relaxed, so completely at home. It filled her with immense joy to think that finally, at last, after months of touch-and-go, Mac McKenzie was settling in. Maybe.

She was on her way out of the bedroom when she turned, irresistibly drawn by the certainty that he was staring at her.

"What," she said, mimicking his earlier challenge.

He let out a moody sigh. "I just hope your Judith moonlights as a guardian angel."

Jane knew exactly what he meant. "Phillip truly isn't a danger to me, Mac," she said, plunging her hands into the pocket of her robe and looking down at her toes. "I, ah, wanted to tell you something concerning him earlier, but couldn't. Anyway, it's academic now, because I've changed my mind."

She lifted her head and said calmly, "The fact is, Phillip —his relations, actually—made me an excellent offer on the house. I . . . I got as far as signing a sales agreement; it's downstairs on the front table."

Mac said absolutely nothing. She saw one eyebrow twitch slightly; but that was all.

So she told him the amount. "You can see how tempting it was," she said with an uneasy smile. "I wanted to stay on Nantucket, but you weren't giving me any encouragement at all. But now all that's changed. It was such a close call. If I hadn't been out of stamps to mail the agreement . . . if you hadn't come here today . . . if I hadn't knocked over the vase . . ."

She smiled lamely. "It's fate, don't you think?" she murmured. When Mac continued to remain impassive, she rambled on about Phillip's aunt and uncle and what nice neighbors they'd have been for everyone, trying feverishly to defend her decision to sell to Phillip and them.

Finally she shrugged and said, "I can't imagine what I was thinking of when I accepted the offer. But you were so determined to shut me out . . . and Phillip was so persuasive . . . and at the time it all seemed so reason-able . . ."

"Because it *was* reasonable," Mac said, sitting up and swinging his legs over the side of her bed. "I was wrong about him, obviously," Mac said without looking at her. "That's a great offer. I thought he'd try to steal the place out from under you. But when his last trick backfired, it must have shaken him. He wants the place more than I thought," Mac added under his breath.

"For perfectly legitimate reasons!" she said. "An aunt! An uncle!"

Mac stood up and reached for his pants. She had to resist an impulse to grab them first and toss them out the window. "What are you doing?" she asked, not knowing what else to say.

When he answered, "Getting dressed," in a flat, unemotional voice it was all she could do not to scream out loud. "Are you *crazy*? You can't just walk out from this. You can't just—how can you? I don't *want* to sell! Don't you get it? I want to stay here! With you!"

He yanked the turtleneck over his head and began tucking it in his jeans. "You signed a sales agreement," he said, hooking his belt up. An angry flush darkened his cheeks. "I don't care if you've handed it over yet or not. At some point you were perfectly willing to sell me out." He stopped himself, got his anger back under control.

"You signed it," he repeated doggedly. "Good for you. It's a great offer. Now you can go back to work, for yourself, doing—what was it?—drawing lipstick and chairs?"

"I've changed my mind!" She wanted to stamp her foot but knew instinctively that it would be deadly to do it. "I don't want to stay in advertising. I could never go back to that rat race!"

She pulled her robe more tightly around her, feeling absurdly at a disadvantage now that he was dressed and she wasn't. "You think I became part of some master plot against you, Mac. But I asked Phillip *specifically* about what would happen if he ever bought Bing's place, and he swore that things would stay the same for you."

"And you believed him."

They were standing face to face now; she could see the distrust, the betrayal in his eyes. "Mac! You have to get over this obsession with Phillip . . . that car episode was a lifetime ago; it's water under the bridge. Your bitterness is eating at you . . . it won't let you trust anyone."

"You don't know who I trust," he said evenly. "Excuse me—whom."

"Who, whom, who cares? Only you, Mac. You're the only one. No one else gives a shit."

Mistake. She saw the veil come down over his eyes; she saw him withdraw completely from the fray.

"You're blocking the doorway," he said coldly.

He was walking away. Again. It was more than she could bear. She slammed the door shut behind her, then slapped herself up against it, barring him from leaving. "No! I have enough phantoms in my life! This time you stay and we talk about it!"

He made a sharp, instinctive move for the door, which infuriated her. She grabbed the doorknob ahead of him. "*Dammit*, Mac—can you hate me so much? So soon?" Her voice cracked, but she rallied, determined to face him down without resorting to tears.

"All right," she said calmly. "Assume I made a mistake. Assume I'm sorry for disappointing you; God knows I am. But I want to know exactly what it is you were hoping I would do. You're so smart. Tell me." She waited for his answer.

His hands were on his hips now, his gaze somewhere above her head. His jaw was clenched tight, always a bad sign. She didn't care. She waited.

"I don't know!" he burst out at last. "All I know is what I *didn't* want you to do. I *didn't* want you to sell to Harrow, I *didn't* want you to sell to anybody else, I *didn't* want you to leave the island."

"Well, what did you think I was going to do? Keep on wallpapering this place for the rest of my life, waiting for you?"

"You? Wait? Your idea of waiting is letting the A&P doors swing open instead of crashing through the glass. Let's face it, lady. Patient, you're not."

"I would wait!" she shot back. "I would wait if I knew what I was waiting for! But *you* can't run from me fast enough. Tell me—what would I be waiting *for*? You to save up your courage?"

"Me to save up my *money*, you twit! Don't you listen, ever? I'm teetering on Chapter 11! Let me try it one more time: *I can't afford you.* Your mother sees it plain enough. Why are *you* so blind? I couldn't afford Celeste, and I can't afford you. *Period.*"

"Oh, this is too Victorian for words!" she said, contempt vying with the faintest glimmer of hope. "I'd be willing to struggle right along with you, but *you*—were you planning to save up until you could afford to feed a proper family? *By then I'll be too old to* have *a proper family!*"

When she thought about it later, she realized that right there was where she'd lost the war. She'd belittled his old-fashioned values; she'd demonstrated spectacular impatience; and she'd grabbed the reins right out of his hands. Not to mention, she sounded like a clinging maniac. Glenn Close, move over.

Still, she could have lived with the episode if Mac had just said something before he walked out; if he had called her a jerk, or a pie-eyed optimist; anything but nothing. Now she had to live with that awful sentence hanging in the air between them, her exit line off the island: *By then I'll be too old to* have *a proper family.*

Jane was still in her robe and pajamas, her hair uncombed, her eyes red from crying, when the knock on the door came the next morning. She knew who it was: Phillip Harrow, come for his signed agreement. She dragged herself to the door like someone nursing a massive hangover.

Phillip looked surprised and puzzled. "*I'm* sorry," he said, all but smacking his head in remorse. "I've got our time wrong."

"No," she said with a sigh. "Come in." She motioned to him to take a seat in one of the wicker chairs in the redone front room. "I just had a bad night, that's all."

"I'm sorry to hear that. Nothing that can't be fixed, I hope."

"Not this time," she said, aching from her thoroughly broken heart. "You've come for the agreement, Phillip. There it is." She pointed to the unstamped envelope still lying on the half-round table near the front door. "But I won't be selling Lilac Cottage to you."

He gave her a cautious, puzzled smile. "True enough; you'll be selling it to my aunt and uncle."

She took the chair opposite his. "Not to them, and not to you. I'm so sorry, Phillip; I feel like such an awful fool. I know that you've got to find a place quickly for your relations, and I know that the cottage would be perfect for them in some ways. But I'm just not ready to sell yet. My emotions are a mess right now," she said disconsolately, trying not to weep.

But the tears ran down anyway. Phillip, looking disconcerted, reached into his pocket and handed her a clean linen handkerchief. "I understand," he said awkwardly. "You've grown attached to the place. You need a little more time. . . ."

"And even if I were going to sell," she admitted, "it couldn't be to you. Mac would never forgive me."

"Mac! What has Mac's forgiveness got to do with all this?" Phillip asked, surprised.

She blew her nose and pulled herself together. "He's obsessed with his access problem. I guess he . . . prefers that you not be holding all the cards," she said diplomatically.

Phillip shook his head thoughtfully. "I can't blame him. The prospect would terrify me if I were in his boots. Okay. Then how about this? A written assurance that if I ever get control of Bing's property—and I don't have the least desire for it anymore—that Mac will have right of way over it. Would that ease us over this hurdle?"

"I'm sure it would help," she said, forcing a smile. But she was dismayed. Now she *would* have to sell.

"There you are, then. We'll just put everything on hold until I've spoken with my attorney. Hold on to the agreement, Jane," he said, standing up and giving her a friendly, beseeching smile. "These guys charge three hundred bucks an hour to run off new ones."

As they were moving toward the door, Phillip hesitated, then said, "One thing I think you should know. Technically, you can't reject an offer if it's for cash and unconditional. Not that my aunt and uncle would press where they weren't wanted. But someone else might. And if Mac told you he didn't like the color of the buyer's eyes . . . well . . ."

He shrugged, then added, "He just won't forgive, will he? He just won't forget."

"No," she said forlornly. "That's not his way."

A little later Jane cleaned up and walked into town on her usual rounds. First she went to the post office, where she mailed a birthday card to her sister, and then she went a few steps farther to The Hub, the news store that served as the heartbeat of the town. She browsed through the latest magazine arrivals and bought her weekly copy of the *Inquirer*—the *Inky,* as it was affectionately known on the island. After that she bought a bouquet of bridal wreath and some loose-leafed lettuce from the local produce truck parked on the cobblestones in front of The Hub.

Many of the year-round tradespeople knew Jane by name; she knew some of them well enough to ask about their children. And there was another, subtler way that told Jane she was beginning to belong: She was able to separate the year-rounders from the summer residents, the summer residents from the day-trippers who'd poured off the first boat of the day and were swarming over Main Street.

Jane lingered in front of The Hub in the perfect June sunshine, scanning the crowd idly, looking for familiar faces. She found one that she held dear: Uncle Easy was sitting on the slatted bench outside The Hub, flanked by his niece, his gnarled hands folded over a cane he kept wedged between his feet. Jane had visited him at his house a few days earlier; in the bright sun he looked older, paler, thinner. But he was still Uncle Easy: sharp as a tack and independent as a hog on ice.

"What the hell have you done to my nephew?" he demanded to know when Jane sat down beside him. "He drove us downtown today; I ain't seen him this foul since the darkest days of his divorce. I reason it's woman trouble, and you're the woman, and you're the trouble."

Jane stammered something dumb, and Uncle Easy said, "What's all this about you've got a buyer for Lilac Cottage? 'Zat so?" She nodded and he leaned on his cane and whispered, "It's Harrow, ain't it?"

Jane nodded again.

"I knew it." He shook his head. "Well, you can't sell to him."

"If he meets my terms, I have no choice."

"Raise the price."

"Then no one else will buy it either. You understand that your nephew is insisting I take the offer?"

"Sounds about right. Mac's cut off his nose once or twice before in his life."

"What should I do? What *can* I do? We had an awful fight over it."

"Better to be quarreling than lonesome."

She laughed ruefully and kissed the old man's sunken cheek. "I'll keep you posted, Uncle Easy."

That evening Jane nestled the Belle Amour and the rugosa roses in a delicate halo of bridal wreath and placed the vase on the table in front of the Empire sofa in the fireplace room. Then she poured herself a very decent-sized brandy and took out the latest book in her soon-to-be-useless library of horticulture. It included a section on budding roses. She sat down with high hopes. How hard could it be?

She read the section through, sipping brandy and sniffing roses as she went. The scent of the roses together was heavenly—so to speak. But it didn't seem particularly erotic. Maybe Mac was right; maybe they'd been destined for bed with or without help. Jane considered the possibility that she was more flaky than psychic, but put it aside. She hadn't been wrong once about Judith and Ben. She knew it, and now Mac knew it.

But she wasn't too sure about the merits of her grafting plan. She wasn't too sure about anything right now. The brandy-induced fuzziness she was feeling was a poor substitute for the truly mystical experience she'd had with Mac the night before. It made her melancholy even to compare them.

Jane closed the gardening book, and her eyes, and laid her head on the back of the sofa. "Dammit . . . dammit . . . dammit," she whispered through a rolling tear or two, and fell asleep.

An hour later she woke up with a ferocious crick in her neck. "Ah . . . geez," she said, wincing and rubbing the area to bring back the circulation. "Talk about your days of wine and roses."

She dragged herself to bed, thoroughly disgusted by her self-pitying mood. Everything that anyone had ever said about being in love was true, except that the highs were higher, and the lows were the pits. She collapsed on her bed, fully clothed.

The pits.

She slept hard, drugged by the brandy, unbothered by dreams, until she woke with a start. Someone was in the house. Her eyes were wide open now. It was a moonless night; the house should have been black. But a pale glimmer, the merest hint of light, seemed to be mounting the stairs from below.

It couldn't be Judith Brightman. With Judith, Jane had sensed only the purest form of passion. What she was feeling now was twisted passion, passion gnawing on its own entrails. If there *was* a force down there, it was undoubtedly an evil one. She got out of bed in her stockinged feet, circling around a squeaky board, determined to meet and defeat the evil once and for all. She felt a crazy kind of confidence, convinced that Judith would protect her: Someone had to bud the rose, after all.

Jane skipped the third tread, the sixth, and the eighth; they all squeaked. At the bottom landing she stopped to listen. It was coming from the fireplace room, a wet and sloshy sound, a vaguely sickening sound. For one ludicrous moment Jane was afraid it might be Sylvia Merchant, come back to haunt her for selling Lilac Cottage. But the smell of kerosene dispelled that fear.

She peered around the corner into the fireplace room. A night-light had been plugged in, casting a dim, innocent illumination over the scene. *Clever,* she thought. *A flashlight might arouse suspicion.* Not that there was anyone around to be aroused.

"You bastard," she said calmly.

Phillip's back had been toward her while he held the old kerosene heater at an optimal angle and poured a steady stream of its contents onto Aunt Sylvia's poor, abused Oriental rug. When he heard Jane's voice, he jerked his head around, as if he'd been caught with his hand in the till. In a way, he had.

She flipped on the switch next to the door; the lamp on the gaming table came on, still dim but bright enough to show the repressed fury in Phillip's face. "Wouldn't you know it," he said with a grim smile. "You're a night person. That really *is* awkward."

"It was you all along," she said, hardly believing that she could have been so blind. "The missing spoon, the fallen bookcase, the muddy laundry. It was you, skulking around, picking on dumb innocent women. What awful form, Phillip. Really," she said in her mother's best voice.

"I disagree. I thought it was all nicely understated. Would you have preferred chicken blood smeared over the wicker?"

She watched in a trance of alertness as he stood the kerosene heater carefully back up and moved a bag of rags soaked with linseed oil closer to the carpet. It was her bag from the basement. He'd brought up her gallon container of turpentine, too, and a can of paint thinner. It didn't take a rocket scientist to figure out the scenario he had planned. Cause of fire: spontaneous combustion. Cause of death: fire.

What a fool she was. She smiled bitterly and said, "You must have been ecstatic when a real ghost showed up to help you out."

"Ah, yes . . . Judith. Cissy told me about her. It was almost *too* perfect. I only wish," he said with a sigh, "that I could have been there to see you two trying to videotape your overwrought imaginations. Priceless."

He stepped away from the soaked section of carpet and wiped his loafers carefully on a dry area. An image of him wiping mud from his shoes in Mac's kitchen on a dry night came rushing back to her. "You pulled the bolt from the railing on the footbridge. You did it just before you showed up at Uncle Easy's party."

"Now *that* was bad form," he admitted, a gleam of malice in his eyes. "In retrospect I ought to have phoned instead. I admit, my feelings were hurt at not being invited."

"You have no feelings, Phillip. Everyone I've met has either told me that or hinted at it, but I was too, too blind to see."

"Yes . . . you're easily dazzled, aren't you? Well, don't be too hard on yourself, Jane. Most people are suckers for smooth talk and good manners."

She saw two inches of envelope sticking out from his blazer pocket and said, "I see you've decided to let me twist your arm into buying Lilac Cottage."

He smiled, appreciating her sense of irony, and tapped the sales agreement with a gloved hand. "It's your fault, you know. You seemed so unsure. You forced my hand; I began to have no idea whether you'd ever make up your mind."

"I'm a Libra. What did you expect?"

"Anyway," he said, "I think the campaign has gone on long enough. I'll give you credit: You don't scare easily. Houses around here get dumped routinely over a squeaky door at night. I never expected you to last this long. Or to cost me this much."

"There is no aunt or uncle, of course," she said, taking a step back when he seemed to approach her. "How do you keep getting in here, incidentally?"

"Key," he said simply. "Sylvia Merchant gave me one many years ago. May I say how grateful I am that you never had the back lock changed?"

She thought of Mac: of how he had insisted; how she'd resisted. "I did put locks on the windows," she said, as if that made her look less stupid. The fact was, it made her look *more* stupid.

Phillip had been jangling something in his pockets. When he brought out a silver lighter, Jane knew that it was time—as Mrs. Adamont liked to say—to fish or cut bait. "Phillip. Don't do this. You're not in that deep yet. Cissy's death was an accident."

He gave her a sharp look. "That's right. It was."

"But there's nothing accidental about arson, Phillip. Why would you do it, anyway—burn down the thing you want?"

He laughed out loud. "Because I *don't* want it, you idiot. I want the land underneath it. Have you ever looked at a land map? If I control your parcel and Bing's—and I will; Bing is shattered and ready to sell—then Mac will fall like a ripe apple into my lap. It'll be a superb property to develop: conservation land on two sides; unlimited ocean views; private, yet convenient. The mind reels at the possibilities."

It was a form of madness: developer's syndrome. Jane was shocked at the grandiose intensity of it. A hundred different things could thwart Phillip's plan; but all he saw was the end product. How he got there was irrelevant.

"Mac will never let you get away with this," she said, backing away another step. "Everyone knows you're bitter enemies. Everyone knows you're after him." She was thinking about the smoke alarm, above her head on the left, with its lid and battery hanging down uselessly. She was wondering if he had a gun.

"Who's bitter?" he said with a shrug. "I had Mac to dinner; he chose not to reciprocate. It's Mac who's bitter. An emotional man, McKenzie. A hopeless romantic." He put the lighter back in his pocket. "Now. Where shall we arrange you?"

And yes, he did bring out a gun: small, silver, fitting. Jane stared at it incredulously, unwilling to believe it had come to this. "Are you *crazy*? If you shoot me, no one'll believe the fire was an accident."

"My lookout," he said coolly.

Jane had no choice but to run for it. She made a break for the kitchen and the back door, stumbling in the dark, but he was right there behind her. She grabbed the door-knob with both hands and tried in her panic to pull it out of the door instead of turning it. It was all the time Phillip needed. He caught her in his arms in a violent grip that hurt her ribs and knocked the wind out of her. It was pointless to scream; she focused instead on fighting back. She freed one arm and grabbed his hair and raked her nails across his neck at the same time that she kicked him viciously in the knee. He let out an oath and pinned her flailing arm under his left arm as he switched the gun from his left hand to his right.

The blow to the back of her head made her see stars. Jane's last thought, as she crumpled in a heap to the floor, was that Judith Brightman wasn't pulling her share of the load.

CHAPTER 25

Kerosene tingled.

That was the sense she got as she lay half-conscious with her cheek lying on a carpet soaked in it. But the tingling passed, and her skin began to hurt, a burning sensation, or maybe that was from the flames roaring at the other end of the room; or the smoke, the black, billowing smoke. . . . She tried to lift her head; she really did not like the smell of kerosene, so unpleasant. . . . And that reminded her, what about the roses? But it was too late, clearly too late. . . .

She managed to drag herself off the wet, stinking carpet just before she heard a "poof," like the sound that briquets soaked in fire starter make when a match is put to them. A friendly sound . . . a summer sound . . . a barbecue sound. She crawled a few steps farther, gasping for air, and then collapsed in the hall. There was no air in the hall, either. How odd, she thought. The world was running out of everything—oil, water, trees. And now air.

Barely conscious, she heard the shattering of glass and assumed it was from the fire, and then heard violent coughing and hacking, and assumed it was Phillip. *He's come back to finish the job,* she thought, angry with him for waiting until she'd fixed up Lilac Cottage before he burned it down.

But the voice that cried her name through the smoke wasn't Phillip's, and the arms that lifted her weren't his, either. And the gasping coughing in her ear—it was the sweetest sound she'd ever heard, the sound of church bells on a Sunday morning. The air when they got outside was even dearer, pure and clean and cool. She sucked a great, long draft of it, then exploded in painful spasms of coughing. Mac laid her down on a carpet of cool grass and immediately ran off and she thought, *How typical.*

She heard more shattered glass, and then the ear-splitting din of Bing's alarm system, the one that Cissy was always setting off accidentally. But then she remembered that Cissy was dead, and Phillip was alive and skulking.

And Lilac Cottage was burning down. She watched with stunned disbelief as smoke billowed out from the back of the house, her charming, magical, thoroughly accursed house. She fell back on the grass and closed her eyes. She couldn't watch.

A minute later Mac had her in his arms again. "Jane! My God. Jane!" he said, pulling her up by her shoulders.

She opened her eyes. "It's all right . . . I'm okay . . . I'm okay. Oh, Mac—you were right; it was Phillip all along. If I could . . . I'd kill him . . . if I could," she said with limp fury.

He kissed her briefly and let her go, taking off on foot in the direction of Phillip's house. Jane tried to call him back, but his name came out a croak. The fire trucks arrived soon after that and the rescue team gave her oxygen while the firefighters took on the daunting task of saving an old wood house from total destruction. Jane sat in the rescue truck, sipping oxygen as if it were Nouveau Beaujolais, and watched, and waited.

And when it was over, she was left with half the house she had.

"If everything looks all right to you, Miss Drew, then just sign here."

It was hard to hold the pen; in her struggle with Phillip, Jane had wrenched her hand badly. It added to the grim satisfaction she took in signing the statement that would

put the man behind bars. Between the criminal suits and
the civil suits—her insurance company would hound him
to the lowest circle of hell, she was told—Phillip Harrow
would not be a bother to Mac, to her, or to anyone else for
a long, long while.

She handed the sergeant his pen and said, "I don't understand how he thought he'd get the house if I was dead."

The officer shrugged. "He had evidence of your intent to
sell. And a house often goes for less in an estate settle-
ment. A burned-out one, even cheaper." He shrugged
again, clearly uncomfortable with the conversation. After
all, Phillip was an islander. Jane was not.

"Well, I really am grateful to Mr. McKenzie for . . . for
bringing him in." She half expected to hear that assault
charges had been filed against Mac.

The sergeant nodded his agreement and said, "Mac's the
guy when you want to get the job done." Wherever Mac
was, at least he wasn't in the slammer.

So that was that. Jane had called her parents and told
them the appalling news. Despite her reassurances, they
cleared their calendars and said they'd be on the island the
following night; she booked them a room along with hers
at the Jared Coffin House.

Jane spent the rest of the day at the cottage, receiving
condolences and picking over the wreckage, deciding
which furniture was salvageable—nothing from the fireplace room—and packing what was left of her clothes for
transport back to her condo in Connecticut. Everything
smelled like smoke except for a load of laundry that was
still in the basement washing machine; Jane took the time
to hang the load on the line to dry.

Mrs. Adamont came by, properly scandalized. "It all
looks so normal from the road, right down to your laundry
flapping in the breeze," she said, shaken by what she saw
inside. "This is not right. This is not what Nantucket is
about," she said angrily.

Jane shrugged philosophically; the shock of it was wearing off, leaving a dull emptiness inside. "Every place has its dark side and demons. Even Nantucket."

Mrs. Adamont insisted that Jane come to stay with her, but Jane begged off. Billy was coming over for a preliminary assessment of the damage, and Jane once again was without a phone. And people were continuing to stop by to express their sorrow; she appreciated that, and wanted to be there for them.

And she was waiting for Mac. It seemed inconceivable to her that after all they'd been through, he wouldn't be by. No heart except a criminal heart was forged of such steel. But Billy came, and Billy went, and twilight fell, and still no Mac. She knew where he was; Billy had told her he was landscaping some new construction near the Quaker Burial Ground. But Mac couldn't very well plant in the dark. On the other hand, Jane couldn't see in the dark either, not without electricity. So she left.

All night long she was too depressed to sleep. At dawn she got up and put on the only clean outerwear she had, a long denim skirt and a gray collarless knit top, and struck out for the nearest beach. She'd taken to walking along the shore recently when she felt moody or out of sorts; there was something about the sound of the sea lapping at the sand that put her thoughts in perspective.

It was a foggy morning in an easterly wind flow, not a good beach day: Jane saw one man, one dog, and that was about it. There was a time when she'd have preferred it that way, but today she felt the isolation deeply. Her heart seemed like a great, empty vessel, without a home, without a dream, without a man to love her. She had survived quite well without them before she came to Nantucket; she would have recommended her lifestyle to anyone. But things were different now. She'd fallen in love, and the love wasn't fulfilled. That, she hadn't planned on.

She walked on alone, the wind tugging and pulling at her skirt like an impatient child. The fog was lowering, bringing with it a mist so heavy it was nearly drizzle. She wrapped her arms around herself in the chill damp air, trying to keep warm, wondering what it was she could have done to make Mac commit himself to her.

She'd played hard to get; she'd played easy. She'd been spirited; she'd been humble. She'd fallen in love with his island, his land, his house, his people, his trees. She'd told him that money didn't matter, and neither did her parents' opinion. She even let him have the Napoleon. And yet here they were, sharing the same little rock in the universe, and still a world apart.

Somehow, she felt closer to Judith right now than to Mac. Judith had understood—the way a man could not—how paralyzing heartache could be for a woman. A man had to climb that mountain, build that bridge, run for office no matter how hard he was bleeding inside, if for no other reason than that other men expected him to do it. Not so, a woman. Her own sex was too sympathetic to her hurt.

What the hell, she thought, staring out at the sea, trying to rally herself back to the condo in Connecticut. *I'll climb the mountain, build the bridge, run for office.*

But the sea seemed to be saying something else. *Without him? Why?*

Why, indeed. Like Judith, Jane had no answer. She wandered onto the wet, hard sand, drawn by the seductive hiss of the water, and then waded into the edge of the sea itself. Her leather sandals became stained dark by the water; it fascinated her. She walked a few steps farther. The hem of her denim skirt turned dark and sluggish, floating at first, then gradually sinking. The sea was still very cold. It crept up her calves, inch by inch. Except that that wasn't true: It was Jane who was creeping, inch by inch, into the sea.

It must have felt this way for Judith, she thought with

surprising detachment. *Colder, though. How far before it was over? Did she walk in over her nose? Probably not; she wouldn't have to . . . her gown would have got waterlogged before that and pulled her under . . . or the undercurrent. . . .*

Suddenly Jane stumbled into a small hole on the sandy ocean floor; her right leg buckled and she dropped waist-high into a cold rush of water. Shocked by the icy sensation, she righted herself and turned to discover how far out she'd waded.

"My God." She fell into a panic that she was reenacting Judith's destiny step by ghastly step, and began racing for the shore. But one doesn't race through the sea, especially in heavy, billowing denim; the wade back to the beach was agonizingly slow. When Jane broke free from the water, she ran like a springer spaniel to high ground, her heart pounding madly from the effort to get there.

She wrung the excess water from the bottom of her skirt, shaking from her experience. She hadn't been so frightened since—*since yesterday,* she thought grimly. Since the ordeal by fire. *And now, by water.* Life on the island was getting a little too biblical for her taste.

The more she thought about it, the angrier she got. If she and Mac had made a commitment to one another, Phillip would've abandoned his plans for an empire, and she would never have had to go brooding on this beach. In short: no fire, no water.

Jerk.

Jane left the beach and went back for her truck, then drove out to Lilac Cottage. In the gloomy fog the house looked forlorn and forsaken; she could hardly bear to look at it. She hurried around to the back door and found, sitting on her back stoop, a gallon-sized nursery pot filled with dirt and with a card stapled to its rim:

*Plant this where you wish. It may not work. It's
late in the season.*

Jane squatted down and brushed a little of the mounded
dirt gently aside to find a small bud rubber-banded to the
stem of another rose. He'd budded Ben's rose onto
Judith's. What had the police sergeant said? *"Mac's the guy
when you want to get the job done."*

So Jane climbed back in the pickup and headed out for
the newly constructed house near the Quaker Burial
Ground. The fog-turned-drizzle had now become drizzle-
turned-rain. The wind plastered her wet skirt against her
legs as she struck out over the grassy cemetery, trying to
remember the location of the new house from when she'd
walked there with Mac months ago. She found the house,
away to the north, but there was no sign there of Mac's
dark green truck.

Judith Brightman couldn't have felt more frustrated
when she'd stood on that rolling earth a century and a half
earlier.

"Jane! For God's sake!"

She turned and saw Mac; he'd stopped his truck in the
middle of Vestal Street and was climbing over the stile,
clearly convinced that Jane was mad.

"Stop!" she yelled back to him, holding out the palm of
her hand; if he got too close she'd never be able to keep
herself in control. "John McKenzie!" she cried. "I leave
tomorrow. Listen to me!"

Her voice rose above the pounding rain, high and clear
and true. "Since I came to this island, I've changed in ways
I'd never have dreamed. I look at myself—and I don't
know myself! I've learned things I never thought I wanted
to know. I've forgotten things that never should have mattered in the first place.

"I've changed, Mac," she cried. "And still you punish
me! No!" she said again when he began to speak. "You had

your chance. You'll tell me about Phillip again. I was desperately wrong about that, and now I'm desperately sorry," she said, her hands beseeching him expressively. *"Still,* you punish me."

His hands were on his hips; he was as soaked through as she was, despite the fact that the rain had begun to tail off as the squall passed over. He wanted to defend himself, she could see that; there was injured outrage etched in his face. But he was holding his peace, abiding by her command, forcing himself to hear her through.

Jane had one last thing to say. She took half a dozen strides closer to him, pointing a finger at him as if she were judge, jury, and prosecuting attorney in his case. "You think you're an oak tree, Mac—so strong, so immutable. *Well, you're* not," she screamed angrily.

She gave him a dark, haunting look and swept a wet lock of hair away from her face. *"You're a human being; that's all you are—and your time here is short, Mac McKenzie."*

A sharp gust of wind, heralding a second squall, flattened the tops of the nearby trees, and was followed by a clap of thunder and a furious downpour. *"I've* changed, Mac," she shouted over the slanting, driving rain. "Now it's *your* turn."

Mac was facing the wind, taking the brunt of the squall like a ship facing it broadside. "I can't, Jane," he said hoarsely, averting his body from the squall's fury. "I *can't.* I've been too long in the making."

A white rip of lightning on the other side of the rise produced another clap of thunder, this time deafening. Jane jumped and Mac said loudly, "This is dangerous! Go back to your truck. *Move!"*

She turned and ran, hardly thinking to challenge him, and sat in her truck, wet and shivering, while a line of black rain drummed the metal all around her with a wild, frenzied beat.

And when it was over, and the sky had lightened up

again to Nantucket gray, she saw that Mac's truck had left, and she was alone.

When Jane's mother saw Lilac Cottage she cried, which Jane thought was very endearing of her. Gwendolyn Drew seemed more emotional these days, and Jane was becoming fonder of her because of it. Jane herself was pretty much all cried out and able to speak calmly, at least about Phillip and the fire. But she kept Mac to herself, like a secret horde of memories boxed up and ready for shipping to Connecticut, to sort out when she had more time.

Jane's father had never seen the before version of Lilac Cottage, so he was much less moved by the tragedy of the fire. Tragedy rarely moved Neal Drew in any case. He was a big believer in not dwelling on the past. As far as he was concerned, you took your hit or you took your winnings, and then you moved on.

So he stood there, this man who was so unstinting in his abilities, so stinting in his praise, and said to his daughter, "You let yourself get emotionally involved with a house."

"Yep. I did," Jane admitted as she idly peeled away a strip of blistered, charred wallpaper in the front room. "It was one of the most satisfying things I've ever done."

She turned and looked at her father. He was standing with his hands in his pockets in the middle of the room, a man of average height wearing modest clothes in an unassuming way. He was the kind of guy you'd walk right past in a bus station; yet she'd spent most of her life chasing down his approval.

"And you never bothered showing it to a realtor first?" he was saying in his implicitly critical way.

"Not unless you count Phillip," she said. "Someone told me he had a broker's license."

"I do not count Phillip," Neal Drew said wryly. "All right, then. You'll leave this part to me. I have the name of a broker in town, very aggressive, with a terrific sales record; he can crunch numbers—"

"Absolutely not!" Jane snapped, amazed that her father still regarded her as an unprofitable subsidiary that needed restructuring. "I've already made up my mind on an agent. She's a decent and well-liked woman who cares as much about who buys a house as she does about the commission they'll pay. After the rebuilding, that's who I'll use. Period."

Jane was damned if she was going to stick Mac with another rotten neighbor.

"Jane, with *that* attitude—well, never mind," Neal said with a kindly pat. "You've been under a lot of stress."

"Stress, shmess! This has nothing to do with stress, Dad! This has everything to do with your trying to run *my* life to *your* standards!" She was taking Mac out on her father; she knew it, and she didn't care.

Neal was clearly taken aback. He gave his daughter a cold, hard stare and said, "Why did you have us come here, in that case?"

"To—because—I don't know!" she said hotly. "Maybe just for once to say 'I'm sorry things didn't work out, kid.' How about *that*?"

Gwendolyn Drew rushed into the room, her radar screen obviously blipping madly, and said, "Hey, hey, you two! This is no time for one of your—"

"Unpleasantries?" Jane asked scathingly.

"—knock-down, drag-out *fights*," said her mother crisply. She slipped her arm around Jane and said to her, "Ignore him, Jane. He's just an old fart. And you, Neal Drew," she said sharply to her husband. "Why don't you make yourself helpful for once in your life? Get that fellow in here to start loading Jane's things into the van."

The two women took a short walk out to the little burying ground behind the house while Jane struggled to bring her emotions under control. It was a beautiful day, awash in sun and richly green, an impossible day to leave.

"You know," said Gwendolyn wistfully as they walked arm in arm, "I had begun to adjust very nicely to the thought of your living here. It has very real charm, this Nantucket of yours . . . and the air is clean and the people are nice . . . and it's a safe place to raise children. . . ."

Jane winced in pain from her mother's well-intentioned words. "Bing never would've lived here year-round anyway, Mother," she said, assuming that her mother had got wind of Bing's intentions.

Gwendolyn Drew looked up at a hawk passing silently overhead. "That's not what he told me," she said quietly, shading her eyes with her hand. "He's in love with you, you know."

But Jane would not be drawn.

They were at Judith's grave, where a fresh mound of rich brown earth covered the rose cutting that Jane had planted there that morning.

Gwendolyn said innocently, "Do you ever wonder about the secrets that have gone to these graves?"

Jane smiled ruefully. "Mother, sometimes you can be positively hysterical." They stood over the grave in a moment of undeclared silence. Then Jane said softly, "No, I don't wonder, anymore."

She looked up automatically in the direction of Mac's house. No sign. Somehow—despite everything she knew about him—she found herself wondering why he didn't come charging down the lane in hot pursuit.

"We'd better get going," she said at last, looking away. "The boat won't wait."

"Jane—don't you want to talk about this?" Gwendolyn asked, distressed to see her daughter in such obvious pain.

"Not for a long, long time," Jane said. "And maybe not even then."

* * *

The five-thirty ferry to Hyannis was the busiest boat of the day. Both levels were filling fast with tired, happy passengers. Jane's salvaged personal possessions, too much for a plane, looked pathetically insignificant in the cargo hold of the boat. The new floral sundress she had on was literally the only wearable thing she owned.

Jane and her mother climbed the stairs and joined Neal Drew, who'd managed to claim a table where he sat comfortably immersed in his *Wall Street Journal.* He looked up at them over the rims of his tortoiseshell half-glasses.

"All aboard?" he said mildly.

It was obvious that he didn't know quite how to handle his daughter and was regrouping. Their speech had been polite and strained since Jane's blowup, with both of them waiting for the next misstep.

"Let's go on deck," Jane's mother said, dragging her daughter outside. They leaned on the stern rail, watching the crowd milling on Steamboat Wharf. Gwendolyn was anxiously scanning the faces below. "What time is it?" she demanded to know.

"Five more minutes," Jane said idly.

"Well, that's it, then. He's not coming."

"Who?"

"Bing Andrews. Before you go biting off my head," she said quickly, "he called me in San Francisco and said he might be on the island today, in which case he'd stop in to say good-bye. Probably we've missed one another."

"Mother—*that* ship has sailed," Jane said morosely. "Get over it." Jane went back to perusing the crowd and was surprised to see a big black dog that she knew well cruising back and forth on the sidelines, checking out the crowd.

"Look!" she cried to her mother. "It's Buster! I can't believe he still wanders this far from home; no wonder he keeps getting arrested." She called his name, yoo-hooing and here-boying to get his attention.

Buster saw her and began barking his Baskerville bark, prompting Gwendolyn to say, "Hush, Jane! Stop encouraging him!"

But it was too late. The dog was making a beeline up the cargo ramp and past the attendant.

Jane said, "Oh *shit*, here he comes!" and took off to intercept him and put him back on shore.

She raced past her father and down the top flight of stairs, got lost, backtracked, and found her way to the lower flight of stairs that led to the hold. She had one hand on the rail at the head of the stairs when she saw him at the bottom, on his way up.

Mac McKenzie. He was in khakis and a denim shirt, his standard uniform, and he looked as surprised to see her as she was to see him.

"Oh! I was looking for Buster," she said.

"I've sent him back."

"Oh. Well, good. That solves that problem."

"And leaves one other."

"How to find a seat when you're the last one on the ferry?"

"How to get you off this boat before it leaves the dock."

They were moving toward one another on the stairs now; Jane down, Mac up. She had no idea why her body was behaving the way it was; she herself was still at the top of the stairs, keeping her emotional distance from this man who'd caused her so much pain.

She watched herself say, "You have about ninety seconds. And as we know, you're not a fast talker."

"I love you."

"I . . . My parents are on board. All my things are on board."

"I love you."

"I can't just walk off this boat, Mac. I can't. Not anymore."

He was on the step below hers, his eyes on a level with hers. She looked into them and saw bottomless depths of love and resolve, and it took her breath away. He cradled her head in his hands and brought his mouth over hers in a kiss that both Janes—the Jane at the top of the stairs and the Jane that he held close—knew was a pledge of commitment. For life.

"Then I'll carry you off," he whispered when he let her go, "and make it easy for you."

He lifted her effortlessly in his arms and carried her down the steps, through the cargo hold, and over the ramp. Jane heard laughter, and then whistling, and finally loud cheering. For a man who rarely left the island, Mac McKenzie seemed to know everyone who worked on the ferry landing. She was too light-headed to remember much of what followed, but she did remember the ramp being raised out of the way, and the great diesel engines of the *Uncatena* being revved up for departure.

And the look on her mother's face as she stood on the afterdeck, watching Mac lower Jane to her feet.

Jane waved and cupped her hands into a megaphone as the black and white ferry began backing away from the dock. "I'm sorry you had to come all this way!" she yelled up to her astonished mother. "I'll call you! Or you can call me at—"

"My place," Mac said, slipping his arm around her waist.

"At Mac's," she yelled, "and we'll talk all about it. And tell Dad I'm glad he came! Truly! And tell him that I'm—"

"Getting married," Mac murmured, kissing her temple.

Jane turned back to him. "Yes," she said, her eyes shining. "I love you very much."

She called out to her mother, who was rapidly passing out of earshot. "And tell him I'm getting married!" she screamed, waving madly. "Not to Bing! I love you, Mother!"

The last, the very last, image Jane had of the scene was of her father, *Wall Street Journal* still in hand, coming out and peering over his half-glasses at the upstart daughter who he insisted ever after must've got switched at birth.

Mac took Jane in his arms and kissed her—more hooting, more cheering—long and hard. "If you hadn't let me carry you off, I would've died," he said in a shaky, joyous voice.

Jane reached into the big flap pocket of her sundress and brought out a small white ticket.

"Round trip," she said with a wicked, provocative smile.

Epilogue

"**N**ervous?"

"What do *you* think?" Mac said, opening his arms to her.

Jane crawled into the macramé hammock alongside him and let him engulf her in a warm summer's grasp. "*I* think you never should've told my dad last Christmas that he didn't know a jacknife from his elbow."

"Yeah," Mac said reflectively. "In retrospect, I should've been more diplomatic. Especially since I was a guest in his mansion."

"His *part* of the mansion," Jane corrected, nipping his shoulder. "It's only a condo."

"A condo that includes the ballroom."

"They entertain a lot. Anyway, Mother tells me he's been boning up on all things green, just to show you. Be prepared for a lively discussion on crop rotation when they arrive tonight."

"Did Gwen tell you she was subscribing to *Parents* magazine? With grandchildren coming at her from all sides, she's decided she'd better do a little boning up herself," Mac said, slipping his hand under Jane's blouse and idly circling her belly.

"*Oh* boy. Maybe we'd better move the guest room from the house to Lilac Cottage."

"What? And wreck your serenity? Where would you paint?"

"I haven't done a watercolor since March. Who has time? With the business starting to take off—look, I've been thinking, Mac." She sat up and swung one leg over his stomach, straddling him. "Let's move the office to the cottage, and add a little shop. I can sell my watercolors there instead of at a gallery, and of course we'd have wreaths and dried flowers and seasonal arrangements. I'll move my studio upstairs. And the small room can be a nursery," she said, giving him a little bounce with her buttocks.

Mac groaned under her weight and said, "Why bother running this past *me*? You do what you want anyway."

She smiled and leaned over to kiss him. "I do not."

He took a moment to savor her tongue before he said, "You're a radical in petticoats. You made me buy a computer."

"I talked you *into* buying a computer. Besides, you don't have to use it; I'm the one who keeps the books."

"I have a son who's a wizard at it and another wizard of indeterminate sex on the way. I damn well better learn to speak their language. I have no choice."

"You're such a fraud, McKenzie. I have to *drag* you away from that thing after supper. It's just a good thing I can still make you a better offer. Like last night."

A remembrance of the night before passed over Mac's face, filling it with a depth of emotion that was almost unbearable for her to behold.

"Is it enough for you?" he asked softly. "What we have?"

"My God, Mac," she whispered, bending over him. "It's life itself."

She gave him a kiss of pure, humble gratitude, for making her existence whole.

"Hey, you two! Cut that out! It's embarrassin'." Uncle Easy was approaching them from the lane that led out to the road, the lane that Bing had granted Mac an easement over, in writing, just the month before. Uncle Easy had his cane with him for his walk, but he didn't seem to need it except as a pointer to scold them with.

Jane hopped out of the hammock and Mac laughed and sat up and said, "You're just jealous, you old rake. Besides, you had your chance."

"At her, or at the hammock?" Uncle Easy said with an irrepressible leer. "All things considered, I'd rather take on the hammock. I could probably get in and out of *that* with a lot less chance of killing myself."

"Uncle *Easy!*" Jane said, blushing all over.

"Ah, yes," her husband murmured in her ear. "This is going to be one interesting dinner party."

"I heard that, Mac McKenzie," Uncle Easy said, though clearly he could not have. He went up to his nephew and gave him a friendly elbow in the ribs. "They thought when you eloped that they got stuck with the son-in-law from hell. Wait till they find out you come with a matching set of relations."

Then he turned to Jane and bowed to her as low as his stiff old frame would let him. "Never fear, madam," he said. "I shall be on me best behavior t'night."

From behind his back he brought out his other arm and presented Jane with a newly cut, pale pink rose. It was a smallish blossom, camellia-like, with its rounded petals opened to show yellow stamens within. "Happy Anniversary," he said shyly.

"The new rose!" she cried. "So it *did* open overnight!"

"Told you it would," Uncle Easy said. "It's a goodish warm day."

She accepted the flower from him and kissed him on his lined and withered cheek, then sipped the intense and spicy fragrance of the rose the way she would a superbly aged wine.

Mac, who'd put his arm around her as he studied the fruit of their labor together, leaned over and took a sniff himself. "Hmm. Definitely essence of aphrodisiac," he said, moving from the rose to her mouth and kissing her in an interested way.

"You two. Honest to Pete. Keep this up and I'm gonna hafta go to Doris's house instead," the old man muttered, shaking his head.

"Don't be silly," Jane said, slipping the rose through an eyelet in the ruffle of her blouse. "Doris would never let you browbeat her the way we do."

"I'm getting out of here," Mac said, covering his head with his hands comically and ducking away. "Yell if you need anything. I think I'll take the tractor over to fill in this one pothole I happened to see—"

"*Mac*," Jane yelled after him. "You *just* put on clean clothes. . . ."

Uncle Easy chuckled and, using his cane now, eased himself slowly into a high-backed wooden Adirondack chair close by. "He's a good kid," he said contentedly. "Always was."

Jane sighed and climbed back into the hammock. After a day of frantic, picky preparations—the guest room was bursting with flowers—she needed the break. All in all, she felt pretty proud of what she and Mac had accomplished together there. She hoped her parents would be able to see the evidence of their year of labor. Lilac Cottage was as charming as ever, a Christmas card come true, especially in December, with a thousand white lights strung around the hollies.

The farmhouse, always picture perfect, now had the finishing touches that made it a home: people. Jerry had come to stay several times—including three weeks in the past summer when his mother was on her honeymoon—and hadn't broken a single bone. Uncle Easy, on the other hand, had broken his wrist in April (pulling out dandelions) and came to convalesce with them. One week led to another, and now he was part of their lives. But he was getting restless; soon he'd be headed back to what he called his bachelor's pad.

Yes: a nearly perfect year. She bent over her blouse to take a whiff of the rose again, thinking that she had no earthly right to ask for more; and yet . . .

Just the one little thing, she prayed meekly. *Just to know that it worked out for them. . . .*

She'd thought about them all winter long, as she and Mac had sat curled up in front of the fire; thought about what an overflow of happiness she had, enough to pass around to everyone, like a gardener who grows too many tomatoes. It worked for Bing: He took one look at Mac and her and turned around and married his senior development officer. Now they traveled all over the world together, a perfect match.

Couldn't it work for Ben and Judith?

She lay in the hammock, half asleep, listening to the lazy buzz of insects, and the sweet songs of the finches in the trees overhead, and the distant sounds of Mac and his beloved John Deere. She must have drowsed off, or thought she had, because when she awoke she saw, or thought she saw, Ben and Judith together.

She was in a kind of flowing, iridescent white, and he was in something neutral, a Nantucket shade of gray. Even from a distance Jane could see her long, blue-black hair, curled and unmanageable. She was taller than he was, but his physique was perfectly suited for sailing: massive across the shoulders, and short bowed legs. They seemed to waver in the noonday heat, like a mirage, and then they were gone.

Jane bolted up from the hammock and cried, "Uncle Easy! Did you see that?"

The old man rolled his head lazily in her direction, and winked.

He drew a circle that shut me out—
Heretic, rebel, a thing to flout.
But love and I had the wit to win:
We drew a circle that took him in.

—Edwin Markham (1852–1940),
   "Outwitted"

Let best-selling, award-winning author **Virginia Henley** capture your heart...